Guardians of the Time Stream

Prequel

Odessa Fremont

By

Michelle L. Levigne

www.YeOldeDragonBooks.com

Ye Olde Dragon Books
P.O. Box 30802
Middleburg Hts., OH 44130

www.YeOldeDragonBooks.com

2OldeDragons@gmail.com

Chapter One

Virginia, 1870

At age fourteen, Odessa Fremont knew that while she had a talent for burglary, that was not her chosen occupation at any time, either in the present or the future.

However, she found exceeding satisfaction in her present position -- hanging upside down outside the window of the headmistress' office at nearly one in the morning, supported by a series of pulleys and sailors knots, attached to the clockwork winder her grandmother, Matilda, had invented. Grandfather Earnest had given her the pulleys to play with and exercise her mind just before he and Granny left for a two-year archeological expedition in South America. The nearly slick, thin-but-tough rope that supported her had been a gift from her brother, Ulysses, six years her elder, just before he vanished. Ess found some poetic justice and equilibrium in using the equipment -- especially since she had managed to keep it hidden from Miss Van Hastings' periodic searches of the belongings of all her students for "unladylike possessions supportive of unladylike actions and unladylike mindsets."

While the headmistress waged a war against her students possessing secrets, Ess had come to realize Miss Van Hastings did not reciprocate. The woman was hiding something from her. Letters from her grandparents came every other month, regular as clockwork, thanks to the relay systems of dirigibles that were allegedly immune to the various political currents that shifted borders in South America with the seasons. The next packet of reports, amusing anecdotes, and sketches of jungles, natives and ruins was overdue by more than three weeks. That was the first clue. The second was that when Ess tried to speak with Miss Van Hastings, the woman fled whenever she saw her coming -- highly unusual, because from the day Ess had entered the Van Hastings Select Young Ladies Academy, the headmistress had felt compelled to criticize and remake her on a daily basis. Up until eight days ago, when all instructions for Ess became the responsibility of the more restrictive members of the faculty.

The third and most important clue: Ess had glimpsed the seal of her grandparents' lawyers' firm on a special packet that arrived three days ago, hand-delivered by a courier riding in the newest model of steam-powered cart. The vibrant royal blue wax was unmistakable. The image imprinted in the wax sealing the packet was large enough to make out the pyramid, scales of justice, and garland of lotus flowers circling the seal. Just like the lotus tattooed on the outside of her right ankle.

Messrs. Endicott, Lewis, and MacDonald had offices for their law firm in six states of the Union. The closest was in New York, necessitating a trip of several days by stagecoach, or else an expensive one-day trip by airship, or two days by train to Miss Van Hastings' boarding school in northern Virginia. If her grandparents' lawyers were here in town -- or her grandparents had sent her to a boarding school in New York or Cleveland or another town where the law firm had offices, they could have come themselves to see her, rather than relying on a courier. Or -- much more fun for her -- Ess could have crept off the school grounds in disguise and walked across town to see them. Mr. Lewis, at least, would have laughed at her disguise. He was the youngest and least stuffy of the three lawyers, though she considered all three friendly.

So, three days now since the packet had come, and Miss Van Hastings certainly acted guilty. Ess considered it highly reasonable to wait three days for the woman to confess her perfidy in hiding communication that only logically had to do with Ess. She now had every right to take matters -- and the lawyers' letter -- into her own hands.

Two rooms away inside the house, a door slammed, and the thin ribbon of light visible under the door -- Miss Van Hastings' house was the most drafty Ess had ever had the misfortune to occupy -- vanished. That meant anyone awake and with a candle had gone far enough away from the headmistress' office that they wouldn't hear Ess moving around on those creaky floors. She was sure now that the dreadful woman wasn't the miser the other students accused her of being, refusing to bring in a good carpenter to fix the creaks and squeaks. The common consensus was that there were some spots in the floors all through the house that could snap any day now and send students and servants falling to the floor below. No, Miss Van Hastings kept her floors creaky and loud to let her track the movements of her students and servants.

"People who don't trust are most often the least trustworthy in their turn," Ess whispered, repeating one of her grandmother's many axioms. She swallowed down the threat of a knot in her throat, part of the ache that had taken root in her body in multiple places ever since her grandparents dropped her here at the Select Young Ladies Academy. How she wished she could hear her grandmother say those words, followed by a wink and a chuckle, and a gesture from Granny to lean closer so they could confer privately over how to deal with the trustless people in question.

Ess twisted her right foot around inside the loops securely holding her in place outside the second story window, and tapped the lever controlling the pulley. It let her down ten more inches before the automatic stop clicked into place. She grinned at this proof that her engineering and calculating skills hadn't atrophied, despite the teachers' insistence that ladies of high breeding did not sully their minds with masculine activities such as mathematics any more complex than dealing with the household account books. Even those activities were to be avoided if at all possible, and left in the hands of a husband, father, or household steward. Ess reached out for the windowsill of the headmistress' office, made sure her grasp was secure, then tapped the lever again. Her arms ached a little as she supported her weight and pulled herself up onto the ledge while the rope-and-pulleys lowered her again. Proof she needed to find some way to resume her physical toning exercises despite being unladylike. In moments she had the sash pushed up, proving what she always suspected about the headmistress' priorities in her household. No locks on the windows on the second floor. After all, every student at the Select Young Ladies Academy believed herself too delicate to climb or, heaven forbid, actually jump from a window.

She dealt with the trap of the creaking floors by climbing onto the sideboard kept in front of the wide windows of the office and walking on it to the tall chest of drawers to the right. Her feet were clad in slippers such as circus acrobats wore -- another gift from Uly -- and made for silent creeping and leaving no discernible footprints. Ess braced her toes on the drawer pulls of the chest, moving quickly in case the furniture here was just as cheaply made as other items in the academy buildings. From the chest she stretched her leg to find secure footing on the desk chair, then slid down into the seat to kneel and lean over the vast desk. Just as she thought, the chair sat on a platform eight inches high, to allow the headmistress to seem even taller to those brought to stand before her massive desk, easily eight feet wide.

From her pocket, Ess brought two glass vials, wrapped in cottonwool. One had an eyedropper as the lid, and the other had a rubber gasket. She used the eyedropper to insert liquid from the first vial into the second, then shook the second until it released a soft, greenish glow. The phosphorescent light would last exactly ten minutes, and Ess gave herself that much time to find the packet and discern what Endicott, Lewis and MacDonald wanted and why Miss Van Hastings kept that communication from her.

"Silly old goose," she muttered, finding the packet on the right of the massive desk blotter with the blue seal carefully peeled off whole. On the right side of the blotter sat the letter in Mr. MacDonald's distinctive blocky handwriting, and directly in the middle of the blotter, an unfinished letter in Miss Van Hastings' loops and curlicues. "When are you going to learn that if you tell everyone to stay out, everyone will try to get in?" Then Ess smiled grimly and picked up her lawyers' letter. It was two pages -- unnaturally short for most lawyers, but her grandparents admired Endicott, Lewis and MacDonald for their ability to communicate clearly, concisely, and in plain English. Ess paused, her hand shaking twice, when it occurred to her that two pages was a long letter indeed for these particular lawyers.

Her hand shook a few more times after the first reading, then both hands shook when she read the letter a second and a third time, just to make sure she wasn't imagining it.

Earnest and Matilda Fremont were missing in the jungles of South America, presumed dead. There was no telling how long this had been, because the latest courier dirigible had been delayed by another of those pesky revolutions that plagued the continent. This time, the rebels had wealthy backers who provided them with battle dirigibles, most likely Southern Army war surplus that should have been destroyed when Lee surrendered to Grant, allowing the war to take to the sky. They had no regard for scientific endeavors and shot down anything that came within fifty miles of contested territory. Ess knew all this from previous letters, but she had assumed the courier airships, armed with the latest weaponry, including flame-throwers, were able to defend themselves. Grandfather Earnest had assured her nothing would get in the way of their regular communications.

When the courier arrived, the crew found the archaeologists' camp in disrepair, signs of depredation from animals and damage from weather, but no signs of attack. They had searched for four days before being forced to leave to avoid an air attack. Endicott, Lewis and MacDonald apologized for the delay in sending the news to Ess --

"Knew it," she muttered. The packet was addressed to her, just like all the others, but Miss Van Hastings had diverted it. Considering how carefully the seal had been pried off, to make sure it was unbroken, Ess considered now the chances were good that the headmistress had been opening, reading, and re-sealing all her mail before passing it on to her. What were the chances she had confiscated drawings and perhaps even small presents, such as dried plants or even animal fur or skins or teeth or bones, sent for scientific curiosity, but all considered unladylike by the interfering woman?

The lawyers apologized for the delay in sending the news to Ess, but they had been busy asking for confirmation of the situation with the war and the diplomats assigned to the surrounding territories. They had been trying to learn about the weather and other information, to determine if perhaps the Fremonts and their associates had been forced to flee for their lives, and were even now making their way back to the United States. They wished to make arrangements to meet with Ess, hopefully with good news or at least more certain information, and discuss with her the arrangements her grandparents had made in the eventuality of their disappearance or deaths. Would one month be too long a wait? If she needed to speak with them immediately, or at any time in the interim, she had only to send a courier by reverse charge mail, and one of them would come personally to meet with her.

Ess had a very good idea of what she would find when she picked up the unfinished letter. Miss Van Hastings had made it very clear how a gently raised young lady of high breeding should react in such distressing situations. During her second month at the Select Young Ladies Academy, Lavinia Pickering's uncle had died after years of convalescence from injuries suffered during the Civil War. Lavinia had avoided him whenever possible, and had loudly declared to all of her friends at the Academy that the world was a better place without the disgusting, sniveling, whining man who always smelled of camphor and whatever new patent medicine was being peddled by snake oil salesmen. Miss Van Hastings had roundly lectured Lavinia for her attitude, insisting that she was speaking from hysteria, that delicate young ladies couldn't bear the traumatic pain of losing a beloved family member. Then she sent Lavinia to her bed for an entire week, to allow her nerves time to recuperate. Ess and several other girls agreed that it was Lavinia's expression of disgust for the Resurrectionists -- a group her uncle belonged to, trying to restart the Civil War -- that actually prompted Miss Van Hastings to lecture her. Rumors said the headmistress' brother was the leader of the local Resurrectionist group. Secret Service or other government agents came regular as clockwork, every eight weeks, to question her if she had seen her brother, heard from him, or seen any of his known associates in the area.

As Ess suspected, when she read through the letter to be sent to her lawyers -- if her grandparents were presumed dead, that made Endicott, Lewis and MacDonald *her* lawyers now -- the headmistress apologized and described Ess's debilitating, nearly hysterical reaction to the news. According to Miss Van Hastings, Ess had to be dosed with laudanum. She apologized in the most flowery language Ess had ever read, as she explained that "young Miss Fremont is in such agony over your news, she has begged me to stand as her intermediary, and deal with you in her stead, until she has regained her strength and her emotional poise."

Ess snorted, grinning at the thought of the reaction of the lawyers when they got the letter. None of them would believe it. They all had told Ess at one time or another that they considered her a most common sense, balanced, and emotionally strong and stable young woman. In fact, they wished more young ladies they met could be like her. It would make dealing with estates and inheritances and bereavement so much less messy and wet for all of them. Ess could imagine some of the pithy comments Mr. Lewis would make, perhaps even being so bold as to call Miss Van Hastings a bald-faced liar.

Although, being a gentleman, he wouldn't say such words to the woman's face.

Ess's inner time sense told her she had just over two minutes left to investigate the desk and its contents further. She found notes of things to say in the letter, and several notes in a different, masculine handwriting, urging her to investigate all of "that stupid girl's assets" before convincing "those interfering Yankees" to hand over control.

Those scraps and notes backed up the dozen or so different scenarios and reasons Ess imagined for why the headmistress hid the letter and lied to her lawyers. Premier among them was keeping Ess as a student at the Academy, to keep the fees for room, board, and tuition coming in. She didn't doubt the woman wanted to control her future. Several of Ess's schoolmates were witnesses with her just two months ago, when Miss Foster of the Boston and Savannah Fosters had made a very advantageous marriage with a young German archduke only four steps away from the throne. They had overheard the headmistress congratulate herself on being instrumental in arranging the match, and earning a large sum of money from the archduke's family and the Foster family, for her services. Ess didn't doubt the headmistress wanted to use every student at her school to increase the size of her bank account.

"I should have turned you in then," Ess muttered as she quickly put the desk back into the same configuration she had found it while the last few seconds of light remained in the phosphorescent vial. "Still, even if we had no proof, someone from the Secret Service would have come out and made life miserable for you. Even a minor flunky would have been satisfactory."

She scanned the desk one last time, nodded in satisfaction, and began her climb back across the furniture to the window. The light from the vial faded quickly while she was still tiptoeing through the clutter on the sideboard. Ess focused on getting to the window and up to the attic where she had stashed much of her scientific and "rambling gear," as she termed her boy clothes and other unladylike paraphernalia, almost from the day she had arrived under Miss Van Hastings' roof. She estimated at least five more nights of visits to obtain all the information and proof she needed to punish the two-faced woman who would give Janus and Benedict Arnold and Iago -- combined -- a run for their money.

Once in the attic, she stashed her equipment behind the panels that hid it, on the off chance a servant actually came up to this dusty, dim room. Ess made a mental shopping list as she inventoried. It wouldn't do to remove the actual letters from and to the lawyers, so she needed to obtain some of the chemicals Granny used to create her copying paper. It was a bother and inconvenience that the copying paper had to be freshly made and couldn't be created in large quantities and kept on hand against need. However, Ess knew where all the required ingredients were kept in the large, airy room that passed for a laboratory on the premises of the academy. Miss Van Hastings presented a façade of a well-rounded education for her young ladies, preparing them to take their place at the head of society.

In reality, the fragments of chemistry, geology, cartography, and biology taught to the young ladies were only to give them a vocabulary to make their husbands and fathers look impressive. None of them were ever expected to put such knowledge to use. None of them were expected to manufacture gunpowder or repair a steam engine or sew a wound. For the sake of appearances, the laboratory classroom was kept fully stocked. Ess made a wager with herself that she could take half of the chemicals and other supplies and even some of the equipment, and no one would notice for a year or more.

"Copying paper," she muttered. "Lots of it -- please, good Lord and Savior, help me find lots of evidence of the noxious Mr. Van Hastings' activities so the Secret Service will cart him away once and for all."

She would prefer the oily young man be locked in an iron box and tossed into the nearest river. Everyone in the school knew when he came to visit his sister because there was always at least one housemaid with a bruised face or the signs of prolonged weeping. He always came wearing a false name and disguises. Ess knew just because she could see through his disguises -- patently false beards, badly dyed hair, monocles and even a ridiculously unworkable metal frame around one leg posing as a mechanical leg -- that didn't mean her fellow students could as well. There was no proof, only speculation. It wasn't like she could carry a camera with her and take photographs for proof without being caught. Although, now that she thought of it, sketches might be of some help in tracking the odious man, if the authorities knew the various disguises he employed. She was rather good with sketching paper and pencils. Why hadn't she thought of that before?

Other than the lack of need or motivation to take the Van Hastings down several notches, until now?

Besides bringing down the nefarious, traitorous activities of Mr. Van Hastings, Ess needed proof of all the lies the headmistress had been telling Endicott, Lewis and MacDonald. She suspected the duplicitous woman had been lying to her lawyers from the beginning, trying to put a wedge between them and Ess. She paused in changing from her boy clothes to her nightgown, robe, and house slippers to mentally slap herself. After all, if she hadn't been so caught up in evading and diluting the woman's every attempt to influence her mind and actions, she might have wondered before now why one of her grandparents' lawyers hadn't come to visit her. Ess wouldn't be surprised to learn that the headmistress had told them she was in a temper -- still -- over being left in the United States while her grandparents went adventuring, and refused to see them, considering them collaborators with her grandparents' decision. After all, Ess had accompanied them on their previous trip to South America four years ago, so why couldn't she accompany them now, when she would have been of help in their scientific endeavors? This was an entirely too believable scenario, because she honestly had been angry with the family lawyers -- they had helped her grandparents in the choice of where to leave her behind, after all.

"You're a fool, Odessa Fremont," she whispered as she slipped down the dark corridor to the stairs. "The situation has changed to something far more serious and dangerous than anything Mama and Papa faced before they died. Act like it. There is no one to stand between you and the cruel world."

In that moment, she made freedom from Miss Van Hastings and her Select Young Ladies Academy her ultimate goal.

Granted, the side benefits were delightful. Aiding the United States government in finally tracking down and capturing the vile Resurrectionist leader, Walter Van Hastings. Exposing Miss Van Hastings' scheming, money-grubbing, politically pandering ways. The delicious freedom to spend the next year or two -- or however long it took to make her way to South America and search for her grandparents -- wearing trousers and pretending to be a boy.

"It won't do to have nothing planned beyond that, however," Ess murmured when she reached her room. She slid the mannequin made of flesh-toned bladders, with a dark wig and dressed in her least favorite nightgown, out of her sheets and under her bed. "Like Granny says, always plan five steps ahead of any situation and any anticipated contingency."

She took another set of vials from the compartment she had hollowed out of the frame of her bed and made enough of the phosphorescent liquid to give herself twenty minutes of light. Using the candle beside the bed would have been easier, but there was the smell of melted wax and a recently doused wick to contend with, if someone were to come checking beds. Every once in a while, when the head housekeeper was in a foul mood, the sour-voiced, skeletal woman would ration candles. She would actually measure the height of each student's candles and accuse them of staying up past the permitted hour of the night. Even the excuse of needing to get in extra study wouldn't protect them from a scolding and confiscation of sweets or presents from families or sweethearts. Ess didn't care about such punishments, but she did want to avoid any notice from the housekeeper. Besides, using the phosphorescent liquid reminded her of her childhood, when all learning had been an adventure and not something regimented and turned boring and useless.

Ess made notes in the secret cypher Grandfather Earnest had taught her, a combination of cuneiform and hieroglyphics, planning out all the things she would like to do and needed to do to ensure her safety, once she levied punishment against the Van Hastings siblings and escaped this prison masquerading as a school. The exercise was so delightful, she nearly cried aloud in disappointment when the light flickered and she had to put her secret journal and the vials away and climb into bed. Ess lay awake past the chiming of two a.m. from the hallway clock, plotting adventures. She would obtain passage by steamship to South America, then assemble a team of guides, porters and guards to get her through the jungle. Or should she try to stow away on the courier dirigible? That would be an adventure all in itself, calculating how much she needed in the way of provisions.

Somewhere between two and two-thirty, her planning turned into a dream. She found her grandparents in a subterranean kingdom where the people ate luminescent fungi and glowed in the dark. Then her brother, Ulysses, arrived at the head of an entire regiment of officers from the United States Air Corps in their dashing gray-blue uniforms.

Chapter Two

Over the course of the next four nights, Ess concentrated on searching Miss Van Hastings' filing drawers and finding every bit of correspondence between her and Endicott, Lewis and MacDonald. She didn't quibble over her luck -- though she did sigh over the woman's arrogant complacence -- when she found volumes of correspondence from the vile Mr. Walter Van Hastings. She made copies of all his letters to his sister, detailing the activities of the Resurrectionists he led, the names of the newest recruits, and boasts about government targets they had crippled or robbed or destroyed outright. Even more loathsome were his boasts of "romantic conquests" of the daughters and maidservants in every household that made the mistake of welcoming him as a guest. Ess made so many copies, she had to sneak into the school laboratory nearly every day to take more chemicals to create her copying paper. Daily, she said a prayer of thanks for her clever grandmother, who had taught her to mix the chemicals and the proper application of the process. The copying paper was dry, and the source paper to be copied was lightly sprayed with a second chemical combination that created the equivalent of a photo negative on the destination paper when the two were pressed together. Several seconds after being separated, both papers were dry again. While there was no telltale smell during the process of copying, making the paper and creating the liquid for the spray was another story altogether. Ess had more proof of the oblivious foolishness of the people around her when no one remarked on or even seemed to notice the slight odors of bitter and pungent chemicals that clung to her after each session in the school laboratory.

Ess set about making a nuisance of herself, importuning Miss Van Hastings and others on the staff twice a day to investigate why she hadn't heard from her grandparents or her grandparents' lawyers yet. No one seemed to notice the change in her personality when she whined and sulked and stomped her feet. Playing the part became great fun, and earned increased mockery of the faculty from her fellow students. Her greatest triumph, however, was discovering several long letters from Walter Van Hastings, instructing his sister on using the school grounds for the Resurrectionist cause.

Ess used the afternoon quiet contemplation time to do a little exploring. While her fellow students found some privacy to sit in clusters and gossip, or indulge in sweets without an adult lecturing them on their complexion, she slipped outside and followed the instructions from the letters. It was ridiculously easy to find the tunnel entrance in the stable. Now Ess understood why students were discouraged from entering the stable, even to visit their own saddle horses. The emphasis on true ladylike behavior had seemed so ridiculously excessive, but now it made sense. All the stable workers were Resurrectionist sympathizers.

She followed the tunnel a short distance from the stable to an opening in the riverbank, where the Resurrectionists could land their rowboats on the pebbly shore. Other branches of the tunnel led under various buildings on the school grounds. Ess discovered that the walls in the large enclosed pavilion used for dances and other social activities pivoted out, revealing hidden storage rooms and large slates for drawing strategies for raids. She made a note to herself to return with a sketch pad and copy the drawings there, for further evidence.

One tunnel went under the building housing the academy's steam engine, which powered various lifting and moving activities on the grounds. It all made sense now. The engine and all the chain drives, conveyor belts and other appurtenances, for lifting water to the upper floors, carrying away soiled linens, and running the lift cars in several of the buildings, gave the Van Hastings a convenient excuse to have as few servants as possible. The fewer people around to see illegal activities, the more secure those activities would be.

Just out of curiosity, she followed some of the pipes carrying steam, to power household devices, or some of the chains leading directly from the engine. No surprise at all, she found nearly half the power of the steam engine was diverted to mechanisms in the tunnels and hidden rooms and for conveyor belts to move supplies, move panels to block tunnels, and pump water from the river to flood other tunnels.

The Van Hastings and their friends clearly considered themselves invulnerable, very smug, thinking they operated unseen under the nose of the government.

"Not for much longer," Ess promised herself as she studied the devices dependent on the steam engine. She had ideas to foul the entire mechanism, perhaps turn around various gears and reverse the controls on valves. It was amusing to think of the chagrin, then frustration, then terror of the Resurrectionists when government agents swarmed down on them. Instead of doors closing and tunnels flooding to protect them, those doors would open wider, the tunnels would stay dry, and others would flood to block their escape.

She refined her ideas as she scurried back down the tunnel toward the main body of the school. Earlier, she had discovered a side tunnel and steam-powered door that would let her out into the gardens. Just how often had the vile Mr. Van Hastings spied on the students while they laughed and frolicked in assumed privacy, even daring to go barefoot or hike up their skirts for games? She took that exit now. No one would scold if they found her wandering the garden in solitude.

Her spirits drooped as she considered all she needed to do to assist the

Secret Service in apprehending this nest of Resurrectionists. While the challenge excited her, and she found much amusement in inflicting frustration on the Van Hastings, her thoughts turned to the unfairness of having to deal with such things at fourteen years of age. Ess planned quite a scolding for her grandparents when she found them. Earnest and Matilda Fremont, brilliant archeologists, scholars, and inventors should have had more sense than to put their only granddaughter into the hands of such obsequious, materialistic, shallow, deceptive people.

No more time to waste on such grumblings and musings. She had a coup to plan, justice to implement, and her escape to orchestrate before she made contact with her lawyers and the government.

~~~~~

The next day was outing day in town. Every other Wednesday, the students were taken to town to allow them to run errands, make purchases, and conveniently encounter the wealthy and influential locals. Ess deliberately sat behind Miss Van Hastings in the long, covered wagon with padded benches that accommodated all the students and teachers. She whined to her companions about how she had a good mind to send a telegram to her grandparents' lawyers while she was in town, demanding they come explain in person what delayed her grandparents' latest communication. She watched the headmistress' shoulders, how they bowed and then stiffened and straightened, and the way she clenched and unclenched her gloved hands.

A few seconds before Ess calculated the woman would turn around and forbid her to go anywhere near the telegram office, she laughed and declared that she had far too many errands to run while she was in town. Why would she want to spend time talking to stuffy, fussy, boring old lawyers? She declared she wouldn't waste another minute worrying about her grandparents. Their last few letters had become positively boring. Why, she wondered aloud, had she ever found the filthy, sweaty, exhausting activities of archeology fascinating?

She fluttered up to Miss Van Hastings soon after arriving in town, and asked permission to indulge in a visit to the ice cream parlor, and then order a new pair of dancing slippers in the shop across the street. The headmistress beamed at Ess so widely, the girl feared the woman might hug her.

"I don't know what mischief you're up to now, Odessa," Fanny Wilcox whispered as the two of them linked arms and scampered across the street. A steam-powered cart whined past them, trailing a cloud of black smoke that most likely came from a faulty seal in the lubrication system. "Whatever it is, you're brilliant. I had the dubious honor of being on the bench facing the nasty old harridan."

She shuddered, her rosebud mouth flattening in distaste in direct contradiction to the merriment sparkling in her eyes. They paused on the steps going up to the shop selling slippers and gloves, and she glanced
~~~~~

around.

"She went white as a sheet when you mentioned sending a telegram to your lawyers. Then you should have seen how beads of sweat broke out on her forehead when you waved it all off. I don't know what that woman is plotting now, but I wouldn't be surprised if she's found a way to sell us all into politically astute marriages, without our parents' permission, and then charging them enormous finders' fees, so she can retire and close the school."

"Maybe turn it into a bordello," Ess offered, and glanced over her shoulder. The prickling sensation in her shoulders had been correct -- Miss Van Hastings stood there in the shade of the awning over the entrance of the tea room. According to the most recent letter from her brother, she was to meet three of his friends there to exchange information and money to aid in plotting the overthrow of the Union. Ess plastered a wide, brainless smile on her face and raised her gloved hand to wave to the headmistress. They were too far away, but she didn't doubt the woman turned red, startled at being caught watching them. In a moment, Miss Van Hastings hurried indoors.

"That might be a better choice than marrying some of the pasty-faced, unimaginative, humorless automatons she's paraded past us lately," Fanny said. The two girls linked arms again and climbed the steps to the door of the shop. "Be thankful you're only fourteen. I will be sixteen in three weeks, and sometimes I positively feel like a prisoner counting the days until the gallows."

"She really couldn't force you to marry someone of whom your parents didn't approve, could she?" Ess supposed she should examine all the files regarding her fellow students, to see what lies the headmistress told their parents, to protect her friends.

"Oh, despite being so clever, you really are an innocent." The older girl patted her hand and stepped to the side once they entered the open doorway. She looked back the way they had come. "A number of us have cottoned to her tricks and schemes. We have something of an underground movement, and meet in the flower arranging classroom every other Sunday night, to compare notes. Then we send letters to our parents or other relatives who might be more prone to believe us. Since we can't get a single letter in or out of the school without the supervision of the teachers, Georgianna's older brother pays for a post office box that we share. We take turns sneaking letters into the mail when we're in town, and checking the box for letters in response to our reports. One of the first things we realized -- or rather, some of the girls who graduated before us realized -- is that the odious woman reads our letters, coming and going, and flies into a rage of offended dignity if anyone dares confront her about it. As if it is not only her right, but her duty to pry into what should be private conversations. Some of our parents have grown quite distrustful of Miss Van Hastings, especially as our letters contradict more and more what she is telling them about our activities and predilections."

"I should very much like to be part of the fun."

"You shall. Some of us noticed she was aiming Senator Wilkerson's son at you at the last cotillion. I wouldn't put it past her to contrive a very long engagement. When it's announced in all the society papers, there's no way you can withdraw without a lot of fuss and embarrassment."

"That fop who couldn't put four words together without gulping? The one who smelled like he gargled Macassar oil, not just bathed in it?" Ess shuddered, and it wasn't in the least for show.

"It's my turn to check the post office box, and you're coming with me." Fanny gestured at a side door that opened into the shop next door. The four shops in a row here were owned by siblings, with connecting doors. They made for convenient exits without being noticed by unwanted watchers across the street.

A little office that arranged transportation by steam ship, dirigible, train and stagecoach occupied a room off the lobby of the post office. Ess said a silent prayer of thanks that Fanny had elected to be her partner for today's excursion. She decided to be flattered that the older girl had chosen to include her in the secret conspiracy among the students.

Now, how could she contrive to help her fellow students not only escape the nefarious schemes of their headmistress, but triumph in a public, embarrassing way, once she had made her own escape?

Her first inquiries in the travel office answered several questions, but didn't provide the answers she wanted. Yes, she could take a ship to South America, either a sailing vessel or a steamship. She had quite enough money saved from her weekly allowance, carefully hidden from the Academy's staff. The teaching staff made a practice of invading the students' pocketbooks, and when confronted with their thefts, claimed they were protecting the girls from carelessness with their funds. Ess hadn't trusted the staff from the first day and contrived several hiding places, so didn't suffer the losses that infuriated her schoolmates. Between that and the bank account her grandparents had established for her -- of which Miss Van Hastings had no knowledge -- she had enough money to pay for passage on an airship all the way to South America. The amount she would need once she arrived was rather nebulous and required further investigation. Common sense said she would need money for supplies and guides and transportation. She would need a translator, unless she managed to make a quick study of Spanish on the voyage south.

However, it didn't matter if she took an airship or a sailing vessel, because no matter how quickly or slowly she arrived, her grandparents' trail would be long gone cold. Once she reached the port facilities, she faced another long wait before heading into the interior. The courier dirigible would leave before she arrived, with a wait of two months between each trip out and back. She would be delayed long enough that anyone sent after her would have time to catch up with her.

No matter how she made her escape, someone would come after her. Miss Van Hastings would continue trying to control every part of Ess's life, or her vile brother would hunt her down in retribution for whatever damage she managed to inflict on the Resurrectionists. While Ess would thoroughly enjoy the Van Hastings knowing she had engineered their downfall, that would be vainglorious, even suicidal. She needed to act as anonymously and undetected as possible. After all, she wouldn't even be fifteen for three months.

Endicott, Lewis and MacDonald would send someone to fetch her home as soon as they learned the truth of her situation. That was the largest reason for acting *before* telling them what she had learned and what she planned. Their sense of responsibility for her was strong and honorable, not through contract, but because they were her grandparents' friends.

Another strike against her plan to go south: the weather. When the ship reached South America, the rainy season would be starting. If she waited too long, to avoid the bad weather there, no oceangoing vessel would be available, as the winter weather made the ocean difficult for navigation.

"Botheration," she said aloud, but not loudly enough to catch the attention of the clerk fussing with his brochures and stamps and other paraphernalia behind the tall counter. She turned and marched out of the little office before the man realized perhaps the young lady wandering his office might have wanted to purchase a ticket. Better to be as forgettable as possible at this point in her planning. What if someone remembered she had stood here, looking longingly at posters of South American voyages?

After that disappointment, Ess found very little amusement in joining the students' plot to circumvent Miss Van Hastings' machinations. She admired the cleverness of the older girls. Her estimation of their common sense and awareness rose quite a good deal after that afternoon.

One thing she was sure of, as she climbed on board the long, sheltered wagon for the return trip to the Academy: she needed to make her break for freedom and bring down the wrath of the United States Government on the Van Hastings as soon as possible. Walter Van Hastings had revealed to his sister the beginning of a plan to assassinate President Lincoln -- for the sixth time since the end of the war. There were rumors he was being pressured by his party to run for President for a fourth term. The Resurrectionists considered him a symbol of everything that was wrong with the Union and hated him for his ability to bring reconciliation to bitter feuds. As long as the benign, caring, no-nonsense man remained in office, the Union would rally against any attempt to splinter it and put the South in power.

The Resurrectionist leaders from ten states were meeting in the pavilion on the far side of the Academy grounds in ten days. That would be the perfect time to bring the Secret Service down on their rebellious, oily heads. The resulting chaos would perfectly hide Ess's escape. Could she prime the steam engine in the cellar to explode? Start a fire? Sabotage the chains and gears and pumps? Flood tunnels that needed to stay open? Something else as a final calling card? Or would that be juvenile and ill-bred of her?

No, she decided as she sat next to Fanny, facing Miss Van Hastings, and smiled serenely at her nemesis. No, indeed, it would not be ill-bred. She knew her grandparents would laugh at her cleverly detailed plan. They wouldn't consider a patriotic act ill-bred at all.

~~~~~

Every third week, the Academy brought in a troupe of highly regarded actors -- stringently chaperoned, of course -- to teach the young ladies the effective use of cosmetics, the language of the fan, and the most modern dances. The next lesson occurred the day after Ess's trip to town. As their teachers took the first group of girls through the intricate steps of a new dance that was supposedly all the rage before the crowned heads of Europe, she worked out another phase of her plan.

Common sense said she should flee to South America in search of her grandparents. They were the only family she had left in the world, after all. Only Miss Van Hastings and the family lawyers, at this time, knew that Earnest and Matilda Fremont were missing, presumed dead. Ess would be expected to flee to join them when she ran away from the Academy, if she didn't know their archeological camp had been destroyed.

Therefore, the common sense step was avoid South America. Ess would delay her trip until next spring, when the seas were more in her favor. Or better yet, perhaps she should hire someone to do the hunting for her and stay in the United States, disguised as a boy, hiding almost under the noses of those looking for her. It was a given she didn't dare go to Endicott, Lewis and MacDonald once she was free of the Academy. They would believe her when she told them about the Resurrectionist activities being carried out under the school grounds, and Miss Van Hastings' duplicity, but they would also put her into another boarding school. If her grandparents wouldn't let her stay at the family home with the household staff looking after her, she wouldn't be able to convince the family lawyers to choose that option for her. If she couldn't join her grandparents in South America, Ess intended to spend the next year or two in freedom.

A brilliant idea came to her as she watched Miss Talbot, the head of the acting troupe, teach a group of older girls how to feign illness, to avoid dancing with some clumsy or socially unacceptable swain. Miss Talbot, with a little paint, a little hair dye, could pass for Ess. She was an excellent mimic in terms of mannerisms, posture, the way she held her mouth or tipped her head. Even without makeup, she could make people doubt the evidence of their eyes.

"Now isn't that a clever, fun idea?" Miss Talbot murmured, dropping into a thick drawl that nearly perfumed the air with honeysuckle, when Ess presented her proposal to her.

Around them, the troupe was packing up their boxes of makeup,
~~~~~

musical instruments, and the diagrams of foot positions that covered the floor. Ess always volunteered to help clean up after lessons, just to talk with someone outside of the school. That helped her now, because no one would remark on her conversation with Miss Talbot. As the days ticked off until the hoped-for raid -- if the Secret Service believed the letters and evidence she sent them -- she grew even more aware of how necessary it was to do nothing memorable or out of the ordinary.

"Darling girl, you have every right to make a run for freedom. None of us have any respect for that woman and her ideas of a proper education for young ladies. Not in the new society being built on the wreckage of that idiotic war. However, we have to be practical, and there is far too much power in money." Miss Talbot fluttered her eyelashes, barely hiding the mischief sparkling in her fern green eyes.

Ess mentally slapped her wrist for not remembering that detail -- her own eyes were hazel. Someone who got close enough would know Miss Talbot wasn't her, no matter how cleverly she disguised herself.

"However," the actress continued, "I have been offered a wonderful touring opportunity in Europe. My career is my top priority while I can still act. Maybe later, when I am reduced to motherly roles, or even teaching..." She slumped her shoulders and pressed the back of her hand against her forehead in feigned distress, earning a chuckle from Ess. "However, I have a friend who is in dire need of a new role, shall we say, to evade an unpleasantly sticky problem. She has the right bone structure, the right height, even the eye color... hmm, the hair will need help, but that is easily remedied."

"What kind of trouble is she in?" Ess glanced over her shoulder to gauge the progress of the others clearing the room. The pavilion was quickly becoming an empty, echoing space again. She found great pleasure in contemplating this place filled with confusion and men shouting and cursing. Dare she hope for some accident, perhaps a malfunction with the steam engine, to cause the pavilion to burn down, or perhaps even explode skyward?

"Three sweethearts in three cities, all believing she has promised to marry them. Honestly, Sarah is too clever for such a mistake. She isn't nearly enough of a success to marry a high-society fool and coast for the rest of her life on her fame, no matter how great the fortune he offers. No, they're all three dunderheads who hear what they want to hear. She needs to either change her name and appearance and start her career all over again..." her smile turned almost feline, "or flee the country entirely, with no discernible trail for them to follow. What she lacks is funds. I was considering offering her a temporary assignment as my assistant, or even my understudy, but your little proposition is far too delicious. Shall I contact her?"

Chapter Three

"Please. How quickly could she be ready?" Ess crossed fingers on both hands behind her back. She had eight days left.

"More important, how can I get her answer to you without arousing suspicion? I've always found that those who have the most to hide are the most suspicious of everyone else."

"You could leave one of your makeup kits with me to practice with, and then send someone in a few days to retrieve it."

"Better yet, I'll leave two. You'll need one when you make your escape." She beckoned and hurried across the pavilion to the doorway, where the boxes of makeup, brushes, face powder and other accoutrements of the thespian trade waited to be loaded into the troupe's steam car.

They made sure that Miss Fernhurst, the pianoforte teacher, witnessed Miss Talbot giving Ess one of the makeup kits and overheard their arrangements for retrieval. She was conveniently there because the woman always scurried around like a ferret, sticking her wriggling nose into everything that didn't concern her. Ess proved her skills as a pickpocket by slipping a second kit out of the box when she dropped the first one and bent to pick it up. Miss Talbot winked and smiled her approval of the sleight of hand trick.

~~~~~

That night, Ess discovered that Miss Van Hastings or her brother had been practicing forging her signature. The worst part was that the forgeries were rather good. Whoever had covered ten sheets of paper with her name, growing closer to Ess's scrawling penmanship with each try, had a future as a counterfeiter.

Ess didn't have nearly enough copying paper and spray to copy all the sheets to prove someone was learning to forge her signature, but further searching negated the need for proof. She found a master copy of a letter, purportedly from her, to go to Endicott, Lewis and MacDonald. Supposedly she was so utterly wounded by the loss of her grandparents that she wanted Miss Van Hastings to become her guardian. All communication would go through her. The lawyers were to transfer all authority over her grandparents' estate to Miss Van Hastings. By the end of the month, she would arrange to empty out the house, dismiss the staff, and sell the house and grounds.

The vision of Walter Van Hastings coming into her grandparents' home and emptying it of the rooms and rooms of books and archeological treasures and all the clever gadgets her grandmother had invented, the shelves and shelves of archives her grandfather kept for his scholarly friends… it sickened
~~~~~

her. Infuriated her. Frightened her.

She couldn't think for several moments. The meeting of the Resurrectionists would be at the same time as the Van Hastings planned to loot the Fremont home. Likely Resurrectionist sympathizers would be recruited to conduct the operation -- and their cause would profit. Ess needed to notify Endicott, Lewis and MacDonald *now* of the deception being perpetrated on them. She needed to go home before the meeting and hopeful raid and looting, and arrange to hide her family treasures.

Ess shuddered, remembering with utmost clarity her grandfather sitting her down in his office, redolent with the aroma of paper and ink, binding glue and leather. He had allowed her several days to accept the inescapable fact of her staying behind when he and her grandmother went to South America. Then he charged her with a number of duties. First among them was a long list of instructions and procedures to follow if anything untoward were to happen to him and Matilda. Top priority was to protect the archives, the record books she was not to read until she had reached her majority. Then he had chuckled and waved a finger in her face and challenged her to resist the temptation to read any of the archives before that monumental birthday.

Hands shaking, Ess silently repeated her vow to her grandfather while she copied the letter to be sent in a matter of days to her lawyers. The most important, the most valuable feature of the letter was the notes written in a second distinct hand, Mr. Van Hastings instructing his sister when to send the letter. There was even a comment about how inconsiderate the elder Fremonts were to die before they could re-educate Ess and turn her into a compliant dupe. They could only hope that their efforts to portray her as fluttery and brainless had convinced the lawyers so they would be glad to wash their hands of her.

Fury finally turned cold enough that Ess's hands steadied enough to copy the letter without any smearing or blurring. Most definitely, she would ensure so much damage to the Academy and grounds and Miss Van Hastings' reputation that no discerning parents would ever again trust their daughter or their wealth in her hands.

When Miss Talbot's courier came to retrieve the first makeup kit, Ess planned to have many letters for her to post. Instructions for her stand-in. More than adequate proof for Endicott, Lewis and MacDonald. Most important of all, multiple letters and proof to go to various Secret Service offices and local officials. Ess would have to leave the grounds of the school before the hoped-for raid, to head off the looting of her family home. By the grace of God, she would be back in time to see the results of her handiwork.

Before the light ran out entirely for that night's foray, Ess found the beginning of a letter from someone inquiring about her presence. Frustratingly, that was all she found -- the beginning. There were notes from Mr. Van Hastings to -- and this raised her ire again -- respond as to the others inquiring about her presence, saying that no such young lady by that name had ever been a student at the Academy. Another note said since this was the third such query from these people, and they couldn't take the hint that their interference was not wanted, he would have to deal with them. Ess assumed the missing portion of the letter, identifying who had inquired about her, had been taken to help him "deal with them."

So, other people were inquiring about her? Ess shuddered, remembering cryptic words from her grandparents about old friends and promises of assistance. Maybe her grandparents had thought she was too young to handle such knowledge? Certainly Uly had been reckless and prone to speaking out of turn and demanding information they weren't ready to give, just before her brother vanished. What made her grandparents think that she was as loud and talkative and brash as her brother? Much as she adored Uly, she wouldn't mimic him because she could see he was rather foolish, despite being six years her senior. Why hadn't her grandparents given her information on these mysterious friends and allies who could be counted on to come to her rescue?

When she was very young, her grandparents had given her a flute and taught her to play certain songs, and certain sequences within the songs, to signal for help. Ess had imagined that her grandparents' friends and allies were somehow invisible. Or perhaps spent their lives in the large dirigibles that could hold entire troops of soldiers or even small villages, enabling them to swoop down without warning whenever she was in need. She had brought the flute with her to the Academy, but one of the headmistress' flunkies had confiscated it within a month of her arrival as "encouraging entirely unladylike positions of hands and mouth." Ess made a mental note to retrieve the flute, to begin playing the signal songs as soon as possible. While she was at it, she would retrieve many other items that had been taken from her and from her fellow students. She imagined leaving everything in a huge pile in the common room in the dormitory, and the other girls descending on the pile of loot like children on Christmas morning.

The light in her glowing tube took on a slightly yellower cast, meaning she had perhaps ten seconds of illumination remaining. Ess quickly put the desk and its contents back as she had found them. There certainly seemed to be more correspondence and paperwork dealing with her lately, like ripples in a pond. She looked forward to tossing several stones into Miss Van Hastings' pond, and planned to linger as close in the area as possible to see the consequences. It would be entertaining, or at the very least, educational.

Footsteps approaching the office startled her just as she climbed off the sideboard onto the windowsill. Her hands trembled just slightly as she slipped her feet into the rigging and prepared to reverse her trip to the office. Voices came closer, and a strip of light appeared under the door. Miss Van Hastings' voice was clearly recognizable -- she was using her normal voice, touched with gravel, not the sweet falsetto used for visiting parents and officials and students who hadn't had the temerity to think for themselves.

The other voice was a man's, also with a touch of gravel, most likely Walter Van Hastings.

This was too good an opportunity to miss. Ess positioned herself above the window, and left it open just an inch, to hear more clearly.

"We need that money now," Mr. Van Hastings said, above the creak of the door opening and the squeaking of the floor. "We can't wait for the sale of the girl's house and grounds. Tell those lawyers to send an advance on her allowance. Not just an advance, but an increase." He chortled, followed by a creaking that sounded exactly like Miss Van Hastings' chair. "Explain to them that the girl's vapors are increasing, and you not only need to pay for the constant visits from the doctor, but you are seriously considering sending her away some place where she can get peace and quiet, rest for her delicate nerves."

"Are we sending her away? Please, Walter, I should like nothing better than to be rid of the girl."

"Why? She's finally docile. You could sell her in marriage without anyone interfering. I suggest you do so before word comes that her grandparents have been found."

"I'd rather sell her into a bordello, like that dratted Minchin girl. Oh, what fun it would have been, hearing her shrieks of fury turn to terror."

"Yes, well." Mr. Van Hastings chuckled, and the sound sent oily shivers up and down Ess's spine. She twitched, hanging upside down in her climbing rig. "The spoiled brat needed to be taken down several dozen pegs. The nerve of her family, pretending they were wealthy and European, and then vanishing when their masquerade folded, leaving you holding the bag and the brat."

"We got most of our money back, though, from the sale." The floor gave off several pops, indicating Miss Van Hastings stood directly in front of the desk -- exactly where students facing her discipline had to stand.

"No, we are better served -- the cause is better served -- selling her into marriage. Or perhaps just into servitude. Another group of people are searching for a final word on the fate of Earnest and Matilda Fremont." His chair creak-groaned, indicating he turned slowly side to side on the swivel. "My understanding is that they are something of rivals, in archeological circles."

"Rivals? Archeologists? What is there to fight over?" Her words were followed by a most unladylike snort.

"You would be surprised, dear sister, how much money is to be made in archeology. Now that the war is over--"

"Temporarily."

"Hmm, yes, temporarily. Now that relations are calm and turning sweet again between the Union and Britain, the passion for ancient civilizations has crossed the Atlantic like a disease. There is great wealth and prestige to be gained from a massive discovery. Great wealth indeed."

"What does that have to do with selling the Fremont chit into marriage?"

"We convince these rivals that the girl was a close confidant of her grandparents, that she knew things they hadn't released to the academic community, and has access to records they have hidden away."

"And leave it up to them to punish her when she doesn't deliver. How delicious!" A most uncharacteristic giggle escaped Miss Van Hastings. "Still," she added, speaking quickly, so Ess wondered what sort of expression her brother wore to prompt that reaction, "what if we're wrong?"

"About what?" His voice tightened.

"The girl's pretentions of being a scholar -- archeology is, after all, a very unladylike pursuit."

"If Queen Victoria has a passion for it, no one dares call it unladylike."

"That is beside the point. Walter, what if the girl *does* have hidden knowledge? Wouldn't it be better to get the knowledge and use it for ourselves? Think how much money archeological discoveries would bring in for the rebirth of the South."

"We don't have the time or the funds or the manpower to invest in such efforts. Sell her to someone who hates her grandparents and would be willing to pay lots of gold right now for the chance of besting them." The chair creaked and the wheels protested, indicating Mr. Van Hastings stood and pushed the chair away. "Now, you're going to sit down and write that letter with all the changes I gave you, and post it tomorrow, first thing. We need that money in hand before the gathering. Don't fail me, sister."

"No, no, of course not. Never, Walter."

Ess took a deep breath and activated the clockwork rewinder to take her back up to the attic. She could still hear the Van Hastings' voices as she crawled back onto solid footing again. Well, it seemed her timetable had to be moved up once again. First step: write a letter to Miss Talbot immediately, and have someone send the makeup kit to her in the morning, rather than wait for the courier. The rest of her letter packets were ready to go, fortunately.

Oh, please, Granny, Grandfather, do show up soon. You have no idea the kind of mess you left me in, when you ran off without me.

Instead of going to bed, Ess went down the dumbwaiter shaft to the locked room where students' confiscated property was held. She planned to leave the secret of the easy access to Fanny, and depend on her to share it with like-minded and athletic students. They could decide how to confound the school staff until the authorities shut down Miss Van Hastings' enterprise once and for all. She couldn't possibly take everything out of the storage room tonight, so Ess would be content with taking just her own property.

Students who had presented properly repentant faces and manners earned back property that had been confiscated. The few who had been obsequious enough to be allowed into the room itself had passed on a description of its contents. The room was full of deep shelves, holding pasteboard boxes arranged in alphabetical order by the students' last names, with their possessions inside.

Ess's sense of elation faded when she found her box and took it down off the shelf, and found only half her confiscated property in it. Only one-third of her books were there. She checked the flyleaf of each, and deduced that only books specifically inscribed to her hadn't been sold. Anything that could be sold had no identifying marks. Her rock collecting equipment, a box of chemicals and a guidebook on conducting experiments, and her flute.

She didn't care about the monetary value of the missing items, but the value lay in the memories evoked. They were precious because her grandparents had given them to her.

Fury prompted Ess to take the entire pasteboard box, when common sense said if she left it behind, empty, no one would realize what she had done. She considered dropping the box into the shaft servicing the dumbwaiter system, in hopes of fouling the ropes, perhaps causing a malfunction in the steam system that powered it. Instead, she planned to steal more boxes, fill them with all her possessions, and use the Resurrectionists' own secretive system to send the boxes to a shipping company in town. Everything would go to Endicott, Lewis and MacDonald. Ess could trust them to keep everything safe for her.

She didn't climb into bed until nearly four in the morning. Ess reached into the secret compartment she had fashioned in the wall behind the headboard, and pulled out the derringer her grandfather had given her for her last birthday. Ess wore the small, deadly accurate gun on her person the day she arrived at the Academy, so it hadn't been confiscated. She had needed to use all her skills of sleight of hand to hide the ammunition, but Miss Deslock had no idea what she was looking at when she opened the box of cartridges and put it aside to be examined later. She turned her back on Ess long enough for the girl to steal it away. Her grandmother had fashioned a holster for Ess that let her wear the derringer under her clothes, if necessary, either strapped high on her chest between her yet-to-appear breasts, or in the small of her back.

"Avoid the obvious whenever possible," Matilda had advised her, on that rainy afternoon when they had thoroughly enjoyed themselves creating the harness that could be adjusted as Ess matured. "No one expects a lady to be armed in the first place, so why ruin the advantage by wearing it in a leg holster or at your hip where any fool with one good eye could see it?"

"Thank you, Granny," Ess whispered as she tugged on the straps that had grown stiff with disuse, and tested the feel of the harness around her upper torso. She was amused to discover that some time in the last few months, her breasts had begun to form. Not enough to be noticeable or require adjustments in her clothes, but they would certainly be a botheration now when she would need to convince everyone around her she was male if she wanted to escape to safety.

~~~~~

Miss Talbot's courier came that morning to retrieve the makeup kit. For a few seconds, Ess feared their plot had been discovered, but the messenger boy was in actuality a young lady, disguised as a boy so utterly convincing that Ess didn't suspect her at first. The "boy" had a cut on his cheek, his hair was short-cropped and tangled with dust and sweat, and his stance was the open-legged, defiant sort of straddle that boys used when they were in uncomfortable situations and wanted an excuse to pound someone. "He" sniffed and wiped his nose with the back of his hand, and then wiped it on the seat of "his" breeches as Ess came down the stairs to the side entrance where merchants and deliverymen were allowed inside.

"Begging your pardon, Miss Fremont, but Miss Talbot is in an awful hurry to get that makeup kit back. Would you mind much if I followed you upstairs?" the boy hurried to say in a scratchy, creaking voice that hinted at impending maturity.

"Oh, very well," Miss Carrvel said with a sigh and a limp wave of her hand, as if she could brush them both off and out of her sight. She walked away to settle down in the chair further down the hall with her knitting, where she could have clear view of the main staircase of the dormitory building, the front door, and the side door. All the teachers who had sentinel duty hated it, and Ess had been counting on that attitude to help her sneak out her letters with the courier.

"I shouldn't have any trouble at all pretending to be you," the courier "boy" whispered, following Ess up the stairs. "Keep moving," she hurried to add, when Ess stopped in surprise.

"You're perfect," she announced, once the actress had followed her into her room and closed the door. Leaning closer, Ess saw they had the same color eyes, and the shape of their cheekbones was similar enough to pass cursory examination. "But what about your hair?" She nearly reached up to tug at the woman's short mop.

"Wig. My hair is nearly the same shade as yours -- a dark red rinse should help put in the highlights. Pardon?" She didn't wait for permission, but reached up with both hands and tugged on Ess's neatly coiled braids, thrust her fingertips into them, even pressed against her scalp. "Nearly the same texture and thickness. We're of a height -- even if we weren't, that could be fixed with shoes."

They had little time to waste, but fortunately Ess had already prepared her instructions for her doppelganger. The actress introduced herself as Sarah Deverall. A friend at the local newspaper had warned her that one of her more importunate suitors was trying to buy an advertisement to announce their engagement. He needed to obtain a photograph that wasn't autographed, and that delay was all that saved her at the moment. The suitor's family was of such high social standing that Sarah couldn't deny the engagement once it appeared in the paper and was accepted as accomplished fact.
~~~~~

"It isn't that I don't like Jacob. I do. I just don't want to spend the rest of my life with him starting next month. I have a long career ahead of me, and I'd have to quit the stage the day the engagement is announced. The worst part of it is that his parents actually like me, and I like them."

"How is that bad? Isn't it better if you like your in-laws?"

"Ordinarily, yes, but I don't want to hurt them. Which they will be -- in more ways than one."

Sarah explained the situation as they searched Ess's wardrobe for several outfits to help convince people she was indeed Odessa Fremont. While Jacob was the impetuous sort who didn't understand that shanghaiing a young lady into an engagement wasn't romantic or welcome, other suitors were of more selfish and violent temperaments. Sarah knew of two who had threatened other suitors, so they didn't dare shower her with gifts after performances, or offer to pay her shop bills. One was likely to challenge Jacob to an illegal duel the day the engagement was announced. The other would either ambush him somewhere and batter him into submission, or simply kill him with a bullet in the back.

"You love him, don't you?" Ess said, once they had made a solid, small bundle of three dresses and matching stockings and gloves. She stepped over to her window and looked down on the grounds. A thick wall of boxwood on the school side of the fence made a challenging target, but she had arm strength built up after many nights of climbing sufficient to toss the bundle over and onto the adjoining property. There was plenty of cover to hide Sarah as she retrieved the clothes.

"I think I do, but... marriage with anyone at this stage in my life frightens me."

"How old are you? If you don't mind me asking."

"I'll be eighteen next month." Sarah tugged her cap back into place, lightly ran her fingers over the seam where her wig was glued to the hairline, and dropped back into her boyish posture. "Now, do we have everything?"

Chapter Four

They ran through the thick bundle of letters, which Sarah tucked inside her shirt, after removing some of the sacking around her waist that hid her hourglass figure. Ess made a note of that trick to use in her own escape. It wouldn't be enough to simply bind her breasts flat, if her hips gave her away. Sarah knew which instructions were to go to Miss Talbot, which were for her, and how to handle the bank drafts to give her access to the ready funds waiting for Ess. Sarah laughed with Ess, when she explained the headmistress believed the allowance sent by her family lawyers was all the money her grandparents had doled out for her. Earnest and Matilda encouraged Ess's love of books and excursions for educational purposes or simply for adventure. They had established a bank account for her to use with no one to gainsay her. Ess had never used it, which meant there was no chance Miss Van Hastings knew it existed.

This money now would help pay for Sarah's flight to South America, to convince the world that Odessa Fremont had indeed gone to look for her missing grandparents. Then Sarah would change her appearance and name once again and take a steamship to England, where she would rejoin Miss Talbot and start her new life safely away from her suitors.

They were kindred spirits, Ess decided a short time later, watching from her window as Sarah scampered through the underbrush next door and retrieved the bundle of clothes. By afternoon, all her letters to her lawyers, various Secret Service offices and other authorities would be in the hands of the Postal Service. Ess hoped she would be just as successful in her own disguise as Sarah had proven to be. Perhaps in later years, when they were older and had found their own successes and reached their goals, they would meet again. She was sure the stories they exchanged would be amazing, amusing, and altogether satisfying.

~~~~~

"Odessa." Miss Van Hastings approached Ess in that waiting quiet before the breakfast bell released all the students to fetch their books and pencils before their first class of the day. Two days had passed since Sarah had taken away the letters.

The quiet deepened, so Ess thought she could hear the breathing of nearly every girl at her round table in the corner. She took a deep breath and ordered her face to remain calm, despite the sudden racing thunder of her heart, and slid out of her chair.

"Yes, Miss Van Hastings?" she said as she turned to face the headmistress.
~~~~~

There was something in the woman's face. A twitching of one corner of her mouth, a matching twitch in the corner of her eye. The way she twisted her handkerchief in both hands, with her arms locked at waist level. The woman was ready to explode in a gush of sarcasm, scolding and indignation, if she followed true to form.

For two seconds, Ess felt her face grow cold and imagined all the blood had left her skin. Had Sarah been caught posting the letters? Or worse, arrested for trying to withdraw money from her secret account?

"My dear child, I fear I am the bearer of grave, indeed sad news."

"Sad news, Miss Van Hastings?" Ess's knees tried to fold, but she caught herself. Indeed, the sudden euphoria of relief nearly lifted her off the floor. Then her mind raced, wondering what disaster in the Van Hastings' plans had forced the woman to tell her the "sad news" right now, ahead of schedule.

Most likely Miss Van Hastings was simply under so much pressure from her odious brother, she needed to lash out and hurt someone. Well, if that was what she wanted, Ess would give her the performance of a lifetime, so she would never suspect she was being played.

"We received word from your grandparents' lawyers that some terrible accident has happened." Miss Van Hastings rested a hand on Ess's shoulder. "You must be brave, dear child. Brace yourself, and be strong."

"Miss Van Hastings, you're frightening me." Ess was so delighted with the quaver in her voice, she almost couldn't get her lip to quiver convincingly.

"Forgive me." She moved her hand to stroke the back of Ess's hair. "I'm sorry to inform you that your grandparents are missing, presumed dead."

"No." Ess bowed her head into her hands, so no one could see her face. Her shoulders shook as whispers circled the room. She went to her knees and dug her fingers into her eyes, to redden them. What heartless twit didn't weep over her missing grandparents, after all?

Granted, she hadn't wept, but she refused to believe Earnest and Matilda were lost, let alone dead. She had been too furious over the Van Hastings' duplicity to allow room for grief.

Within half an hour, Ess was ensconced in her room, tucked up in bed with soothing tea and offers of sweets from the girls on her floor. Miss Deslock stood guard outside her door to drive away offers of company. Miss Van Hastings had been all too quick to accede to Ess's announcement that she preferred to be alone.

"She *wants* me isolated," Ess mused. She tugged a private journal from its hiding place in the bottom of a drawer, and made notes of this latest step in the Van Hastings siblings' assault on her life and freedom. "She wants me weak and weepy and dramatic? Fine."

The soothing tea smelled suspiciously of an herbal mixture her grandmother used to give her and Ulysses when they were much younger, to make them sleepy and quiet. Usually when scholarly friends met in their house for days at a time, or when childhood escapades resulted in injuries that needed serious doctoring. Ess poured the tea into her chamber pot and obligingly pretended to be asleep every time someone opened the door to check on her. When they woke her for lunch, and then for dinner, she spoke in whispers and blinked rapidly to force tears, and only nibbled on the toast and poached eggs and creamed fruit they brought her. As soon as she was left alone, Ess chewed up the food and spit it out into the chamber pot. Miss Deslock seemed entirely too pleased at this false evidence that Ess couldn't keep anything down.

"Well what shall we feed you at breakfast, if you have become so queasy?" the woman said, removing the tray of the remains of Ess's dinner. Her lip curled as she watched the housemaid carry away the covered chamber pot.

"Please, I would prefer not to have any breakfast at all," Ess said, curling up on her side and hiding as much of her face as she could in the pillow and her tangled hair. "I think I will never be able to eat again. I just want to sleep."

"Sleep you shall," she said. "Drink the nice fresh pot of tea I brought you, and we will see how you feel at lunchtime tomorrow, shall we?"

"Yes, please. Thank you for taking such good care of me, Miss Deslock. I shall never forget it."

From the nasty smirk on Miss Deslock's face as she left the room, Ess guessed she was deep into the plots and actions of the Resurrectionists. She could only hope the woman ended up in a federal prison somewhere for the rest of her life.

"No, indeed, I shall forget nothing," Ess whispered as she slid out of her bed and listened to the woman's footsteps fade, heading down the hall. With all the girls in bed for the night, there was no need to keep away visitors. Miss Deslock was indeed an arrogant fool, thinking it was more important to keep people away from Ess, than to keep her in her room.

All her preparations were ready. She slipped into her boy clothes that had served her so well during her midnight rambles through the school grounds, and pulled out three bags with long straps for going across her chest. Everything she could not live without, that she refused to leave behind in her enemies' hands, went into those bags. Within half an hour, she had made her way up the dumbwaiter system to Fanny's floor, crept into her friend's room, and slid a note with instructions for getting into the storage room under the older girl's pillow. Then Ess went up to the attic, retrieved all her sneaking and skulking gear, and took the dumbwaiter down to the cellar. She hurried through the secret tunnels, adjusting valves, jamming levers, and trickling sand into gear boxes. The damage she did tonight wouldn't be noticeable for several days. Pressure would build up, closed off tunnels would slowly fill with water, and sand would slowly gum up the works. All were small things that combined into a large disaster for the Resurrectionists.

Ess just hoped she would be able to get back here in time to witness it all.

Two hours later, she stowed away in a long train of wagons pulled by a steam engine, going to a manufacturing hub three counties away. The sacks and bales of cotton and hemp fiber made a relatively comfortable nest, if slightly aromatic. Ess was most definitely pleased with this first step in her plan of retribution and gaining her freedom. She knew better than to hope that this success would endure for however long it took to find her grandparents, so she had better enjoy it for as long as it lasted.

~~~~~

Ess withdrew funds from the local bank as soon as it opened that morning, then bought a third class ticket ten minutes before the first morning train was due to leave. She chose a seat that gave her a good view of both doors, tucked her bags under her seat, and curled up to sleep. Whenever the train made a stop to take on more passengers, she roused enough to register how many people boarded, then she closed her eyes and went back to sleep. The fifth stop was just after ten-thirty, and she opened her eyes to see two elderly ladies clamber up the steps. Three men with the big rectangular cases of traveling salesmen huffed and grimaced at the delay. As soon as the women entered the car, the men pushed past them, nearly shoving both elderly women against the wall. Ess put her feet down on the floor and looked down the length of the carriage. There were three empty seats left, close together. The salesmen scrambled to grab those seats, put their cases against the windows, rather than in the overhead rack, and then sat down with their feet in the aisle. From the tenor of their conversation, they continued a discussion that started before the train pulled into the station.

When the two elderly women tottered up the aisle, the men glared at them and refused to move their feet. The one in the blue-striped boater raised his voice to talk over her, when the smaller of the two ladies asked in a quaking voice if he would kindly move his feet. Several people in the car spoke up, telling them to move their feet, they had no right to block the aisle, and if they didn't let the ladies past someone would call for the conductor. Both ladies visibly shriveled when the salesmen looked them up and down and grudgingly moved their feet out of the aisle.

Ess noticed that no one with an empty seat by them offered to share it. The whistle pierced the air, three short blasts, signaling the train was about to start. The doors at the end of each car automatically locked to prevent passengers moving between cars while the train moved at the new, faster speeds approaching forty miles per hour. The ladies paused, four seats from the end of the train, and their faces crumpled with consternation.

"Here," Ess said, surprised to hear her own voice, and stood. She bent over and yanked her bags out from under her seat and stepped out into the aisle. "You can have my seat. I figure you want to sit together?"

"Oh, thank you, sonny," the taller of the ladies said, blinking rapidly, her eyes glistening wet. She let out a little gasp as the train started up, jolting the car.
~~~~~

"You're such a fine gentleman," the other lady chirped, once the two of them were settled in the seat. Ess grabbed hold of the ceiling bar running the length of the car, to stay upright. "You tell your mother she did a good job raising you."

"I would, ma'am, but my grandmother raised me." Ess ducked her head and tried to sound younger, shyer. She knew better than to look around the car. The people she had shamed by helping the ladies would be glaring at her. She caught some mutters from the salesmen about being "too big for his britches," before the rumble of the wheels on the rails grew loud enough to muffle most sounds.

The ladies tried to talk to her, but they soon gave up, tittering behind their gloved hands, when it was obvious neither side could hear the other.

"Here, now, what's this?" the conductor said, coming through the door and nearly running into Ess. "Shouldn't be standing up like that, boy."

The ladies beckoned for him and he bent down to listen. There was much gesturing and indignant expressions and pointing at the salesmen and the seats occupied by baggage instead of people. The conductor looked over his shoulder at Ess several times. When he finally straightened, he gestured for her to stay there, then went down the aisle, checking and punching tickets. He had some words to say to the salesmen, and from the indignant expressions in their corpulent, reddening faces, Ess thought they had been scolded at the very least. They took their feet out of the aisles and turned to face forward now, but she suspected they would turn back to their former positions as soon as the conductor left.

Third class was the last two cars in the train before the baggage cars. The conductor reached the end of the car and came back to the door where he entered. He looked Ess up and down, eyes narrowed, then crooked his finger and beckoned for her to follow him. He inserted a three-pronged key in the lock for the car door, slid the panel open, then stepped aside and gestured for Ess to go ahead of him. She was almost disappointed at how safe the crossing was between cars. Six chains on either side attached the little balcony-like structure at the end of each car, so that someone would have to make some effort to slide between them and fall off the train. She stepped to one side so the conductor could get to the door of the next car and unlock it. He said nothing, just beckoned for her to keep following. They passed out of third class, into the three cars of second class. The front of the second class section was only sparsely occupied. The seats were farther apart and had cushions instead of plain wooden slats, and the backs extended higher to support passengers' heads.

Wonder of wonders, the conductor opened a bin at the end of the car next to the privy closet, and a fog of cold air rolled out of it. He pulled out a bottle of dark liquid and cracked a smile for the first time.

"Compliments of Sanderville and Tuttle," he said, and handed it to Ess. "Not too early in the morning for a cold sarsaparilla?"

"No. Thank you much, sir." Ess fought not to giggle. It wouldn't do to reveal herself as a girl, though a bottle of sarsaparilla was an unexpected treat. Miss Van Hastings considered the beverage plebian and uncouth for a lady to drink. "Am I wrong, sir, to think the ladies are... someone important?"

The conductor glanced over her shoulder at the other passengers, then gestured with a tip of his head for her to take one of the empty seats. First he pointed out a niche in the wall where Ess could insert the neck of the bottle and pry off the cap. She found that quite clever. It had been several years since she had ridden in a train. Her grandparents had borrowed a friend's steam car to drop her at the boarding school on their way to New York and their ship to South America. The changes in train travel astounded her. She saw now she had mistakenly assumed that all large mechanical and scientific advances would be limited -- or perhaps reserved was a better word -- for bigger things, like military and government needs, for the convenience of the rich or the scholarly elite. Why shouldn't technological advances be used to help the common people?

"The truth of the matter is... well, the ladies are in the employ of the railroad. Messers Sanderville and Tuttle like to keep an eye on how the passengers are treated and how they treat each other. Those gentlemen who aren't such have been banned from riding in second class."

"Are the ladies to test who has manners, or keep an eye on people who are most likely to cause trouble?"

He winked, told her to enjoy the better seat for the rest of the journey, and headed for the door leading to the first class section.

~~~~~

Ess stepped down from the second class carriage and looked right, to see the three salesmen grumbling and stomping together as they walked up the pavement toward the station. They stopped short, staring, their heads turning from her to the clearly marked second class carriage and back. Ess knew better than to meet their gazes. Better that they think she didn't see them. She slung her bags over her shoulders and hurried up the walkway out of the station.

From the station, she could have borrowed a horse or even indulged in a steam car. One of the experimental short-distance rail cars went near enough to her grandparents' house. Any of those options could have saved her time, but they would have meant encountering someone who might remember her later, or even worse, recognize her as the Fremonts' granddaughter. At the start of her long journey, she couldn't afford even the smallest careless mistake.

Ess walked, reaching her destination late in the afternoon, as the shadows began to lengthen. Most of the windows had been shuttered and the shutters nailed shut for the duration of her grandparents' absence. Inside, three of every four rooms was awash in dust sheeting. Ess hated the thought of seeing all the bookshelves hidden, the furniture turned into great lumpy
~~~~~

ghosts -- but she hated worse the risk of the Van Hastings coming with falsified documents and hauling away all the contents of the house and then to sell the house, to fund the Resurrectionist cause. Just slightly more painful was knowing that the loyal staff, who occupied the quarters a short distance from the main house, would lose their home and employment if the protective steps she had taken failed.

Giles was sitting on the front porch as he always did at this time of the day, watching the play of colors on the horizon far across the sprawling lawn where guests used to play endless games of croquet or blind man's bluff. The bald old man had been bent and walked at a rapid totter, with a voice like a saw catching in damp wood, for as long as Ess could remember. He acted as secretary for both her grandparents, hired temporary household help when they had academic gatherings, and made travel arrangements. He had earned the years of idleness and rest while Earnest and Matilda were in South America.

She wondered if the news had even reached the household staff that her grandparents were missing, presumed dead.

Ess studied Giles as she walked up the long flagstone path from the road, though at first all she could see was the shiny dome of his head. She found it difficult to fight off tears. This was not the homecoming she had hoped for. When she was perhaps twenty yards from the place where the path split, leading either to the side and the kitchen door, or the front porch, that shiny dome rose above the ornate, white-painted spindles and railing of the porch. She picked up her pace. A choked bubble of laughter escaped her when she realized she couldn't remember how to run like a boy.

"Odessa Vivian Fremont, what in tarnation are you doing here, now, dressed like that?" Giles' voice boomed across the wide lawn. He stomped to the edge of the porch, with the energy of a man one-third his age, despite his arthritic knees and ankles that made him walk bent like a kangaroo.

~~~~~

Hilda, the cook, Bridget and Thomas, the married couple who took care of the outside of the house, and Peggety and Waldo, the married couple who took care of the inside of the house, gathered around the dinner table with Giles and Ess. She told them everything, trying to concentrate on the true crimes against the nation and the lies the Van Hastings had told to Endicott, Lewis and MacDonald. The effort not to whine about all the petty injustices she had suffered since her grandparents left her at the Academy actually hurt. These people knew her, had helped to raise her, had participated in all the glorious adventures her grandparents thought necessary for Ess's education. Thomas and Giles had arranged for her to study the inner workings of the new steam engine before Dr. Rasmussen even had permission for his experimental rail transportation system within the confines of town. Hilda had felt it necessary for Ess's education to learn how to make all sorts of delectable treats heavy on butter and sugar and exotic flavorings imported
~~~~~

from other countries. Ess needed to feel their sympathy, but knew that spilling all the sordid, nasty details would waste time. They had a house to protect.

Endicott, Lewis and MacDonald had informed the family retainers of her grandparents' disappearance. A letter had come from Miss Van Hastings two days ago, contradictory and confusing, until Ess's narration of all the details. Looking through the letter, Waldo and Giles agreed that the Van Hastings were trying to get a picture of just how many people were at the house, perhaps even estimate what kind of forces they needed to overcome any resistance the staff might offer.

"I say we need to move the really valuable things -- all your grandparents' research notes, their library, Miss Matilda's equipment. Give them nothing to find, if they have the gall to show up here with false documents," Hilda said, settling down next to Ess after refilling everyone's coffee. "The furniture don't much matter, in the long run."

"She's right." Giles saluted Hilda with his cup. "Those scoundrels sound greedy enough, they might just jump the gun once they figure out you've flown the coop. I say we stash the valuables wherever we stash you, girl."

"I am not going into hiding." Ess held her breath and looked around the table. The six adults just looked at her, not one jumping in to lead the argument. "I have to find Uly, so we can hunt for Grandfather and Granny together. I can't do that if I'm sitting in a warehouse guarding crates of books and papers."

"She sounds just like her father," Peggety murmured. She dabbed at her eyes with the corner of her apron.

Ess just crossed her arms over her chest and leaned back in her chair. Peggety was the last person to be sentimental like that. When she met the older woman's gaze, she burst out in titters. Soon everyone was grinning.

"Everyone needs to take a long trip to parts unknown to visit old friends," Giles announced. "Resurrectionists are nastier than the Borgias, and some of them are dangerously intelligent. It won't take much for them to realize that we had warning. Some things I've heard tell me they don't care about justice when they punish people for confounding them. Everyone should be long gone before someone comes to either loot the house or take revenge."

Silence. Ess looked around the table at the dear, elderly, familiar faces.

She had done this to them. She couldn't breathe for a few seconds as the enormity of what she had done crashed down on her, made heavier by the knowledge of the fun she had had with her plotting and tricks and disguises.

Chapter Five

"I'm sorry," she managed to say in a reasonably calm voice.

"Now then," Hilda said, slipping an arm around the girl's shoulders, "it's all right. You did marvelously handling those villains. We'll have a bit of excitement, a bit of adventure, and come home in a few months -- a year, then?" she said, frowning, when Giles shook his head. "Keep in mind, Giles, we're all well along in years. These old bones aren't up to traipsing all around the world like we did when we were Ess and Uly's ages. My goodness, the adventures we had." Her eyes seemed to change, seeing something not in the room, able to look right through Ess. "Someday, girl, when you're a little older... well, there are things your grandparents should have told you before they left, but how could they know this misadventure would happen to them?"

"You don't think they're dead, do you?" Ess had to ask.

"Earnest and Matilda Fremont, dead in some God-forsaken South American jungle." She let out a snort that earned giggles from Peggety and Bridget. "Wherever they are right now, whatever adventures they're having, they'll have an incredible story to share with all of us, and a good laugh."

"Hilda is right. Knowing some of your grandparents' secrets would have made this moment easier to bear. Maybe avoid some problems," Giles said, glancing around the table and meeting the gazes of others, each nodding agreement in turn.

Ess fought down a surge of frustration at this sign she was being left out of something important.

"Your grandparents chose not to tell you, so out of respect for them, we can't tell you. However." He held up a hand, stopping Ess when she opened her mouth to protest, that her grandparents' disappearance had to change things. "When we rejoin in a year's time, we'll tell you, whether Earnest and Matilda have reappeared or not."

"Who knows?" Bridget said, passing Ess the dish of her special shortbread. "You might just find that scapegrace brother of yours in a year. I wouldn't put it past you to figure out where he went."

For some odd reason, Thomas and Waldo both glared at Bridget, as if she had said something she shouldn't have. She wrinkled up her nose at them both and winked at Ess as they both bit into the rich, buttery, sugar-dusted shortbread.

The seven of them worked through the night, making arrangements and boxing up all the precious books and papers and scientific equipment. Thomas and Waldo went to the neighbors at dawn and borrowed horses and wagons to haul the crates away. Each couple would be entrusted with a wagon load. Hilda had friends in Cleveland and she had the task of heading north and finding a place they could all use as a safe hiding place for themselves and the crates. Once each couple had their load safely stashed, they would meet Giles in Parkerton, twenty miles north, where he would arrange for a post office box they would all use for communication. Ess wanted to return to the Academy to see if the Secret Service showed up on time for the meeting of the Resurrectionists. If they didn't respond to the letters she had sent, then she needed to add to the sabotage she had done. She would meet everyone in Parkerton in five days, to make final arrangements before disbursing for a year. Giles knew where Hilda was going, the people she would confer with, but the others didn't. He would keep in contact with Hilda.

Later, Ess decided everyone agreed with the plan and picked up their parts a little too easily, as if they had long experience in similar activities. That should have been the first clue that her grandparents' situation and the people they associated with were far more serious than she ever could have guessed as an adventurous fourteen-year-old.

~~~~~

Three days after she fled the Academy, Ess returned under cover of darkness, travel-worn and grimy, and certainly smelling like a boy. She bought provisions in the next town over, including an insulated bottle guaranteed to keep the contents as cold or as hot as they were when poured in. She arrived after everyone was long asleep, and easily crept through the vaunted security precautions Miss Van Hastings claimed were stronger than what protected President Lincoln. She moved like a shadow through the tunnels, filling her bottle with cold water from the ice room off the kitchen, and taking provisions to last her until the Resurrectionist meeting was over. She climbed to one of the attics in the central building on the school grounds. The gables had slotted vents and provided her two lookout points in each direction. Ess had a bird's eye view of the main building of the school grounds and anyone who came in or out.

To her delight and surprise, Mr. Endicott himself arrived just before noon that same day. Ess calculated the law firm should have received her first letter by then, with the proof that the Van Hastings had been forging her signature, keeping information from both her and her lawyers, and lying to both sides. The letter informing the lawyers she was running away from the school and heading to South America wasn't due to arrive until the day after tomorrow. Ess watched a maidservant scurry out to greet her lawyer and flutter around like all the scatterbrains the Van Hastings preferred to employ. They were all easily intimidated into silence, unable to understand what went on around them, and therefore unable to report on their actions to parents or the authorities. The silly girl took Mr. Endicott into the building. Ess scrambled across the attic until she reached the fireplace ventilation shaft
~~~~~

leading directly to the formal office used to impress important visitors. It had grand decorations, and comfortable chairs, made for entertaining. Unlike the office where Miss Van Hastings handed out discipline and carried out her brother's assignments to support the Resurrectionists.

In the warm months, a metal-lined shaft guided hot air out of the room, passing through the attic, while another shaft, equipped with a steam-powered circulation fan, sucked chill air upwards from the ice room in the cellar. The metal was just loose enough to vibrate and aid in conducting sound. Ess had learned that handy detail in her earliest exploration of the school. She wished now she had let some of her schoolmates in on the secret, just in case Miss Van Hastings escaped punishment and the school stayed open. Her schoolmates deserved every tool possible to defend themselves. Her grandparents always maintained that those with great wealth, with great talent, with great influence, had a responsibility to help others when they had the means and ability to do so.

That settled it. Ess decided she would sneak down to one of the schoolrooms tonight to steal paper and ink and write a long list of instructions for Fanny.

Right now, though, she settled down at the opening of the ventilation shaft and prepared for an entertaining time. Miss Van Hastings would likely fall back on the befuddled, well-meaning, tearful, misunderstood, frail female mask that she wore so well and deployed like a weapon of war against all men. Or she would play the role of the abused, falsely accused martyr who would willingly suffer great indignities for the protection of her beloved students. Which would it be? That all depended on Mr. Endicott's first salvo in the pending war. Ess was pleased that her lawyers had reacted so quickly. When her first letter had arrived, Endicott, Lewis and MacDonald had likely called a hasty meeting to thoroughly discuss her accusations and proof. The nice thing about the three gentlemen was that they all respected her, despite her youth. They wouldn't discount her claims as hysteria or "female vapors." They would believe her and act on her reports. She simply hadn't expected Mr. Endicott, the senior partner and patriarch of the firm, to come here. Ess estimated he had taken either a midnight train or had justified the expense of an airship ticket, to arrive at this time of the day.

"Why didn't you bring authorities with you?" she mused as she heard the housemaid settle Mr. Endicott in the grand office. The girl fluttered around, offering him drinks, to take his hat, and asking if he was comfortable. Then she assured him as she brought in lemonade and sugar cookies that Miss Van Hastings was on her way, she was momentarily indisposed and caught up with school business that couldn't be put aside.

"Is there some sort of crisis occurring?" Mr. Endicott asked.

Ess grinned, recognizing his tone of voice. She had been privileged to witness a public forum when she was eight, when Mr. Endicott led a team of churchmen in a debate with a group of self-styled academics and philosophers. The debate had centered on the newfangled -- asinine, in Matilda's words -- proposal that the Bible was merely a collection of myths, no more valid than Greek, Egyptian, or any other mythologies ancient people created to explain the workings of the world around them. Ess had been allowed to attend the debate, though it was sure to last long into the night, with foul tempers and fouler language. Mr. Endicott had been splendid, earning her undying admiration by staying cool and dignified while others lost their tempers. He ably reduced his opponents into muttering, snarling, twitching confusion with his cool, mildly scornful tones and glances, and his ability to use their own words against them. He rearranged their own statements to show the foolishness of what they insisted had to be truth -- with no proof, other than that they chose to believe them. Ess heard echoes of that night in his voice now, the chill scorn, the offended dignity, the implied message that he needed to fix a shameful mess before it spread any further. Miss Van Hastings would come away from this encounter feeling as if she had been hit with the newest, fastest steam engine.

"Mr. Endicott." Miss Van Hastings sounded rather breathy. Ess wondered if she had run from somewhere else in the school, or simply played a new role. Did she have any inkling what had brought the man here? "Sir, what a pleasant surprise. You caught us at a rather... how shall I say it? A disorganized time."

"Yes, I can imagine," Mr. Endicott said. "Trying to locate a student who escaped your clearly faulty security precautions could put the entire school in an uproar."

"Escaped?" Her tittering laugh rattled up the ventilation shaft. "Sir, you make it sound as if our school were a prison. No student, I assure you, has any reason to leave us, except that her education has come to an end and she is ready to take her place--"

"At least you have the sense not to lie to me about that."

"Sir!"

Ess had a clear image in her head of Miss Van Hastings sitting up straight, shoulders back, eyes wide, feigning shock that a gentleman of Mr. Endicott's stature would be so rude as to interrupt her.

"Madam... I have to wonder if you recollect exactly who I represent."

"I must assume--"

"One of my favorite professors, when I was studying for the bar," he said, not quite covering up the second gasp-squeak of indignation at this second interruption, "cautioned us never to assume, and never to *say* we assume anything. Excuse my language, but to assume is to make an ass out of you and me." A dry chuckle escaped him.

Ess wriggled a little, wishing she could be hanging outside the window, watching Mr. Endicott at work, that calm, ever so slightly smug and confident little smile tugging at his usually somber mouth, the sparkle of mischievous malice in his eyes. She had been privileged to see him at work during a trial or two, and the energy that nearly crackled off of him as he dismantled his opponent's arguments and witnesses one by one had fascinated her. She rather thought he enjoyed himself hugely during those times. She hoped he was enjoying himself, taking Miss Van Hastings apart, little by little.

"Sir, really, if you must be so rude, perhaps I should ask you to leave and return when you are inclined to be more civil."

"Madam, the next time I return to this mockery of a place of education, it will be with the sheriff and an order to close it down."

"Really, sir! You offend me. What have I and my staff done to bring such -- such accusations?"

"You don't know who I represent, do you?"

"No, and whoever they are, you can be assured your client's daughter shall never be welcome in these hallowed halls."

"My clients are the Doctors Fremont. Earnest and Matilda Fremont. Their granddaughter, Odessa, fled your so-called school three days ago, after posting to me quite an interesting report on your activities." He paused. No sounds filtered up through the ventilation shaft and Ess bit her lip in consternation. Being unable to see expressions was quite disappointing. "I have here a list of her possessions which you illegally took from her, and which she was not able to retrieve before fleeing. I am here to demand their immediate return. Promptness and cooperation will go far in mitigating the charges which are even now being filed with the local and state authorities, and reported to the major newspapers throughout the country."

"News --" A thud punctuated Miss Van Hastings' gasp. Ess imagined she had dropped with unladylike speed and weight into the nearest chair.

Ess muffled a chuckle behind her hand and settled into a more comfortable position, though she doubted she would hear anything else useful while the headmistress collected herself. She wondered what Mr. Endicott would have said and done if she had told him about the Resurrectionists, and that she had sent other kinds of proof to the Secret Service. He might have delayed, just long enough to consult with those authorities. Perhaps he would have acted even more quickly, afraid for her safety if the government should take action immediately? Ess decided she had been wise to limit what she told her lawyers. She wouldn't want him to give any warning to the Van Hastings that they were about to lose much more than wealthy students and their reputation.

Miss Van Hastings alternately played the falsely accused innocent and misunderstood mentor, as Mr. Endicott went through the list of confiscated items, including a recounting of how each personal possession had been taken away. Ess felt some chagrin as she listened to Miss Van Hastings berate the maidservants, three in a row, who were sent to fetch the box, and reported that the box wasn't there. Finally the headmistress excused herself, her voice tight with a mixture of emotions, all negative, and went to investigate for herself. Ess considered for maybe ten seconds climbing down and secreting herself outside the gates, to wait for Mr. Endicott when he left. She decided against it. This was all too much fun, despite the knot of guilt that Giles and the others had to flee the family home to protect themselves from possible retribution by the Resurrectionists.

Besides, she wanted to see the fireworks when, or if, the Secret Service showed up. Mr. Endicott would sweep her away to "safety" at the New York office. He would be scandalized by her boy clothes and somewhat filthy condition. Despite his admirable qualities, he was rather a fuddy-duddy, a little too concerned with propriety. He most certainly would not allow her to remain in the vicinity to watch the fireworks, and to intervene if the Secret Service for some reason did not appear in time to capture the Resurrectionists.

Miss Van Hastings did not return to the office -- Mr. Van Hastings came in her stead, after leaving Mr. Endicott sitting for nearly half an hour. Ess shivered in anticipation, when the odious man introduced himself with oily charm. Didn't he realize he was up against one of the finest legal minds in New York? Ess pressed her ear closer to the opening of the vent and wriggled in pleased anticipation.

"Sir -- Mr. Endicott -- my sister is so dreadfully upset by the discoveries and events of the last hour, she is quite indisposed. You can understand that though I do not become involved in the affairs of the school, for propriety's sake if nothing else, I must intervene here. The unpleasant truth is that Miss Fremont was one my sister's most troublesome students. She stole from her classmates and bullied the younger girls and frightened them into compliance. Above all, she was the most abominable of liars. Sadly, that was one of her few talents. She quite excelled at it."

"Indeed. That is not the young lady I had the distinct pleasure of watching grow up under the tutelage of my scholarly clients, who I was indeed delighted to call my friends. Her sense of justice and fair play was always displayed most admirably." Mr. Endicott used a calm tone of voice that made Ess think he paid more attention to the lint he picked off his cuffs than the words he said.

"Indulge me here, sir, and consider the possibility that the young lady learned at a very early age to dissemble, to play a part, if you will, to please whoever was her audience." Mr. Van Hastings' voice was tight enough to be used as a cutting thread for wax or soap.

"Indulge me in turn, sir, when I counter that I have more than enough evidence of duplicity on the part of you and your sister to close this school tomorrow, if I felt necessary."

"Duplicity?" He chuckled. "Sir, your sense of humor is indeed the driest I have ever had the pleasure to encounter. What duplicity?"

"To begin with, not telling Miss Fremont about her grandparents' disappearance until only four days ago."

"Is that what she told you? Sir, we told her the day your letter arrived. She had an emotional outburst, locking herself in her room and breaking crockery. It was most unpleasant and disturbing to all her classmates."

"Indeed? Then why do I have in my possession instructions written in your handwriting, essentially ordering your sister to keep the news from Miss Fremont for as long as possible?" A pause, when Ess couldn't hear anything, though she could imagine Mr. Van Hastings struggling for words. "Oh, did I forget to mention that thanks to her grandparents' scientific discoveries, Miss Fremont had the ability to make perfect copies of all your letters, in which you lied to my law firm, and you spelled out the exact steps to be taken to carry off your deception and confiscate all her grandparents' possessions? Perfect copies that any handwriting expert and police officer and judge in the country will be able to look at and compare with your handwriting and verify that yes, you wrote those letters and no one else. Convenient, wouldn't you say, that she could make copies so the originals would stay in your possession, and you would never suspect?"

"Indeed." He cleared his throat, several times. "Well, sir, doesn't that just prove what I have been saying? A more deceptive, scheming, sneaking troublemaker my poor sister has never before had to endure. How did the girl obtain those letters she claims -- *claims*, sir, and has not proven -- she copied in my sister's office? How indeed, except by sneaking and breaking rules, going where she had no permission? I would hazard she left her bedroom when she was not supposed to, and broke a dozen other house rules at the same time."

"Illegal actions have often been accepted when employed in self-defense, sir. Indeed, many can argue that the war for independence was an illegal act, that our forefathers owed their very lives and all loyalty to the crown of England. They had the duty as well as the right and responsibility to stand against the tyranny and intolerable treatment from the authorities who owed them justice and respect. Just as Miss Fremont had every right to expect dignified treatment and honesty from this school and everyone involved in its operations. When those rights, duties and expectations were violated, she had every right to strike out to right the balance again and obtain her freedom."

"Her freedom." Mr. Van Hastings' snort was loud enough to be heard in the attic. "You sound as if you are delivering a much-rehearsed speech."

Ess found it fascinating that the longer the odious man spoke, the stronger the Southern accent grew in his voice. She didn't doubt Mr. Endicott noticed -- he was a most observant man. She regretted not telling him about the Van Hastings' connection with the Resurrectionists. Surely he could use that bit of knowledge now, to further irritate and perhaps even confuse his opponent.

"A speech to be delivered in court, perhaps?" Mr. Endicott said. "Should we need to go to trial, Mr. Van Hastings? Or will it be sufficient to try your case in the court of public opinion?"

"No. Please!" Miss Van Hastings sounded even more breathless than she had before. "Here, I found as much as I could from the list. The box is entirely missing from the room where we keep the students' possessions for safekeeping when they are punished for misbehavior. I couldn't begin to tell you what happened to it. But here -- here are what things I could find."

Ess listened as Mr. Endicott checked the items against the list. Her pearl earrings were not returned. She didn't doubt they had been sold, or else they were in Miss Van Hastings' jewelry box. Her glass pen, fashioned to look like the reeds used by the ancient scribes of Egypt, was also among the few items not returned. Several more items were also not returned, all of them worth some good coin. The worst blow was learning the most important item on her list, her flute, wasn't returned. Ess found it odd that Mr. Endicott seemed particularly disturbed, almost upset, at its absence. He asked several times, even going so far as to interrogate Miss Van Hastings when and why the flute had been taken from Ess and where it would have been put. Why, she wondered, did it mean so much to him that she didn't have the flute? Could he possibly know about the signal songs her grandparents had made her learn?

Mr. Endicott finally left, refusing all offers of refreshment and hospitality. Ess wondered if the Van Hastings understood just what an insult that was. They promised to have the entire school searched to find the last few missing items and the missing box, and vowed all of Ess's classmates would be questioned, to see if any of them knew how she had vanished from the school grounds and where she might have gone. Ess thought Mr. Van Hastings sounded pleased to learn Mr. Endicott did not know her whereabouts. She thought about Giles' warning that the Resurrectionists were vindictive, nasty folk, striking back at anyone who stood in their way, even if only by accident. Maybe Mr. Van Hastings hoped to send his cohorts hunting for her, to punish her for the trouble she had caused them.

She moved to the ventilation portal to watch Mr. Endicott leave. He had hired a steam-powered cart and seemed quite handy with the technological requirements, pouring water into the tank, tending the vents, and springing up handily into the single seat, despite his advanced age of sixty-three. There was a covered box behind the seat, and she theorized it was for carrying luggage or equipment or perhaps folded open to form a seat for more passengers, riding sideways.

Mr. Endicott and the hired cart trundled out through the school grounds gates and turned down the shrub-lined path aiming for the main thoroughfare. No one in the school could see him, unless they climbed up this high to join her. She watched him go, thinking about all that had been said and unsaid in the meeting she had overheard. She had learned a great deal, and the general results pleased her. However--

Everything skidded to a halt in her head as she watched the top of the box behind Mr. Endicott flip open, staying attached as it folded down the long side. Probably attached by hinges. A man sat up and Mr. Endicott hit the brakes as he looked over his shoulder, making the steam car jerk to a stop. Ess clenched her fists and fought the urge to shout her vexation -- her lawyer and the strange man were too far away for her to read their lips. She couldn't even see Mr. Endicott's face clearly enough to guess what was said. The two talked, then the man in the box pulled out something from his coat and unfolded it. She caught a glimpse of a flash of sunlight on metal.

"Please, oh, please," she murmured, as possibilities crashed through her head. Could that be a badge? The kind of badge a government official, an agent of some kind, would have in an identification folder? Was the Secret Service here already, preparing to invade the school grounds -- or was it only her imagination? Did she see what she merely wanted to see?

Whatever the man said, without the assistance of a gun, Mr. Endicott seemed to cooperate. He moved around to close the lid of the box and took a seat on it, holding onto the back of Mr. Endicott's seat, and the cart continued down the path to the main road. Ess stayed at the ventilation slats for a short while, on the off chance they would turn around and return. Then she prepared to wait until nightfall, when she could sneak through the house, refill her water bottle, and perhaps find something to occupy herself until the Resurrectionists' meeting, just one more night away.

~~~~~

Ess spent the day sleeping, aided by the thick heat collecting in the attic during daylight hours. She spent most of her night rambling. She visited the school, borrowed a sketching book and a handful of pencils from the art studio, and played harmless but utterly satisfying tricks on loathed teachers and fellow students -- taking supplies from desks and hiding them in other desks or on top of shelves where they were visible, but no one would think to look right away. She took stashes of sweets and liberated a number of bottles of spirits from teachers' desks. The necessity of a sip of spirits to help them get through classes seemed like an indication of their unsuitability as teachers, to Ess's mind. She smiled and admitted that yes, she and her fellow students were a handful. What could anyone expect, when young women left their homes and families, expecting to have an education, to be thoroughly modern women and prepare themselves for an important part in the world of the future... and they were forced to conform to mental corsets made for someone else's shape? Just like a voluptuous girl's body rebelled when she tried to wear a corset made for a girl with no hips or bosom, their minds and souls rebelled. They could only *pretend* to be well-read, only *pretend* to understand the sciences and fields of engineering that were exploding across the entire world thanks to steam technology and air travel.

Ess mused on the subject while she traveled the tunnels and made sure of the sabotage she had set in slow motion days ago. What did the situation at the school say about the parents who knew their daughters' minds and souls were being stunted, and yet left them there under Miss Van Hastings' tutelage? There couldn't be that much prestige in saying a young woman had
~~~~~

graduated from the Academy, could there?

"It doesn't matter," she told herself as she checked a gear box and heard the faint grinding and scraping sounds that indicated the sand she had trickled into the mechanism was indeed gumming up the works. "In another few days, it shall all be over."

She added more sand in some places, drained out oil in others, and found that the water filling several escape tunnels had reached a truly satisfying depth. Ess borrowed tools from the tunnel toolboxes, slid down the slope of the riverbank, and pried open the seams in the handful of hidden rowboats. They wouldn't sink right away, but when the fleeing Resurrectionists leaped into them, they would founder.

Satisfied with a good night's work, Ess went back through the tunnels to the school building, refilled her water bottle, confiscated a bottle of milk and a large chunk of ice, dumped out the bread that had just been set out to rise for the morning baking, and snagged half a roast chicken and an entire apple pie. Some might call it stealing, but she reasoned the school owed her meals, if nothing else.

Ess fell into a doze under a cool stream from a ventilation shaft opening. The rumble of wagon wheels and clopping of shod hooves on the gravel drive approached the school grounds and woke her. She could make out very little in the dimness between moonset and dawn, and the wagons didn't have any lanterns on them. With very little starlight left, she could make out only shapes and shadows. Two wagons, and perhaps a dozen or so men. No one came to any of the doors of the school buildings to see who was there -- that told Ess these people were expected. They said little, and what they did say was spoken in muffled voices. The men went straight to the barn that hid the main entrance to the Resurrectionists' tunnels. She found it interesting that they didn't drive the wagons inside, but left them in front of the doors and unloaded the wagons. A large trap door took up more than half the open space in the floor of the barn, and was operated by steam and gears, creating a ramp down into the tunnels. In the quiet before dawn, Ess heard the grumbling and grinding and hiss of the mechanism at work. She grinned, congratulating herself on her sabotage, when the sounds turned strained and then stopped, followed by curses.

Chapter Six

Another group arrived, most on horseback, but two steam carts among them. A lantern appeared in the doorway of the building where Miss Van Hastings and the senior teachers lived, but Ess wasn't at a good angle to see who it was. Several men let out muffled curses and darted into hiding behind the wagons and steam carts. Then one man left the group of the newest arrivals and stomped across the school grounds to the door, hissing and gesturing angrily. Miss Van Hastings' distinctive snapping voice responded.

"Botheration," Ess muttered. The Resurrectionists couldn't possibly be starting their meeting today, this morning, could they? The wretched men couldn't abide by their own arrangements, having to arrive half a day ahead of schedule. Why?

Maybe... maybe there was a traitor among the Secret Service, and someone had managed to warn them that the jig was up? Maybe they just needed more time to assemble for their meeting, so that such large numbers arriving all at once wouldn't attract so much attention?

Whatever the reason, Ess knew she wouldn't get much sleep, if at all, today. She knew the tunnels running below the school very well. In many places, the pipes and gears and belts and such running the various mechanisms underground ran alongside the tunnels where the men traveled about, and there were access hatches at regular intervals. Ess knew she was small enough to travel through the mechanism tunnels, allowing her to remain unseen while she could observe everything the plotters did and said. She had a brand new sketching book and a handful of sharp pencils. Why not sketch the faces of the men who came for the meeting, so if any of them escaped she could give some help to the Secret Service?

Miss Van Hastings had grudgingly complimented Ess on her ability to draw lifelike portraits with simple pencil lines, no need for watercolors or chalk to fill in the details. She had managed to turn the compliment sour by remarking that if Ess failed in making a decent marriage, she might earn a living as an assistant to an artist, or perhaps working for a newspaper or a retailer with a large catalog to produce each year.

Her entire sojourn at the Academy crystalized into that experience for Ess. If Miss Van Hastings had simply left the compliment be, if she hadn't felt the need to grind her students under her heel, to remake their minds and spirits to suit her purposes, if she had simply been a little kinder, they would not be in this place, in this moment in time. Ess never would have suspected the woman, would never have spied, would never have found the letters, would never have learned about the Resurrectionists.

What would her grandparents say about all this? She mused on that as she prepared her "campaign" in the tunnels and shadows. Earnest might wax philosophical, and conclude by admonishing Ess to be careful how she treated everyone she encountered, even in the most casual and temporary fashion. She had no idea who she might encounter at a crucial moment who would remember, and make future decisions based on how she had impressed them.

~~~~

By midafternoon, Ess felt sure she had sketched every man in the tunnels. She gladly retreated back to her original hiding hole. Her activities had left her feeling bent and cramped and achy-exhausted. She searched the main kitchen during a lull between cleaning up from luncheon and beginning preparations for dinner. The chickens in their enormous roasting pans were just starting to send up a fragrance that made her mouth water, and twice as much bread as usual was baking -- perhaps to feed the men in the tunnels -- and a peek in the icebox revealed the makings of a massive custard and a huge bowl of strawberries, cleaned and glistening with sugar. Ess wanted to sabotage the kitchen, if only to make the Resurrectionists go hungry tonight, but she had learned some caution during the day. Several near misses had frightened her. She heard the men discuss plans for where they would go next, who they planned to attack, to rob, and several government officials and offices they would strike at. This was no longer a game. She felt rather grimy in soul as well as body, as she confiscated a bucket of water and hauled it up to the attic, to wash and make herself a little cooler. What had she been thinking, making this her own private war of petty retribution?

Maybe… maybe she should change her plans and attach herself to Giles when she met up with him again? Giles knew all her grandparents' friends, especially the secret ones. Surely they would have more resources to find out what had happened to Earnest and Matilda than Ess ever could, even if she went to South America and retraced all their steps. What had she been thinking? Yes, it was all a fine adventure, in theory, but she wouldn't be fifteen for another few months. They should concentrate on finding her brother and then seek their grandparents, no matter how long it took to find Ulysses. Never mind that she had proven herself far more mature and responsible than Ulysses. He was her brother, an adult now, and people wouldn't give a second glance at a brother and sister traveling together. While grimy boys living on the street were often invisible, Ess couldn't depend on people to ignore a boy traveling all alone on a ship to South America.

"Botheration," she muttered. Ess pulled her last pieces of clean clothing on her still-wet body and lay down in the nest of cushions she had fashioned for herself.

At a time like this, her grandmother would scold her for complicating things, for making a muddle of something that, with a little clear thinking, would turn out to be simple. Then Matilda would gently cuff the back of her
~~~~

head and admonish, "And just how much praying have you put into this effort? The world doesn't rest entirely on your shoulders, young lady. You can't solve every problem before you turn eighteen, as clever as you are. Present your puzzle to the Good Lord, and then wait, however long you must, until the solution arrives."

"The waiting is the hard part, Granny," Ess muttered, and closed her eyes. A tiny giggle-snort escaped her, when a dizzy sensation immediately wrapped around her in the darkness behind her eyelids. Definitely, she had exhausted herself today. If she was lucky, most of her muddled thinking came from weariness and hunger.

~~~~~

The rattle of multiple wheels and hooves on the gravel in the yard below yanked Ess into full waking. She blinked and sat up, confused as she stared around herself. Everything was in twilight. She must have slept at least four, five hours. Trembling in anticipation, she hurried to the ventilation slats with the best view of the main yard of the school. When she was two steps away from it, she heard the thudding of a fist on a door, underscored by the sounds of dozens of feet running across the gravel. Ess looked down.

Everywhere she looked, men in dark blue uniforms with gold trim spread across the school grounds, going into buildings, surrounding buildings. More men arrived while the man who had knocked on the main building door -- conspicuous because he was not in an army uniform, but a brown suit -- waited for someone to answer.

A maidservant answered, freezing in the doorway, her eyes and mouth so wide with shock Ess could see them from her perch in the attic. Then the girl let out a shriek and darted back into the building. She tried to slam the door, but the man stopped her. A moment later he had one arm around her waist and the other clamped over her mouth. Her eyes got even wider. Then he nodded to the soldiers and stepped into the building, carrying the maidservant with him. Four soldiers followed him inside.

Ess wanted more than anything to go down into the tunnels and watch the soldiers round up the Resurrectionists. She was sure it would be like chasing down rats with torches, and pitchforks ramming into the openings of their dens for good measure. Common sense said anyone caught running through those tunnels would be considered an enemy of the Union. If they didn't cooperate immediately when ordered, they would likely be shot. She would just have to trust that the Secret Service knew what it was doing.

Still, she positively, physically ached with the waiting.

Ess found some entertainment in the uproar as all the students fled screaming from the dining room on the first floor of the main building, out the double doors onto the veranda. They huddled together like so many fancy-dressed, shrieking chickens, gathering the youngest girls into the middle of the group. To her disgust, the older girls quieted down quickly enough when they caught sight of the soldiers. Several of her classmates were
~~~~~

foolish enough to suddenly turn to giggles and making eyes at the men guarding them. Ess muffled some laughter of her own when someone barked an order, clear through the chaos of shouting and banging of doors and distant gunfire, and the six soldiers circling the group of students turned their backs on them.

Miss Van Hastings and the teachers were herded outside next, kept in a group some distance from the students. Ess couldn't make out what the headmistress said, but it sounded as if she were sobbing and babbling. The soldiers didn't actually believe her patently false tears and terror, did they?

Scant moments later a man staggered from the barn, shoving aside the sliding doors, followed by streamers of smoke. At first she thought his clothes were on fire, but more smoke gushed out after him. Five more men erupted from the thickening clouds, staggering and choking and swearing -- abruptly cut off as half the soldiers in the yard turned sharply and raised their rifles at them.

"Hmm, miscalculated," she muttered. "Or maybe not." The sabotage she had performed underground had finally caused the machine to seize up and the gears to burn out and the oil to burst into flames. Either way, she was satisfied with her handiwork.

As the minutes flew past, more men came into the yard, either up through the tunnel and trap door in the floor of the barn, or herded from various other buildings spread across the school grounds. Ess couldn't discern if anyone was soaking wet. Perhaps the hatch into the flooded tunnels hadn't opened? Or maybe no one had tried to escape that way.

Mr. Van Hastings was very easy to identify. When he stepped into the yard, his sister erupted in louder shrieks of fury. She dashed toward him, pointing a shaking arm. Sobbing hysterically, she went to her knees halfway across the yard, collapsing in a puddle of skirts.

"Well, you are quite an actress, aren't you?" Ess said, disgusted by the two soldiers who hurried to stand over her and pointed their rifles at Mr. Van Hastings. He responded with curses and pointing in his turn.

The man in the brown suit apparently was the leader of the government forces. Soldiers and other men in plainclothes -- agents? Detectives? Spies of some kind? -- turned to face him or moved out of his way as he crossed the yard. He gestured and two soldiers each separated Miss Van Hastings and her brother from all the others, then escorted them in their leader's wake into the main building.

Ess counted the prisoners as they were shackled and loaded into wagons. Some of the Resurrectionists fought and swore. They earned blows, sometimes with fists to the face, sometimes rifle butts to the backs of their heads. Some were gagged. Ess focused on their faces until the twilight thickened too much to make out details. Even when the soldiers brought enough torches into the yard to illuminate it as bright as daylight, she couldn't be sure of all the features to identify each man she had studied and sketched during the long day hiding and creeping through the tunnels. By her count, at least ten of the Resurrectionists hadn't been caught. Whether they had found a hiding place in the tunnels or had escaped into the countryside, maybe even managed to get into a rowboat and cross the river before it sank -- she hoped all of them sank -- she couldn't be sure. Most of the serpents had been caught. That was all she cared about.

However, that didn't mean she had to leave the situation there. Why else would she have risked her freedom, maybe her life, spying on the rebels all this long, hot, grimy, cramped day?

~~~~

The Secret Service searched every building, every room on the school grounds the following day. Ess barely got her small camp disassembled, scattering the cushions of her nest among the other detritus in the attic, and took to the dumbwaiter to hide just before three soldiers came up into her attic hideaway. She decided the safest place to be was following on the heels of one of the search parties, gambling that they wouldn't look over their shoulders, but always ahead into the next unexplored room and hallway and attic. She spent much time crouching in one dumbwaiter or another, listening to the soldiers talk, learning their names, hearing them talk about their families, about what other teams had discovered in searching the school grounds, and what they thought of Miss Van Hastings. To her disgust, while many soldiers doubted the woman's claims that she was unaware of most of her brother's actions, the leader of the raid, Agent Randolph Sutter, seemed to accept her claim. The school would remain open, although many of the parents were retrieving their daughters in the next few days.

That evening, Ess returned to the attic that had been her headquarters when she had been merely spying on Miss Van Hastings. She watched cart after wagon after cart pull out of the yard, loaded with prisoners and evidence, and crate upon crate of weapons taken from the tunnels. She was certainly disgusted that she hadn't found the weapons cache, because she would have liked to have confiscated more ammunition for her derringer and sabotage some of those guns. When night fell, leaving only a few soldiers standing guard, she took the dumbwaiter system down to the floor housing the older students, and crept into Fanny's room.

Her friend didn't disappoint her. She reacted calmly when Ess whispered her name and shook her shoulder, sitting up in bed and reaching for the matchbox to light her bedside candle. Her look of surprise changed instantly to delight, and she shook with silent laughter. Many of their fellow students would have shrieked and erupted with dozens of questions at the top of their voices, or even called out in alarm, running to tattle to one of their teachers that the runaway had returned.

"What have you been doing and where have you been?" Fanny whispered, and tucked up her legs, making room for Ess to sit on her bed. "Are those boy clothes really as comfortable as they look? What heaven, not
~~~~

to have to worry about skirts or heels or your hair. You didn't cut your hair did you?" She sighed. "Listen to me, sounding like an absolute ninny. Oh, but Ess, the things that have been happening the last few days!"

"I know." She hooked a thumb upwards at the attic. "I've been watching."

"You rascal." Another delighted chuckle. Then Fanny's eyes got big and her mouth dropped open for three long seconds. "You... Odessa, you didn't have anything to do... no, how could you have... but I heard some of the agents talking. Someone informed them..." She shivered slightly. "Is that why you ran away? You discovered Miss Van Hastings was helping the rebels, so you had to tell on her?"

"At least someone believes that she was involved, instead of being used. Honestly, what is wrong with men? Flutter your eyelashes, squeeze out a few tears, and pretend you're a brainless featherhead, and everyone believes every lie that drops out of your mouth."

"What do you think she's been teaching us all this time?" The momentary fear fled, replaced by sparkles of mischief, though dimmer than usual.

"So you overheard things. I was hoping you'd be clever enough to pay attention. Tell me everything."

Miss Van Hastings was reportedly infuriated that parents were demanding refunds of fees paid in advance. The soldiers were ostensibly there to guard Miss Van Hastings from reprisals by the Resurrectionists, since she had loudly and repeatedly and wetly proclaimed that her brother had bullied her into silence and cooperation. She seemed to be genuinely dumbfounded when confronted with the existence of the tunnels under the school. Some of the rebels were dead, drowned in the flooded tunnels. Others were vilely sick, poisoned by smoke when the machinery in the tunnels burned up, and some were injured when gear boxes and mechanisms exploded, shooting cogs and gears and rods and belts in every direction. Ess had seen several bodies on stretchers, but she had assumed those men were injured while resisting capture. She felt a little queasy at the thought she had killed someone. Still, that left maybe ten or a dozen Resurrectionists still unaccounted for.

The most disappointing discovery was that the proof she had sent to the Secret Service reinforced Miss Van Hastings' claims that she was her brother's puppet or dupe or pawn. All the instructions how to falsify financial documents and the bookkeeping of the school, and what lies to tell people -- all in his handwriting. What would it take to convince the authorities that the sister was just as culpable, just as involved as the brother? Ess considered walking up to one of the soldiers and demanding to be taken to Agent Sutter, but what good would it do her? Who would believe the testimony of a fourteen-year-old girl? She would have to explain how she had come to overhear the conversations, and that would require admitting she had been hanging upside down from the attic window. No one would believe her. Even if they did, once they learned her grandparents were presumed dead and her brother had vanished, they would place a guardian over her. If she had to have guardians, Ess wanted Giles and Hilda, but would anyone give her that choice?

No, she would simply have to hope and pray for justice to fall on Miss Van Hastings, preferably brought about by her own actions in the future. Ess wouldn't gamble her freedom just to give the headmistress one final push toward punishment.

Past midnight, Ess finally stepped out of the school for the last time. She would have liked nothing better than to climb up to her abandoned bedroom and curl up in her exceedingly comfortable bed, even if it had been stripped down to just the mattress, and sleep until she had caught up on the hours she had sacrificed over the last three weeks. That wasn't wise. Another day skulking in the shadows, hiding from another search of the grounds, and stealing food wasn't palatable to her. As the students were removed by their parents, and the population dropped, her movements would be easier to detect. No, it was better if she left now.

Two steps across a narrow gap of moonlight, heading for the bushes where she could slither under a gap in the fencing, a clear, metal click-snick stopped her. Ess began raising her hands even before she recognized the sound of a rifle cocking.

"Turn around slowly, lad," a man ordered in a quiet baritone voice.

Ess held her breath, waiting for the moment the bright moonlight revealed she was a girl underneath her slouch cap and baggy, grimy boy clothes. The soldier looked her over, head to toes and toes back to head, then the hard line of his mouth in his square-cut face softened. He gestured with a tip of his head for her to move out ahead of him. The big, heavy hand resting on her shoulder didn't feel threatening. Then again, she might just be so tired right now, she wasn't sure of what she sensed. For example, there was an odd sense of relief that she had been caught, and that didn't make any sense whatsoever.

The soldier guided her to the main classroom building. Light spilled out when the door opened, and Ess discovered that the first floor had been turned into a sprawling office for the Secret Service agents. The leader, Sutter, stood over a long table formed of four student study tables placed end to end, with maps and diagrams and papers everywhere. He worked in his shirtsleeves, his shirttail tugged out on his left side. He glanced up at Ess and the soldier's entrance, turned away, then turned back a few seconds later, his frown deepening.

"You picked the wrong time to come thieving, boy," he said, his voice a smooth, low baritone.

"Wasn't breaking in, sir," the soldier said. He guided Ess down into a chair, then finally removed his hand from her shoulder. "Caught him sneaking out."

"Out?" The left corner of his mouth crooked up. "Think you found our ghost?" He walked over and settled down on the side of the table directly in front of Ess, leaving about six feet of open floor between them. "What's your story, lad?"

"What ghost are you talking about, sir?" Ess asked. She didn't have to try to disguise her voice. It was rough with exhaustion and thirst.

"Never mind. What were you doing hiding in the school?"

Ess tried to sit up a little straighter. The exhaustion ached in her back and ribs, and the movement made the drawings tucked into the inner pocket of her coat crackle. She nearly smiled -- this was the perfect opportunity to get the drawings to the Secret Service, let them know some men escaped them.

Or maybe she was just so tired she wasn't thinking clearly?

"Looking for you, sir. You're Agent Sutter?" Ess did grin now, when the agent grunted in surprise and sat up a little straighter. He glanced at the soldier, who had taken up the post in front of the door.

"I am. Why are you looking for me?"

"Mr. Oppenheimer asked me--" She glanced around, pretending to be afraid of being overheard, while her mind scrambled for more to add to her lie. Mr. Oppenheimer had left two years ago, before Ess came to the Academy, but the girls loved to giggle about him even now. The prevalent theory for why he had left suddenly, in the middle of a school session, was that he had worshiped Miss Van Hastings from afar, until he finally got up the courage to approach her. Either he had fumbled badly with his courtship and fled in embarrassment, or Miss Van Hastings had driven him away with scorn.

"Oppenheimer?" Sutter frowned, then nodded twice. "I know the name. Former teacher. What about him?"

Ess crossed her fingers, praying that Sutter and the Secret Service didn't know Mr. Oppenheimer had fled the country, back to his native Bavaria.

"He's still sweet on Miss Van Hastings. That's why he had to run away, you know. Her brother threatened to skin him alive. Said he wasn't good enough for his sister."

"What did he ask you to do?"

Ess reached into her coat and drew out the packet of drawings. "Mr. Oppenheimer has been watching, and he drew pictures of all those men who were here. He was some glad when you hauled away the teacher-lady's brother." She offered a mischievous grin, hoping it looked sufficiently boyish to suit the agent. The longer she sat under his unflinching regard, the more fidgety she felt. Any moment now, her cap would burst into flames, revealing her long hair tucked up underneath it, and the agent would finally realize she was a girl.

Chapter Seven

"Interesting," Sutter said, glancing down at the pictures. He started to say something more, then stopped, frowning deeper as he leafed through the drawings. "Why did he want you to give these to me?"

"Said you didn't get everybody. Mr. Oppenheimer, he wants them all hauled away."

"Why didn't he bring them himself?"

"Scared." She shrugged.

"Uh huh." More scratching of papers against each other as he flipped through the sketches.

Ess watched him, putting some sketches aside after frowning at them longer than the others. She guessed he was putting aside the sketches of the men who hadn't been captured. Mission accomplished, even if she hadn't set out to hand over the sketches today.

"What's in the bags, lad?" he asked, startling Ess, so she realized she had started to list to one side and her eyes were closing.

"Clothes. All I got in the world, sir. I didn't steal it. Swear."

"Uh huh." His mouth softened again. "Did this Mr. Oppenheimer pay you to play messenger?"

"Not until I get back to him." Ess flinched as a drop of sweat rolled down her right temple. She tried to remember if she still had some coins in her pocket. Maybe she should have said he paid her, or couldn't pay her, or she did it because he was nice to her or something else? What if Sutter wanted her to lead them to the nonexistent Mr. Oppenheimer?

"Hungry?"

"Starving."

That earned a chuckle from the agent. He didn't look quite so grim now.

"How about Mr. Oppenheimer?"

"Sir?"

"Is he hungry? I figure a man who could get close enough to get detailed pictures like these, well, he must be close enough to see everything going on here. Maybe so close, he's afraid to move, afraid to get caught. Maybe he's stuck, caught somewhere, and can't leave until the excitement dies down." Sutter leaned closer to her. "He can't afford to be caught by either side." He sat back and his eyes narrowed as he looked her over again. "Did he explain to you what's going on?"

"A little." She shrugged. It was hard to think of more lies, more embroidery for the story, as her grandmother would have put it, when her stomach had awakened and taken over most of her concentration.

"What exactly is contained in the 'little'?"

Ess shivered and hunched down lower in the seat, none of her discomfort play-acting. "Miss Van Hastings and that man who kept coming to visit, they pretended not to be Southerners, sir, but they were. They tried to talk like Northerners, but they slipped. Mr. Oppenheimer found the tunnels just before he got sacked for trying to sweet talk the lady. He figured the man was making her do things she didn't want." Ess nearly gagged at offering more support for Miss Van Hastings' lies. Maybe this was what her grandfather sometimes had lectured her and Uly about, when warning them not to lie, because each one required more lies to support it and turned into a tangle.

"How did he find the tunnels? What was he looking for?" Sutter asked, when she had paused too long. Ess shrugged, earning a groaning sigh from him. "What will it take for Mr. Oppenheimer to come out of hiding?"

"Don't know, sir."

"You're exceedingly polite and well-spoken for a boy who looks like he's been relegated to the barn or the back alley all his life."

Ess hunched over more, and braced for something physical -- maybe the worst danger of all, hands grabbing her, searching her, peeling away her cap to reveal her tightly pinned braids, or discover her different shape under her clothes. She should have asked Sarah for that padded corset that filled in her hourglass shape and flattened her hips and bottom. Was it too late to catch up with her before her steamship sailed?

"It's late," the soldier offered. "We could lock the boy up, feed him, give him a place to sleep. Maybe if he doesn't come back, this Mr. Oppenheimer will get worried and come looking for him. Boy can't know much more than he's already said. This man sounds like he'd know a lot you'd find useful, sir."

"Indeed he would," Sutter mused, narrowing his eyes more as he studied Ess.

A quick snatching motion with his hand earned a squeak from her. She dodged, falling off the chair, but not before he caught hold of her right hand. Ess shuddered as he pulled her back up to her feet and turned her hand over, studying her fingers.

"Your Mr. Oppenheimer isn't the artist." Sutter's smile was smug, yet oddly compassionate. "Is he?" His fingertips running over her middle and index fingers made her shiver more. He pressed on the dent on the first knuckle earned from gripping the pencils tight all day, the smears of lead on her fingertips from rubbing at various places to create shading. She hated being so close to him. Any second now, those incredibly quick, alert eyes would decipher that her cap wasn't quite as floppy on her head as it should be, and yank it off, revealing the bulge of braids that it covered.

"Sir?" she whispered, and forced herself to meet his gaze. Her grandparents had several traveling magician friends, and they had confided one of the secrets of their trade was to distract the audience away from what they were doing, to give them something else to look at and suspect, so they didn't see the actual sleight-of-hand trick happening right under their noses. As long as she met Sutter's eyes, he wasn't looking at any of her other features.

Sutter let out another loud sigh and nodded to the soldier. Before Ess could anticipate his next move, the agent gave her a shove, right into the soldier's grasp. She fought a sudden urge to weep in relief when he told the soldier -- Cosgrove, she learned his name was now -- to take "the boy" to the kitchen, feed him, give him a bucket of water for washing, and find a room where he could spend the night comfortably. There was plenty of time in the morning to continue the questioning. It was obvious, Sutter added as Cosgrove led Ess away, that "the boy" was on their side. They just had to figure out who he feared more, to get him to talk. Maybe someone on the staff knew who he was and could answer some questions, fill in the blanks. In the morning.

Ess did not want to be here in the morning, and she most certainly did not want to stand under the scrutiny of any of the teachers or housekeeping staff or -- God protect her -- Miss Van Hastings herself. A woman as scheming as the headmistress, who would sell out her own brother to protect herself, might just be observant enough to see Ess under her disguise.

Praying, she decided nearly twenty minutes later, truly did work. God did hear. Ess nearly laughed aloud, nearly dropped the armful of blankets and the net bag of bread, apples, cheese and the bottle of cold milk Cosgrove had made her carry after a detour through the school kitchen. The soldier nudged her with the bucket of water he carried, to get her to go through the door of the storage room holding all the boxes of confiscated personal items.

"It's not that bad, lad," Cosgrove said. "The only room in the entire bedeviled place without a window. Agent Sutter just wants to make sure you're here in the morning, that's all."

Ess bit her lip against laughter, and stumbled into the room. Cosgrove put the bucket down nearly under the hatch for the dumb waiter. He glanced at it once, frowned -- maybe he came from a home that didn't have such conveniences -- and stepped over to the oil lamp hanging from a chain in the middle of the room. After he lit it from the candle he carried, he stepped back to the door. He waited until Ess spread out the blankets, just around the corner from the door, behind the first rack of shelves, where she wasn't so visible.

"Be a good lad and eat your dinner and get some sleep. Hear me?" He winked at her when she just nodded, then stepped back and pulled the door closed. A moment later, the key turned in the lock.

Ess knew better than to assume they would simply leave her alone for the rest of the night. Especially with the oil lamp burning like that. She was proven right twenty minutes later, when another soldier opened the door, leaned in, and studied her for a moment. Ess was in position, leaning against the wall, slouched down and feigning sleep, a fragment of bread in her hand,

and the bottle of milk empty and lying on its side. She had kept most of the provisions for her journey. This new soldier also glanced at the hatch for the dumb waiter, glanced again at her, again at the hatch -- it was quite frustrating, watching the flickers of his eyes as they shifted back and forth. Finally a little smirk twisted his mouth and he stepped into the room, lifted the glass chimney on the lamp, and blew out the flame. He said not a word as he stepped out and pulled the door closed, and clicked the key in the lock extra loud.

"Bully," she muttered.

Just what did that smirk mean? Did he know what a dumb waiter was, and he was going to scold Cosgrove for putting her in a room with such easy escape? Or did he think that she didn't know what it was, and laughed at her as a stupid, lower class boy who didn't recognize an escape route when it was feet away from his grasp? Ess waited another half hour, just in case. No one came.

In the dark, she rummaged through the boxes of her former classmates, finding enough items -- decorative pillows and favorite clothes taken away as punishment -- to approximate her shape hidden under the blankets on the floor. She took the dumbwaiter down to the next floor and climbed out a window. She crept through the shadows, halting at every rustle of leaves, to a low point in the fence and hedge separating the school grounds from the next property. She tossed her bags over the fence and hedge, and crawled under.

By dawn she was miles away, safely tucked up in a wagon in a long line pulled by a steam cart. For all she knew, it was the same train of wagons she had used for her original escape less than a week ago. Ess burrowed in deep, to hide behind the bundles and crates and barrels. When the wagon stopped, she could climb out, hidden behind the high fence of the freight yard, and find her next mode of transportation to Parkerton, where Giles and the rest of the household staff were to meet. Ess looked forward to telling them about her adventure and rejoicing over the downfall of so many Resurrectionists. Maybe they could help her find a way of ensuring Miss Van Hastings was duly punished. For now, though, she made herself as comfortable as she could for the long journey.

She didn't manage to fall asleep right away, though the rocking and creaking and groaning of the wagons around her was soothing. Ess thought about her brother, speculating on where he had vanished to. She had memories of hushed, urgent voices in the middle of the night, and before that, arguments between Uly and their grandfather. Her brother was up to something and Ess's impression was that while Earnest approved of the principle, he was disappointed in how Uly carried out whatever escapades were getting him into trouble. Thinking back now, that struck her as somewhat strange, for the very first time. Was she mistaken, or were her grandparents not as upset as they should have been when Uly vanished?

Maybe they knew where he had gone?

"Doesn't matter now, does it?" she muttered in the stuffy darkness. "I need to find Uly, then we can go find Granny and Grandfather together." Her efforts to dredge up everything she could remember from those tumultuous days immediately before and after her brother vanished only served to push her over the final ledge into sleep. Her dreams were full of finding her brother, then losing him again, as soon as she reached for his hand. In the last dream before she woke, Uly hung by his knees from a trapeze bar suspended from an airship. He played his flute, demanding she play the signal song before he would pull her up into the airship with him.

Ess woke thirsty and hot. She put replacing her flute at the top of her list. There was no telling when one of her grandparents' secretive friends might be nearby. How would they know who she was and that she needed help if she couldn't play the signal songs?

Her narrow escape at the school taught her never to assume that silence meant safety. Ess peered in all directions to make sure no one was watching before she slid out from under the wagon cover into the rutted freight yard. The driver had parked near the gates, which hung open, undoing all the security offered by the yard proprietor. What good was it to park the wagons of freight inside a fenced-in yard if people could just walk through the gate? Ess glanced around and saw the wide porch full of tables, where a handful of men were eating. She ducked into the shelter of the fence and peered through a gap in the thin wooden slats. Perhaps the security wasn't quite so bad, because anyone sitting on the porch could watch the gate of the yard. If she tried to walk out the gate, she would be seen. Claiming she was leaving, not breaking in, would just land her in deeper trouble.

The seat of one of the wagons parked up against the fence in the back of the yard was just high enough for her to stand on it and haul herself up to the top of the fence. Ess hated leaping where she hadn't had a chance to look ahead, but the fence was thin enough it wouldn't hold her weight for long. Indeed, it started to wobble just in the few seconds she hung there, pulling her legs up so she could roll over the top and drop, to follow the bags she had tossed over. Her ankles hurt when she hit the hard ground, but her boots proved sturdy enough for the task and she did manage to land on her hands and feet instead of on her face or her side. Ess stumbled for the first dozen steps before the ache faded and she was sure she hadn't broken her ankles.

An hour later, an elderly lady driving into Parkerton with a wagon full of bales of wool and buckets of berries offered her a ride in return for her help in unloading at the general store. Ess gladly took the offer. The lady, who had introduced herself as Mrs. Hopkins, was chatty, filling her in on the exciting events of the last few days, since she didn't recognize Ess as being from around there.

"What did you say your name was again, boy?"

"William, ma'am. Ma calls me Willy." Ess offered a shy shrug and grin.

"She says it's 'cause she doesn't know, 'will he do his chores on time or not?' I'm trying to do better." To her relief, the lady chuckled.

"Where is your mother?" Mrs. Hopkins glanced over her shoulder from the driver's seat. Ess sat far back on the folded down tail gate of the wagon.

"We're staying with my Pa's brother. Pa is looking for work in Washington, all the rebuilding. He's a carpenter." She waited until Mrs. Hopkins turned around to look, and hooked her thumb back down the road. "Uncle Reuben's a nasty cuss. Told me I could come to town and gave me five whole cents for candy, but he didn't tell me what a long walk it was."

"I'm surprised at him, letting a boy your age wander around alone, with all the outlaws suddenly coming out of holes in the ground."

"Outlaws, ma'am?" Ess was just relieved that Mrs. Hopkins hadn't asked why she was carrying her bags, if she was just walking to town for candy. Maybe the elderly lady wasn't as observant or as smart as she appeared. Personally, Ess thought it a little chancy that she would let a stranger climb into her wagon, even if she did need help unloading it.

"The saddest thing. A gentleman staying in Mr. Alberts' hotel was accosted by a group of ruffians and when they didn't get what they wanted -- my friend, Mrs. Crabtree, says the argument went on for what seemed like hours -- they shot him. They threw him into the street and they shot him while he lay there in the dust. Dr. Alberts -- that's Mr. Alberts' son -- he doesn't think the poor man is going to make it." She *tsk*ed several times. "Rumors are, all the men had the most disgraceful, thick Southern accents, and the man they shot even called them Resurrectionists. What is the world coming to, when those rebels are still allowed to run around free in this country, trying to stir up all that disgraceful, terrible war, all over again? Someone should lock them up and throw away the key."

"Yes, ma'am, it's horrible all right." Ess shuddered and fought the urge to jump off the tail of the wagon and run the rest of the way into town. It was still several miles away, according to Mrs. Hopkins, and the wagon was rolling along at a good clip. Going on her own two feet would only leave her sweaty and filthy and exhausted. No one would take her seriously if she staggered into town looking even more ragged and filthy than she already was. She gripped the wooden slats on either side of her and prayed all the rest of the way. *Please, Lord Jesus, please, don't let that man be Giles. Please. Please. If it is Giles, don't let him die?*

How could the Resurrectionists have caught up with him, and so quickly?

Ess fought the rising queasy sensation that this was yet another mistake she had made that had caused trouble for those she loved.

~~~~~

Dr. Alberts had his surgery in a wing of the hotel built on four years ago, according to Mrs. Hopkins, which connected the hotel and the pharmacist's shop. Dr. Alberts' sister and aunt ran the pharmacy. That would have been a
~~~~~

scandal twenty years ago, again according to Mrs. Hopkins, but "times, they are a'changing, and we do so appreciate having one of our own dispensing patent medicines and compounding whatever good Dr. Alberts prescribes. It's a feeling of comfort, don't you think? Someone you know is more sure to do a good job."

Ess nodded and murmured agreement, and plotted how she could get into the convalescent room, if she couldn't find Giles, just to assure herself the shot man wasn't Giles. Mrs. Hopkins informed her the convalescent rooms were on the first floor of the hotel, set aside for Dr. Alberts' patients when the hotel expanded. She seemed to find great pride in saying the word, "convalescent," almost as if it gave the town as much style and class as having a doctor and a pharmacy. Ess had a good idea in her head of the layout of the pharmacy, surgery wing, and hotel, just from the elderly woman's good-natured gossip. All she needed was ten minutes, twenty at the most, to get in and see how Giles was doing -- and assure herself the wounded man wasn't Giles at all.

The wait wasn't long, once she said goodbye to Mrs. Hopkins and found the hotel, because whoever built the wing for the surgery seemed to have a dislike for windows. Ess found it entirely too easy to creep through the shadows, without even having to bend over, and sit in a deep pool of darkness in the corner between hotel and surgery. The windows on this side of the hotel were wide and short, high in the wall, most likely just to let light in, but not to provide a view. Especially not a view into the narrow alley. She climbed up on the roof of the surgery, then into the hotel by stepping onto the balcony running along the second floor -- "Just like those big city hotels have, so people can look down on the street and catch the sunrise," Mrs. Hopkins had declared with such delight and pride, Ess fully expected to find out she was related to the Alberts by blood. From there she popped the frail lock on one of the french doors that let into an unoccupied room. All the hotel guests were either in their rooms for the night or finding entertainment at the small, new music hall at one end of the street, or the saloons at the other end. The town had three saloons, proving just how large it had grown -- again, information provided by Mrs. Hopkins. Ess speculated that the woman had provided quite a bit of information to enemy forces during the war, so Rebel spies had left the town entirely alone.

Once inside the convalescent rooms, she found the injured man readily enough, and let out a long, loud sigh of relief, crackling a bit at the end with a hint of a sob. By his thick red hair alone, the man with bandages across his face and chest wasn't Giles.

"Vivian?" the man whispered.

Ess gasped and stepped back away from the bed, realizing too late that she had come too close, so the feeble illumination from the shielded nightlight had touched her face. Then a second later she realized what he had said.

"Why did you call me that?"

"You're Vivian and Edward's... no, you're not the boy, Ulysses. Too young. But your face, all the best parts of them, in one face." A chuckle escaped him, ending in a cough that sounded wet, like it would bring up blood at any moment.

Ess hurried to help him sit up, and caught up one of the towels sitting on the low table beside the bed. The man pressed it over his mouth and shuddered and gasped. She cringed when he took the towel away and it was spattered with bright speckles of red.

"That's Matilda's spirit in you, isn't it?" he said, his voice harsh, like he had splinters in his throat. "The girl's name -- can't remember the girl's name. By the Great Machine, how the years have fled by."

"How do you know my parents?" Ess helped him sit back, after tugging the pillows into position to support him. When he gestured at the nightlight, she took it down from its arm on the wall and raised the shield to give more illumination.

He was pale, making darker contrast with the red splotches of exertion on his face. Something niggled at the back of her mind. She thought perhaps she had seen his face once, long ago. Or maybe not him -- maybe a photograph? She tried to imagine him changed to gray tones, or sepia. Was it a tintype, or something newer?

"It's all right," he whispered and patted her hand.

Ess was surprised to see she had come to perch on the side of the bed, within reach of him.

"You think you know my face, but can't remember when or where. It's all right, Odessa. Yes, I remember your name. Your mother was the whimsical one, naming your brother Ulysses and you Odessa. How she loved Greco-Roman mythology. Much more fascinating and easier to understand, she said, than the Egyptian and Incan and Norse that was spoon-fed to us since our cradle days."

"How did you -- I know how, the Resurrectionists." Ess muffled a growl of frustration that she feared might erupt into a shriek that would bring the doctor running. She knew she had very little time until he or his assistant came in to check on their patient. She had spent the whole evening watching them, learning their routine. While she admired their diligence, it frustrated her. Especially now, when there were so many questions rising up in her mind that she needed to ask this man. "Who are you?"

"Your brother called me Uncle Darius. I haven't seen your parents since your mother was expecting you, but your father kept me informed up until the... well, even the most cautious archeologists run into nasty surprises left by the ancients." He patted her hand again. "You're here for Giles, aren't you?"

Chapter Eight

"Is he here?"

"I'm sorry. He was supposed to meet me yesterday. I suppose I got a little anxious, and that made me careless. One of those scoundrels recognized me or one of the signals I put out, so Giles could find me. He didn't tell me much, couldn't get much into the telegram, but I'm guessing the drop box and communications links were for you. What sort of trouble have you gotten yourself into?" His voice trailed off so it was little more than a breath on the last few words.

She told him in as few words as possible, because her inner time sense told her she had run out of room to dally. Darius agreed, her first priority was to find Giles. He feared that Giles had been detained by the same trouble that had him asking for help in setting up a mail drop in the first place. He promised he would work hard to regain his strength and have answers for her when she returned -- hopefully with Giles and a fascinating, most likely frustrating story to tell.

Ess slipped out of his room and down the short hallway to the staff stairwell -- another sign of just how prosperous the town was, Mrs. Hopkins would say, "Just imagine being able to have stairs just for the servants and one for the guests" -- and down the hall to the empty room. In moments, she slipped down the back of the surgery wing and into the darkness. In the shadows, she had to navigate mostly by feel, the ground under her feet and the walls on either side of her. Ess was surprised to step out into the weak spill of moonlight and find everything blurry. She blinked and felt warm wet trickle down her cheeks. What was she crying about? She didn't have time to think about it, maybe didn't even want to understand all the reasons. One thing she promised herself -- she would return quickly and have more time to talk to Darius.

"At the very least, he might be able to help me find Uly," she muttered as she looked in all directions, including up. As she had learned recently, more things slipped past people who didn't look upwards as well as to either side. Then she crossed the side street, heading for the outskirts of town.

~~~~~

The smell of burning still lingered in the air as Ess came down the road to her grandparents' home. She had passed through town and scavenged a newspaper from the trash barrels behind the Star City Restaurant to find out if anything noteworthy had been happening in town. She had to dig out five newspapers, because food smears and grease stains seemed to be all aimed at the story about the raid and fire at the Fremont house. Ess knew better than
~~~~~

to risk being recognized by lingering close enough to the agitated groups of people in town to hear what they were saying. She knew better than to approach the house through open country in the light of day, so she had to stay in the shadows, in town, until it was safe to walk the three miles home. Why not learn everything she could and be prepared for what she might find? Common sense said something had happened at home to keep Giles from meeting her and Darius as planned.

The newspaper story had prepared her, but not nearly enough. The damage was minimal. One corner of the huge porch, where friends had gathered to play music together or hold long, involved, scholarly discussions, looked like it had been bitten off with flaming teeth. One of the tall, thin windows was covered with boards, and black smears peeked out from the edges. According to the newspaper report, a party of horsemen had ridden into town late at night, demanding directions out to the Fremont place. They were rude enough in interrogating the townspeople -- who was at the house, had the granddaughter returned, had any lawyers come through town? -- that they attracted the attention of the sheriff. When they raced out of town, the sheriff had called up half his deputies and followed them. They were close enough on their heels to fight the fire before it did much more than cosmetic damage.

However, they were too far away to cut short the fatal gun battle between Giles and the invaders.

Ess let herself into the house using the hidden doorway in one of the outbuildings, and took the secret passageway in the underground maze that connected all the buildings on the property. She searched the house the best she could, but found nothing that Giles might have left behind to indicate his arrangements to make contact with Hilda, Bridget, Thomas, Peggety and Waldo. There was nothing left in the house other than dishes and clothes and furniture. Everything she valued had been removed into safekeeping and storage by the loyal family retainers.

The worst pain of all was knowing she didn't dare linger in town for Giles' funeral. She couldn't even take the risk of sneaking into the funeral parlor to make her final farewells. Giles wouldn't want her to waste time "maundering" over him. Her only chance at getting answers and reconnecting with people who knew her and could help her was to return to Darius and stay with him while he recovered.

~~~~

When she returned to Parkerton, Ess discovered the hotel and Dr. Alberts' surgery were overrun with strangers, well-dressed people with stern faces, men and women who asked questions and seemed to be everywhere, watching in every direction. Even up. Ess found Mrs. Hopkins, spotting the woman's wagon coming into town. She followed until she could pretend to accidentally run into her. Mrs. Hopkins recognized her, and offered to pay for her candy and give her a ride back to her "mean old skinflint uncle's place"
~~~~

in exchange for help unloading the wagon. Ess accepted, though the gossip that would soon spill from the woman's lips was the more valuable payment, in her estimation.

Darius -- though Mrs. Hopkins didn't know his name, just the poor man who ran afoul of the Resurrectionists -- had died the morning after Ess visited him. Dr. Alberts said there were internal injuries he hadn't been able to stop bleeding. Whoever the stranger was, he was an important man in academic circles. Judging by the serious intensity of the well-dressed people now filling the town, asking questions, examining his body and teaching Dr. Alberts medical procedures he had never heard of, he was someone important. Speculation ran rampant through the town about who exactly these powerful, scholarly people were. They said they were archeologists, but Ess suspected no one in town really understood what archeology was. She wasn't about to offer facts to straighten out Mrs. Hopkins' impressions that it was something akin to fortune telling. Archeologists could simply pick up a piece of old pottery or look at a cave drawing and know about the lives of the people who had created them, including personal details like how tall they were, what they liked to eat, and how many children they had. While Ess thought it would be amusing to see what her informant could do with the truth, she didn't want to attract attention to herself by revealing her knowledge. After all, she was just a dirty, bored boy from out of town, a stranger, staying with relatives who didn't really care about him.

If she educated Mrs. Hopkins, by nightfall the archeologists investigating Darius' death would hear about the boy who knew so much... but that wouldn't be a bad thing, would it? If they were friends of Darius, then they might be friends of her grandparents. They were archeologists, after all.

Maybe they were archeologists. What if they were simply another division of the Resurrectionists, trying to find out through a façade of civilization and scholarly activity what they hadn't been able to learn through using guns and bullets and fire?

Ess finished unloading the wagon, picked out her candy, and let Mrs. Hopkins buy her a sandwich and a shaved ice in a paper cone before they headed out of town. She had time to embroider the tale of a skinflint uncle before they reached the point on the road where the elderly woman had met her before.

"I'm sorry, ma'am, but it wouldn't be good if my uncle saw you with me. He's that cussed mean. If he knew people were nice to me, then he'd think I was saying bad things about him."

"The truth is often cruel. What self-righteous people never seem to understand is that if they would act civilly and with consideration and kindness to all, they wouldn't have to worry about what people said or thought about them." The elderly woman sighed and tipped her head to one side, smiling softly at Ess. "I will be coming back in three days with another wagon load, if you happen to need to take another long, dusty walk into town."

"That'd be very nice, ma'am. I thank you kindly." Ess bobbed a little bow, trying to make it awkward, like a boy who knew manners but rarely had reason to use them. She gestured off down the side road into the woods. "I gotta be back before dark. You got a long way to go yet before you're home?"

"Hardly any time at all. You take care of yourself, lad, hear me? And if it won't get you into trouble, give my best to your mother."

"Yes, ma'am, I surely will." Ess walked backwards, watching the wagon trundle down the road. Mrs. Hopkins looked backwards several times, and each time Ess waved to her and the woman waved back. She stepped into the cover of the trees, still watching, until the wagon vanished down the road. Then she waited in the shadows, for another hour, in case Mrs. Hopkins decided to come back and risk rousing trouble from the skinflint uncle by confronting him.

When it was safe, Ess headed back down the road to town. She would get as close to the archeologists as she could and ask her questions and maybe, just maybe she would confront one of them. If God was good, the person she approached would also be a friend of her parents, would see Vivian's and Edward's features mixed in her face, and believe her story. She wasn't sure even now if she wanted to be taken under anyone's care -- other than being dirty and dusty and hungry, she rather liked being on her own. That, and the lack of books to read, and the fear of someone being horrified to discover she was a girl under the filthy boy clothes.

The steam carts parked in front of the hotel and surgery were gone. The well-dressed strangers were gone, and no lamps gleamed in the windows of the surgery or the pharmacy next door. Ess shivered with the certainty that once again, her timing was off. What could she have learned from these people? Certainly they could have done something about Giles' death, at the very least. How was she going to make contact with Hilda and the others, without Darius or Giles?

She waited in town five days. The archeologists never returned, and she learned they had taken away Darius' body. Hilda, Thomas, Bridget, Peggety and Waldo never made an appearance. Ess considered traveling to Cleveland and looking for Hilda, as that was the only destination she knew about. However large and growing the city on the shores of Lake Erie might be, surely it couldn't be so huge she wouldn't be able to track down the woman who had read her faerie tales.

Ess formulated her new, revised plan of action. She would have to hurry, but she thought she could reach the port before Sarah's steamship sailed. She would need the shape-altering corset if she wanted to carry off her disguise as a boy indefinitely. After that, maybe Cleveland. She had plenty of money. Enough to travel in some comfort, to purchase the clothes of an upper class boy. Certainly people would be more willing to answer the questions of a boy who looked like he came from wealthy, powerful people. Not like they would with a girl, or even a young woman. Their first questions would always be to ask why she was traveling alone, where her parents or escort were. Ess thought about being able to get a room in a hotel and indulge in a hot bath, and not having to skulk in the shadows again. Definitely, she needed that corset. From there, she would make up her plan as she went along.

All except one detail.

Wherever she went, she would look for the men who had escaped Agent Sutter's raid. She would do what she could to trip them up and let the government know where they were. Perhaps she was wrong, thinking that they were responsible for killing Giles and most likely Darius, but what if they had been acting in retaliation, somehow suspecting her escape was related to the capture of so many of their fellow rebels?

They had to be punished. She had to be part of that. She owed Giles, if no one else. She owed Darius, because he knew who she was, and suddenly that struck her as a very rare thing. What if the day came that there was no one in the entire world who knew who Odessa Vivian Fremont was?

~~~~

Ess felt as if she had been shaved bald and her suit of upper class boy clothes felt stiff and unwieldy as she strolled -- or at least tried to stroll -- casually along the pier leading to the great steamship *Allegheny*. She had three hours until the ship left port, with Sarah on board. Still, despite her discomfort from walking about in broad daylight when she was used to staying in the shadows, there was something exciting about the situation, too. She had to constantly remind herself to tip her hat to ladies, but if she forgot once in a while, well, what boy remembered that courtesy every time? Even more of a conscious effort was not brushing her hand over the back of her head every time she took her hat off, checking that yes, her thick mass of mahogany curls had indeed been cut off. There were no braids to fall down and betray her masquerade.

The steamship line that owned the *Allegheny* and five others was relatively new, backed with the new money and new millionaire families that had arisen, profiting from all the technological advances created by the Civil War. It was christened the Atlantic Venture Line and for now its sole port on the American side of the Atlantic was Charleston. Ess considered the owners very wise to practice slow growth. It seemed every year there was a new advance in steam engine design, and it would be a tragedy to invest in a large number of ships, only to have their design be considered obsolete in a handful of years. She had heard rumors that the Atlantic Venture Line was considering expanding to airship travel. During the war, airships had been used for military tactics only, and limited to government use in the first few years of rebuilding, simply because airships were so prohibitively expensive. Also, the only trained airship crews were military men. In the last few years, the airships were being used for courier work, when speed was an absolute
~~~~

necessity, and in dealing with transport of vital supplies. Some merchants were investing in small airships when speed in getting their items to market was important enough to balance out the cost. Ess had even heard that the wealthy had their own airships. She had heard that European countries were adopting airships more quickly than in the United States, and some governments even looked down on the Yankees for holding to steam engines in ground and water transportation. For herself, she preferred the slower means of transport offered by ships and trains.

The steamship line turned every debarkation into a holiday atmosphere. Bands played and vendors with carts sold shaved ices and lemonade. Children in their Sunday best dashed about, chasing gulls and jumping over the thick cables that snugged the steamship to the pier. Their parents sat in the shade of the pavilions marked for passengers and chatted, waiting as their names were called, their tickets confirmed, and porters took charge of their piles of trunks and baggage. Everything was done in an orderly, almost leisurely, but highly efficient fashion. Ess noted the bright buttons on the uniforms of the ship officials, the porters, the lady hostesses, all the polished brass of the carts and the railings on the various gangplanks, and speculated that one of these days, the Atlantic Venture Line would figure out how to bring the look of a posh hotel lobby to the pier. They certainly had the atmosphere down pat.

Pavilions were marked with letters for the last names of the passengers, assigning them their waiting areas. Ess almost panicked for a moment when she couldn't remember Sarah's last name. Then she laughed at herself -- Sarah would be using *her* name. Sarah had assured her that she would have perfectly legitimate-looking documentation, proving who she was. A technician for her acting troupe had been a forger before the war, creating false manumission papers for escaped slaves so they could get jobs and live openly and freely in the North. Sarah claimed that his papers were so good, a group of escaped slave hunters had found a man and his family and tried to haul them back to Alabama and their owner, but the police officers who looked at the papers tossed the slave hunters in jail for attempted kidnapping of a free Negro family.

"Excuse me, ma'am," Ess said, taking off her cap and bowing her head to a woman who looked like a superior sort of governess, keeping watch over two little girls, sedately licking their bright red shaved ices. "Could you tell me where the pavilion--"

"Pardon me," the governess said, bending with a handkerchief to wipe the face of one little girl before the red syrup dripped from her chin to her pinafore.

The action of bending took the woman's head out of Ess's line of sight, revealing the sign for the pavilion she wanted, letters E through H.

"I just found it. Sorry for bothering you." She winked at the little girls, who giggled back at her, slipped her hat back on her head, and picked up her pace.

The steamship line official standing in the gate of the pavilion had his back to her, so Ess didn't need to stop and identify who she was looking for, as she had to do at the checkpoint at the head of the pier. She blinked and looked around, waiting for her eyes to adjust from bright sunshine to shade, and her heart skipped a beat when she recognized her navy blue- and white-striped traveling dress. For a dizzy moment, she could actually believe she saw herself sitting in a corner where the afternoon light spilled into the pavilion, over the shoulder of her double, illuminating the pages of the book she read. Yes, she would be doing the exact same thing -- enjoying a few moments of solitude, escaping the noise and activity of the people around her by diving into a book.

"Miss Fremont?" she said, stepping up directly in front of Sarah and taking her hat off again. Ess could barely hold back her grin as her double slowly looked up at her and no recognition showed at all for a good eight seconds -- she counted. Sarah's mouth started to open in surprise, then amusement lit her eyes.

"Hello there, boy. I didn't expect to see you down here." Sarah raised herself slightly from her seat as she closed the book and looked over Ess's shoulder at the other people occupying the pavilion. "Was there something I forgot back at the house?" Whatever she was looking for, she settled back in the seat and patted the cushioned bench next to her. "Is there a problem?" she whispered, as Ess took the seat.

"I was hoping I could borrow that clever corset you used for your disguise. I need to pretend to be a boy for a while longer than I planned."

"Fortunately, I don't have it with me." A bird-like chuckle escaped her when Ess blinked, confused. "Well, it wouldn't do to open my trunks here, in front of all these people, and dig it out. Think of the grannies who would be scandalized, seeing my unmentionables even for a moment. Or just thinking they saw my unmentionables. People would remember seeing a boy taking underpinnings from a young lady, tucking them under his coat, and walking away."

"Sorry. Didn't think that far."

"Yes, I can imagine you've been having a wild ride the last week or so."

"Why?" Ess felt as if suddenly her face and back were covered in nervous sweat. "What have you heard?"

"A few rumors, and Miss Talbot let me know about the raid on the school, so I would be able to speak knowledgeably -- to a point, at least -- if someone should ask me about the situation. I'm still not sure if I should envy you all that excitement, or pity you."

"Both." She breathed a little easier. "If you don't have it, and if you will loan it to me, how do I get it?"

In moments, Sarah had obtained pencil and paper from the porter at the pavilion gate. She wrote down several addresses where Ess could catch up with Miss Talbot, and the dates she would be there. Then she wrote another note for Ess to present to the man who guarded the ladies of the theatrical troupe, to let her backstage to reach Miss Talbot. Moments after the two girls hugged and wished each other luck and Ess exited the pavilion, the porter called for Miss Odessa Fremont to prepare to board. Ess nearly turned around to respond to her name.

"Not anymore," she told herself, and picked up her pace. The sooner she got away from the steamship and the pier itself, the safer she would be. If someone who knew her well enough to see through her disguise had come to the pier to keep her from sailing, all would be lost. All it would take was a few seconds of inconvenient timing -- first arriving in time to see Sarah and realize that she was not Ess -- then arriving at the perfect time to see Ess disguised as a boy. How many times, after all, had friends of her grandparents seen her coming back from madcap adventures with Uly, dressed as a boy? Just a lucky glance, a moment of recall, knowing what kind of tricks she was most likely to play to disguise herself -- all combining to end in disaster. She had to leave. Quickly.

Ess focused on the people around her and pretended to be a boy heading for one of the carriages or horses tied up in the waiting area beyond the pier gates. She tried not to think about the next step in her roundabout path until she was safely away. Disaster could still strike. If her mind was full of planning how to get to Boston to catch up with Miss Talbot, she might forget *not* to react if someone called her name. Just a momentary lapse, just a pause to respond, could ruin everything.

Once away from the pier, she breathed a little easier. She retrieved her bags, took a trolley car to the train station, found a seat in a shadowed corner where she could see everything and no one could sneak up on her, and finally relaxed. Just a little. Just long enough to catch her breath, to think, to cool down from the long, hot walk. She really did miss her street urchin disguise, so much easier to move in. Upper class boys had just as much weight and restriction from their clothes as girls did. She would never envy all boys their freedom of clothes and movement ever again.

Getting to Boston in time to meet up with Miss Talbot and obtain the corset wasn't a problem. The cost of a ticket -- even in a sleeper car -- wasn't a problem, either. Ess had plenty of money. She didn't feel entirely safe, even with the money belt around her waist and the packet of bills sewn into the stiff bands around her upper chest. The sooner she made arrangements to deposit the money, yet have access to it no matter where she went in the country, the better.

Chapter Nine

What she should do once she had the corset and took care of her money... that was the problem. How exactly was she to find Uly's trail without running into people who knew her? Even if they weren't fusty, old-fashioned sorts, they would want to watch over her and load her down with advice and cautions for her grandparents' sake. Even for her parents' sake. Ess shivered, remembering Darius saying he knew her parents, he could see their faces in her face. Odd, how she was more used to being identified as Earnest and Matilda's granddaughter than Vivian and Edward's daughter. When she found her brother, people wouldn't be so interfering. Ulysses Fremont would not be the most responsible guardian, but people would step back and give them leeway because, after all, he was her elder brother. Finding Uly and gaining that freedom, however, was the problem.

A newspaper headline, displayed on the counter of one of the many stations where she had to change trains, provided the answer. Ess nearly laughed aloud when she realized how oblivious she had been. The headline announced another spectacular capture by the Pinkerton Agency. That was the answer -- she would hire a detective.

As she settled into her seat on the train with a box lunch she had bought from a cart vendor outside the station, she decided that solved another of her problems. She knew a detective required a retainer against expenses. She had to arrange for a way to get updates on the search from the agency, and leave money on deposit to handle all expenses. Why not leave *all* her money with the agency? That would save her some fussing and planning, and she could be guaranteed that no matter how long it took, she would have the funds to keep the search going for her brother. Maybe there would even be funds left over when the Pinkertons found Uly and they were reunited, to use in the hunt for their grandparents.

~~~~~

Two weeks later, Detective Horace Winslow showed Ess into the Philadelphia office of the Pinkerton Agency. She was now a widow named Flora Lewis, courtesy of Miss Talbot's wardrobe and makeup kit. As far as she could tell, the man didn't seem at all suspicious. Ess followed Miss Talbot's maxim that a little went a long way. Better to have a few lines around her eyes and mouth and present a well-preserved façade, rather than such heavy age makeup that it threatened to cake and crack and fall off at the worst possible time. Besides, this disguise was for everyday living, and not convincing people sitting twenty rows back that she was an elderly woman. The iron-gray wig itched, the rolls of cloth to enlarge her hips, bosom and
~~~~~

bottom were hot and heavy, and the borrowed black clothes smelled of camphor, but other than that, Ess was delighted with the disguise.

"Ma'am," he said, shuffling through the pages of notes he had made after they had talked for nearly an hour, "has anyone ever pointed out what a fine, analytical mind you have?"

"Sometimes." She effected a delicate shrug. "I assume this means the information I was able to give you is useful?"

"Useful?" He chuckled and sat back in his chair, crossing his arms over his chest. His bushy brown moustache, dusted with gray, stretched in a charming way when he smiled as broadly as he did. "Somebody would think you've been doing some detective work of your own."

He rested his hand on the stack of pages with all the information Ess had been able to recall about her grandparents' South American expedition, as well as the things Uly had been doing, the things he had mentioned, in the weeks before he disappeared. To complete the disguise, she had included information on herself, the events at the Academy and the things Fanny had told her that the girls had speculated when she vanished. If she had the Pinkertons looking for the entire Fremont family, surely that would stop them from suspecting that their elderly client was one of the missing Fremonts, wouldn't it?

"This is a grave concern, sir. The girl needs her older brother, at the very least. The two of them were deprived of their parents at an early age. They need their grandparents back safe and sound. Unfortunately, what news that comes north indicates many of the countries in South America are in turmoil once again, making the area even more unsafe for Mr. and Mrs. Fremont. Rebels and native tribes on the rampage have no respect for academics, no matter how well-respected they are in the archeological field."

"As a good friend of the family, you're right to be concerned. I sure hope those two youngsters appreciate how much you're investing in this search." His left eyebrow raised as he glanced over her once again, sitting as upright and prim and poised as she could manage when there were rolls of cushion between her bottom and the chair. "You must realize, though, that eventually we're going to look a little further into your connection to the family."

"I hope that only happens when you've found them and reunited them, and you're bored with nothing else to investigate."

That earned a chuckle from him that made his shoulders shake. Ess decided she could like him very much. He seemed a common sense sort of man with a good sense of humor, who wouldn't be too scandalized to learn she planned to spend the next several years as a boy.

"I assume, sir, the funds I will put aside will be adequate, and the proposal for payment and making contact will be as well?"

"Oh, certainly, certainly. We've had other clients through the years who are constantly on the move. You realize, the further out west you move, the longer it'll take to get a response to you. Especially if we have a report to send through the mail, instead of just a telegram."

"I've added that to my calculations. With any luck and God's grace, the next time I contact you for a report, you will be able to arrange a meeting with at least Ulysses Fremont, if not his sister."

"Something tells me he's going to be the easiest one to find." Horace winked at her.

Ess couldn't breathe for a moment -- he hadn't seen through her disguise, had he? Was he playing a game with her?

"Why is that, sir?"

"Just from the outline of what you told me about the boy, he sounds like a rascal without much brains. Got fed up with being kept under tight reins, decided to run off west to seek his fortune. The West is a pretty big place, lots of wilderness, but you'd be surprised how easy it is to find someone if you know something about their character. There are only so many places that suit specific types. Besides, we have offices and agents everywhere. Won't take more than a few weeks of telegrams, checking with the local sheriffs, asking at boarding houses, to eliminate where he didn't go and get a clearer view of where he did, if you catch my drift. We'll find his trail. South America..." Another shrug. "That's where most of your money is going to be spent."

"I have more than enough, I should hope." Between the money she had taken from her grandparents' home and her own bank account, she was quite well off. No need to waste money on luxuries, however. She calculated that if she needed to raid her bank account again, or even contact Endicott, Lewis and MacDonald for more extensive funds, enough time would have passed that she would be allowed to stay free.

"More than enough for... oh... I'd say six years of intensive investigation, traveling fees, boat fares and the like. Meanwhile, the bulk of your money will be sitting in Mr. Hoffstead's friendly bank across the street, earning interest, to help carry you through a few more years."

Ess had several uneasy moments, positive her disguise would be pierced, as they went through the process of signing the contracts and finalizing their methods of communication and code words, so the Pinkertons would know she -- Mrs. Flora Lewis -- was contacting them and not some imposter interfering in "family matters." Several times, Horace had to step away from his desk, go into another room for papers to sign and check on records, verify where other Pinkertons were currently assigned, or confer with one of the other agents in the office. Each time, she expected him to come back without his charming, lazy smile, as he demanded the truth.

Detectives couldn't possibly take it very well if their clients lied to them from the beginning, after all.

That evening, however, Ess boarded a train to Pittsburgh, where she would debark in the early morning darkness and find some secure place to shed her disguise. She would leave Mrs. Lewis's costume in a storage locker, paying a yearly fee. With any luck, the people running the lockers would be amenable to accepting shipments from her and storing them in the locker as time went on. After all, while she might collect clues and important items along her way, she would need to travel lightly and couldn't afford an increasing amount of baggage.

In Pittsburgh, Ess mailed a long, detailed letter of explanation to Endicott, Lewis and MacDonald, thanking them for their diligence in looking after her affairs, and apologizing to them for a number of lies she had chosen to tell them. She promised to keep in contact with them, and to answer all their questions as soon as she had some solid proof as to her grandparents' whereabouts.

She fell asleep tucked into the dark corner of the second class carriage with Detective Horace Winslow's words ringing in her memory. If only, at her first scheduled check-in, two months from now, they had found her brother. Life would be more complicated, with needing to keep Uly out of trouble, but much simpler and somewhat safer, at the same time.

Ess's next stop was Cleveland. It was a much larger city than she had anticipated, thanks to the shipping companies using the port city as their headquarters for much of the Great Lakes region. Trains also used it as a hub, and several airship companies were preparing to build skyscrapers to rival those in New York, to use as docking towers. Ess gave herself a week to do some preliminary searching for Hilda, based on what she had heard the woman say about friends and connections and places she had visited in the growing city. Her efforts were futile, and she considered hiring another detective simply to track down Hilda, but several incidents frightened her away.

With all the growth in the city, there was a desperate need for manual laborers in all areas. Children as young as five years old were put to work hauling water, picking up stones to help clear building sites, pulling wagons and carts to haul away debris or bring in building materials. One too many times, a foreman who called to offer work to the "boy" who obviously had nothing to do but "walk around town, getting in the way and pestering people," got angry when she refused to come work for him. There seemed to be some competition among work crews to get laborers. She overheard some women, trying to do their laundry in an alley, discussing rumors that wives and children were being threatened to make men switch their allegiance from one foreman and employer to another. Ess could easily envision a lone boy with no adults to protect him, being kidnapped and forced into labor. Twice, someone had grabbed her by the arm and tried to drag her toward a group of boys hard at work, insisting that her father or uncle had already accepted her day's wages, and threatening to call the police if she didn't cooperate. The first time, Ess shouted for the police herself, and the man let go. The second time, she used a boxing trick her grandfather had taught her and put the man on his back. Workers gathered around laughing as she fled.

From there, it was easy to imagine what would happen to her if her captor found out she was a girl.

So Ess fled Cleveland, silently apologizing to Hilda, and vowed that when she found Uly, the two of them would return and look for the cook who had been like a second mother to them. Now, however, it was time to turn her face westward and begin her own search for her brother. She made a map and a list in her head, all the places Uly had wanted to see someday, all the things he wanted to do. They had spent many happy hours in the attic that was their playroom and sanctuary, looking out over the fields and making plans for adventures, just the two of them together.

Most definitely, she would make her brother regret having his adventures without her.

~~~~~

Ess bought a third class ticket from Cleveland to Toledo and switched trains from there to go to Dayton. The engine sounded strained when she walked down the platform to get into a car near the end, and Ess spotted tiny geysers of steam escaping from some of the pipes leading from the boiler to the pistons. Places where there shouldn't have been any pressure release valves. Before she could step off the platform to get a closer look, the conductor called for everyone to board -- or get left behind. Ess scolded herself silently for thinking anyone would welcome her curiosity. She was just a lone boy, after all, far too young to know anything about steam engines or trains in general.

She listened for the laboring sound of the engine, the unsteady pace, and thought she felt extra moisture in the air from too much steam escaping. That boiler was going to run dry before they reached Dayton.

When the train slowed to a stop in a stretch of train tracks with nothing but prairie, untouched by plows or towns, in every direction, Ess wasn't surprised. She got up on her knees and lowered the window to stick her head out to listen to the engineers and the conductor arguing. A few men got out of the first and second class carriages, walked up to the front of the train, gestured and talked for a little while, then went back to their cars without doing anything. She supposed they weren't too proud to admit they didn't know anything about engines.

She recalled a discussion between her grandfather and some of his more philosophical friends. Philosophical, according to her grandmother, meant they preferred to sit and discuss the world's problems rather than get up and do something about them. The topic that day had been over the ethical divide between those who knew to do right and chose to do wrong, and those who knew what needed to be done to make the world a better place, had the necessary skills, and yet chose not to use those skills. There was entirely too much of a growing trend, according to her grandparents, of people saying that because a problem did not affect them directly, they were not responsible for fixing it. "No concern of mine" was the phrase they had heard so many
~~~~~

times, when other people walked past a bad or pitiable or simply disgusting situation, and didn't stop to offer help. Her grandfather and his friends decided that those who could fix a problem and chose not to were worse criminals than those who chose to do evil.

"Botheration," she muttered, knowing exactly what her grandmother would say if she argued that getting involved in the steam engine problems might threaten her disguise. Matilda Fremont would retort that if Ess's disguise was that fragile, then it wasn't worth maintaining in the first place.

Slinging her one remaining bag over her shoulder, because she didn't trust the few people sitting in the third class carriage with her, she slipped out the door. From there, she ducked underneath the guard chains and hopped down to the ground without the aid of the folding steps. A line of train workers in a bucket brigade were manually filling the boiler when she walked up the short line of the train to the front.

"Excuse me." She tugged on the conductor's arm after she had stood beside him for several minutes, watching the exercise, and he neither acknowledged her presence nor told her to get back on the train. "When we were at the station, I noticed some steam leaking in the..." She trailed off when the man turned sharply to glare at her.

"Where?" he barked, instead of telling her she didn't know what she was talking about, she was just a dirty boy.

Most likely he was frustrated enough to snatch at any helpful idea. While Ess walked up to the side of the engine and pointed out some of the pipe joints where she had noticed the little geysers, he shouted for the men to stop filling, that it wouldn't do them any good. The engineer and another man, covered in coal dust and likely the head stoker, sauntered over to the array of pipes that fed into the piston works, while the other three men dropped their buckets and settled down on the ground. Ess heard them muttering, punctuated with crude laughter. From the reddening of the conductor's ears, they were probably mocking him for listening to a passenger who was just a boy.

The engineer took a massive wrench from a loop in the leg of his overalls and tested some of the places where Ess had seen steam leaking out. All the pipes moved easily. His face grew redder with each joint he tested, until he raised the wrench as if he would dash it to the ground, then let spill a stream of curses. She was impressed -- she recognized French, German, and Irish curses all mixed together. Then amazingly, he let the arm holding the wrench drop to his side and grinned at her.

"Got a good eye, lad. Let me guess, you want to be an airship captain someday, love tinkering with gizmos." He wiped his hand on the seat of his overalls and held it out to shake hers.

"Uh -- well -- not quite, sir. My Pa, he was an inventor. I love gizmos, but I don't know what I want to do just yet."

"Was?" the conductor said.

"Died of his wounds from the war a month or so back. Collectors took everything to pay his debts." She hooked her thumb over her shoulder in a westward direction. "I'm hoping to catch up with my big brother. It's been a while since we heard from him."

"Where's the last place he's been?"

"He was heading for Springfield, last I knew. He wanted to see where Mr. Lincoln came from." That much was true. Ulysses admired President Lincoln greatly and couldn't wait until he was old enough to vote, if the great man was still running for office by then. Three assassination attempts had followed the bullet that had put him in a clockwork wheelchair, and each one left him weaker.

The engineer and the stoker and the other three men got to work, tightening the pipe joints and sealing the leaks with a putty-like substance that hardened when touched by steam. The conductor meanwhile became talkative, regaling Ess with stories about Springfield. As the hometown of President Lincoln, it was a focal point of the Union as it rebuilt. There was talk of making it an even more important hub for commerce and travel and culture than Chicago or New York or San Francisco all put together. Her brother might still be in Springfield, with so much work to do, so much growth taking place.

"That's the last of it." The engineer stepped back, wiping his greasy hands on the sides of his overalls. "Wish we had that newfangled telegraph that you can hook up to any line."

"Portable?" Ess liked the sound of that.

"Not every train has them yet," the conductor said, nodding. "I know what you're thinking, Harry. I want MacPherson's head as much as you do. This is exactly the sort of thing the big bosses were afraid of when they sacked him."

"Today was the last day for the man at the Toledo station on day shift," the engineer explained as he bent to pick up tools and the bucket of sealing putty. "His job is to check all the seals on the steam pipes, make sure nuts and bolts and such haven't worked loose on all the connections. He was sacked, given two weeks' notice, for being drunk on the job one time too often."

"Yep," the conductor said, stretching the word out into a sigh. "That's just the sort of nasty trick MacPherson would pull. Doesn't care who he hurts, just as long as he can hurt someone." He turned back to Ess and winked. "Thank the Good Lord for your sharp eye, lad. Wouldn't have done us a lick of good to put all the water from our reserves in the boiler if the steam just kept leaking out again."

"Don't suppose you want to ride up front with us?" the stoker said, stepping over to join them. He held out a bottle of something that dripped condensation, that all the other men had been drinking from. "Go on, it's just ginger beer. You earned it, boy."

Ess thanked him with a nod. Her thirst and the marvel of having something cold overrode her hesitation over drinking from a bottle five other people had already put to their mouths. There was likely a foot of insulation around the cold box, to keep ice from melting into thin air, sitting so close to the firebox and the boiler. The ginger beer was strong and bubbly and a delightful treat, washing away the dust in her mouth.

"Not that we think you'll have to fix anything else, but an extra pair of eyes would be a help," the engineer said, nodding. "Maybe keep you with us as a good luck charm, what do you say?"

Ess wasn't sure what exactly a boy would say, offered the treat of riding with the engineer, even if the engine was dirty and hot and noisy as she expected. Too much excitement or words that were too polite would ruin her disguise. She just grinned and nodded hard. That must have been right, because the conductor and engineer both laughed and clapped her on the back.

She was gritty and gray with coal dust and sweaty and windblown, and ended up tucking her cap in her trousers pocket because it kept blowing off. Thank goodness she had chosen to cut her hair short. All in all, despite the filth and noise, she thoroughly enjoyed the ride in the engine. Any conversation had to be conducted in shouts, so her throat hurt by the time the train pulled into the Dayton station. The engineer and stoker were both talkative, eager to educate her on their beloved engine and trains in general. Ess found it quite informative.

The stoker showed her to a washroom where she could take a basin bath and change her shirt. Ess hesitated, dreading the difficulty of trying to wash, which she needed desperately, while men were in the room. Fortunately, the kindly man just shoved the door open and told her to come to the ticket window area when she was done, that he doubted any of them would be back for a while, and the clerk behind the window would take care of her.

"It's going to take some time to figure out the words for the telegram, and we have to write up a blasted report on what happened. That MacPherson is probably long gone, but that doesn't mean we can't send the sheriff and some company men on his trail for what he did," he added.

"At least he didn't try to make the boiler blow, mess with the pressure gauge so it didn't read true," she offered.

"Aye, there's that. You've got a two-hour layover until your next train leaves, so we should be done and back to look after you before then."

"You don't need to," she said, cringing as she felt her face warm. Now was not a good time to blush. "I'm used to taking care of myself."

Chapter Ten

"Lad, we pay our debts. We owe you a good dinner, at least. If you want to know the truth." He grinned and leaned down closer to her. "I wouldn't be surprised if the boss-man offers you a job as inspector. That'd be the life, don't you think? Ride all day long, get off at stations, look around, see how the maintenance fellows are doing their jobs, looking for shortcuts and short-shifting, report on how the rest of us do their jobs."

"Why would you give that kind of a job to a boy?"

"MacPherson didn't notice you noticing the steam leaks, I figure, or he would have fixed things, or done something worse, like you said. Nobody notices boys. Some of our best inspectors are old ladies working on their knitting the whole while."

"That's true." Ess grinned, remembering the ladies she had given her seat to, and how that had earned her a cold drink and a better seat.

The stoker patted her head, gave her a shove through the washroom door, and announced he was late. He ran, heavy boots pounding on the wooden boards, before Ess could reach back to close the door.

She took the time to rinse out her filthy shirt and peeled out of her trousers and give them a good shaking, to get as much coal dust as possible out of the fabric. Ess laughed at herself in the polished brass sheet mirror before she washed. Her face was dark gray, with pale circles of clear flesh around her eyes where the goggles the engineer had loaned her had kept her skin clean. With some regret, she put on her clean shirt, tucked her still-damp shirt into her bag, and headed around the back of the station to the ticketing area. This station was large enough to have an indoor waiting area. Maybe she could find a private corner where she could spread out her shirt to let it dry more before her next train departed.

The man at the ticket window was short and spindly-looking. He had to perch on a stool to reach over the counter and hand tickets through the cage bars. He couldn't have been more than twenty-three or perhaps twenty-five, his hair slicked down and his tie tied in a precise knot, and his posture on his stool was perfect. Ess cringed when she got her first look at him, expecting him to treat her in just as prissy a manner as he looked.

"You're Joshua?" he called, frowning so his forehead filled with wrinkles, when she approached the ticket window.

For a second, Ess almost forgot the false name she had given the conductor and the others. She nodded. To her amazement, the constipated look fell away entirely, replaced with a wide grin, and he reached through the bars, offering his hand to shake.

"Pleased to meet you. I hear you're helping put the final nail in that rotter MacPherson's coffin."

"Oh, I think it was obvious enough he did it, without me pointing it out. I just helped find the problem faster so the train wasn't so late."

"Maybe so, but you're still a hero. Wouldn't be surprised if they don't offer you a job. The big bosses are always talking about needing sharp eyes and sharper minds, and they don't much care how old you are or whether you wear trousers or a skirt. Once all the hoopla over airships dies away and people settle back into common sense, trains are going to be the hearts what pump the lifeblood of this country, so we need to prove we're the best passenger line of all, before that day comes. Am I right, or am I right?"

He spouted more fancy talk like that, in between inviting her to sit inside the ticketing cage with him and sharing a cold bottle of lemonade. In between hearing about the trouble MacPherson and "rotters who think just like him" had caused the railroad line, Ess learned that Archie, the ticketing agent, was the nephew of one of the owners, and he was working his way up. She guessed that despite his connections and his fancy talk, he was well-liked, simply because of how he treated her.

With twenty minutes before her train to Indianapolis was due to leave, Angus, the conductor, came running to Ess with a certificate. It had a red wax seal and was signed by Mr. Armbruster, a member of the board of directors, who was at the Dayton station on an inspection tour. The engineer and conductor had been holed up with him the whole time, reporting to him. The certificate granted Joshua Lewis first class passage on the train line all the way to Springfield, and half-price tickets for him and his brother for the next two months, wherever they wanted to travel. On the back of the certificate was a written offer of employment for Joshua and his brother if they were of a mechanical mindset, once the brothers were reunited.

"It wasn't that much," Ess protested, fighting not to let her hands shake and wrinkle the certificate. "I just did what was right, what my Granny would want me to do."

"Not as many people as should, have that kind of mindset nowadays," Angus told her. "Your pa was a veteran. War orphans deserve our help and our gratitude, the big boss says. And like Archie here probably told you, we're always looking for sharp eyes and loyal hearts."

She still stammered her thanks when Angus gruffly pointed out she was wasting time and would miss her train. He cuffed her gently across the back of her head, nearly knocking her cap off, and trotted with her all the way to the train, where he guided her up the stairs into the first class compartment. Then he handed her a canvas sack he had been carrying.

"Not quite the fancy lunch we promised you, but it'll serve." He winked, grinned at her stumbling thanks, and hurried out of the carriage. Just a few seconds later, the carriage jolted and the engine whistle shrieked, and Ess settled back in her comfortable seat.

The sandwich was massive, enough for two meals, heavy with slices of chicken and soft cheese and a spicy mustard that bit at her nose. The peach was as large as her fist and juicy enough she didn't need anything to drink. The conductor who came through the car twenty minutes after leaving the station was a young man, around Archie's age, and seemed to know who she was. He winked and gestured for her to put away her ticket and the certificate while she was still pulling them out.

"I am going to be quite spoiled," she mused. "Odds are against me being rewarded so well every time I do something right. Is the world really such a nasty place that people make a fuss over those who do right?" She sighed and settled back in her seat to watch the landscape speeding by the window. "Granny... I hope I always make you proud of me. Even if I end up being punished for doing what's right."

~~~~~

In Springfield, an ambitious project had captured the imagination of the entire city. A tower twenty stories high, to be serviced by the newest design in steam-powered elevators. It would serve as a docking tower for two airships at a time, with ramps to allow passengers to disembark without having to land the airship. Part of the tower would serve as a hotel, while the other would house government offices. The tower was actually two buildings, with an open space between them, connected every third floor by an open platform that would support gardens and open air cafes. Ess found the whole concept fascinating. She took a job with a dozen other boys hired to haul sealed buckets of drinking water up and down ladders all day for the construction workers. Naturally, she was expected to haul more than just water, but she didn't mind, because the construction workers took the boys under their wings, watching out for their welfare, paying them to run errands for them -- haul their wash to the laundry or buy them a plug of tobacco or order a hot meal for them to pick up on the way to their boarding houses.

The elevators were installed before the final two stories were enclosed, and Ess was scolded just as often as the other boys, and many of the construction workers, for stopping often in the course of her errands to watch. The coils of cables and piles of pulleys and the massive engines in the basement of the building and miles of pipes captured her imagination. She tried to calculate what kind of power would be required to keep the elevator running at peak calculated speed. A team was training to monitor the boiler and the mechanisms full-time during the installation. The few times she overheard the instructions and the questions the workers asked, she decided she wouldn't have such an exacting duty for all the money in the world.

Ess's evenings were spent roaming the city, listening to the gossip, the rumors, asking questions. There was no sign of her brother. She wasn't entirely disappointed. At least Uly hadn't been caught in one of his escapades.

As fall approached, she reluctantly admitted she needed to decide where to go next, and what she should do to find work. Soon the skyscraper
~~~~~

construction would be finished. Should she stay in Springfield and find some sort of work -- maybe hawking newspapers, driving delivery wagons, acting as a courier for businesses, or some employment that would put her indoors in inclement weather? Thanks to the extra money earned running errands for the construction workers, and the cheap, clean little rented room barely big enough for a bed, she had been able to save almost a third of what she earned.

The day the water boys were dismissed, they were all handed vouchers, allowing them to come back on the day of the dedication of the building in two weeks' time. They would be allowed to perch on the garden level of the third floor and look down on the ceremonies in the square fronting the tower. The owners of the building were delighted and proud to announce that President Abraham Lincoln himself had agreed to return to Springfield to dedicate the building, which would include a memorial for his late wife and young son Willie, who had died while in his first term of office.

A chance to see Abraham Lincoln was reason enough for Ess to linger in Springfield and pass up a job offer that would require her to go to Missouri. One of the boys she had worked with had an aunt who ran the laundry at the largest hotel in Springfield, and chances were good the president would stay there. Ess gladly went to the hotel with Roger to apply for work in the laundry, under his aunt. They would get that much closer to the president than the other boys in their work team. She learned young boys were made for filling in a dozen different odd jobs every day, in hotel operations. She ran errands for everyone on the staff. Right now, with the weather pleasant, she didn't mind. When winter came, however, she hoped the hotel would either provide her winter clothes or the fare to take a streetcar.

Four days before President Lincoln's train was due to arrive, Ess stepped out of the newspaper office after dropping off an order for ads, and nearly ran into a man with a familiar face. At first she couldn't place where she had seen him. He turned to one of his four companions, all dressed in rusty black, fine clothes, and made a comment, his face twisting into a sneer. She remembered that expression from the tunnels below the school grounds. Ess recognized the other four men. All of them were Resurrectionists. All had escaped the raid led by Agent Sutter.

What were the chances the Resurrectionists were here by mere coincidence, rather than in anticipation of President Lincoln's visit?

She gnawed on how to get warning to someone with the power to either stop the president's visit or increase his security, without jeopardizing her own freedom. It wasn't as if she could simply walk up to the head of hotel security and inform him that Resurrectionists were in Springfield, preparing to kill Mr. Lincoln. There was likely an office of the Secret Service here in Springfield. Being the president's hometown made it a target of the disgruntled and vengeful. The chances were very good an office or several had been assigned already in the new tower. Getting into the tower and finding that office and telling someone raised the same questions. Who would believe a boy with no credentials and no adults to back him up? Granted, Aunt Hazel had taken Ess under her wing from the day she started working for her in the hotel laundry, but what was the word of a laundry woman against five well-dressed men who likely had false papers and false names and legitimate business in town to justify their presence?

Ess prayed twice as hard as usual in her morning prayers, and when she went to services the next morning at the little church four blocks away from the hotel. Oddly, she lost some of her anxiety about the whole situation. Maybe she had come to the point of giving up and placing everything in the hands of the Almighty, and that sense of peace was actually just relief from giving up the burden?

After all, why should she worry? The Secret Service had grown skilled at protecting the president. They had plenty of experience. The years of rebuilding the country after the war had churned up enough unrest to toss a veritable sea of lunatics and disaffected against the shores of Washington. Every time the president left the White House, someone tried to break through to hurl abuse at him, or bombs, or take a shot, or sometimes they just settled for throwing rotten produce. Three failed assassination attempts over the last two terms of office surely proved the Secret Service knew how to perform their job.

As Ess looked over the congregation from her perch in the little balcony adjacent to the organ loft, she mused that there was always a first time for a fatal mistake. Should she simply sit back and trust that having prayed hard, the Almighty would take care of President Lincoln? Or should she fall back on her usual tactics of disguise and sneaking and leaving letters full of information for the proper authorities to use? It was too bad she couldn't disguise herself as a man. She would need more than Miss Talbot's long vanished makeup kit to help her pass through security and talk to whichever agent headed the president's security detail. No, she needed someone who resembled a Secret Service agent. Someone like that man sitting in the shaft of sunlight coming in through the side window. She had kept her eye on him during the service as the rising sun sent different colors of stained glass across his features. Right now, the light was nearly golden, instead of the splotches of blue and crimson and green that had covered his face until now.

Ess caught her breath as the man's features seemed to jump out at her. Wouldn't it be funny if she could persuade him to impersonate a Secret Service agent -- specifically Agent Sutter? A moment later, she threw that thought away. There was nothing in the world that could persuade a man who was a merchant of some kind, maybe a banker, or some highly placed office worker, to carry on such a masquerade. Especially so close to the president's arrival. He would consider it treasonous. A lone boy who approached him for the first time, even coming from the church service, could have nothing to convince him.

"Start over, Odessa," she muttered as the preacher raised his hands, gesturing for everyone to stand for the closing prayer. She grimaced at herself, realizing she had missed out on the last twenty minutes of the sermon, caught up in her worries and plotting.

Despite knowing it was useless, Ess managed to exit the balcony at the right time to follow Agent Sutter's doppelganger from the church. No wife or children or colleagues walked with him. While he nodded to several people who wished him good morning, no one stopped him to chat, exchange greetings or invite him for Sunday dinner. That was odd, she knew, because Sunday was the time for decorous courting under the careful eyes of parents. Handsome, prosperous-seeming young men were always invited to spend Sunday afternoon with the families of eligible young ladies. She had seen it happen without fail the entire time she had attended this church, and the man who looked like Sutter certainly fit the bill.

She couldn't recall seeing him at church before today, so maybe he was new to the city, new to the church? Despite knowing better, she picked up her pace once they were out on the pavement and heading away from the church, toward the hotel, where she had to go on duty shift immediately after dinner. Odd, that the man was heading there.

Unless… Ess grinned at how her heart picked up speed, and so did her feet. Following her intuition, she crossed the street and hurried ahead, so she could stand and lean against a gas lamp pole and watch the man approaching her on the other side of the street.

That man was not Agent Sutter's doppelganger, but Agent Sutter himself.

Ess ran ahead to the hotel, positive that was exactly where the Secret Service man was headed. Her plan unfolded in her head with delicious ease. All she needed now was to obtain decent drawing paper and pencils, and find time to draw from memory the five men she had seen on the streets of Springfield. Then she would slip the drawings under the door of Agent Sutter's room. He would have to recognize those faces, and from there she could leave the president's protection detail in his capable hands.

The most difficult part of her task was to contrive to be in the lobby when Sutter returned and checked at the front desk for messages. Ess doubted he would be so foolish as to leave his key with the front desk clerk as some people did, but rather carried it with him. She was right, but the small risk of getting caught standing in the lobby, watching guests, paid off. She saw the number on the box the clerk reached into, to retrieve several telegrams and hand them to Sutter. Interestingly, the clerk addressed him as Mr. Pierce. So, even the Secret Service felt some need for deception and subterfuge. Ess ran off with a skip in her step to her Sunday dinner with Aunt Hazel and Roger, and then a full day of laundry duties.

Finding decent paper that would support a drawing was easy enough. The hotel provided fine quality paper for its guests. Ess couldn't find a stationer's store to obtain the artist's pencils she wanted, but the hotel also opted for the highest quality in that small detail, too. She finished one sketch of the leader of the Resurrectionists during her supper break and hid in the linens storage room after her duties were over, to work on the others. There was no use in going to her tiny boarding house room and wasting time walking that she could use in drawing. Actually, staying past midnight at the hotel suited her plan perfectly. She was able to slip up the staff staircase without anyone noticing her and walk down the dimly lit, carpeted hallway to Agent Sutter's room in nearly perfect safety. There was always the night guard to worry about, but she knew the man on duty tonight. He came often to the laundry to share supper with Aunt Hazel, so the laundry boys and girls teased her about her sweetheart.

Heart thumping, Ess paused two steps from the door of Agent Sutter's suite of rooms, clutching the carefully folded sheaf of sketches. She said a quick prayer, much like the others she had muttered through the day, that her plan would be enough, that her sketches were accurate enough, and that he would act on them and foil the Resurrectionists. Taking a deep breath and holding it, she bent over to shove the papers through the gap under the door.

Too late, she saw the strip of light under the door -- Sutter was awake. Ess's heart tripled its pace and she nearly tripped over her own feet as she backed away from the door. She strained her ears to listen for the door to open, for him to shout after her, but her heartbeats blocked all sound except the unnaturally loud thumps of her boots on the runner down the center of the hallway. Somehow she made it back to the staff stairs and down again without falling or raising an uproar. That close call convinced her that she couldn't follow her original plan of sleeping among the dirty linen until it was time to go to work in the morning. She had to get out of the hotel, in case Sutter started a search for whoever might have slid the sketches under his door. If no one knew she was in the hotel past her working hours, then she wouldn't be suspect, easy as that.

Nothing, she realized, as her heart seemed to jolt to a stop and she nearly slipped on the bottom step of the stairs, was ever easy.

Directly in front of her, in the wide entryway where the hotel staff entered and deliveries were made, stood the night manager, Mr. Filipont, talking with two of the Resurrectionists. In that moment Ess paused, he reached out to shake the hand of one man, and the other grinned at something Mr. Filipont said and clapped him on the shoulder. This was no polite inquiry for information. Besides, what law-abiding, polite citizen asked to talk to the night manager of a large hotel at one in the morning? Even if there was need, why meet in the staff area?

Ess felt nearly sick with a mixture of disappointment and relief.

Disappointed because she liked Mr. Filipont. He had shaken her hand when she and Roger had officially joined the laundry room workers. Just last week he had commended them all on handling a mess made by a French family whose children had become violently ill from a surfeit of "your filthy, plebian sweets," as the sneering father had stated multiple times before departing. Mr. Filipont had treated them all to chocolate bars, and they all had laughed when he noted that American constitutions were certainly stronger and able to enjoy such "filthy, plebian sweets," without any harm. Besides, Mr. Filipont's mutton chop whiskers made him look like a chipmunk, and who could dislike a man who looked like a chipmunk?

Relieved... because she had considered, more than once, confiding in him about the Resurrectionists she had seen, and asking his help in getting the information to the Secret Service. Up until this moment, she felt something like guilt at not trusting someone she liked.

"Thank You, blessed Lord," she whispered once she made it up to the second floor landing. She walked backwards with her heart thudding in her ears again, and no sign anyone had noticed her momentary appearance on the bottom of the stairs.

Ess went down the main stairs, creeping as slowly and quietly as she could in boots that suddenly felt as heavy as if the soles were bricks. Her back hurt from bending over, to present as small an image as possible. She still couldn't breathe easily when she made it to the ground floor and crossed the blessedly empty lobby, and slipped out the front door.

What was she going to do? What if Agent Sutter showed those sketches to the management of the hotel? Would that halt the Resurrectionist plot altogether? Would the night manager panic and follow Miss Van Hastings' example by throwing his co-conspirators to the wolves to save his own neck?

Why would he need to save his own neck, if no one told the Secret Service that he was on cahoots with the Resurrectionists?

"Botheration," Ess muttered, and a moment later snorted laughter at herself as she hurried down the darkened, quiet streets. She would just have to get to work a half hour early in the morning, get hold of more hotel stationery, and write a note to Agent Sutter to slip under his door again. She needed to do it before he awoke, and do it this morning so he had time to work around whatever treachery Mr. Filipont had perpetrated against the president.

Despite the shocks she had endured, Ess found it amazingly easy to curl up on the comfortable, clean mattress in her tiny room and slide into sleep. She nearly didn't get her boots off, and she felt only a momentary flicker of shame that she was sleeping in her street clothes and hadn't washed her face. Her landlady took great pride in clean sheets, and Ess felt she betrayed her by inflicting dirty clothes on sheets that were still stiff from hanging on the line, and smelled of sunshine. Then sleep took her before she could get past that momentary bit of discomfort.

Chapter Eleven

"Fancy meeting you here," Agent Sutter said, as Ess slipped around the corner into the laundry room, half an hour before she was due to start feeding coal to the enormous boilers.

She turned to flee, saw him nod to someone over her shoulder, and felt the presence coming up behind her -- but still tried to run. Big, strong hands caught hold of her by her shoulders and she had a momentary vision of being flung over the musclebound man's shoulders and hauled away. Where, she couldn't imagine right that moment.

Sutter got up from the table where Aunt Hazel kept track of how many sheets and towels and pillowcases and washcloths went through the laundry each day. He moved with an almost feline, stalking grace toward Ess, a smile growing on his face just as slowly.

"I recognized your hand, the moment I saw those sketches. And the faces of the men. What sort of reward should we give a boy who is so diligent in his patriotic duty, Collins?"

"You could let me go," Ess offered, keeping her voice low. Despite herself, she shuddered. Collins' hands tightened on her shoulders. She couldn't exactly explain that she wasn't afraid of him, but of Aunt Hazel or one of the boys she had worked with for so long, walking into the room. The unholy fuss that would result would ruin everything.

"I don't think so. Come along with us."

Colins moved her aside as easily as if she were made of paper, so Sutter could walk past her and out the door. The big man shifted his grip so his hand rested on one shoulder, an arm around her, and his grip just as implacable even if it appeared a bit friendlier.

"I'm going to lose my job if I'm late," Ess said, as they guided her to the staff stairs.

Of course, it made perfect sense for the Secret Service to use the back stairs, to keep the general public from seeing them in action.

"Or don't show up at all?" Sutter paused on the third step and smiled over his shoulder at her. "Have you considered that these men might recognize you from the school and realize you betrayed them, or just *fear* you *could* recognize them and betray them, and they would try to kill you just to keep you quiet? Your life is in danger. Why worry about a job?"

"Nobody notices boys, especially boys with no one and nothing in the world," she countered, as they started up the stairs.

"Secret Service agents and traitors threatening the wellbeing of our country notice everything," Collins said, his voice just as big and deep as his bulk indicated. His hand lifted once, clapping her on the shoulder. "Don't want to lose someone as clever as you, lad. Especially with all the help you've given us."

"Who did you ask, to track me down?" she asked, after climbing two flights of stairs and coming out on the third floor, where the agent's suite was. Ess wondered for a moment if the president would be staying on this floor as well. Was it already emptied out in preparation for him, for security? She couldn't remember if the amount of laundry had been dropping off the last day or two. Why was she wasting her thoughts on such details?

"No one." Sutter glanced at her again, his smile thin but somehow begging her to share in a joke she didn't quite understand. "I knew who to look for, when I recognized your drawing style." He paused to slide his key into the lock. "It didn't take much thinking to deduce who would have access to hotel stationery and who would be able to move about after midnight and find out what room I was in, without being chased out by hotel security. I only had to describe you to the agents who have been here two weeks already, checking out everyone who comes into the hotel."

"Good." She was so relieved, she didn't resist as Collins nudged her through the door.

"Good?" Sutter's eyes narrowed and he reached blindly for the desk chair, to pull it out and sit down while Collins closed and locked the door. "What else have those clever eyes seen, Joshua? If that's your real name?"

"Mr. Filipont, the night manager. I saw him when I was leaving last night -- this morning -- he was talking to two of the Resurrectionists. They seemed to know each other."

"You're sure?" Sutter didn't strike her as doubting her, but simply asking because he had to. Ess appreciated that subtle difference.

"Innocent men don't come to the delivery door of a hotel at midnight and ask to talk to the night manager."

"Boy's got a point," Collins said with a chuckle in his voice.

"More important, why didn't Buckley notice the meeting?" Sutter said, his face shifting slightly, not so much a change in his expression, but an impression of cold and hardness settling over it.

"Housecleaning time again?" The big man had the door open before Sutter could do more than nod.

"Housecleaning?" Ess asked.

"What did you do when you saw those men talking?"

"Went back up the stairs -- I was just coming down from giving you the sketches -- and up to the second floor and down the main stairs and out the front door. Why?"

"Agent Buckley has night watch duty over the delivery door. If he saw you coming out soon after those men met, and if he is a traitor, he might have you marked as trouble."

"So I lose my job either way," Ess muttered.

That earned a brief chuckle from him. "If it's any help, there's a reward for helping to capture traitors and stop plots against the president." He gestured at a padded bench against the far wall. "Have a seat, boy. Make yourself comfortable. Until we root out all the conspirators, you're here for the duration."

"Did you describe me to Mr. Buckley when you were looking for me?" She gladly sat down, surprised at how her legs still trembled, to the point they ached a little.

"No, thank goodness." He watched her for a few moments, his smile growing wider.

"What's so amusing?"

"I was just thinking how furious I was, when I realized I had the artist in my hands back at the school, and how easily you escaped. You knew that school inside and out, didn't you?" A chuckle escaped him when Ess just shrugged. "You have quite a talent. Much training?" Another shrug. "We could use good sketch artists like you, for situations where a camera is just too cumbersome. But when you're older. Can't send a little lad like you into danger." Another chuckle. "Not that you haven't been in danger already."

"How old do you think I am?" She was genuinely curious.

"Hmm... twelve, maybe."

"I just turned fifteen." Ess nearly laughed, when she realized that her birthday had passed and she had been too busy looking for clues to Ulysses' trail, and being on her own, to notice or even complain.

"Really." Again that narrow-eyed, considering look. "I wonder how long you can manage to pass yourself off as much younger than you are. When do the men in your family start growing beards or their voices start changing?"

"Why?" She sat up straight, astonished by the flash of insight. "Are you -- are you offering me a job? With the Secret Service?"

"You've proven your courage, loyalty, patriotism, and morals. The ugliness of the war behind us has proven we need people from all walks of life, to root out our enemies. As you said, people don't notice young boys. They also tend to ignore women in many places. The Pinkertons have had incredible success with women agents, and someday we may have women serving the country in the Secret Service."

"Imagine that," she murmured. The "someday" kept her from confessing that if she accepted his job offer, he would indeed have a woman in the Secret Service. Something told Ess that Agent Sutter's superiors weren't quite that enlightened yet. Still, it was something to consider against the future.

Three taps on the door alerted them both, just before Collins entered the room. His expression had changed from genial giant to something cold, so serious that Ess suspected what had happened before he spoke.

"Hawthorne went to relieve Buckley half an hour ago. Not at his post. They found him two alleys away, his throat sliced." Collins glanced at Ess. "Stone cold. Need a doctor to know for sure, but Hawthorne guesses at least eight, ten hours."

Ess knew it would be little comfort to the somber men who seemed to communicate in silence, to point out that Agent Buckley had not been a traitor after all.

She didn't have to think long to realize that if the plotters had spotted the agent watching the delivery door of the hotel, then they could know who other agents were. They might have seen her come down the main stairs last night, and someone might even now be wondering what a laundry boy was doing, coming out the front door of the hotel hours after his shift was supposed to end. Someone might be watching the laundry, and wondering right now why "Joshua" hadn't reported in for work. Maybe Mr. Filipont had been given instructions to talk to her when she came in and he was about to leave his post and go home. Maybe...

Her head hurt from all the possibilities, and most of them unpleasant and frightening. Ess drew her legs up against her chest, her heels resting on the bench, and shivered, feeling colder than she had felt since... she couldn't remember the last time she had felt this cold. Not even when she realized Giles and Darius were dead and quite possibly she was to blame through some stupid mistake, something she should have done and hadn't known to do, some miscalculation.

"Uly, where are you?" she whispered, and startled herself, speaking her brother's name aloud.

Yes, she realized, she wanted, needed her brother. He might be a scapegrace and a rascal, and had gotten into some kind of trouble and vanished without warning, but he was her big brother and he would protect her and she needed him. After all, despite all the amazing things she had accomplished, the adventures she had had, the scrapes she had endured, she was only fifteen.

"Who's Uly?" Sutter asked, his voice softer, with a weary roughness. Somehow he had crossed the room and stood in front of her bench without her realizing.

"My brother. I'm looking for him. He vanished two years ago." She shuddered, queasily glad she hadn't had breakfast yet. "He's all I have left in the world."

For the first time since sneaking into Miss Van Hastings' office and reading the letter from her lawyers, Ess truly felt she was alone.

"Well, we might just be able to help with that." He tried to smile. "After all, we're the Secret Service."

"After you protect the president."

"Good lad," Collins said.

~~~~~

Ess found it slightly amusing that both men were surprised that she could read and write. Maybe it was odd that a boy on his own had managed to obtain an education. Did they think boys without family lived in trees and
~~~~~

ran with wild animals, like some of the Indian fables or the legends filtering east from the western plains? She wrote notes to Aunt Hazel and her landlady, to cover her absence, and to let Collins get into her room and remove her few possessions. Ess suspected the man would search the chest where she kept her clothes and journal, but she hoped her impressions of him were correct and he wouldn't be so nosey as to read her journal. That would give away everything.

As the long day passed, she met the rest of the team of agents who had come to Springfield weeks in advance of the president's visit. Most of them were friendly enough. A few were openly scornful of her identification of the Resurrectionists -- until Sutter revealed how she had provided sketches of all the men he had caught in the raid on the Academy. He didn't indicate to her that he connected her with the letters and evidence that had brought the Secret Service down on the Van Hastings. Ess wondered when he would confront her and demand the whole story.

After they made sure the president's visit went off without a problem.

Some of the men ignored Ess once her presence in the suite was explained, while others hesitated every time they opened their mouths in front of her. There was nowhere for her to go, except perhaps hide in the bedroom, and she could still hear everything they said in the front room of the suite. The rest of the team immediately took her under their wing, understanding that a boy needed something to occupy him and keep away "the fidgets," as Collins said. He went to a stationer's and purchased a sketchbook and proper artist's pencils and a watercolor kit for her. Another man brought in a stack of penny dreadfuls, tales of the Wild West and detective stories in the tradition of Mr. Poe, to entertain her.

She found more than enough entertainment observing the Secret Service agents at work, the private language they seemed to employ at times, and the tricks they used such as changing into hotel livery when they needed to check on a room or some operation within the hotel. Agent Ashmore was in charge of picking up their food at restaurants and storefronts all around the city, a different location for every meal, to hide exactly how many agents were coming in and out of the hotel and staying there. Ess had the impression that only four men were staying here in this hotel. The rest of the team were scattered throughout the block surrounding the building the president would be dedicating in just two more days.

Ess tried to help where she could, giving more intimate details of the operations of the hotel than strangers could obtain. She sketched floor plans and revealed several not-quite-secret passages that the laundry crew used to get around faster. Sutter winked at her, as if they shared a private joke, when she pointed out all the dumbwaiters throughout the hotel, some large enough to carry a grown man at a pinch. When Ess thought about it later, she decided that yes, it was a private joke between them. She was grateful that he found her escape from the Academy amusing now.

That night she slept in one of the two beds in the bedroom. Several times she was aware of agents coming in and taking turns using the other. From comments she had overheard, the men were used to sleeping on the carpeted floor and in the chairs. She was grateful that she didn't have to share a bed with one of them. While she had no intention of ever revealing she was a girl, she didn't like to anticipate their reaction if any of the agents who were, in essence, protecting her, ever found out the truth. There was something chivalrous about most of them, and she didn't like thinking of them being uncomfortable on her account.

In the morning, Ashmore brought a fancy suit of boy clothes with breakfast, and she had to hide in the wardrobe while several of the boys she used to work with hauled up a huge brass bath and enough buckets of steaming water to fill it. Ess had to fight laughter when she overheard a familiar voice grumbling that for all the hotel's bragging that it was the most modern and luxurious of all the hotels in Springfield, it still didn't have indoor plumbing and hot water that could be pumped up to the top floors, like two hotels just on the other side of the square.

She would have stayed in the bath for a full half hour, if she had been permitted, but the fear of one of the men coming into the bedroom to fetch something terrified her into speediness. Still, she didn't mind. The new suit of fancy clothes felt wonderful, like a reward for her cooperation. Ess had to laugh, to realize that while she enjoyed the freedom of her shabby clothes, there was something almost decadent about sturdy, fine cloth trousers and matching coat, a silken vest and fine broadcloth shirt. The sturdy shoes were almost a revelation, after making do with shabby cut-down boots and triple thickness of socks to make them fit securely.

Ess stepped out into the main room of the suite to present herself for inspection. Everyone approved, and no one gave her an odd or suspicious look. So, her disguise held firm, despite losing the shielding layer of grime in her clothes and on her face, and without her sloppy, loose cap shadowing her face. Several of the other agents teased Ashmore that he was wasted as an agent, he should consider becoming a gentleman's gentleman, he had done such a good job estimating her size. He laughed and pretended to preen at their comments. Ess supposed that such a good idea for heights and weights in people was a valuable asset for an agent.

"May I ask now why I need to be dressed up like I'm being shipped off to finishing school?" she asked, when the comments ceased and the agents turned back to the diagrams of the hotel floorplans.

"Finishing school?" Sutter's thin, slightly tense smile curved up just a little. "Girls go to finishing school."

"I feel like a girl, all gussied up this way," she retorted, and didn't mind when her face warmed. The agents around her laughed again. She scolded herself to be careful of such slips in the future.

"We need your sharp eye." Collins pulled out his pocket watch, glanced at Sutter, and the senior agent nodded. "Come along, lad. No time to waste." He beckoned and stepped to the door.

Ess only hesitated a moment, though a dozen questions rose to her lips. They weren't planning on taking her out of the hotel in broad daylight, were they? She thought being immured in the suite all day yesterday, the pains they took to hide her presence from the hotel staff, was being totally wasted now. Muffling a sigh, she snatched up the new cap that matched her suit and slipped it on over her still-wet hair. Collins said nothing as they strolled down the main stairs and out the front door. Ess tried not to look around. From the corners of her eyes, she watched for people watching her. No one seemed to give her a second look, but if they were conspirators, they would be careful not to give away anything by the slightest gesture or word, wouldn't they?

Collins explained once they were two blocks away from the hotel and the train station was in sight. She would be positioned where she could see the platform and everyone who got within fifty feet of it. Ess's job would be to watch for the Resurrectionists, plain and simple. The other agents who were already getting into position would take care of pinpointing anyone who looked suspicious and handle them.

"What if I see one of them? How do I let you know?"

That earned a grin from Collins. He taught her a simple series of hand signals, much like the finger language used by the deaf to communicate, but broader, to be visible and readable from a distance. He also gave her two small mirrors, to catch the sun and get the attention of the agents who would be on the ground.

"He's coming by train, isn't he? The newspapers said the president was coming by airship, to land out on the parade grounds, but he's coming by train instead."

"Clever lad." He nodded. "It's too easy to shoot an airship out of the sky, launch bombs into the structure, send it crashing down. Trains are still safer, just because they're already on the ground and they can be armored."

By the time President Lincoln's train came into the station, with a reassuring lack of pomp and circumstance, Ess had already perched on the ledge of the water tower two hours. Her fine new suit seemed to be far too fancy for such a job, until she realized that the cloth was nearly the same shade of weathered, dark gray of the paint of the water tower. She was nearly invisible, and if she sat still and didn't attract attention with movement, she would be. Besides, no one really looked upward unless they were given a reason.

Ess held still, though her bottom ached from sitting for so long. She suspected that sitting down had been a mistake. What if she needed to move to follow someone who looked suspicious, until she got at a better angle to identify him clearly? Her fears and questions didn't go away, even as the ramp was put up to the door of the front car of the train and soldiers filed off, spreading out across the train platform and through the station, before

President Lincoln rolled off the train in his wheelchair. She almost forgot to watch for the Resurrectionists as she studied the clockwork mechanism that gave the wheelchair the ability to move independently. A thick crossbar on the back probably took the place of the key, and through the gridwork of the shield around the mechanism, she could see thick coils of springs. It probably took a strong man to sufficiently wind the clockwork. President Lincoln steered the wheelchair with a long lever that came up between the supports for his legs. She shuddered a little in sympathy when he came out into the sunshine and she saw how emaciated and pale he looked, compared to the tinted drawings she had seen of him through the years. Rumors said he had an illness that should have killed him years ago. Ess had heard many people say that it wasn't the doctor's skills, the constant medical attention necessary after the failed assassination attempts that kept him alive. Rather, his dedication to the Union, to ensuring the healing and repairs after the devastation of the war, kept him alive despite everything done to him.

~~~~~

"I'm not so much a gargoyle, am I?" President Lincoln asked, his eyes bright with amusement that gave a lie to the sickly pallor of his face.

Ess stumbled into the room, half-expecting a dozen soldiers to leap from hiding and arrest her. Sutter had gestured for her to go into one of the meeting rooms on the first floor when she and Collins returned to the hotel, and she had thought there was more work to do, one more conference regarding hotel security. She saw Mr. Lincoln's wheelchair before she saw him, and stopped short, long enough for the president to turn around, see her, and smile.

"Sir. I'm sorry, sir." She glanced over her shoulder and was stunned to see Collins wink at her as he pulled the door shut behind her. "I didn't know -- I thought--" She gave up, knowing whatever she said to explain her mistaken ideas would only make her sound like a babbling fool.

Abraham Lincoln leaned back in his wheelchair and chuckled, the sound warm and healthy. Comforting. He held out a hand, beckoning, and Ess finally unlocked her legs and crossed the room to him. She sat down on the chair set facing him and let herself breathe a little easier.

"You, young man, are in very good odor with our estimable Mr. Sutter. He thinks very highly of you, and I wanted to thank you for your cleverness and your help." He winked and leaned forward and softened his voice. "Just between you and me, I am most grateful to have had my traveling plans rearranged. My boys are mad about airships, but I prefer to keep my feet on solid ground." He patted the arm of his wheelchair. "So to speak."

"Yes, sir."
~~~~~

Chapter Twelve

"Now, I should like to hear the full story behind how you found yourself able to identify some men who have been high on the 'shopping list,' shall we say, of the Secret Service. Mr. Sutter said he made your acquaintance when he conducted a valuable raid of a Resurrectionst stronghold some months ago. Start from there, if you don't mind."

Ess froze, again. She didn't dare tell the truth, yet how could she justify lying to the president of the United States? That was nearly as bad as lying to her grandparents -- which was usually impossible, anyway -- or to Reverend Crenshaw, back home. The last few months of living a lie, of lying to everyone around her, everyone she liked, the friends she had made working in the waterboy gang and now here at the hotel laundry, pressed down on her with an incredible weight that nearly brought tears to her eyes.

Yet what could she do? Admit she was a girl and be scolded for immodest behavior, scolded for taking foolish risks that just a few moments before she had been commended for as bravery? If she let them put her back into skirts and send her to another school, even if all they did was contact her family lawyers, she would never find Ulysses.

Forgive me, Lord, for lying. Please, let me be as honest as possible?

Slowly, picking her words with care, she related how she had found the tunnels under the school, how she had overheard Mr. Van Hastings giving his sister orders for preparing the grounds for the meeting. She told how she had put sand in the gears and played with the pressure on the steam engine that served the school and the Resurrectionists' hiding place, and how she had played a dangerous game of Hide'n'Seek in the days before the meeting, spying on the Southern traitors as they arrived, so she could sketch them.

"How did you know the Secret Service would show up to capture these men?" Mr. Lincoln asked.

"I didn't. I could only hope... oh, yes, well..." Her mouth felt too dry to speak for a moment. Ess swallowed hard and tried not to fidget. She wondered if this was how Paul felt when he was on trial before Agrippa and Festus, or when he stood before Caesar. Would it be blasphemous to ask God for the right words in this instance, too? "There was a student who decided the headmistress was hiding things from her, so she spied and found letters and evidence and she was the one who sent the letters to the Secret Service, letting them know about the upcoming meeting. I helped her get the letters to the postal service, so I knew what was going on."

"Clever. I should like to meet this young lady. I assume she is no longer a student there?"

"No, sir. She ran away. She discovered the Van Hastings were forging her signature and lying to her family lawyers and trying to take over her grandparents' estate, to finance the Resurrectionists."

"And so you helped her get a little vengeance."

"A great deal of vengeance, sir."

That earned a wider grin and the president's eyes sparkled. Ess relaxed. If she had made Mr. Lincoln laugh, that was a good thing, wasn't it? When he asked what she did once she escaped Agent Sutter, she gave a vague description of coming west to look for her brother -- after all, he deserved as much truth as she could spare -- and deciding Springfield was a good place to start, because Uly was a great admirer of Mr. Lincoln. That earned another chuckle from the great man. Ess told about working on the airship docking tower and moving on to the laundry with Roger. She finished by seeing the five Resurrectionists in town just a few days ago.

"So it was all just coincidence or luck that you discovered Mr. Sutter and his men were staying in this very hotel, and you gave him the sketches?"

"Oh, no sir. I was in church and praying that God would help me, because I knew no one would believe me if I just went to a government office and said what I saw. I was praying, and I was sitting in the balcony and the light from the stained glass window was touching Mr. Sutter and I..." She shrugged. "I recognized him from the school, so I followed him and when I realized he was staying here, I knew what to do." She shivered a little, chilled by the resentment that suddenly surged up inside her. If God would answer her prayer about finding someone to tell about the traitors, why wouldn't God answer her prayers about finding her brother, or having someone find her grandparents alive?

"Which brings us here to this moment." Mr. Lincoln sat back, clasping his hands in his lap. His mouth quirked up and his eyes narrowed just a little, so Ess felt as if he could somehow see through her. It made her want to fidget. "What was your name again?"

"Joshua, sir." A sudden dropping sensation took her breath away. Why would he ask her that? Wouldn't her name have been at the top of the report Sutter gave him?

"You're sure?"

"Sir?"

He raised a hand and a door on the far side of the meeting room opened. Ess flinched, realizing the door hadn't been entirely closed. Sutter walked in, and that dropping sensation increased, making her slightly dizzy. Why had he been listening at the door? Tears prickled at the corners of her eyes. The new clothes that felt so fine now felt like a trap. How could she flee, vanish into the streets, wearing such clothes? They would make her stand out like a beacon on a hill.

"I'm curious. What do you plan to do when you can no longer disguise yourself as a boy?"

"Sir?" Agent Sutter said, stopping so abruptly he seemed to lean forward for a second. His eyes widened and he stared at Ess.

"I'll ask you again, young lady, what is your name? Your real name," Mr. Lincoln emphasized.

He laughed softly, shoulders shaking, as Sutter stared, looking back and forth between Ess and the president.

"Odessa Vivian Fremont, sir," she admitted, bracing herself for a torrent of questions.

Ess saw the moment Agent Sutter made the connection, the moment his frown relaxed into understanding and his eyes widened. Then he grinned and she couldn't decide if she should be relieved or perturbed by him.

"I assume you are the student who discovered your headmistress was lying to you, so you spied on her and found the information you sent to the Secret Service?" Mr. Lincoln asked. When Ess confirmed that, he demanded the story. He laughed at some of the details she gave, such as her system of pulleys and ropes so she could hang outside the window, and he was intrigued, asking for more details, when she explained the chemical-infused paper that let her make exact copies of documents so no one would know she had found them.

That led to explaining who her grandparents were and what they did, and how they had vanished. There were several knocks on the door during the tale, and each time Mr. Lincoln gestured for Ess to stop while Sutter went to deal with whoever was at the door. She didn't know whether to feel proud or guilty, to know that the president was delaying important business to listen to her story.

"How did you guess, sir?" Ess had to ask, when her story was finished and neither Mr. Lincoln nor Agent Sutter had any more questions for her.

"That you were a girl? You carry off the charade very well, but I had the pleasure of meeting several clever young ladies during the war, who were quite effective spies, switching from trousers to skirts at just the right time to let them get through enemy lines. And quite frankly, as I have lost some use of my body," again he patted the arm of the wheelchair, "I like to think the Good Lord has granted me keener perceptions to make up for it." He tipped his head toward Agent Sutter. "What shall I do, Miss Fremont? One of the men I count on to keep me safe and fight the treachery in our country has proven himself blind as a bat. I feel quite betrayed, somehow."

Agent Sutter just grinned and shook his head.

"Now, I think we need to take some time and find a suitable reward to thank you for the great help you have been -- and, I must admit, the help I hope you shall provide this country in the future. The conspirators have yet to be found, and if they realize by now that their plot here has been discovered, they will likely flee town. That means it will be some time until they are caught. You could be in some danger, if they ever discover your part in this. Agent Sutter, I would highly recommend you find some employment for this clever young lady, if you know what is good for you."

"Yes, sir, Mr. President." Sutter winked at Ess. "You are most certainly right."

"But -- I'm sorry -- I mean, I'm grateful, Mr. President," Ess said. "I need to find my brother, and my grandparents."

"Hmm, yes. Family should always come first. The situation in South America has grown quite uneasy, and dangerous for foreigners. I wouldn't recommend heading down there for some time to come. Agent Sutter, can you find something for this young lady to do that will give her the flexibility to look for her brother, at least?"

"I think I can arrange that," Sutter said.

"Very good." Mr. Lincoln held out his hand to Ess. She leaped up from her seat to shake his hand. "If you will excuse me, Miss Fremont, there is business to attend to. We need to figure out how I can dedicate this building and draw out the Southern plotters without getting me shot at again."

~~~~~

Ess was relieved to get her old clothes back, so she could attend the dedication ceremony with the water boys. Roger was all agog when he saw her, waiting for the boys to assemble in the lobby of the tower. He ran up to her and punched her in the shoulder, scolding her with delight for vanishing without warning. Then he spilled the news of Mr. Filipont being arrested for stealing from guests. A number of items belonging to the Secret Service agents were found in the manager's office, when Mr. Filipont went off duty.

"Can you believe someone being that stupid?" Roger crowed.

"I can't believe Mr. Filipont would do something so low." Ess imagined her friend's reaction if he ever found out the real reason for the man's arrest.

"Mr. Wilkinson let slip that he thought that's why you up and vanished -- you fingered him." He searched her face as they crossed the lobby to the lift doors. He smirked when Ess couldn't respond.

Agent Sutter had said that was the story they would spread abroad, that one of the laundry boys had spotted the night manager taking keys and going into people's rooms during the day. The plan was to simply let people make what inferences and connections they wanted. It explained her absence, at least, and gave convenient excuse for removing Mr. Filipont with the least amount of fuss. Ess hadn't expected the hotel staff to make the connection so quickly, but she felt rather proud that Mr. Wilkinson, the head bookkeeper, thought highly enough of her to give her credit.

There was a chance, Sutter had warned her, that the rest of the plotters might decide that the unnamed laundry boy had seen much more than stealing from guests, and would come look for him. After the dedication ceremony, she would vanish for good, moved several states away, and given a new identity. She devoutly hoped it wouldn't require her to put on skirts again. She rather liked the freedom and anonymity afforded by trousers.

"It was you, wasn't it?" Roger pressed.
~~~~~

"I'm not saying anything." Ess winked at him. His mouth dropped open, then he hooted and punched her again in the shoulder.

Several of their fellows from the water gang showed up then and joined them, and Roger had the discretion not to say anything more. Mr. O'Malley, one of the foremen for the tower, showed up on the heels of the last boy and gathered them all together, checking their names against a list, then guided them past two Secret Service agents standing guard in front of the lift doors to go up to the third floor garden platform. Ashmore was on duty, and he winked at Ess as she passed him.

"You got in good with them government men, didn't you?" Roger whispered as their gang crowded into the lift.

Ess just smiled. She muffled a chuckle as she thought of Ashmore's reaction when he found out -- if Sutter hadn't told the rest of the team yet -- that she was a girl. Then her stomach tried to do a flip when the lift jerked and they were suddenly rising upward. The others let out yelps and hoots of surprise, and one boy behind her even said he wanted to try that again, when the doors slid open on the third floor. Mr. O'Malley just chuckled and shook his head, and herded them out onto the garden platform, where they could have a bird's eye view of the dedication ceremony.

They spread out along the railing to look down on the square in front of the building, chattering and pointing out men in the crowd who had been part of the construction team. Ess moved to the position Sutter had asked her to take, and palmed the two small mirrors tucked into her pocket. From this position, she would be able to see most of the square, and had the right angle to catch sunlight on the mirrors for signaling the agents mingling with the crowd, if she saw one of the Resurrectionists. One mirror was for focusing a patch of light on the man she identified, and the other was to signal an agent. Ess thought the arrangements clever enough, but the flaws in the system were too evident. What if the day turned cloudy? What if the man she saw moved away and she couldn't reflect light onto him? What if someone were watching for this tactic, because they knew the Secret Service used it for security during outdoors ceremonies? What if someone identified her as the source of the signal and followed, or even attacked her?

What the Secret Service needed, she decided, was a system of communicating in code that only they could hear, something like the telegraph, but without wires. Perhaps something hidden in a man's hat, that tapped out the message softly enough only he could hear. Better yet, if they could find a way to transmit voices to individuals' ears, without the people in between them hearing. Ess knew Grandmother Matilda was clever enough to come up with something like that -- if she weren't fighting for her life in some South American jungle right now.

"Look at that," Martin crowed, pointing, and shouting to be heard over the brass band that struck up a tune almost directly underneath them.

President Lincoln came out of the doors on the other side of the tower, four soldiers escorting him, and the wheelchair rolling along without anyone pushing.

"You ever seen the like?"

Ess bit her lip to keep from saying yes, she had seen the wheelchair up close, and the clockwork mechanism was rather loud. The springs were just as large as she had imagined them, and it had taken all her self-control to keep from asking Mr. Lincoln if she could examine it.

The other boys pressed up against the railing to hang over and point and comment and cheer as the president rolled up the ramp to the platform. Ess ignored them and tightened her grip on the mirrors. She prayed she wouldn't need to use them as she surveyed the crowd below her. Methodically, she swept her gaze across the informal, crooked rows of spectators, then shifted to studying the people who were still approaching the square.

She nearly missed the man, first because she was so high up and the angle changed his features, and then because he was dressed as one of the workmen. Ess supposed later, thinking over the events of that morning, they all should have expected the Resurrectionists to wear disguises. While well-dressed, prosperous-looking men were granted some freedom from suspicion, there was anonymity in the rough clothes of a construction worker as well. Especially since the men who had helped to build the airship docking tower and office building were being recognized today in the ceremony.

However, there was no mistaking that crooked smirk and the feather-fine, ginger-colored hair. It stuck out even more when jammed under a workman's cap, or perhaps her higher angle just made it more noticeable against the dark, dust- and mud-smeared jacket. That swagger that had made that particular Resurrectionist stand out among his fellows in the lantern-lit tunnels under the Academy was even more pronounced as he strolled along among the workmen entering the square. Ess grinned as she noticed another detail that should have given him away -- all the other workmen were talking to each other, while this man walked alone, unacknowledged.

Her hands shook for a moment as she slipped the mirrors into position, and found the sun to get the right angle. Ess thought a simple prayer of "help," as she moved her left hand to create the sequence of short and long flashes to catch an agent's attention. For a few heart-stopping moments, she couldn't see anyone, not a head tipped back or a hand raised, to acknowledge her signal. Then she saw Collins. He patted the top of his head. She waved her hand in the direction he was to look, and turned her mirrors.

For three seconds she thought the man she had seen had moved out of the square. She nearly cried out in relief when she saw he had stopped only a few paces away from where he had been when she took her gaze off him. She had to reflect sunlight from one mirror onto the other to get it to go at the right angle. The splotch of light landed dead center of his chest.

"Whatcha doing?" Roger asked, moving over next to her.

Ess realized she stood out somewhat, because all the rest of their gang had jammed together a good ten feet further down the railing, where the view of the president was better. She snarled frustration when Roger cast a shadow over her mirror. Before she could snap at him to move, he stepped away.

"Who's he?" he asked, stepping around behind her to look over her shoulder.

Collins, Parker and McTavish converged on the Resurrectionist from three different spots in the square.

"Who's who?" She concentrated on holding her hand steady and keeping the splotch of light on his chest.

"You're supposed to get it in his eyes," Roger said with a chuckle. "It'll take forever to light him up. Except maybe he's got matches in his pocket. Then he'll spark fast for sure."

"I don't want to--" Ess gasped as the man she marked turned, taking a step forward, and the light beam hit him in the eyes. She couldn't seem to lower her hand fast enough, before he looked up, and their gazes met.

The Resurrectionist glared at her. Without thinking, she adjusted the mirror to put the sun back in his eyes. Roger laughed. The man below her moved again. Again, she put the light in his eyes. Then the three agents were on him. Collins and Parker, both big men, grabbed hold of him by his upper arms, while McTavish got in front of him. From her perch, Ess could see the gun he slipped from inside his coat and showed the prisoner, effectively silencing him, but she thought no one on the ground, even standing next to them, could see it.

"What was that about?" Roger said with a gasp, as he and Ess turned to watch the three agents hurry the man out of the square.

"He was the man I saw Mr. Filipont giving the stolen things to."

"You got to *work* with the Secret Service, didn't you?" His eyes huge, Roger stared at her. When he turned, his mouth opening to most likely shout something to the other boys, Ess caught hold of his arm.

"No, you can't tell. It's bigger than this," she said in as quiet a voice as she could manage.

"Bigger? It's huge!" Roger clapped her on the back. "Why do you get to have all the fun?"

"Fun? Worrying that some gang has probably marked me for death because I fingered a couple of thieves? Oh, yes, uproarious good fun," she snarled, effecting the British accent and curled lip of Miss Hamilton, who had made the girls' lives miserable for half an hour every other afternoon at the Academy, teaching them how to serve tea.

"What's got your--"

Ess didn't hear the rest of his words as she caught sight of another familiar, scarred face glaring up at her. Before she could even think to find another agent to signal, the Resurrectionist darted under the bridge between the buildings. Panic froze her for two crucial seconds. She slid the mirrors into her pocket and ran for the lift. She grabbed the lever to call the car to that floor, half-expecting the doors to slide open. Someone must have sent it down to the ground floor. She was positive Sutter had said the lifts would be locked so no one could get higher than the third floor until after the ceremony.

"What's got you so riled?" Roger demanded, chasing after her.

A bell chimed inside the wall as Ess turned to him. She opened her mouth to tell him to go back and watch the ceremony, because she certainly didn't have time to explain anything. The fact was, she had no idea what she was going to do, but maybe she could point the Resurrectionist out to someone if she got down to the ground quickly enough.

The doors slid open with a hiss of steam from the mechanism. All she saw at first was the scar running from chin to cheekbone, icy white against the flush of the Resurrectionist's skin. He cursed and lunged, reaching for her. Ess stumbled backwards.

Roger hollered like a dozen Indians and flung himself into the man's chest, leading with his head. The two collided and went down.

"Run!" Roger gasped, landing astride the man's chest.

Ess ran for the door to the stairs before she could even think of trying to get in the lift. A gasping laugh escaped her as she thought she could kiss Roger for his help. She had never had such a good friend, and so clever, to leap to her defense. What would he do if he learned she was a girl? She would have to tell him if she had kissed him, wouldn't she? Better not do that.

In what felt like only a few steps, she reached the door of the first floor and slammed into it before she could turn the doorknob. She gasped, shoulder reverberating in an odd aching-numb combination, and out the door. She found Ashmore staggering to his feet in the lobby, with a bloody nose. Foster shouted his name and darted in through the lobby doors. They both saw Ess, and before she could say anything, the landing door slammed open behind her. She turned as the Resurrectionist staggered out, glaring at her. He lunged, swinging with both fists. One got her in the chin, the other against the side of her head and she went down, everything going gray for a few seconds. The sounds of struggles and curses and fists slamming into flesh seemed to come from far away until the world righted itself around her again. Ess sat on the floor, turned sideways away from the struggle. By the time she got herself turned around, Ashmore was sitting on the prisoner's back, pressing his shoulders down into the floor, while Foster stepped back and pulled out a revolver.

"Are you all right, Josh?" the agent asked.

Ess nodded, feeling a little breathless. She regretted the movement when it sent up a clanging of out-of-tune bells in her head. She pressed her hands against her temples and groaned. That earned a fierce grin from Foster.

Chapter Thirteen

Aunt Hazel was stunned speechless when she and Roger were escorted into the hotel suite on the first floor where President Lincoln had retired, after the dedication ceremony went off without a single noticeable interruption. Roger had a black eye that he sported proudly, shoulders back and a cocky strut to his stride. He winked at Ess, who stood with Ashmore, now assigned as her personal bodyguard until she left for the position Sutter had found for her. He smirked up at his aunt, and the proprietary hand resting on the boy's shoulder visibly trembled as she made a curtsey to the president and guided Roger in bowing. Ess counted the seconds, deciding this was a new record for the sharp-tongued but loving laundrywoman to hold that tongue.

"Ma'am, I understand you are responsible for this fine young man who leaped into action and helped in subduing one of the men who came to harm me and disrupt the ceremony. You have done an admirable job. Roger, I hope you continue to listen to your aunt's guidance, and you will consider a position, when you are grown, where your sharp wit and your fists can be put to the best advantage."

"Sir -- thank you, sir," Roger managed to say, and only hesitated two seconds when Mr. Lincoln held out his hand to shake theirs.

Aunt Hazel's gaze met Ess's as the two of them turned to leave and she flushed red and her mouth dropped open. She started to say something, then just sighed loudly and shook her head and crooked her finger for Ess to follow. No one disobeyed that finger unless he had a desire for a tongue-lashing that made the boilers and the wringing equipment in the laundry vibrate. Ashmore must have understood that, because he didn't try to stop Ess, but followed her when she turned to hurry out of the room.

"Just what trouble have you been getting yourself into?" Hazel gasped, when Ashmore closed the door behind him and Ess and the four of them stood in the hall a few steps down from the doorway. Despite her exasperation and what Ess hoped was relief glittering in her eyes, she kept her voice down.

"Joshua here was a big help in identifying several dangerous individuals plotting against the president's life," Ashmore said. "Your lad was a big help as well." He winked at Roger, who grinned widely enough Ess thought she could see all his teeth.

"You're not coming back to the laundry, are you?" Hazel waved her hands to brush away Ess's response, and reached out to hug her. "I have the awful feeling you're tied up in whatever trouble dragged away Mr. Filipont. Stealing from guests' rooms, my--" She froze, her arms tight around Ess, breathed twice, then slowly stepped back, but kept hold of the girl's shoulders. Her gaze bored into Ess's face, and in that moment she knew the loving, rough-edged woman had guessed her secret. "You little minx," she whispered, shook her once, and finally let go.

"Unfortunately," Ashmore said, as that rapid exchange took place, "Joshua here is in danger because he identified five conspirators, but only two were captured. We're moving him to a safe place…" He pulled out his pocket watch. "In half an hour. If there are any other goodbyes you need to make, lad, now's the time."

"No, Aunt Hazel and Roger are really my only good friends." Ess exchanged grins with the woman. She wondered if Roger would ever know the truth about her, or if his aunt would keep it to herself as a good joke.

The joke was on her, she decided a short time later, when Ashmore escorted her to the little pantry that served the president's suite, and she saw the costume she was to wear to get her to the train station. Full widow's gear, including a clever hump to strap to her back. Between her veil, black lace fingerless gloves, cane, and an ear trumpet to hang around her neck on a string of jet beads, Ess thought she would either smother from the multiple layers or be crushed under the weight of the disguise. Maybe Sutter was getting revenge on her for tricking him? Then again, she thought the joke might be on his fellow agents. He and the president knew she was a girl, but the others didn't. Would he ever tell any of them, or even just Tuttle, who was to escort her to safety, that his charge had been a girl disguised as a boy disguised as an old woman?

Ashmore looked apologetic when he returned to the pantry once she had donned her disguise. At least, she thought he did, until she caught one corner of his mouth twitching in merriment. She wouldn't be able to say goodbye to the rest of the Secret Service detail, and he promised to pass along her thanks and farewells. Then he shook her hand, gave her a large envelope with Sutter's instructions, and turned her and an enormous black carpetbag over to Tuttle. In moments he was gone, and her most recent adventure seemed to officially end with the click of the door closing behind him.

"I hear you're a dab hand at traveling by dumbwaiter," Tuttle said, a grin lighting his dusky, sharp-boned face.

"You should have told me about that before I got weighed down with this rig." Ess couldn't help grinning back at him.

"Just up one floor, and then I'm to escort you down the stairs and raise an unholy fuss about transportation to get you to the train station. You're a deaf, rich old lady with wits just slightly less feeble than your body, and I am your longsuffering servant taking you home after a long visit with your favorite granddaughter."

As he spoke, to Ess's delight, his voice changed, taking on a Creole drawl. He bowed and offered her a hand to climb up into the dumbwaiter, warned her to stay in it until he let her out, then slid the hatch shut. Dozens of questions circulated through her mind, and she had sufficient time to discard most of them as impolite, while she waited to be free from the cramped box. Perhaps on the journey to New Orleans, they would come to know each other well enough she could ask some of her questions without being rude. Then again, she might decide that if they became friends, she wouldn't need to know.

Unfortunately, Tuttle informed her on the leisurely stroll -- he strolled and she rode in a borrowed wheelchair with thick tires -- to the train station that she would not end up in New Orleans. That was simply what the tickets for Madame Beaujolais said. At the last train stop before entering Louisiana, at the discrete and secretive hour of two in the morning, she and Tuttle would part company. She would return to her boy disguise -- currently hiding in her enormous carpetbag -- and get on the next train going north, while Tuttle would hike to the Secret Service office in the next town.

Once they were settled in their private compartment on the train, comfortably sprawled in the cushioned seats facing each other, Tuttle gave her the rest of the details of Sutter's arrangements. Ess was to join up with a traveling circus troupe in Indianapolis. The owner and ringmaster was one Alexander Stockwell -- although that wasn't the name he had been born with, nor wore while he served with distinction during the War Between the States. He had been involved in a complicated spying operation whereby he and several of his men pretended to turn traitor to the Union and became the secret weapon for one of Jefferson Davis' advisors. They learned all they could of the rebels' communication routes, the meeting places where airships sent by Queen Victoria's government brought in supplies past the air and sea blockades, and uncovered the names of several traitors in key positions on the Union side. Stockwell was the only one who survived the mission, and he lost his left leg from the knee down. The explosion that destroyed a rebel outpost and cost him his left leg also disfigured him so he was nearly unrecognizable. With a huge reward posted by the Resurrectionist leaders for information leading to his capture and torture and execution, Stockwell had taken on a new name to go with his face, cut all ties with his past, and took on a new occupation. A traveling circus afforded great opportunity to go everywhere, to be entirely visible and yet not be noticed by the very people on whom he spied.

"Your job," Tuttle explained, as the clacking of the train wheels threatened to lull Ess into a doze, "is to hide, learn some useful skills--" He grinned. "Sutter's exact words were, 'let the lad figure out what's useful and what's just plain fun.' Most important, you're to keep an eye on Stockwell. Only a fool believes that his disguise is perfect. Stockwell's no fool, but a few years of safety make a man relax and get careless. Sutter thinks you have eyes fresh enough to see what others might miss."

"That's a tall order," Ess mused. She tugged on the black lace gloves, idly wishing they would stop itching. Something in Tuttle's voice when he talked about the war hero had caught her attention. "You like him, don't you? Stockwell, I mean."

"My big brother was part of his team. Rupert thought the world of him. They were in an ambush long about five months before they got the assignment to go deep into enemy territory. Rupert got shot, shattered both his legs falling from the lookout spot where he was sharpshooter, keeping the others safe. Most men in that situation would have figured he was dead already. Left him for the crows. Stockwell led the charge to go back for him, carried Rupert out, then he raised an unholy ruckus and wouldn't let the surgeons cut off his legs. Dragged in a doctor with some newfangled ideas about infections and germs and setting bones." Tuttle sighed and leaned his head back and closed his eyes for the first time since boarding the train two hours before.

"Rupert swore he'd go through Hell and back for his commander. All the men did." He opened his eyes, and the intensity in their dark depths made Ess catch her breath. "Here's something you need to understand, boy. Only you didn't hear it from me, got it?"

Ess nodded and leaned forward, anticipating how Tuttle lowered his voice, and leaned forward in his turn.

"Sutter thinks the world of Stockwell, and he's got a world of guilt and regret riding his shoulders. He was shot up bad in a snatch-and-run operation just four days before the team got their orders to go deep. He was sick with a killing fever and blood poisoning that would have taken another man. Stockwell's doctor friend with the miracle medicine and crazy, newfangled ideas was in charge of him, otherwise Sutter wouldn't be here today." Tuttle's mouth softened with fondness that mildly surprised Ess. "So you can understand that he didn't get sent on the mission, and he sure as shooting couldn't join them when he was back on his feet."

"My grandfather would say that he has too much pride," Ess offered.

"How's that?"

"Sutter thinks -- maybe he hasn't put it into words -- but it's there in the back of his mind, that if he had been there with them, some of them might still be alive. That's pride, don't you think?"

Tuttle nodded, soft laughter flowing out of him, wiping away some of the grief that she could see lingered even this many years after his brother's death in the mission that only Stockwell survived. She had some new understanding of Sutter, too. It pleased her that the agent trusted her enough to send her to a man he admired and worried about. Stockwell wouldn't be her keeper. She would help keep him safe. Ess laughed as she realized something.

"What's so funny, lad? Sutter warned me you're a clever one. What sort of mischief are you dreaming up already?"

"I was just thinking that this is perfect. What boy doesn't dream of running away to join the circus?" She laughed with him, though the sound turned wistful when Tuttle sprawled out more on the train seat opposite her. Ess could not relax that fully, because the false hump strapped to her back made lying down awkward.

Being caught by the remaining Resurrectionists would be even more awkward, painfully so. Ess was willing to pay the price for her safety and her life.

~~~~~

Three days later, after four train changes and a costume change, Ess stepped onto the platform of the Indianapolis station. Totally alone, burdened with a carpetbag that was much lighter after discarding her widow's clothes two stations ago, exhausted and hungry, she felt an odd kind of exhilaration. Some of that could be physical lightheadedness, but the last few days of solitary travel had given her time to think and work out a plan of action in her journal. She had a token Sutter had given her, a wooden disc with Greek letters, that she could use at any Secret Service office in the country to claim help, or simply to get communication to Sutter. He had made her promise she would keep him updated on her search for Ulysses and their grandparents, and promised he would help if he was able. He had winked when he said it, and added, "Within reason." Ess wore the token around her neck on the same chain that held the key to her storage locker. Already she could see she had been wise to set up that protection, because any step along her journey so far could have resulted in being robbed or simply having to abandon something for the sake of escape.

"Earnest MacDonald?" The deep voice came from the shadows of the stationhouse. A moment later, a thump-creak-wheeze followed, as Ess turned to identify the voice.

A tall man with broad shoulders, piercing ebony eyes, and an imposing mane of silver-white hair stepped out into the noonday sunshine. He took long strides with a visibly rocking gait. Ess realized the thump-creak-wheeze came from his left leg when he took a step. He wore tall, heavy, glossy black boots with thick cuffs reaching to his knees. His trousers were nearly as glossy, and Ess wondered if they were silk. He had a crimson leather belt with an enormous buckle that could pass as a saucer for a grand set of dinnerware. Between the burn scars mottling the left side of his face, looking like a wax mask that had partially melted and what was clearly a mechanical leg, this had to be Alexander Stockwell. Ess decided not to be flattered that the owner of the circus had come to meet her himself. He had probably done it out of necessity. Anyone Sutter sent to him for safekeeping probably received such treatment.

"Yes, sir," she said, and held out her hand to shake. She had chosen to be Earnest because that was her grandfather's name, and close enough to Ess she knew she could respond to the name with minimal trouble.

"So," Stockwell drawled, looking her over, head to foot, taking in her travel-worn, patched trousers and use-softened boots, sweaty shirt, and the
~~~~~

carpetbag that had been turned inside out, changing it from widow black to battered, cast-off, patchwork. "So another adventure-minded boy runs away to join the circus."

"Yes, sir." She couldn't repress a grin, tipping her head back to look up at him in her turn.

"I hear you're a troublemaker." He gave her hand an extra squeeze and tug before releasing it. Ess decided she had passed the first inspection or test. There would likely be more.

"Oh, no, sir. Trouble finds me." She shrugged. "I just don't bother to run away from the fight."

Stockwell tipped his head back and let out a burst of laughter that was half roar. He turned on his good leg and gestured for her to follow. "Don't dawdle, lad. Not much time to get you settled before we have to prepare for the afternoon show. I hear you have some mechanical skills. We'll apprentice you to the man who keeps our steam engine and all our tricks and traps and gimcracks running."

His leg wheezed and groaned louder as he took the steps leading down to the yard in front of the station two at a time. Ess had to hurry to keep up.

"How are you with horses?" the big man threw over his shoulder, while gesturing at a small gig hitched to a huge horse more suited to knights in armor than pulling a carriage.

"Driving them?"

"Feeding, grooming, riding. You're small enough, look like you have some grace. Care to learn tumbling, some bareback dancing, jumping, that sort of thing? Maybe get up on the trapeze?" He stopped two steps from the gig and turned sharply to face her, eyes narrowed and mouth a flat line.

"I'll learn anything you want to teach me," she blurted, feeling breathless from more than just running. That lightheaded feeling had returned, and she suspected it was more than just physical.

Stockwell snorted and nodded, his face brightening in a grin that did odd things to the creases in the burned side of his face. "You'll do, lad. You'll do."

~~~~~

The Countess was the only name Ess ever heard used for the woman who stood as mother for most of the circus workers. She was tall enough to look Stockwell in the eye, with an olive complexion and jet black hair with intriguing white streaks in it, and a way of braiding her hair to take advantage of those streaks to look mysterious. The Countess assisted in training the acrobats and performed as a magician in the sideshow. What Ess found fascinating was how the Countess could slide from one foreign accent to another, first French, then German, then British, then Russian, and each one sounded perfectly natural to her. Then again, what did Ess know about accents and what was natural? She was only fifteen, and despite her grandparents' many scholarly visitors, she hadn't seen much of the world.
~~~~~

"Earnest, is it?" the Countess said.

Stockwell had instructed her to get Ess set up with a bunk, more presentable clothes, and then introduce her to Gus before the afternoon crowds started arriving. Then he walked away.

"Yes, ma'am." Ess had the sensation the tall, elegant woman could see right through her.

"This way. I think you and Jasper will become friends quite quickly." She beckoned with a tip of her head and set off through the maze of tents and wagons that made up the circus backstage. "I must warn you, the quarters are cramped. You don't need them except for sleeping, but..." A soft, lazy sort of chuckle escaped her. "Perhaps I should apprentice you as a magician, as well as with the horses. You like illusions, do you?"

"I suppose I do. I haven't seen magicians perform much."

"Performing, not watching." Another chuckle. "Yes, you and Jasper shall be good, instant friends. If you do not become the worst of enemies," she added after a brief pause.

The Countess led her to an enclosed wagon that had most definitely seen better days. It might have once been part of the parade that traditionally took place from the train to the fairgrounds where the circus would set up, but only streaks of the gilding and bright paint remained on the weathered wood. Some boards had been replaced, and others had black that Ess thought might be burn marks. The wheels looked rusty and the wood inside the metal rims was battered, the bright paint worn off years ago, and splintering. They were massive, maybe eight feet in diameter, and made up most of the height of the little wagon. Ess thought she would have to bend over when she climbed up the four fold-down steps into the wagon. The Countess rapped four times on the door, then pulled it open.

Ess had a moment of discomfort -- no locks on the door of what would be her home, her bedroom, for the foreseeable future? She supposed she had made mistaken assumptions, that a man who still faced threats from wartime enemies would maintain some simple security precautions in his circus. Such as locks on doors. Then the Countess gestured for Ess to climb up the steps, and the girl looked in and had another moment of disorientation. The wagon seemed to be a storage locker for the entire circus. Ropes, pulleys, stakes, toolboxes, bolts of canvass. The wagon was jammed full. Everything was neatly stowed, but crammed in as tightly as possible. Two-thirds up the sides of the wagon, three bunks hung over the supplies, bolted to the walls. Each bunk had a thick mattress, blankets and a pillow piled neatly on one end, with a small trunk attached on the other end. Ess saw the lock on each trunk, and understood.

"Cramped quarters, but as I said, you'll only be here to sleep," the Countess said. "Jasper has that bunk," she said, gesturing at the far wall. "Nobody else is in here with him, so you have your pick."

Ess chose the opposite wall, leaving the third bunk, on the short wall between the two, for the next person to join them. The Countess showed her where the key for her trunk was tucked between pillow and blankets. Ess shoved her carpetbag into the trunk, and was just stepping down from the wagon when a boy a little taller than her came running up. Eyes wide, face flushed, he looked caught somewhere between fury and panic. The Countess crossed her arms and waited for the boy to skid to a stop before her. Then she raised a single pointing finger, silencing the boy when he opened his mouth in what looked like a protest.

"Jasper, this is Earnest. He will be working with Gus and learning acrobatics. Shouldn't you be painting your face right now?"

"But--" Jasper gulped, and gestured at the wagon behind Ess and the Countess.

"Listen to me, my dear, and listen carefully. Earnest is in the same position as you. It is high time you had an ally and a partner in mischief. Do you understand me?" She gestured back and forth between the two of them as she spoke.

Slowly, the color receded to normal in Jasper's face, and his mouth relaxed into an astonished smile. He looked back and forth between Ess and the Countess several times, then tipped his head slightly to the left... and fluttered his lashes.

Ess gasped, and it was as if the light had suddenly changed, or perhaps a screen from a theatrical performance had been lifted, revealing what was only partially visible a moment ago.

Jasper was a girl.

Ess laughed and held out a hand. A moment later, Jasper clasped her hand and they shook. The Countess chuckled, then gave an imperious wave of her hand and Jasper ran back the way she had come. When the woman beckoned, Ess followed along at a trot.

"Yes, I think you will do very well with illusions. What trouble are you fleeing, my dear, to be so skilled at disguise at your age?"

"My grandparents are missing and the boarding school where they left me tried to turn me into a porcelain doll with sawdust for brains."

"Why anyone wastes time sending their daughters to school if they want only decorative pieces, I will never understand." She gestured at a massive, much-patched tent where great gouts of steam escaped through the seams and the sound of wheezing and grinding erupted, louder as they drew closer. "Ahead is the domain of August Wheeler, one of the mechanical geniuses of our time. Like many geniuses, he has no use for money and is quite mad. A safe, amusing kind of madness, fortunately." Her eyes half-closed and her shoulders shook a few times in silent laughter.

Chapter Fourteen

"Ma'am... how did you guess?" Ess asked, pitching her voice low and slowing her steps. The Countess slowed her steps as well, to her relief. "What telltales am I giving off, that you could tell?"

"There is a new catchphrase that is coming quite into vogue. 'It takes one to know one.' I have had to resort to disguise to smooth my path in life, and to avoid the... shall we say, depredations of those who consider the world their hunting grounds, and women in general their assigned prey."

"Experience, then." Ess nodded.

"I promise you, my dear, you shall gain all the experience and skill you will ever need, before you must leave our company."

August Wheeler, who insisted Ess call him Gus from the start, was not what she expected. Then again, she had gone back and forth in her imagination between a hulking blacksmith, skin turned to leather by the heat of his forges, covered in sweat and soot, and the opposite extreme of someone very thin, whipcord muscles and nearly dandified with cleanliness as he worked. Gus was slightly on the short side, balding, with a scraggly, lopsided, carrot-colored goatee, crystalline gray eyes, and covered in freckles. He wore a pair of leather and glass goggles over his eyes when Ess and the Countess approached him, and another pair of goggles on top of his head, with multiple lenses on pivots to adjust for different aspects and intensities of sight necessary in his work. Despite his long, heavy canvass sleeves, leather gloves, leather pants and leather vest -- as she learned later, very necessary protection against the hot metal and glass he worked with -- he never seemed to sweat.

"Gus!" In contrast to her elegant manner of speaking and moving, almost gliding across the circus grounds, the Countess had a bellow worthy of a stevedore. It was necessary, with all the clattering and wheezing and hissing and sizzling and banging going on.

The engineer looked up from the massive steam engine sitting on an iron cart with eight wheels thicker than Ess's thigh. He frowned a moment, then somehow moved his goggles up onto his forehead without dislodging the other pair. A grin cracked his grease-smeared face.

"Ah, yes. The lad. Alex's friend -- friend of Alex's friend. What did you say your name was, boy?"

"He didn't," the Countess said, nudging Ess to step forward. "His name is Earnest, and the rest the two of you can handle. Please make sure to show Earnest where the cook tent is, and make sure you get something to eat yourself, before this afternoon's performance. I recommend you take some time off this afternoon and watch the show yourself for a change. Titania will get her feelings hurt if you don't show your face backstage at least once every blue moon."

"Yes, your royal highness. Your wish is my command." Gus swept her an elegant bow, holding it without a twitch until the Countess chuckled, winked at Ess, and strode away. He grinned like a boy poised on the edge of mischief as he straightened. "Welcome to the circus life, Earnest. No need for last names, especially since we all need to change both sets regularly. Since you've been assigned to me, I assume you have no mechanical or engineering training whatsoever."

"More theory than anything, but my..." Ess felt suddenly unutterably weary with the lies she had been telling in the last few months. "Granny loved to tinker and experiment and invent, and I used to watch her. I know enough to look at steam leaking from pipes and guess what kind of trouble we'll have. And I'm rather good with pulleys and such."

"How so?" He gestured across the workshop area. Shelves and tables, all on wheels, formed a lopsided circle, enclosing what seemed to be his designated work area. Gus led her over to a set of bins in a rack on wheels and pulled out handfuls of pulleys and bits of rope and hooks and other pieces of hardware, then tossed them on a nearby, somewhat empty table. "Show me what you can do."

Ess hesitated for a moment. How well she got along with her new teacher might very well depend on what she did, what she revealed, in the next half hour. Almost without conscious choice, she picked out the right number and sizes of pulleys and hooks to join them together and lengths of rope to reproduce the system she had used to get herself up and down outside Miss Van Hastings' office window. Gus let her work in silence for the first ten minutes, which she appreciated -- but she felt the weight of his regard, and from time to time her fingers slipped.

"I'm guessing you actually used this, meaning it worked. What did you used to do?"

She grinned. If Sutter trusted Stockwell, and the circus owner trusted this man enough to assign her to work with him, learn from him, maybe the best tactic to take with him was honesty. To a point, of course.

"I used this to slide down from the fourth floor to spy on the office of the headmaster of my boarding school." She winced when her finger caught on a rough piece of metal in the pulley she was trying to thread rope through. "In the middle of the night."

"Just hang there and listen and watch?"

"No." She succeeded with that pulley and picked up the next to feed the rope through that one, in and out, twisting, and back into the first. "It turned out my suspicions were right and she -- he and his sister were hiding my mail from me, lying to my guardians." She grunted as she tugged on the rope to make sure it would move, but not too smoothly. Resistance was a key factor in making the twisted mechanism work properly.

"All right, I can see how you get down -- what did you do when you wanted to leave your perch in mid-air?" Gus stepped up and tugged on various parts of the mechanism, testing.

"Do you have a clockwork winder here?"

He tipped his head to one side, narrowed his eyes, then grinned. "Let's say I don't. What does it look like and how does it work?"

The clockwork winder Ess had used, which she had been forced to leave in the storage locker because it was just too big to haul across the country and back, had been created by her grandmother. Chances were good there was nothing exactly like it in the world, because Matilda Fremont had a knack for designing things not quite like what anyone else was inventing. However, that didn't mean someone the Countess had called a genius hadn't devised his own version.

The winder was deceptively small. Matilda had designed it so the case opened up, with prongs on the spool that folded out, expanding the amount of rope it could hold. The gears were thick, strong enough to take considerable weight and resistance. The number of pulleys in Ess's contraption made it possible for it to handle her weight and perhaps two more girls her size.

Ess spent time explaining to Gus how the casing opened and the prongs folded out and snapped into place, then asked with a gesture to use the large slate and stick of chalk lying on another table nearby. She sketched the inner workings of the winder, the placement of the cogs and gears and ratchets that could control the speed with which the mechanism wound up rope, and most important, the multiple layers of springs, so that when the tension provided by one ran out, another was ready to take its place.

"Huh," Gus said, after she had finished. "Clever. Who made this?"

"My Granny."

"Think you can reproduce it?"

"From memory?"

"Unless you can get into her workshop and steal the schematics, yes, from memory." He laughed, a hearty bellow that was surprising for his frame. He certainly had the blacksmith volume, if not his size and build.

"Why?"

"Well, to prove you can do it, first of all. And second, because I love to get my hands on a new toy. Even if you can only remember half of what your Granny did, we'll have a jolly time working out the missing parts and making adaptations of our own. Doing is half the fun of learning." He rubbed his hands together in visible anticipation, his eyes lighting up, again reminding her of a little boy ready to jump into a massive mess. "I can already think of a dozen stunts and tricks we can offer our clowns and acrobats, using the winder to help them. The children will love it."

"Children?" Ess hated feeling as if she should know what he was talking about, and being entirely lost, left behind in the conversation.

Gus snorted and gestured around his work area, ending with the massive, hissing steam engine. The motion guided her to look at the dozen or so pipes running from the engine, a short distance to where they went under the back wall of the largest of all the circus tents. Ess guessed that was the main performance tent.

"We pride ourselves on all sorts of wonders and tricks. Steam-powered carts that race around the ring fast enough to make grown men faint with fear. Explosions that catapult the acrobats high into the air, to grab onto a trapeze or turn a dozen somersaults before landing in a net -- or even on one of their fellows' shoulders. All sorts of gizmos that play music and spin around. Even wonders like that grow old -- or other circuses try to copy them. One catapult, anyone can do. It's the waiting for the steam pressure to build up again to shoot someone else that causes problems. Gertrude here --" He patted the side of the steam engine and didn't even wince, though Ess knew the boiler had to be hot enough to scald the skin off his palm and fingers, "-- she can provide enough constant steam to shoot two acrobats at a time up into the air, and only ask for two minutes, tops, between each throw. Plus keep the clown cars and whirligigs going at the same time. This gizmo of your granny's is small enough, we can hide it under a cape or a fluttery costume. No one will see it. No matter how many spies from other circuses attend performances, trying to steal my designs and copy our tricks." He chuckled, his expression an odd combination of malicious and delightfully mischievous. "What do you say, boy? Up for the challenge?"

Of course Ess was. Even if she wasn't, she wouldn't have said so. Trying to recreate the winder would make her feel a little closer to Granny, and she certainly liked Gus enough already to want to be part of his "tricks."

Gus led her to the cook tent next and introduced her to a table full of men and boys, all of them nearly done eating their lunch. Even the biggest and oldest of the men just grinned and nodded to Ess when the circus's engineer referred to them all as his apprentices. Some of those smiles faded, though, when he announced that she -- or rather, Earnest -- would be joining their ranks and had a few interesting tricks to share.

Others weren't happy to hear Ess had joined them, as she met various members of the circus troupe. First she went through the cook line to fill her plate and then watched a performance through a slit in the tent, on a perch high above the ground equivalent with the middle trapeze. It didn't take long to theorize that those particular people were the newest members of each group Ess was to join -- the acrobats, Gus's apprentices, and the boys who hauled water and feed for the many animals who performed in the ring. Ess was certain their smiles dimmed when they decided there wasn't enough room for all of them, and a new boy in the troupe meant someone would lose his job. One person she couldn't figure out was Durgen, whom she met after the evening performance, when she and Jasper were folding up a massive, billowing cloth. Lighter than air, slicker than silk, the clowns played a game of Hide'n'Seek in it for a good ten minutes, to the delight of the children.

The big man seemed to slide out of the shadows and stand there on the very edge of the torchlight behind the main tent, where the two girls worked, laughing as the slippery cloth kept evading their fingers, as if it had a will of its own. Ess felt first a prickling in her scalp. She couldn't turn around because it would mean losing her grip on the cloth. The sensation of insects trying to burrow through her skin grew stronger the longer she couldn't satisfy herself that no one was watching her. She fought the feeling, telling herself it was the unfamiliar surroundings, the long day -- and yes, the growing certainty that while Stockwell and Gus and the Countess, the powers of the circus, welcomed her with open arms, others wanted her to leave without even taking the time to get to know her. Then Jasper glanced over Ess's shoulder and her face lit up.

"I wondered when you would bother to show your ugly face," she said, dropping the rasp that she maintained in her voice most of the time. "Earnest, behind you stands the biggest, meanest, smelliest roustabout that ever manhandled an elephant or held up the center pole without help. Durgen, this here is Earnest. He joined us today. Gonna be working with Gus and Violetta."

A grunt came from the darkness behind Ess, sounding vaguely like "Pleasetameetya."

The two girls struggled for a little longer, until they managed to fold the long, slippery cloth three more times. Jasper let out a gasp and tugged the bundle from Ess's hands, pressing it tight against her chest and squeezing billows of air out of it.

"That's done it for tonight. Wish Gus would come up with a gizmo to fold this hellhound mess for us, like he keeps promising." She gestured with her chin and Ess ran to pick up the massive canvas sack that the cloth went into, to keep it clean until the next performance.

While they worked on sliding the cloth into the sack, Ess managed to look where Jasper had been directing her comments. Sure enough, a big, dusky-skinned man was barely visible at the edge of the torchlight. His eyes seemed to burn, or maybe it was just the golden flicker of the lamp flame reflecting there. Ess didn't like the way he stood, feet apart, arms crossed over his chest, mouth a flat line, or the way he seemed to be staring at her every time she glanced at him. What was wrong with him? More important, why did he just stand there, watching and frowning, when anyone could see they needed help? Was he one of those people who refused to help until he was asked? Or just so oblivious, so caught up with the thoughts in his head, he never noticed what was going on around him? Somehow, she didn't think anyone could survive as a circus roustabout by being oblivious, ignoring people and things. That was a surefire way to get himself hurt.

"Don't suppose you came to help us out?" Jasper said, once the canvass sack was tied up tight to keep dirt out. She turned to Durgen and fluttered her eyelashes.

The big man stepped further into the light. Muscles rippled in his jaw and his stare turned into a glare. He tipped his head at Ess. Whatever the question he was asking, she couldn't understand. Jasper did, though.

"Earnest is sharing my bunk, so be nice. You'll be running into him a lot from now on."

Ess fought the gut instinctive urge to skip back a few steps when Durgen stomped toward her. She held her ground, wishing she could understand whatever game Jasper was playing. What was her bunkmate's real name, anyway? Then the big man grunted again, bent, picked up the canvass sack with one hand -- it had taken both girls to manhandle it and slide the cloth inside -- and stood, flinging the sack over one shoulder. He gestured with a jerk of his chin and stalked off into the darkness again.

"What is going on here?" Ess asked in a low voice.

"I think you are going to be my best friend in the entire continent," Jasper said with a definitely feminine giggle. "Durgen is jealous."

"Of what?" She nearly yelped the words, only remembering at the very last moment to lower her voice.

"He knows I'm a girl. Imagine what he's thinking, a nice boy like you, sleeping just five feet away from me. We were working together nice and friendly, even laughing, when he showed up. The man's jealous." She slapped her knee. "I never thought I'd see the day."

"Are you going to tell him I'm a girl, too?"

"And spoil the fun?" Some of the merriment sparkles left her eyes. Jasper shrugged. "Someday. A few days. Unless you don't want me to?"

"I'd rather no one know but the Countess and Mr. Stockwell. But if it'll save trouble with your sweetheart--"

"Oh, he's not my sweetheart. Not that he'd admit it. Might finally rile him enough to get him to say something." Jasper's grin turned mischievous and boyish again. "Don't wait up for me, hear?" Before Ess could respond, she ran off into the darkness, following Durgen.

Ess sighed, shoulders drooping in a sudden wave of weariness that made her bones ache. The day had been too long, with too much change and excitement crammed in. She thought she would enjoy however long Sutter wanted her to stay with the circus, and she thought she could count Jasper as her friend. The resentment she sensed from others in the circus troupe would probably fade once they realized they weren't going to be replaced. Still, there was that uneasy feeling that had nothing to do with the first silent, testing days at the Academy, when she was the new girl and had to prove herself worthy to be accepted among her schoolmates. She thought maybe she could trace the genesis of that sensation... to Durgen's presence. Granted, the feeling of precariousness added to her situation didn't go away when he walked away, but yes, she thought he was the source.

Understanding why took her until she had retrieved her bucket of washing water from the massive tank that one of Gus's pumps kept filled, and another one of his gizmos kept at just the right temperature for washing. Ess walked slowly back to the little wagon, watching the bucket so it wouldn't swing too far and slop out that lovely, steaming water. It would feel so good to wash her entire body in warm water and be thoroughly clean before she climbed into clean sheets, and stretched out on that mattress that certainly looked blessedly thick and comfortable. Stockwell took care of the members of his circus troupe. That had been her first impression, and what she had seen during the long day had borne it out.

With Jasper as her roommate, she could even give her body-changing corset a thorough washing, really wring it out and let it hang up to dry, instead of just a rinse and blotting it on her blankets when she got up in the morning, and putting it on damp. While their quarters were certainly cramped, crammed full of circus supplies, there was room to walk on the floor, crates to use as chairs, and plenty of spaces to spread out the corset to dry. Definitely, her situation had improved.

Ess added another point to that list of positives when she got back to her quarters and found a deadbolt on the inside of the door, meaning she could keep people out if she wanted. Most definitely, she wanted. It was a matter of moments to find the little oil lamp in its protective wire cage, strike a spark to light it, and then close the door and slide the deadbolt. A groan escaped her as she slid out of her dusty clothes and then peeled out of the corset. There were plenty of spare buckets and basins in a stack within arm's reach, just as she thought she remembered from this morning. Ess took a basin, put the corset in it, and spilled a third of the bucket of water on it. Then she set about soaping herself down, groaning with pleasure as she washed off the sticky, dried sweat sensation.

For the first time in a long time, she studied her body, assessing herself. Was she strong enough to handle the work at the forge, the tools, the physical work Gus had promised to put on her? Was she agile enough to learn basic acrobatics, even learning to stand up on the back of a horse trotting around the circus ring? To her dismay -- it couldn't be her imagination, could it? -- her hips seemed a little rounder, and so did her budding breasts. Maybe it wasn't her imagination for the last few weeks that her corset felt a little tighter. Why did she have to keep growing? Why couldn't she stay a girl who could pass for a boy? Eventually, she would have enough of a woman's figure, she wouldn't be able to go about in daylight in her disguise, just at night. What use would she be to anyone then? Especially if she hadn't been able to find her brother or their grandparents by then?

"That's it," she whispered, as she slipped into the long man's shirt she slept in, and reached for the clean underdrawers.

That was what worried her about Durgen, she decided. He obviously knew Jasper was a girl, but how did he learn? She imagined a handful of unpleasant, embarrassing scenarios where Durgen walked in on Jasper while she was washing, catching her in wet underwear, seeing her without the protection of the bands flattening her breasts. Was Jasper being careless, or did Durgen stick his nose where it didn't belong? Ess glanced at the deadbolt, wondering how strong it was.

Right that moment, she knew she didn't want Jasper to tell Durgen she was a girl, too. Let the man learn to be jealous and trust his sweetheart. Or maybe he would be jealous enough not to be her sweetheart anymore. Maybe Jasper would be better off without him. Ess had been told many times by her grandparents not to rely solely on first impressions, even as they counseled her to trust the instincts the Good Lord had granted her. No matter how things turned out, Ess didn't like Durgen. The less he knew about her, the better.

She remembered to look in all directions, even up, after she slid aside the deadbolt and opened the wagon door, before she stepped outside to empty the bucket of dirty water. All was quiet, except for the rumbling and far off hissing of the steam engine. Most of the lights in the circus grounds had been doused. She stood in the doorway for a few minutes, listening, wishing Jasper would come back to their quarters so she could close and lock the door for the night. Ess knew she wouldn't sleep well as long as that deadbolt wasn't in place. She said her prayers silently and turned the lantern down so it was nothing more than a thin line of glowing wick, barely enough light for Jasper to make her way from the door to her bunk.

Please, Savior, keep me safe. Help me fit in. Help me watch out for Mr. Stockwell. Please help me find clues to Uly's trail, and would it be too much trouble for Uly to come here to the circus and find me, so I don't have to keep looking? I'm not a very good hunter, and I don't know when I can check in with the Pinkertons again to see what they have found. Please keep Granny and Grandfather safe, and help them find their way out of South America, so we can be together soon. While this is great fun, pretending to be a boy... I think I could get tired of it soon. Especially if I can't pass as a boy for much longer.

Sighing, Ess climbed into her bunk. Another complaint to add to her growing list was that she couldn't say her prayers aloud, for fear someone would hear her. She always felt much safer, more sure of the Good Lord hearing her, if she could say them aloud. Scolding herself not to think about the unlocked deadbolt -- which entirely defeated the effort -- she curled up and pressed her face into her pillow, and waited for Jasper to come back to their quarters.

The next thing she knew, it was morning. Ess silently laughed at herself, her worries, and laughed aloud when her stomach grumbled. Jasper was already out of her bunk -- at least, Ess assumed Jasper had come back to the trailer because the lantern had been blown out and her blankets were tumbled, showing someone had slept in her bunk. Ess slid her legs over the side of the bunk and reached for the clothes she had hung up on the wall of crates, ready to be put on. The door opened and Jasper staggered in, carrying two buckets of steaming water.

"Good, you're awake. What is that contraption?" She pointed at the corset.

Jasper admired it, and expressed some envy of Ess having "such interesting" connections, to obtain such helpful equipment. She made no pretense of turning her head to give Ess some privacy to actually put on the corset, and winced a few times in sympathy over her struggles to get it on.

"I swear, the wretched thing heard me thinking that it was getting too tight for comfort," Ess grumbled as she tugged the last hooks together over her breasts.

No, definitely it wasn't her imagination last night. She did seem to be "blossoming," as pretentious, overly dramatic Miss Hochschtetter had called the transformation into a mature female figure.

"Then it decided to shrink while it was drying last night," she finished, as she reached for her shirt.

"What a funny creature you are," Jasper said, and bent to tug her boots on. "Do you actually think that things can think?"

"It's called animism, and no..." She sighed and picked up her trousers. The trailer was all well and good when they were in their bunks, but with all the crates and bags and the limited open floor space, their sleeping quarters seemed very crowded. What did Jasper do when the weather was foul and she didn't want to be shut up in the dining tent with other circus folk? "No, I don't actually believe inanimate objects can think, but it's nice to be able to blame something besides my own body suddenly taking on a growth spurt. At the most inconvenient time, too."

"How long have you been hiding out as a boy?"

"It feels like forever."

"Are you in trouble? In danger?"

"I wasn't, but things happen." Ess finished with her belt buckle and sat down on a convenient crate. "Granny would say trouble gathers around you, the more lies you tell. It's a law of nature or something like that. Some longing for balance and clarity in the spiritual realm, putting increasing pressure on you to tell the truth."

"Sounds awful."

"It can be." She grinned. "However, adventures and troubles ensure you meet the most interesting people. I'm curious -- what's your real name?"

"Jasmine."

"Pleased to meet you, Jasmine. That makes some sense, actually, choosing a boy name that it's easier, more natural to respond to." She held out her hand and they laughed softly as they shook hands. "I'm Odessa."

"How did you turn that into Earnest?" Jasper wrinkled up her nose.

"First, it's my grandfather's name, and then my family calls me Ess, so it's close enough to Earnest, I should respond to it faster." Her stomach rumbled loudly.

"We'd better hurry if we want to get in and out of the cook tent before the bully boys get in there." She leaped to her feet and stepped up onto a crate, to quickly stow her nightshirt and soap and other items in the trunk at the end of her bunk, and lock it.

Ess followed suit, and felt only slightly better about leaving the trailer unlocked. After all, there was equipment in there that others in the circus might need during the day. She tugged her cap down tighter on her head and followed Jasper out the door.

"Are there some mean workers we need to avoid?" she asked, her voice softer, as the two of them hurried through the dewy circus grounds, following their noses to the cook tent.

"Some people are enormous grumps first thing in the morning -- and they smell. It's just polite, don't you think, to wash before you go to breakfast?" She winked.

The Countess was already seated at one of the long tables, eating alone. Only a few other people were going through the serving line, and all of them were still wearing their nightshirts, sloppily tucked into trousers, with here and there a single suspender strap holding up the mess. Ess muffled a chuckle when she remembered what Jasper had said about washing before breakfast. The Countess gestured for the two girls to join her. She was nearly finished with her meal, and had a day book, quill pen, and a glass inkwell full of iridescent red ink open in front of her. Ess tried not to look like she was trying to read what the woman had written and was allowing to dry. She didn't feel like explaining that for fun, her grandfather had taught her to read upside down as easily as right side up -- and backwards in mirrors, too. After a few tries, she gave up, because it looked like the Countess wrote in a foreign language Ess couldn't identify.

Then she had no chance to even try, because the Countess put her through a series of questions, determining her education, her physical training, and how she had liked her first day in the circus. Then she laid out Ess's schedule. Mornings were for training with the acrobats. They would be concentrating on horseback tricks for now, because Perdita and her husband had just announced they were expecting their first child. Ess had to be ready to take Perdita's place in two months, when the doctor said she could no longer be allowed to do handstands on galloping horses or leap through hoops or other strenuous, jolting exercises.

Chapter Fifteen

"I don't envy you one lick," Jasper said, and shuddered with exaggeration. Then she grinned. "I am as clumsy as they come."

"When it comes to bareback riding, granted," the Countess said. "You have your family's sharpshooting skills and cleverness with numbers, and unfortunately, your devil-may-care attitude."

"Got the unholy luck to go with it, to keep my head on my shoulders," she retorted, leaning back in her folding chair and hooking her thumbs through her suspenders in a pose of bravado.

"Anyone who trusts to luck is a fool," the woman said without any change in her slowly elegant tones. Ess saw a spark of something in the Countess' eyes, though, that made her think she was either irritated with Jasper's attitude, or feared for her.

"I know," the girl said, lowering her voice and losing a few degrees of the cocky grin. "Got the family smarts to keep my skin whole, just got to remember to use them."

"Indeed you do. Speaking of family smarts." She tipped her head back, gesturing with her chin at the serving line.

Ess turned to look and saw McGuillicutty, the chief cook, stepping out from behind the long steam-heated tables with a tray.

"Off to work." Jasper scooped up her dishes and held out her hands for Ess's and the Countess's as well.

In moments she had deposited their plates and mugs and utensils in the dishwashing bins that had a continual stream of steaming water flowing through them -- Ess thought that entirely clever -- and hurried to take the tray from McGuillicutty. Then she hurried out of the cook tent, calling out greetings to the clumps of circus performers coming in for breakfast.

"What does Jasper do?" Ess asked.

"He's Stockwell's assistant. Runs errands, carries messages, learns the business, the bookkeeping work and such. And, unfortunately, will soon be joining the trick shooting team, both in the ring and in the side show exhibitions." The Countess shuddered delicately. "Come along. You need to be fitted for your harness and riding shoes before training starts. Your afternoons and evenings will be spent with Gus, tinkering and making noise and keeping the steam at the perfect pressure for all the toys needed for performances."

Ess waited until they were out in the open and no one was close enough to overhear them before she asked her next question. "What kind of trouble is Jasper in that she has to hide out here?"

"Family trouble." The Countess responded with only a second or two of hesitation. She had an enviable talent for speaking without moving her lips, her voice clear, yet so soft Ess thought no one standing more than two feet away could have heard her. "Stockwell is her grandfather. His enemies from the war weren't satisfied with believing he had been killed. They went after the whole family."

"Resurrectionists are my enemies, too." She had to resort to pretending to rub at her mouth to hide the movement of her lips. Ess resolved to learn the Countess's trick. It would come in handy in situations where she wouldn't want people to read her lips and understand what she was saying when they couldn't hear her. After all, if she proved herself useful and trustworthy, Sutter might move her on to bigger, more active, dangerous assignments.

Ess started her training with a few advantages, the first being that she liked horses and rode bareback quite often as a child. Her brother had been an adventurer, and as their grandmother often accused, had a goal of breaking all his bones before he became a man. Ess had insisted on following in her big brother's footsteps, to the point of disdaining a saddle except when she needed to appear in public and in skirts. She had held onto her bareback skills, despite the equestrian training of the Academy, which insisted that "true ladies" rarely rode faster than an elegant, dancing walk around the park. While the Academy did win dozens of ribbons for equestrian skills, most of them were for the horse's conformity to standards of breeding, gait, and what the riding masters called equestrian dance.

Ess decided she could handle this part of her duties quite well, and have fun at it, until Roscoe Fletcher, the riding master, told her to stand up on her horse's back. When she hesitated, while the big gray gelding galumphed around the training ring, the skeletal black man flicked the end of his long training whip-pole at her. She flinched and twisted out of the way, nearly falling off, while the gelding didn't even flick an ear. Ess held onto the mane as she contorted, trying to get to her knees. She couldn't seem to ignore that whip tip that hung two feet over her head as the horse completed another circuit of the ring. That made finding her balance and levering herself to her feet even harder than if she had tried it without anyone watching her.

Halfway to a standing position, with her knees and back bent and a few strands of mane sticking to her sweaty fingers, Ess felt her center of gravity shift. Holding her breath, refusing to let out a yelp for help, she froze. Gut instinct said quick movements would only make things worse.

Gut instinct didn't factor in the horse's continued jolting, jerky steps, in that awkward place between trotting and galloping. One foot lost contact with the horse's back, despite the nubby leather sole of the riding shoe that, Roscoe had promised, would grip the horse's hide better than glue.

Everything slowed as if mired in molasses in winter. Ess twisted, jolted by another horse step. An image of sliding down those heaving flanks and going under, to be trampled by those big, black, shod hooves, made her heart race.

Think, think, think, she snarled silently in her head -- still refusing to make a sound, and entertain anyone who might be watching.

Roughhousing memories with Uly came to the fore and her body remembered, despite the years. Ess's foot came back down, sideways on the horse's flank. She kicked, pushing off hard with that foot to guide her angle, and shoved with the other leg, twisting herself in mid-air. She curled into a ball, hitting the sawdust of the ring with her shoulder and rolling twice, to sprawl out on her back, the air knocked out of her. Applause somehow penetrated the hammering of her heart in her ears as she struggled to remember how to breathe.

"Very good," Roscoe bellowed, taking his own sweet time to cross the ring. He held out his hand to help her up, but only after Ess had sat up and remembered how to breathe. "Knowing how to fall without getting hurt is half the battle in learning trick riding. Willy, me lad," he said with a fake Irish accent. He turned and gestured to one of the older men who stood on the sidelines, tending to the horses. "The harness, if you please."

At first, Ess couldn't figure out what the tangle of leather straps and buckles hanging from the rope on the long pivot arm was for. Then as Willy and two other men brought a long pole and settled it into a metal tube set into the center of the ring, and attached the pivot arm to it, she caught on. Astonishment warred with relief when she understood, but both feelings were overtaken by anger.

"Why did you make me try standing up without it?" she demanded, as she responded to Roscoe's imperious gesture, and approached him in the center of the ring.

"Fear is a better teacher than hours of lectures." He was so calmly matter-of-fact in his explanation, she thought she could hate him. It would have been better if he had been amused, as if he had been pulling a trick on her. "Besides, I needed to see if you knew how to fall, or if I'd have to waste a couple days teaching you that before we got you in the harness and moved on to having fun." He winked at her.

"Fun." She snorted and turned around, raising her arms to let him adjust the straps of the harness that would keep her in the air whenever she slid or fell -- or as she later did a few times, bounced off the horse's back.

Ess hated admitting he was right. There was something almost amusing about losing her balance and suddenly finding herself swinging in a wide arc on the end of the rope. When she had time to think later, grateful for the steady supply of hot water that eased some of her bruises and aches, there were similarities between Roscoe's teaching style and her grandfather's. Earnest Fremont liked to hand his grandchildren massive books, or give them a vague assignment to research something, and then set them free to read and find their own answers. They could write down all the questions they wanted on whatever subject he had given them to study, but they were to try to find the answers for themselves. Roscoe had a tendency to give instructions but few explanations until after Ess had learned through -- repeated, aching, clumsy, embarrassing -- failure.

After nearly an hour of private lessons, bumping and bouncing and falling and twisting and managing to stay on her feet for two complete circuits of the ring, the equestrian team came into the tent for rehearsal. Ess was sent up a pole to sit on one of the acrobat perches and watch.

"Will I have to copy everything I see tomorrow?" she asked, as she snapped off a salute.

Roscoe's responding laughter was deep and lazy, with malicious undertones that didn't fool her for a moment.

The next two weeks were essentially a repeat of her first morning in the ring -- learning to stand on horseback until the team came in to rehearse, then sitting in various spots, giving her different perspectives, while she watched them rehearse or work out new tumbling tricks. After four days, Roscoe took the supporting harness away, and Ess learned how much she had come to depend on it to keep her from going under the horse's hooves. She only fell off the horse five times, and agreed that learning how to fall was the largest part of the lessons. After that, once she could find her balance and keep it no matter how the horse changed his gait, Roscoe started her on tricks. When she could hop from one foot to the other, leaping up high in the air and kicking her legs wide apart in between, and then stand on her hands on the horse's back, then Roscoe graduated her to working with the team. She had to learn Perdita's role perfectly, after all, and only had six weeks in which to do it.

Afternoons with Gus usually ran between the extremes of silent contemplation of the various parts of the steam engine, and frantic, greasy, sweaty activity during performances. Ess started out as one of the stokers, hauling buckets of coal and pumping water into the boiler. Then she kept busy getting her hands caught constantly as couplings were shifted for one mechanical trick after another. If the clowns weren't getting ready to race around the ring in their steam-powered carts, the ladder for the firemen clowns had to be raised and lowered by steam so that it seemed to have a life of its own. Gus gave Ess two pairs of gloves and thick canvass and leather coveralls just for performance times, because each performance resulted in getting thoroughly soaked and near-scalded by the steam from the pipes and unscrewing connectors. She had a third set of gloves and coveralls for the lulls between performances. Then, she either followed him around and he explained what he was doing to repair the latest breakdown, or she tried her hand at diagnosing a mechanical problem on her own.

Between dinner and the evening performance, Ess became the Countess's assistant and errand runner. She helped the woman set up for her magic act, and learned various tricks just through putting props in their places and then watching the Countess run through them. Dampness in the air or heat or dust could affect how sensitive pieces of equipment performed, so they had to be checked every day. The Countess commended Ess for her sharp eyes and the sensitivity and dexterity of her hands. She promised that when they had some leisure time, riding the train to their next performance venue, she would teach Ess sleight of hand tricks with cards and coins and scarves, and "useful skills," such as picking locks. Ess looked forward to that.

~~~~~

At first, Ess was so busy she forgot why she was at the circus. Then the weight of guilt and sense of uselessness smothered her when she remembered -- Sutter wanted her powers of observation and analysis watching for trouble sneaking up on Stockwell. Knowing the circus owner was Jasper's grandfather put a little extra weight on the assignment, because Ess genuinely liked her fellow imposter. She had even more reason to protect Stockwell because she knew how it was to feel like everyone in the world had been taken away from her. First her parents, when she was almost too young to remember them. Then Uly. Then her grandparents, then Giles and the rest of the household staff.

Her sense of uselessness faded as Ess settled into her new life. Stockwell was everywhere. She wondered that she hadn't heard the wheeze-creak of his mechanical leg more often, because he wandered the entire circus grounds from sunup to sundown. She saw him a dozen times a day, watching the acrobats rehearse or checking with Gus on the engine and progress on new ideas for performance "tricks and traps." When she didn't see Stockwell striding from one place to another, dealing with minor crises or vendors or town officials, Ess could see Jasper acting as her grandfather's second pair of legs, carrying messages or fetching something he needed or making deliveries. As long as Jasper was running, in a good mood, then Stockwell was safe and all was well with the circus. As an added benefit, when the girls settled in to sleep, Jasper chatted about what she saw and heard and what her grandfather had done of note during the day.

Ess liked the quiet time at night, after the lantern was blown out and she and Jasper lay in their bunks, talking quietly until they fell asleep, both of them exhausted from their rapid pace during the day. She had never really had a friend to chatter with, though she had certainly had friends at her grandparents' church and then at the Academy. She learned anything she wanted about circus life from Jasper.

In return, Ess talked about her grandparents and Uly, her grandmother's scientific experiments and inventions and her grandfather's scholarly and philosophical friends. Jasper was fascinated by the clockwork rewinder Matilda had made, and the chemicals that let one paper be copied perfectly onto another. Discussions of the patterns of history, the high tides of creativity versus the low tides of oppression of thought and spirit didn't interest her much.

The only thing Ess didn't like about sharing quarters with Jasper was
~~~~~

that Durgen showed up at least once a day, glowering at her as if she was in his way. Plus he came up in the conversation at least twice a day. Every other night, Jasper was delayed returning to their little wagon because she met with Durgen to whisper and kiss and talk about whatever minor crisis had threatened the circus that day -- and plans for a future together.

"How old are you?" Ess had to ask, the first time Jasper confessed that they had kissed four times the night before, blushed, and went into wriggling raptures, lying on her bunk.

"I'll be eighteen in December. I'm more than old enough to know my own mind." Jasper wrinkled her nose up at her, then a moment later relaxed back into her delighted grin.

Ess bit her lip to keep from retorting with words her grandmother had used for a girl in their church who thought she was in love: Yes, but how can you know *his* mind?

She had an awful suspicion what Durgen had in mind, if he knew Jasper was Stockwell's granddaughter, and his most likely heir.

Jasper and Durgen's romance was none of her business, but if the big, glowering man had designs on owning the circus someday, then that could be considered a threat to Stockwell. Especially if Durgen manipulated Jasper and broke her heart along the way. Ess resolved then to include Durgen's name and his relationship with Jasper in her first report to Sutter. The circus was headed for Detroit once they finished up their two-week run in Indianapolis, and there was a Secret Service office in an airship docking tower office building in the center of the city. Where it lay in relation to the fairgrounds where the circus would set up, Ess had no idea. She would simply have to find out. Hopefully it wouldn't be too far away, because she did have duties that took up most of her time.

~~~~~

As their assigned assistants, Ess and Jasper rode in the front car with Stockwell and the Countess as the train pulled out of Indianapolis two hours before dawn, after their final performance. Both girls curled up on the thick couches of the car that served as office and living quarters for Stockwell, and went right to sleep.

The girls cooked breakfast in the little kitchen in Stockwell's office car. While the Countess and Jasper took care of cleaning up, Stockwell took Ess aside for the first private conversation they had since he fetched her from the train station. He emphasized that she not let slip to anyone that she had been sent by Sutter. The story was that an old Army friend had sent her, to hide from creditors and people with old grudges to settle.

The Countess settled Jasper and Ess at one end of the car, while the supervisors of different divisions within the circus came up to the car to meet with Stockwell to handle circus business. While men discussed numbers and costs and damages and risks, the girls learned magic. Ess delighted in the sleight of hand tricks, and especially in how easily she caught onto them. She
~~~~~

would make an admirable and successful pickpocket, if she should ever have need, according to the Countess.

~~~~~

The first day in Detroit, Ess took a detour during an errand through the city, to visit the Secret Service office and deliver her first report for Sutter. The agent at the desk barely looked up when she walked in and handed him the sealed envelope. He did look up, though, after seeing the name and the sequence of numbers that Sutter told her to put on all correspondence with him. She assumed the numbers were a code and guaranteed delivery straight to him. The big, battle-scarred man looked uncomfortable in his neat, pressed suit, and his expression clearly said he couldn't understand what a young boy in a slouch cap and oversized jacket could be sending to a Secret Service agent in Washington.

Ess supposed that his entirely too readable face, his inability to hide his emotions or thoughts, was exactly why he was assigned to a desk, and not out in the field, or even working in disguise. A man who gave away what he thought or felt was predictable in his actions and reactions. He could never have the advantage over criminals.

She hurried through the rest of her errands, because she was to meet Jasper when she finished. She found a telegraph office and sent a message to Detective Horace Winslow at the Philadelphia Pinkerton office, asking for a report, using the password that proved she was indeed Mrs. Flora Lewis. The telegraph office operator very kindly agreed to let Ess use his office for delivery of the response. If there was anything to report.

Two days later, Ess returned to the telegraph office, and found a message waiting, simply saying, "U vanished after original ruckus. SA hotter. No details." Sighing, she thanked the man in the office.

She would wait two more months and try again, when she knew the circus would be in a town long enough for her to receive a report through the mail. The entire situation was discouraging enough that she didn't enjoy her duties behind stage during the afternoon performance. Gus even remarked on her seeming rather sulky, and that frightened Ess a little. The inventor engineer was a brilliant man, and a fascinating teacher, but oblivious for the most part when it came to the people around him. For him to notice Ess's low spirits meant she was far too obvious.

Being obvious, and being distracted by her disappointments, could end up being dangerous for her.

~~~~~

Two months later, the circus performed in Philadelphia. Ess borrowed a widow costume from the Countess -- her mentor did not ask why she wanted to use the clothes -- and she visited the Pinkerton officer personally as Mrs. Flora Lewis. Detective Winslow wasn't present, but her password convinced the man on duty to open the files and give Ess a report.

So far the Pinkertons had tracked down four of the men Ulysses Fremont had argued with just before he vanished. All of them were hangers-on, bystanders, not really involved in the original argument. All of them agreed that the men who accosted her brother had accused him of either taking something that didn't belong to him, or of being where he didn't belong. Ess couldn't believe her brother would ever steal. However, she could believe that he would poke and prod and sneak in and spy where he had no business. They had both been raised to be curious and to follow their curiosity. That testimony was all the Pinkertons had been able to scrape up so far. They noted that people in town found it odd that the men who started the ruckus were all outsiders and seemed intent on harassing "one of their own," as one of the witnesses put it.

As for her grandparents, a series of telegrams to diplomatic offices and shipping lines and a representative of the airship courier line in the United States had yielded discouraging news. Tensions had escalated all through the regions of South America where her grandparents had planned to travel during their two-year expedition. All access to the mountains where her grandparents had vanished had been cut off. After three attacks on the courier airships, the company had decided to suspend all operations until they were assured of safer conditions.

~~~~~~~~

Late November, the circus traveled through Virginia, heading for warmer winter venues in Georgia and Florida, and heading for Texas. Ess had dared to confide in Jasper about the Academy, making her friend laugh as she described the various teachers. They were given an entire morning of freedom from their duties -- Ess, because the acrobats couldn't practice, as one horse had turned up lame and another was too far gone with a foal to perform -- and the girls hurried off to hire a gig and visit the town where the Academy's students did their shopping. Ess was disappointed when the only difference in the town after all this time was that the streets were muddy from constant rain. She supposed the change was mostly in her, rather than the countryside.

She was surprised to see the long covered wagon full of students come into town. Miss Van Hastings had never allowed the girls to go outside in inclement weather. It wasn't the fear of rich parents being upset that their daughter had developed a cold. Rather, the housekeeping staff didn't like mud on the floors, or having to wash and dry student cloaks after going out in the rain. What had changed at the Academy? That was definitely the wagon. The false family crest Miss Van Hastings took such pride in was clearly visible on the wagon.
~~~~~~~~

Chapter Sixteen

"You had to wear a uniform?" Jasper said, staring as the girls sedately filed off the wagon, their cloaks only going to their knees. Cloaks and poke bonnets were uniformly silver-gray. The full skirts were a uniform dark blue, with white ruffled pinafores. The skirts raised to stay out of the puddles, as the girls hurried to the wooden sidewalk, revealed uniform black boots and blue-and-white striped stockings.

"No, we didn't." Ess shrugged the collar of her jacket higher around her ears and tugged her cap down lower as she crossed the street for a closer look. She was halfway across the street when she confirmed what she had suspected -- she recognized none of the girls who got off the wagon. Something odd was going on.

Was it possible that Miss Van Hastings had been deposed after all? Had Sutter finally gotten tired of waiting for the Resurrectionists to return for the supplies left as a trap under the school, and had her arrested?

"Shall we charm the ladies?" Jasper said, when Ess shared her thoughts.

"Charm?"

Her friend winked at her, tugged off her cap, raked her fingers through her hair to straighten it, and sauntered into the first shop, where several of the uniformed, unfamiliar students stood in a cluster, giggling. Ess realized they were watching her and Jasper. The girls actually blushed when Jasper bobbed a shallow bow to them and addressed them as lovely young ladies.

"I wonder if you would help me and my brother. Our family is considering opening a mercantile here in your lovely town, and it is vital to learn what the residents here want most in a store."

While their outward appearance had changed, the general mindset of the Academy's students hadn't. A little flattery, a chance to talk about clothes and sweets and jewelry, and they gladly babbled about anything and everything. Every question she and Jasper asked about the Academy itself, the girls answered without hesitating. Yes, Miss Van Hastings was still in charge. Yes, most of the students had only started attending this fall, after a massive changeover following a huge ruckus in the summer. The school grounds were a mess. Some girls believed there had been actual explosions. Soldiers had found rooms under the school and set off bombs to destroy them. The conveniences had improved greatly, because someone had been stealing the steam power that should have gone to heating and cooking and laundry. The school was greatly reduced in size and in the incomes of its students' families. Hence the uniforms. Rich girls could afford to compete with each other in their wardrobes. The daughters of merchants and town officials were supposedly happier wearing uniforms, as equality was good for building character.

"It just means they find other ways of dominating each other," Jasper remarked, as she and Ess left the town behind them. They didn't have much protection in the slight awning of the gig, and didn't much mind the misty rain in their faces and clinging to their clothes. "Clothes are harmless. Other ways..." She shrugged.

"You sound like the voice of experience."

She sighed. "We used to be rich. I had to go to a fancy school. Before those filthy Southerners came looking for Grandfather." She swallowed hard. "I should be thankful, I suppose. I much prefer wearing trousers and traveling all over the country."

Ess patted her knee, fighting the urge to wrap an arm around her shoulders. Now was not the time to risk prompting a spate of tears. Jasper hadn't seen her father in two years, and various aunts and uncles had scattered throughout the country under false names. Her mother had died in childbirth, and some odd remarks Jasper had made prompted Ess to think the circumstances of her death were suspicious.

They parked the gig half a mile from the school grounds and walked through the woods to get close enough for a good look. Ess looked for signs of exploded tunnels. She saw no trenches as they approached the high wooden fence around the school grounds. Either she had been mistaken, estimating where the tunnels reached, or the soldiers dismantling the Resurrectionist warren hadn't discovered the false walls and tunnels. She turned around, sighting various landmarks as they walked, and gauged where they were in relation to the river. If she wasn't wrong, a tunnel was directly under her feet. Ess muffled laughter and considered how she would tell Jasper -- or maybe she shouldn't tell her?

Ess froze. That shiver up her back had nothing to do with the chilly, damp weather. She turned, putting her back to the fence only a dozen feet away from them.

What if there were Resurrectionists hiding in those tunnels that hadn't been destroyed?

"What are you doing here?" a familiar male voice said, as a big shape dressed in homespun and leather stepped out from a thick mass of shadows and bushes. Collins slowly lowered his pistol to his side. "Does Sutter know you're here?"

"No." She glanced at Jasper, who watched the gun rather than the man. "We're set up nearby. I just wanted to see what happened."

"Not smart." The Secret Service agent gestured with the gun, shooing them away. "What if those men you identified for us are in the area? If I could sneak up behind you, so could one of them. Sutter'd have my head if anything happened to you."

"All right." She bit her lip against laughter when the man's eyes suddenly widened and he stared at Jasper, his gaze taking her in from head to toe several times. Was the big man blushing?

Ess thanked Miss Talbot and Sarah once again, for the use of the corset that flattened her shape. Jasper had been filling out over the months. She wouldn't be able to disguise herself as a boy much longer. Plus, the damp made their clothes cling to them a little, decreasing the effectiveness of their baggy clothes to disguise their shapes.

What she found amusing was that Collins could tell Jasper was a girl -- if that was what that darkening of his cheeks meant -- but he hadn't been able to tell Ess wasn't a boy.

"Should I draw a map for you and send it through the post?"

"What map?" Collins said.

"Of the tunnels you haven't discovered and exploded yet." She took a step toward the trees.

Collins sighed loudly. "Come with me."

Elliott and two men she didn't recognize were brewing coffee inside the tunnel mouth overlooking the riverbank, when Collins led the two girls to what was obviously the agents' headquarters. The cover of vines and shrubs and the wooden panel, cleverly covered with dirt and moss and grass, had been removed. It was a quite sizable cave, and deep enough that the rain didn't get inside. Elliott recognized her, and Ess decided to be flattered.

Collins gestured everyone out of the shelter and rummaged through a trunk to find paper and one of the newfangled pens with a barrel of ink attached to it. He gestured at a table of planks and hauled over a folding camp stool from the fire pit at the mouth of the cave.

"What sort of trouble has this scamp been getting you into?" he asked, after Ess got to work drawing.

"Oh, no trouble at all." Jasper sweetened her voice into a drawl. "He's actually been assigned to keep me out of trouble."

"I'll believe that when he -- excuse me, when all unholy heck freezes over." Collins caught Ess grinning at him and he scowled, even as a flush crept up his cheeks. "What are you staring at, boy? Get to work."

Ess muffled laughter, and got back to work. She tried not to listen as Jasper fed Collins one ridiculous story after another about the "trouble" that she kept her out of. They were all silly pranks, mostly consisting of sneaking away from her make-believe governess and guards while her powerful government official father -- "I'm not at liberty to identify my dear daddy, you understand," -- took a long-term tour of the Southern states. Ess fought not to listen, because every time she did, she had to muffle giggles that would certainly shred her disguise as a boy.

Collins took it upon himself to lecture her, once she was finished drawing, trying to impress on her the seriousness of the position she had been entrusted with. Then he escorted them to the thicker woods where they had hidden the gig. The sight of the small cart and the placid horse somewhat mollified him. Jasper fluttered her eyelashes at him as he helped her up into the cart, which just raised another blush.

"What interesting friends you have," Jasper murmured, once they had put several miles of laughter-strained silence between them and the school. "If I don't miss my guess, those were federal agents, keeping watch. What haven't you told me? Who made the tunnels?"

"Resurrectionists. That ought to answer everything." Ess regretted her sharp tone as soon as she saw the happy flush fade from her friend's cheeks. She let go of the guiding reins with one hand and squeezed Jasper's hand. "I'm sorry. There's so much I'm just not allowed to tell, but… well, we have more in common than you think."

"More than I used to think," the other girl murmured. A moment later, she squeezed back. "We're a pair, at the very least."

~~~~~

For Christmas, the Countess gave Jasper a sapphire gown trimmed in layers of ivory lace, and matching dancing slippers. She gave Ess a new journal and two books on the ancient civilizations of South America. That made Ess pause to think about just how much she gave away with the few things she had said about her life. She worried that perhaps the Countess had seen her journal, so she knew there were only twenty blank pages left.

Then Ess had more to worry about, when she got back to their quarters after the Christmas day dinner and discovered Jasper and her new dress missing. It wasn't hard to guess that she had slipped away to go dancing with Durgen.

Over the months, Durgen appeared to have thawed toward her, but Ess didn't trust him. He wasn't friendly, but at least he didn't stare, with a fire in his eyes as if he would like to kick her out of his way like a puppy. She was still convinced that he spent far too much time with Jasper, and volunteered for too many chores or errands that kept him close to Stockwell. Every time she looked, he was watching the circus owner. What was he looking for? What did he expect or even want to see?

She hurried to change into her nightshirt and slipped into her bunk. The weather had turned constantly damp and chilly, and while the crates and sacks filling the wagon provided some insulation, the oil lantern didn't make up for the lack of a stove. Ess slipped her legs down under her blankets and nearly let out a yelp when she touched something smooth and chilly that crinkled. Her heart was still racing as she reached down and pulled out the envelope with her false name written on it. For a few moments, she just looked at it. Who would hide that envelope in her bunk?

When she opened it, she found the letter was from Sutter. He thanked her for raising the question of Durgen. He hadn't responded to her concerns until now because finding information on the man had taken longer than usual. That in itself raised red flags. Thanks to the sketch Ess had sent of Durgen, with the last report she had turned in on the roustabout's activities,
~~~~~

Sutter had been able to determine that he was not, as he claimed, honorably discharged Navy Lt. Willard Durgen of Connecticut. No one who knew the lieutenant during the war had heard from him in years, or had any idea what had become of him. He hadn't gone home, hadn't contacted his family since the end of the war. Whoever now wore the name had taken it up some time between the real Durgen's discharge and when he joined the circus.

Hard thudding on the door of the wagon interrupted Ess before she could finish the letter. Before she could think to respond or roll out of her bunk, the door was yanked open and Stockwell leaped into the tiny, cramped living space. His gaze landed on Jasper's empty bunk. In his hand, he held a sheaf of papers, and just a glance revealed the top was covered with the same square, bold handwriting of the letter Ess was reading. She swung her legs over the side of the bunk and pulled one of her quilts up around herself.

Stockwell turned slowly. Instead of the fury she expected, his face was pale and his eyes held an aching and fear she hoped never to see anyone else suffer.

"She's with him, isn't she?"

"I'm sorry. She promised me they didn't do anything but--" Ess sighed. "Kiss."

"Sutter told me you've been watching him. I'm glad you were worried, but..." Stockwell closed his eyes and leaned back against Jasper's bunk.

"I should have said something to you, instead of telling Sutter."

"Jasmine is your friend. You trusted her. I trusted her. The problem is that Durgen was here when I bought the circus. I thought he was safe. I didn't accept new workers for months, just so I could make sure none of... none of *them* caught up with me."

"What if he isn't a Southerner? What if he's just someone who knew the real Durgen died and took over his identity?"

"He has a reason for lying to us, but I'm not willing to risk my granddaughter's life that it's a good reason." Stockwell crumpled up the letter in his hand and thumped his other fist against the side of Jasper's bunk.

"What are you going to do?"

"Besides order her to stay away from him?" His mouth stretched in a mirthless smile, grimmer than any frown he could have worn. Ess imagined he had worn that expression when he headed into a battle that had a very good chance of killing him.

"She won't like it. She probably won't listen."

"I know. I need you to keep watch over her. Don't stop her from sneaking out to meet him, but don't let her ever be alone with him." He reached out his hand, and Ess gave hers into his grasp. "Can I count on you?"

"Yes, sir."

~~~~~

Wherever Jasper and Durgen had been heading, Stockwell found them and brought his granddaughter back. Ess was still awake, trying to read one
~~~~~

of her new books, when Jasper stomped into the wagon, swathed in a deep blue velvet cloak -- borrowed from the Countess's costume trunks, likely without permission -- and fighting not to sob aloud. Her face was red, but as she peeled off the cloak and flung it down on a nearby crate and tore off the false braids that looked like a crown, Ess could see her friend was furious, not tearful.

"What did Durgen do to you?" Ess said, choosing not to let Jasper know that she knew, and certainly not to reveal her part in destroying her romantic adventure.

"Nothing!" Jasper flung the braids down to the floor. "He would never hurt me! I don't care what he says -- Durgen loves me."

"He who?"

"Grandfather."

If her red face and trembling hands weren't proof enough, now Ess knew her friend was furious beyond all self-control. Jasper would never make such an enormous slip and refer to Stockwell as her grandfather. Not when she was aware and thinking clearly.

"Did he catch you sneaking away?"

"Halfway to town." Jasper clenched her fists and closed her eyes and she shuddered all over as she muffled what would have been an ear-splitting scream in any other situation. "I don't care what his government friends say. He has to have a good reason -- he'd tell me the truth if he could -- Grandfather can lie about his name and where he came from, why can't he?"

Ess wondered if she would ever find it funny that she could follow what Jasper meant without any trouble, amid all the "he" and "his," interchanging between Stockwell and Durgen. The most important thing was relief. Stockwell had given Jasper someone to blame, the agents who were still his friends, still protecting him, and not Ess.

"What has Durgen been lying about?" she asked, knowing when Jasper calmed down, she would be suspicious if Ess didn't ask questions.

While Ess helped Jasper get out of her pretty new dress and petticoats, her friend did calm down and explained the sequence of events, and what Stockwell had told her on the wet, windy ride back to the circus camp.

"Perched on the back of his horse like a sack of potatoes!" she fumed.

Ess forbore pointing out that she would have been flung face-down if she were a sack of potatoes, and Stockwell had probably made her sit behind him, holding onto his belt.

Durgen had stopped at a roadside shelter a little less than halfway to town, ostensibly because the wind was getting fierce and the rain heavier, and the little awning on the gig didn't provide much protection. He was very protective of Jasper's pretty new dress, which the girl appreciated. Ess felt slightly sick to her stomach when her friend's fury cooled and she described her sweetheart's care for her clothes. From what Ess had learned, eavesdropping on her grandmother's friends, men rarely paid attention to women's clothes. When they did, they were trying to sweet-talk a woman into doing something, to cover up an enormous mistake, or they had been trained to pay attention after years of marriage. Durgen's actions certainly raised more red flags for Ess. She knew better than to point out the anomaly to Jasper, though.

Durgen and Jasper had sat and talked in the darkness of the shelter -- and kissed, Jasper admitted, blushing -- until the rain slowed. Durgen had just picked up Jasper to carry her through the mud and puddles back to the gig when Stockwell caught up with them.

"Oh, he was wonderful!" Jasper stroked the front of the blue dress, straightening it on the hanging rod, before moving to suspend it from the empty bunk. She sank down on a nearby crate. "He didn't move a muscle, just stood there and listened while Grand -- while Stockwell handed down his decree. Then he said, 'Sir, I understand she's your granddaughter and no one will ever be good enough for her, but we're in love, and sometimes that's more important than anything else in the whole wide world.' And he bowed and he just stood there and watched when I was heaved up on the back of the horse and we raced off." Jasper let out a little sigh and slumped dramatically, face flushed.

"How does he know?" Ess whispered, as a chill shot down her back.

"Know what?"

"How does Durgen know you're Stockwell's granddaughter? Did you tell him?"

"No, I--" Jasper frowned. The flush faded from her cheeks. "I know I never told him."

"How did he find out, then?"

"Maybe Grandfather let it slip." She shrugged, but it wasn't the flighty gesture Ess had seen her use before. There was something defiant, maybe even troubled in the uneven twitching of her shoulders, and the frown that dug lines around her mouth and across her forehead, just for a moment. Jasper jerked herself up from the crate and climbed up into her bunk. "I've certainly been slipping up enough. It's infuriating."

"Did Durgen really tell you he loves you?" she had to ask.

Granted, it was romantic and could even be called desperate, that Durgen announced he and Jasper loved each other, but Ess suspected it was very different from the man telling the girl he loved her.

Jasper's eyes lit and she opened her mouth to answer -- and stopped. Ess was relieved to see frown lines return, glad her friend hesitated and really thought before answering.

"Well, no..." The frown turned into a pout and she thumped her pillow a few times. "We're not allowed to go anywhere near each other. It doesn't matter that we're in love -- yes, Durgen loves me, even if he's never said it. Didn't he tell my grandfather that we were in love? That ought to count for something."

Ess climbed into her bunk and tugged the blankets up. She felt far colder than the rain and damp and howling of the wind outside could account for. She watched Jasper struggle to get comfortable in her bunk, pulling up the blankets and thumping her pillow to fluff it a few more times.

"What are you going to do?" she asked, as Jasper leaned out of her bunk to reach for the lantern and blow it out.

"Keep seeing him, of course." The other girl offered her a flat-lipped smile. It was so different from the mischief-filled smirk Ess had seen when Jasper had defied orders before, the change made her shudder. Then the light vanished, leaving them in cold, windy darkness with the rain drumming down all around them.

~~~~~

Ess took her derringer out of its hiding place, safely wrapped up in her extra socks and underclothes, loaded it, and adjusted the holster to ride low on her leg. She had to rip a hole in the pocket of her trousers so she could get at the pistol. If she needed to use the gun, she certainly couldn't ask the enemy to wait while she unfastened her belt and reached down the leg of her trousers, could she? Fortunately, one of the guns she was assigned to use when she filled in for another performer during sideshow exhibitions -- wearing an enormous fake beard and boots with high heels to make her four inches taller -- was another derringer. At her next sharpshooting practice, she palmed several bullets at a time, to give her a supply of ammunition.

She looked for Durgen whenever she had reason to move around the circus grounds. Her focus turned to always knowing where the man was, what he was doing, and who he was talking to. Jasper spent most of her day with her grandfather, as his assistant, and Stockwell didn't let her go running around on errands any longer. Ess could imagine the seething silence in the office, in direct contrast to the explosions of complaints when she and Jasper were alone together at night. The Countess said nothing, but once when Ess was following Durgen during a free hour, she ran into the Countess, also watching him. The woman looked at her, nodded, her gaze dark and penetrating, patted Ess on the shoulder and walked away.
~~~~~

Chapter Seventeen

By New Year's Eve, Ess had several pages of notes on Durgen's activities to turn in to Stockwell. The big roustabout had always been a sociable type of person, exploring the towns where they stopped to perform, making friends with the locals, buying drinks for his new friends and handing out complimentary tickets to the circus. Ess had thought it was just good business, a sign of loyalty to Stockwell, to constantly drum up business and make a good impression wherever they went.

What if Durgen was meeting his contacts, passing along information, in every town? Perhaps he hadn't been assigned to watch Stockwell at the start, but he was a general spy for the Resurrectionists. What if Stockwell's enemies had deciphered his false identity, and with the worst kind of luck already had Durgen in place when their enemy bought the circus? The only other explanation was that Durgen was simply a bad apple who had agreed to spy on the new owner. Maybe he felt some resentment for the changes Stockwell instituted when he took over the circus.

"He has something of a reputation as a show-off, a braggart," Stockwell said, when Ess made her report to him.

He nodded and winked, but it wasn't his usual jaunty, encouraging expression. This last week of silent arguing between him and Jasper was taking a toll. Ess felt a twinge of guilt, blaming herself -- yet she knew she had done the right thing. If she hadn't mentioned Durgen to Sutter, and Sutter hadn't investigated, they wouldn't know Durgen was a liar and a danger.

"If I had learned he had his sights on Jasper, and didn't know what our friend discovered, I would have excused it as simply the kind of man he is. He likes to be admired. I would have still told him to stay away from her, and threatened to shackle her in my car for the next ten years, just because he's not the kind of man she should love. Knowing this casts a whole new light on the situation. Never mind my fury at being deceived."

"I should have told you as soon as I found out," Ess offered.

"No." His smile had a touch of sadness. "How were you to know? She's your friend, and I'm glad you have each other. Better that she's furious with me for a while, than to destroy your friendship." He patted Ess on the shoulder.

"So what are you going to do about Durgen? How do we prove he's passing information to others?" She gestured at the report in his hands. "He goes to the same saloon in town at the same time every day. While he talks with different people every day, he goes up to the same bartender and shakes hands with him each time." She shook her head. "I can't help feeling they shake hands a little too long. Maybe I'm just suspicious--"

"No, that's an old, time-honored method of passing messages."

"What are we going to do?"

"You," he gripped her shoulder, so she had to look him in the eye, "have done more than I would have asked or expected. I think I shall take a drive into town and send a telegram to thank Sutter for his help, then do some shopping. Presents and treats for the party, something to get that dratted girl to smile at me." He winked again. "You, if you would--"

"Keep Jasper in my sights?" she guessed.

Stockwell nodded and squeezed her shoulder once more before releasing her.

Ess was headed for the cook tent when she saw Durgen heading there. The knot that had settled in her stomach while she talked with Stockwell effectively killed her appetite.

The thundercloud on Durgen's face, the snapping tightness of his stride, caught Ess's attention. She shuddered, wondering what had set the man off now. Jasper had remarked a few times over the last week that Durgen was angry -- not with her, but with everyone else at the circus. He spent most of their time together holding her a little too tightly, and when he kissed her he seemed angry. Ess had noticed bruises on Jasper's upper arms a few times and blamed Durgen. She hadn't been sure what to do about it, other than mention the bruises in her report to Stockwell. She doubted the circus owner had read that far in her report. He might go after Durgen with a whip, when he did.

The knot in her stomach turned cold, and gut instinct told Ess she did not want to be in the cook tent with Durgen right then. She decided to head back to her quarters and tie a handful of bullets into a handkerchief and tuck the bundle in the pocket without the hole. She just hoped she wouldn't need them any time in the near future.

Jasper let out a yelp when Ess pulled the door of their quarters open. The lantern hadn't been lit, and in the dim daylight streaming through the door, Ess saw the tears glistening on her friend's face.

"Did he hit you?" she demanded, and leaped into the car, leaving the door hanging open. She wrapped her arms around Jasper and didn't care who saw them.

"Nearly," Jasper admitted through gulps that fought back sobs.

"Promise me." She grasped the other girl's shoulders and made her look her in the eye, just as Stockwell had done just a short time before. "Promise me, if he ever raises a hand to you, you don't wait for him to hit. You take a knife to his gut. You hear me?"

Jasper went stone still, eyes wide, the tears stopped for a moment, not even breathing. Then she closed her eyes and swallowed hard and nodded. Ess pulled her close again and rocked her. The rain came down then, pulling a gray curtain around their cramped quarters. She decided in that moment she would never spend another winter in the southern part of the country ever again. Seasons needed to be more defined. Winter required snow, not constant rain and chilly winds and everything gray. At least in a northern winter, the sun came out.

As the rain thundered down harder, Jasper gained the courage to speak. Halting, stopping sometimes to swallow or rub her eyes, she told Ess about her argument with Durgen. He insisted that it was time for them to run away. Time for her to stop being a child, put skirts on, and act like a woman. His woman. If "that old fool" was going to get in their way, then they should leave. Durgen had errands to run, to get back what Stockwell owed him, "even the score," and then they would leave. When Jasper hesitated, frightened by the fire in his eyes, his venom toward her grandfather, Durgen shoved her hard against the wall of the boxcar where they had been talking. He bent down so their noses touched and snarled for her to stop being a baby and choose.

"And if you're as smart as you think you are, you'll choose me and get out with your skin whole," were his parting words as he stomped away.

"Your skin whole?" Ess shuddered. If that didn't prove Durgen was there to hurt Stockwell, she didn't know what would.

"I'm an idiot." Jasper sounded steadier now. "How can he love me if he hates my grandfather like that? What does he think he's owed?"

"Has he said yet that he loves you?"

Jasper's silence was all the answer she needed.

"You listen to me." Ess sat back, judging that Jasper wasn't going to dissolve into sobs, that the crisis moment had passed. Time to start thinking hard and mount a good defense. "Durgen was just playing with you, to spy on Stockwell and hurt him. Yes, he was," she hurried on, when Jasper shook her head. At least her eyes didn't fill with tears again. "I know he was, because Stockwell asked me to follow him, and Durgen went into town every day and passed messages along."

Jasper's utter stillness proved she was thinking hard and fast.

"Tell me," she finally said.

The rain stopped and the sun had come out by the time Ess finished telling Jasper everything she had seen while following Durgen around for the last week. Even if the sun wasn't bright, it was brighter than it had been for the past three days. Ess dared to hope the puddles might start to dry up. She thought about lighting the lamp and closing the door, so she and Jasper could keep talking in privacy.

"What's wrong?" Jasper asked, when Ess shuddered at the next thought that came to her.

"He's going to come looking for you once he calms down. When did he tell you to be ready to leave?"

"Tonight." She wiped away the last few tears. "I'm not waiting for him to come look for me. At least he stays away from me if he thinks I'm with

Grandfather."

"Then that's where we're going."

Stockwell wasn't in his train car office. Ess had hoped he would wait until the weather cleared before going to town to telegram Sutter. Why did they have to be so far away from Washington? What if Durgen had contacts in town and they interfered with the telegram, or even told Durgen Stockwell was sending for help? Even if he used code words, a telegram sent to Washington would raise a red flag for Stockwell's enemies.

Ess made Jasper promise she would stay there in the office and not come out, even if Durgen stood outside and bellowed loud enough to shake the car off the rails. That earned a weak grin from her friend. Ess checked that her derringer was set in its holster as she hurried across the circus camp, praying Stockwell was still there. She checked with Bascomb, head of the roustabouts, then the men walking the horses outside, now that the weather was clearing. One of them thought he had seen Stockwell with the Countess. Ess ran to the Countess's car. No one there, but as she left, Gus hailed her, and when she asked, he said the Countess and Stockwell had left maybe twenty minutes before.

"Decided to go to town, take advantage of the nice weather while it lasts," the engineer said.

Ess thanked him and headed across the open area between the cook tent, the exercise ring, and the practice tent. What should she do now? Go to town after Stockwell? He had the two-man gig. Maybe she could talk Bascomb into loaning her one of the performing horses. Her bareback skills meant she wouldn't have to waste time saddling the horse. Anyone watching might even assume she was taking the horse out for more exercise. Maybe if she rode fast enough, she could catch up to Stockwell and the Countess before they got to town.

"You," Durgen growled, emerging from the cook tent as Ess skirted around it.

She ducked, sensing the hand reaching for her arm before she saw it. Not fast enough. His hand caught hold of her shoulder with bruising force, then she smelled him. The combination of sour sweat, beer and something she could only identify as dirty salt was unique to the big, scowling man.

"Where is she?" Durgen said, yanking Ess around hard enough her boots tried to slide out from under her in the mud. She shoved away hard, willing to land in the mud rather than fall against him.

"Where is who?" She staggered, catching herself before she fell. Several people out in the open looked up, pausing in their errands. Gus stopped on his way to his tent and looked back at them.

"Where is Jasper?" He reached for her again.

"You leave Jasper alone. Stockwell told you not to talk to -- talk to him." She nearly laughed at the close call, referring to Jasper as "her." Her friend would not appreciate that slipup at all.

"He's not here." Durgen sneered.

"Leave the boy alone," someone called from behind Ess.

"Mind your own business!"

Others drew closer, some of them jumping in, telling Durgen to leave Ess alone. His response was to curse at them. When Ess tried to back away, mistakenly believing the big man was distracted, he lunged, grabbing at her again.

"Leave the boy alone!" Gus shouted, stomping through the growing crowd. His big boots spattered mud.

"You're all idiots!" Durgen caught hold of Ess's shirt by collar and front buttons and yanked hard, pulling in opposite directions.

The material tore with a shriek. She nearly choked, fighting not to echo the sound. Gus and two other men leaped on Durgen, wrestling her free of the man's grasp. Ess staggered back, pulling the shreds of her shirt up into place, but all she felt under her fingers was the material of the corset. She couldn't seem to do anything but stand there, arms crossed over her chest. Technically, she was still decently clothed, but she felt naked, and growing more naked by the second as everyone's gaze seemed to land on her.

"What is that?" Wilcox, another of the roustabouts, stared at Ess. He barely noticed when Durgen shoved him hard enough to make him stagger, sliding in the mud.

"That's a girl," Durgen said with a sneer, followed by a stream of filth describing Wilcox's family defects.

"You just figured that out?" Gus startled Ess's brain back into motion with a bellow of laughter. He winked at her when she turned and stared at him.

"You big, smelly, drunken bully." Glenda, one of the trapeze artists, stomped through the ring of onlookers and flung her shawl around Ess. "If you don't like a girl dressing as a boy, you take it up with the boss, you don't go ripping off her clothes."

"You knew?" Ess whispered. Glenda winked and put an arm around her.

"Admit the big idiot saw what the rest of us missed? Not on your life," she whispered.

Durgen stomped toward her, reaching again for Ess, spilling curses, but Gus and several others came between them, forcing him to stop. Durgen's cursing grew louder, until his voice cracked and he actually went silent, his face going dark red. Others weren't so silent. Ess was relieved that some actually laughed, a few were astonished, but didn't seem upset. She should have known circus people would be far less stuffy than other people at the revelation that a boy was actually a girl in disguise.

"Jasper is a girl!" Durgen barked. He lashed out, lunging at Bascomb when he laughed.

"Most of us know," Gus said. "And we don't much care. She's a good worker, and she must have a good reason for hiding."

"Did you know she's Stockwell's granddaughter?"

That struck everyone silent.

Ess pulled free of Glenda. The acrobat woman let her take the shawl with her. Ess watched Durgen, who fortunately seemed to be glaring at everyone but her. She felt sick to her stomach as she backed away, trying to still her spinning thoughts enough to plan what to do next.

She couldn't push her mind past the last three words he had said. Again: How did Durgen know? Jasper swore she had never told him. Was that proof Durgen worked for the enemy? If he knew Jasper was Stockwell's granddaughter, maybe he knew Stockwell's real name.

Ess ran for the horses trotting around in the muddy, makeshift corral, disturbed by the shouting. She fumbled with the shawl, tying it around herself so she was decently covered. Her hands shook a little, but she managed to grab the top bars and vault over the barrier. Misty, her favorite of the ring horses, trotted up to her. Ess pulled herself up onto the horse's back and nudged her toward the gate. Kicker, one of Gus's apprentices, shouted her name and swung the gate open just before she had to slow Misty and turn her to handle the latch. She thanked him with a salute and then wove her fingers through the coarse mane of her mount. All that mattered now was catching up with Stockwell. She prayed Durgen didn't realize she had fled on horseback to look for the circus owner. More important, she prayed he wouldn't find Jasper before help could come.

She had barely come around a bend in the road, a large stand of trees hiding the circus grounds from sight, when a man on horseback crashed out from among the trees in front of her and out onto the road. Ess nudged Misty hard, yanking on her mane to get the horse to swerve out and around him. He shouted, waving his arms as she passed him -- and calling her Joshua. She nearly lost her balance as she turned to look at him.

"Tucker?" She shook her head and faced forward. That couldn't be one of Sutter's men. Could it?

"Slow down there, lad," Tucker said, his voice rattling as his horse galloped up alongside Misty. "What's the brouhaha you left behind?"

"Sutter put you on guard?" She hooked her thumb behind herself, barely waiting for the agent to nod. "Durgen is on the warpath. I need to tell the boss -- I need to get him back there, before Durgen kidnaps his granddaughter."

Tucker's usually smiling face darkened and he concentrated on the road ahead of them as the two horses raced side-by-side. Then he nodded. "Three more of us on duty. I'm going back -- you warn Stockwell." He saluted her before yanking up hard on the reins and turning his horse in a wide arc. Ess found it hard to breathe for a moment. She blamed the momentary misting in her eyes on the wet wind slapping her in the face.

Chapter Eighteen

When Ess reached town, Stockwell and the Countess were still sitting in the gig. She guessed from the way he gestured, pointing out different storefronts and other buildings up and down the street, they were planning their route. Her throat closed up, so she couldn't have shouted if she wanted. Then a moment later, as Stockwell turned and looked right at her and rose from the driver's seat -- meaning he recognized her on Misty -- she decided it might not be wise. Who knew if Durgen's contact here in town wasn't waiting, wasn't ready to take action at the first sign of trouble? The Southerners seeking revenge might be here in town right now, gathering enough manpower and firepower to attack.

Stockwell stepped down from the gig and took a few steps to meet her as she brought Misty down to a trot. He reached up and caught hold of the horse's forelock as she came to a stop.

"Durgen's on the warpath." Ess swallowed hard. Her voice sounded like it was made of sand. "He's got Jasper scared to death -- wants her to run off with him. She's hiding in your office. Don't know how long that'll hold. He's bellowing all our secrets."

"All?" Stockwell's eyes turned cold and glittering in his weathered face.

"Everybody knows we're girls, and he told them she was your granddaughter."

The Countess swore, an elegant, long string of French and Spanish and German, and other words Ess didn't recognize, but she was pretty sure they were poisonous, too. When Stockwell gestured, Ess slid down off Misty's back. He swung up in her place. He barely reacted when Ess told him about Tucker and three more agents, sent by Sutter to keep guard. Stockwell nodded to the Countess and some silent communication passed between them. In moments, he was racing down the road on Misty.

The Countess demanded all the details as she and Ess turned the gig around and headed back down the road to the circus camp. It didn't take long, and for half the ride they were both silent, pushing the horses to run faster. The thudding of the horses' hooves and the harsh bellows of their breathing seemed to fill the world.

Few people were visible when Ess and the Countess came through the gates, and no one seemed to notice as the two of them careened through the mud. Maybe that was because everyone was running, or at least walking quickly, away from the public area of the circus grounds.

"Waste of time," the Countess muttered as she reined the horses to a stop. "Where is Jasper?" She shook her head. "You already said. She is our priority.

Let Stockwell take out the trash."

They ran around the outside of the circus community, to avoid attracting attention. Ess half-expected Durgen to jump out of the shadows and grab hold of her, shake her, and demand to know where Jasper was. She was oddly disappointed when they reached the door of Stockwell's train car and found the door closed and no one in sight.

Gunshots erupted maybe fifty yards away, with several other cars between them and the noise. Men shouted and cursed, several women screamed, and there was the sound of running feet and loud thuds of large objects, perhaps even bodies, banging into even larger objects.

"Idiots," the Countess said as she jumped up the first two steps to the landing in front of the door. She turned the door handle and pushed, and it stayed closed. She pushed again as Ess climbed up behind her. Three sharp knocks on the door -- no response.

"It's me," Ess called through the door

"Oh, yes, that's clear as mud," the woman said under her breath.

"Your grandfather's dealing with Durgen right now. You're safe. I have the Countess here with--"

The door swung open, hard enough to bang hard against the wall. Jasper grabbed hold of them both by their wrists and pulled hard, so they stumbled through the door. Ess managed to grab hold of the door handle and fling it closed.

Jasper didn't cry, but she clung to the Countess. The woman wisely said nothing, just led the girl back to the couch where it was apparent she had been curled up, waiting, probably hearing too clearly all the noise and uproar outside. Ess saw a snowstorm of salt water taffy wrappers on the floor. More gunshots rang out, still sounding far enough away that she didn't worry too much about a bullet coming through the window at any time. The three of them stayed away from the windows. All the shades had been pulled down, and only a small lantern was lit.

Ess leaped up when a thought occurred to her. She turned the shield on the lantern so only a thin line of light escaped, and handed it to the Countess. Jasper let out a little cry when she walked over to the closest window and tugged up on the thin rope controlling the shade, but the Countess hushed her. They waited while Ess went around the car, checking the locks on all the windows.

"Very smart," the Countess murmured when Ess came back and sat down on the edge of the long couch with them.

"Didn't think of that," Jasper admitted, her voice raspy. Had she been crying this whole time?

Ess admitted she felt a little disappointed. Jasper was older than her, and she thought the older girl had more sense than that. Then again, Jasper had been fooled by Durgen, and up until the last week, had every reason to believe he was wonderful.

The sound of excited, alarmed voices, men and women, broke into her thoughts. Ess got up and went to the door. The Countess and Jasper stood, but didn't say anything. Ess gestured at the lantern and the Countess picked it up and turned the shield, casting a little more light across the train car. The voices drew closer, and footsteps became clear, slopping through the mud and gravel and then crunching through the cinders surrounding the tracks. Ess jammed her hand into her pocket and through the hole, drawing the derringer. Jasper let out a little gasp and Ess glanced over her shoulder at the two of them. The Countess nodded, and her smile seemed grimly satisfied, through the shadows.

"Joshua! Open up," Tucker shouted.

Ess reached for the lock. "He's a friend -- Secret Service," she hurried to add, forestalling the protest she could almost feel sticking in Jasper's throat. She flung the door open and stepped back as men leaped up the stairs.

They cradled Stockwell between them. The smell of gunpowder was strong, and blood, and oddly the stink of lubricating oil and scorched metal. Ess stepped back out of the way. She recognized Pucket. The other two men were dressed like him and Tucker, in long, mud-smeared dusters and high boots, with rifle holsters across their backs and pistols at their hips and the grimy look of men who had been camping in the open in the rain. However, they were total strangers to her.

Gus and McTavish, his right-hand man, bustled into the car, along with several others, all jabbering and shouting. Doc Simpson limped up to the door of the train car just as the traffic cleared and Ess was about to shut it. He winked at her and hauled himself up the steps, his mechanical ankle and foot creaking louder than ever in the damp weather.

By the time Ess had the door locked again and turned around, they had Stockwell stretched out on the couch Jasper and the Countess had been using. The circus owner was conscious, and seemed to be struggling to get his own coat and shirt off. Now that she had a chance to look at him more than once, Ess thought his only injury was to his upper arm. It looked more like a deep gouge from a bullet through the meaty part of the upper arm. Lots of blood, but she didn't see any fragments of bone. Damage to the bone was always a bad thing, from what she had heard.

A shrieking of gears cut through the voices, different people calling orders and asking questions. Gus stepped up and pushed aside Jasper and two other people. Everyone froze, and a few people, including Doc Simpson, took a step back when Stockwell's leg stiffened and pivoted up a good six inches off the couch and vibrated, then bent and tried to kick, then slammed down into the cushions.

"Help me, Mac," Gus said, and threw himself down across Stockwell's leg. That action muffled the shrieking and grinding of gears and springs.

Then Ess understood -- Stockwell's clockwork leg was malfunctioning.

"Where's his toolkit?" she said, yanking Jasper out of the way.

Pulling her away from the odd sight of Gus and McTavish fighting with Stockwell's leg seemed to help Jasper. She looked around as if she had forgotten where she was, then dove at one of the drawers underneath a window seat. She pulled it open and Ess snatched up the leather satchel, something like a doctor's house call bag.

"Good lad," Gus grunted, when Ess dropped the kit down on the floor next to him. "Trade with me." He pressed down hard on Stockwell's leg just below the knee. "Sit."

Ess landed as hard as she could, pressing her bottom into the column of the mechanical leg. McTavish had hold of his ankle and foot and was sitting on the floor, pushing down with all his weight. Gus pulled out a screwdriver in one hand and needlenose pliers in the other.

"Someone slit his pants," Gus ordered.

"Got it," Stockwell said, and slid his knife from the sheath at his hip with his left hand. In moments, cloth shrieked and he exposed the cuff that the stub of his leg slid into, to hold the mechanical leg in place.

Ess tried not to stare, but the harness of wide, soft straps and buckles that fastened around Stockwell's waist and then attached to the cuff fascinated her. With the cloth torn out of the way, the sounds of springs breaking and gears breaking off their teeth was even louder. Gus dove in, prying up panels and yanking wires and springs and gears. He worked in a frenzy, tossing aside whatever he pulled out, until with a shriek of tortured metal ending in a crack-snap-click, the tension rattling through the leg died.

"May I have at my patient now?" Doc Simpson said, breaking the sudden, overwhelming silence that enfolded them all.

McTavish let out a crackling chuckle and levered himself up off the floor. He offered a hand to Ess, and Gus held out a hand to her, and both men pulled her to her feet.

"Hold on a second there, Doc," Stockwell said. He slit his pants further, revealing the large buckle on his hip, which proved to hold most of the harness together once he had unfastened it. "Sorry about ruining your Christmas present," he added, baring his teeth in a grimace for Jasper.

"Oh, Grandpa..." she moaned, and dropped down to the floor next to him. Her mouth trembled too hard to let her smile last more than a few seconds.

Tucker and Pucket and the other two agents retreated to the doorway, while Gus and McTavish got the mechanical leg off and unceremoniously dumped it on one of the quilts Jasper had been wrapped up in a short time ago. Ess kept herself busy gathering up the scattered bits of gears and springs and other pieces of metal Gus had tossed aside. The first rule the inventor/engineer had taught her was never to waste anything, no matter how damaged.

"This ought to keep us busy for a while," Gus announced, as he and McTavish bundled up the pieces of leg and got out of the doctor's way.

Jasper held onto Stockwell's good hand. She looked utterly miserable, but Ess was proud of her friend that she didn't blubber and wail and call attention to herself.

"Before we do anything else, who can be trusted and who can't?" Tucker said, beckoning for Ess to come over with him and the other three agents.

"Pardon me," Gus said, frowning at the four strangers, as if he had just begun to wonder what they were doing there.

"Gus, these are Agents Tucker and Pucket of the Secret Service," Ess hurried to say. "I'm sorry, I don't know you two, but if Sutter sent you, then…" She shrugged.

"Secret Service, huh? My, what company you do keep, lad." He winked. "Or should I say 'lass,' now?"

"Please, Gus…" Ess cringed, dreading seeing the look of comprehension on the agents' faces.

"Right. More important things going on right now."

"What about Durgen? Did you catch him? Did he actually shoot the boss in his mechanical leg?"

"Someone else did it," the shorter of the unnamed agents said. "Popped up from behind the colonel," he nodded at Stockwell, "and hauled out a rifle while Reese and Pucket wrestled Durgen to the ground."

"But you got him?"

"Bascomb has him trussed up tighter than a stallion about to be gelded," Doc Simpson called out as he finished washing up the gouge in Stockwell's arm. "Someone should have tried that tactic to cool his temper years ago."

That acerbic comment earned snorts and grins from most of those present. Tucker started by explaining that Ess -- still referring to her as Joshua -- had been sent to stay with the circus partly to hide her, but partly to keep an eye on Stockwell. The Secret Service had been alarmed from the moment Ess included Durgen in her report, mostly because of the inconsistencies in the few records there were relating to the man. When Sutter sent his last letter to Stockwell, he had assigned the four agents to keep watch, until they had a definitive decision on Durgen, who he was or wasn't.

"It's not over, now that we have him," Stockwell said, after discussing the lunatic game of Hide'n'Seek with Durgen and his unknown ally in the mud and rain among the tents and train cars. "Durgen's contacts in town have to know by now what's happened here. Can't hunt them down without making more noise and fuss. Just spreads."

"Begging your pardon, Colonel," the agent who had been silent until then said. "We can't let them spread the word you're still alive. They'll just keep hunting."

"Can't stay with the circus. Whoever was backing up Durgen has probably gotten to town by now. Short of cutting the telegraph wires, not hell of a lot we can do." He patted the hand Jasper had kept on his good arm the whole time Doc Simpson worked on his wound. "Sorry, Junebug. Gotta fly again."

"It's all my fault," Jasper whispered.

"Stuff and nonsense," the Countess said.

"That's the problem with civilization," Doc Simpson offered. "If we were still at war -- heck, those lunatics are still fighting the war -- but if our old unit was still together, we'd have no problem riding out and hunting them down." He finished cleaning up the detritus of his doctoring and stood, wiping his hands on a towel tucked into his belt. "Civilization just gets in the way of doing what needs doing. In war, people knew why we were fighting, and they knew what side they were on. Made things simple. Easier to find who was against you before they even started shooting at you."

"The problem with civilization," Stockwell said, sitting up and wincing a little when he put pressure on his bandaged arm, "is that a lot of people become casualties who don't even know there's a battle. Only a few of you here know what's behind all this ruckus--"

"We're starting to guess," McTavish grumbled.

"You're safer if you don't know." He frowned and glanced toward one of the closed windows.

Ess heard running feet in the cinders and gravel, then a skidding sound and a thud just before someone banged on the door at the end of the car. Several voices shouted, and there was the sound of more people running to the car. She couldn't make out what they were saying. Gus swore and threw himself at the agents standing in front of the door. They parted barely in time and let him out. Obviously, he understood.

"Stay here," McTavish barked, catching hold of Ess and pulling her up on her tiptoes to look him in the eye.

"What's happening?"

"The boiler. Some hellfired fool has jammed the boiler."

Then everyone fled, including Doc Simpson. Tucker looked back once and nodded to Ess. He held up one of his guns, making as if he would toss it to her. She drew her derringer. He gave her a grim smile and pulled the door closed.

"Lock it!" he shouted as he ran with the others to deal with the new crisis.

Silence filled the car. Ess settled back from the door and lit another lantern so she would have light to see by as she checked her derringer's load, then pulled out the extra ammunition and set it up on a table next to her, where she could get at it faster and easier than from her pocket.

"First thing you should do," Stockwell said, breaking the silence inside the car that seemed to muffle the shouts and alarm bells on the other side of the circus grounds, "is change the name."

"Name of what?" Jasper asked.

"And start all over again, building our reputation from scratch?" the Countess said. She pulled over a chair from the desk on the opposite wall and settled in squarely where she could face him. "I don't think so."

"With everything happening here today--"

"My dear man, scandal and rumor and the curiosity of the crowds will only be good for us. There is nothing you can do to a circus' reputation to hurt it -- unless the ugly rumors are true, of course." She snorted and gestured to wave away the very thought.

"You're giving her the circus?" Jasper's voice cracked. "I'm so sorry! I was so stupid--"

"You were not, and I don't want to hear you berate and blame yourself any further, do you hear me?" The Countess waited, holding Jasper prisoner with her gaze until the girl seemed to calm a little bit, then nodded. "Very good. You are a good-hearted child, and you were deceived. You were used. Durgen is a scoundrel of the lowest sort, along with those cretins who insist on punishing your grandfather for doing his duty to his country. If it were against the law to believe in love, to want to fall in love, where would our world be today?"

Jasper had no answer for that. Ess stood guard, moving from window to window, peering out through thin gaps in the blinds, keeping her gun ready. She found some comfort in the fact that the voices didn't get any louder and she couldn't hear the piercing shriek of escaping steam, meaning the boiler was not yet ready to explode. As the minutes crept past, Stockwell and the Countess conducted their business, following through on arrangements they very obviously had discussed years ago. Jasper acted as their hands and feet, fetching papers from various drawers, moving a small table over so they had a surface to write on, preparing pens and finding an inkwell.

"What's that?" Jasper said, in the quiet after the multiple sets of documents had been signed.

The Countess looked up from blowing on her signature and frowned, then tipped her head to one side. Ess thought the voices had grown louder on the far side of the circus grounds.

A gunshot rang out. Without thinking, she flung the door open and went to her knees, taking shelter behind the half-wall around the platform, and searched in every visible direction. The tents and train cars blocked all sight of whatever was happening in the engineering tent. She couldn't see any flashes of light, no sign of flames or explosions. So what was happening?

The car jolted underneath her. Ess braced herself on the guardrail and looked down. Gravel and cinders rolled out from under the end of the train -- no, she adjusted her perception -- the train car was moving.

More gunshots rang through the thickening darkness, answered a moment later by a rumble of thunder.

"Is the train in danger?" Jasper asked, coming to the doorway and getting to her knees to stay down behind Ess. "They're moving the train to get away if the boiler explodes?"

That made sense, and yet it didn't.

"They would tell us," Stockwell said. He swung his good leg and his stump over the side of the couch, and swept all the signed, half-dried documents into a stack, then handed them to the Countess. "Get our girls off the train now."

The Countess only hesitated a moment, regret flickering across her face. She unbuttoned her blouse and slid the signed papers in between her waistband and corset, then buttoned up again as she turned, snapping out orders to Jasper. Ess stood to step back into the car and the next moment fire streaked across her cheek. Jasper screamed and pulled her into the car. Ess raised her hand to the stinging line across her cheekbone and it came away bloody.

That was a bullet.

Ess's knees tried to fold, and buzzing filled her ears. She watched stupidly as Jasper pulled a crude-looking wooden leg and cuff from a long drawer under a window seat and handed it to Stockwell. The Countess gathered up jackets and emptied papers from Stockwell's desk into a sack.

"Come along, girls." She gestured at the door, then stopped, frozen, with her hand pointing directly at Ess.

Another gunshot and the sound of breaking glass snapped Ess out of her stupor. The Countess went to her knees, wrapping herself around Jasper, who went down with a shriek and covered her head. Ess and Stockwell locked gazes. His pleaded, yet remained stern, even grim. She nodded and raised her gun.

"Go!" he shouted, as he struggled to get the cuff securely fastened around his stump. "Inez, please!"

The Countess pulled herself to her feet, hauling Jasper up with her. She reached back, brushing her palm across Stockwell's cheek, then stumbled for the door.

Ess swallowed hard and stepped out onto the platform, standing upright when gut instinct screamed to drop to her knees and hide. The train had doubled in speed, no longer creeping along at a foot or two per second, but yards now. Soon, it would be too fast to jump without injury. A flash of light warned her. Nerves snapping, she swung her arm around and shot blindly, even as a bullet screamed past her and ricocheted off the side of the train beyond her.

"Now, now, now!" she shouted, shooting, fighting to hold her arms steady.

Behind her, Jasper screamed and the Countess's skirts brushed against her legs and the two leaped. From the corner of her eye, Ess saw them fall down the incline on the other side of the tracks, putting it between them and the shooter. Gasping, she stumbled backwards into the shelter of the car.

"Go!" Stockwell roared as he pulled himself to his feet.

"No bullets." She staggered back to the place where she had left her ammunition. She scooped up a handful and snapped the chamber open.

Chapter Nineteen

Someday, a quiet part of her brain insisted, guns would hold more than eight bullets at a time, or there would be an invention that would attach a pre-loaded chamber to a gun. Her fingers shook as she slid the bullets into place and said a quick prayer she would live long enough to invent such a device.

"Now." Stockwell yanked her up to her feet as she snapped the chamber closed. The car rattled and swayed underneath them as they staggered together to the door.

Despite the sheets of rain now coming down, obscuring vision, they clearly had left the circus grounds behind in the time it had taken to load her gun. No gunshots rang out, forcing them back into shelter. The car bucked and swayed under them, and Ess looked down at the tracks. The ties and the cinders and mud between them flashed by in a blur.

"Too fast," Stockwell growled. He kept his grip on Ess's shoulder. Maybe he thought she would try to jump, without even knowing where she would land?

"We'll be crossing the river soon," she said, feeling as if she could breathe again as she remembered that detail. "The trestle is low to the water. I remember Gus laughing about it, asking what the railroad company thought it would do during flood season. We can jump in the water without getting hurt."

"Too fast."

"No, but the water--"

"Before we get to the river, there's a huge boulder. Whoever built the tracks here decided it was easier to put in a hairpin turn, instead of blasting and maybe changing the course of the river. We have to slow down to navigate that turn."

"So we jump off when whoever stole the train slows..."

The grimness of Stockwell's expression made her feel as if she had inhaled ice, and then she understood. Chances were good whoever had started the train had set it to increase speed, then jumped off. Maybe they were the same people shooting at whoever tried to jump off. There was no one in control of the engine. Even if she could climb up in all the wind and rain, walk the length of the car, jump down, and cross the two flatcars still loaded with equipment, then climbed over the coal car, and reach the engine, she wouldn't know what to do to slow the train. Stockwell had to know, as the owner, but he couldn't climb with that false leg. Not like he could do with his mechanical leg.

"How soon--" The car seemed to leap up underneath them and crash down again on the tracks. She clutched at Stockwell and he held onto her with one arm, grabbing hold of the doorframe with the other.

"Maybe a minute, at this speed. That was the warning bump."

"Cushions." She shoved herself away from him and stumbled across the jolting, swaying car, to snatch up the long cushion off the couch. "We have to try something!"

"Couldn't make it any worse." He offered her a grim smile and stepped past her to pull up the other long cushion. He pulled out packing straps from a crate next to the door and folded the cushion around her longwise, buffering her from hips to shoulders, wrapped the strap around her, slipped both ends into her hands. "Go!"

Ess couldn't do anything but stand there, shaking her head. The seconds ticked by with maddening speed. Stockwell cursed and wrapped the cushion around himself and held onto both ends, his arms crossed, and shoved her out the door. Ess stumbled, and for a moment her bulk caught in the opening where the steps led down. She saw a flash of lightning, the landscape lit up in blue-white, and the river stretching out ahead of them and reaching to the right. Then Stockwell roared something and pushed her and she fell, screaming.

Despite the thick cushion, which she somehow kept around herself by her fingers digging holes in the thick cloth, Ess felt every rock and bump and dip and fallen tree limb as she rolled and bounced down the incline of the tracks. Water and mud soaked into the cushion and thickened it and slowed her descent, until she rolled to a soggy, sloppy stop. Then she couldn't seem to move her arms, couldn't unbend her fingers, and wasn't at all ashamed as gasps and sobs wracked her body.

A massive explosion lit up the sky and the scream and screech and rolling banging of the train tumbling off the tracks filled her ears and made the ground shake. Shuddering, stunned silent, Ess unfolded her stiff fingers and let go of the cushion. Every bit of muscle ached and shrieked as if on fire as she sat up, shaking, and turned toward the sound.

Fire lit up the landscape as oil spilled from tanks and flames leaped from the shattered engine and the coal car continued tumbling, four more rotations before rocking to a stop. Part of the train trestle looked shattered, hit by one of the flat cars that lay on top of it, broken in half. Ess could only guess that momentum had kept it going when the heavier cars skidded off the track at the turn. She saw the monolith of the massive boulder Stockwell had mentioned. In the flickering flames that doggedly hung on despite the torrential downpour, she swore the boulder looked as if it had cracked in half.

Stockwell. Where was he? Had he gotten off the train in time?

She should get up and look for him -- but she couldn't. It took everything she had to sit and watch as the rain drowned the fire, even where oil and coal fed it. She was sitting in water. If she waited a little longer, even just to catch her breath, she thought the river would rise and catch her and sweep her away.

Would that really be so bad? Just go to sleep.

"Don't be stupid, Odessa Fremont," she scolded herself, sputtering through the water sheeting down her face.

Ess tasted salt. That made no sense. She wiped across her face, and in the flickering light from the oil fire she caught streaks of red. That was blood she tasted. Blood on her face. She was hurt, cut. Oddly, she couldn't feel the injury. The pounding of the rain probably made her numb.

"Move," she scolded herself aloud. Maybe she had hit her head hard enough to affect her thinking? Her head tried to spin and twist right off her neck as she struggled to her feet.

She staggered a few steps to the right, then corrected to the left, as the gray air turned to charcoal. She saw upright shapes moving in the darkness, weaving in and out among the streaks of watery moonlight that pierced the shredding clouds. Ess stood still, watching, feeling as if her brain was wrapped in cottonwool and the water that filled her ears and eyes and weighed down her clothes slowed every thought.

Cold horror thickened the muzzy slowness in her brain. Ess bent over, feeling as if she had been kicked in the ribs and she couldn't get her lungs to work. A whimper escaped her as she easily envisioned Stockwell lying in a crumpled heap in the mud and water and debris from the train wreck, caught between dead and alive. She should do something, but she didn't know what. Or how.

She stayed still, waiting, shivering, wanting to run, afraid to make a sound. Where was her derringer? She had put it back in its holster, under her clothes. There was an awful, aching, deep bruise on her hip where her holster belonged. She pressed her hand against the spot -- *Please, Savior, God, let that hard lump be my gun?*

Ess couldn't remember if she had any ammunition left. The dark shapes kept moving, walking past her. *Please, don't let them turn. Don't let them see me.*

She went to her knees, pressed her face into her thighs and shuddered, and bit her tongue to hold back the cries.

Light shot through the darkness, shredding it, glistening on water and mud. Ess kept her head down, trying to breathe softly, trying not to move, straining her ears. She shuddered as footsteps squelched through the mud all around her. More light spilled around her. She could feel it touch her. She saw the shadow of her hunched body.

"Joshua?" A semi-familiar male voice brought warmth to the ice in her blood. "Josh, lad. Speak to me." Then big hands caught hold of her shoulders and hauled her to her feet, lifting her up like she was nothing but a drowned kitten. Pucket grinned down at her, and another searcher came up behind him, spilling lantern light into Ess's eyes. Pucket's grin melted into a grimace, and he swept her up in his arms.

In moments, Ess found herself tossed up into the arms of someone on horseback. The galloping motion tried to turn her stomach inside out and the dizzy feeling grew stronger, until she couldn't keep her eyes open -- but closing them just made things worse. She dug her teeth into her lips to keep her mouth closed and fight the whimpers that kept rising with every breath she took -- along with her gorge. She would spew at any moment, and it didn't matter that she hadn't had anything to eat in what felt like days. The very thought of eating made her stomach knot.

Through the grayness filling her eyes, she made out lights and the blare of voices assaulted her ears. She fought as the arms released and she slid downwards. Liquid touched her lips and she choked as fire slid down her throat. She tried to twist free and hands caught hold of her.

"Hold still!" Doc Simpson's voice grated against her ears. "Listen, you have to drink -- Lad, you need to --" He muffled a curse when she managed to get her hands up and pushed away the container of fire. Glass shattered. Hands grabbed her, arms and legs and shoulders and wrists, and pressed her flat. Ess opened her mouth to shriek, and fire spilled down her throat.

She swallowed to keep from choking. It kept coming. She swallowed again and the fire went up into her nose and spilled sour-smelling liquid down her chest and oddly, the spinning slowed. Her stomach went numb in spots. The shuddering twisting her limbs relaxed.

"That's it," the doctor murmured, his voice soothing now. "Just a couple more swallows. There's a good lad."

"Not," she whispered, as the glass pressed up against her lips again. She swallowed, finally recognizing the liquid as whiskey. Warmth spread through her limbs and the spinning of the world beneath her slowed. She felt as if she would melt in another moment.

~~~~~

Ess's head ached abominably when she woke. She blamed the whiskey, until she pressed her hands against her throbbing head and felt bandages. Then she opened her eyes, and found them obscured with gauze. She lay still, trying to assess her condition. In some spots, she felt as if she had been battered to a pulp. Wherever she was, she lay on a thick mattress. The sheets were soft and smelled of chamomile soap. Or maybe that smell came from her. Shreds of the day before returned slowly through the churning of her stomach and head. Someone had washed her, because she felt clean and dry and warm.

Clean.

Holding her breath, she moved her hand under the sheet and pressed it against her hip, then ran her fingers up her side. Her corset was gone, along with her muddy, dripping clothes. She wore nothing under a thick cotton nightshirt.

Just who had undressed her, and who had uncovered her secret? Yes, Durgen had announced it, but Ess hoped her friends in the circus troupe -- her family for the last six months -- would have protected that secret.
~~~~~

"Don't be an idiot," she whispered. There was nothing she could do to change the past, no control over the reactions of others. All she could do was deal with the situation facing her now. If Sutter and President Lincoln weren't offended by her masquerading as a boy, and even seemed to find some use for her in disguise, then there had to be others who would accept her.

If they wouldn't accept her, she would just pack up and move on.

No matter her situation, she was in charge of her own recovery. Taking a deep breath, Ess pressed her arms under herself and pushed, slowly, until she sat upright. She took deep breaths, fighting the slight swimming sensation. Not as bad as yesterday, but enough to worry her. Just how badly had she bruised her brain when she hit her head hard enough to need all these bandages?

"Here, now," Tucker said. His voice came through the bandages clearly enough. Boots clomped on a wooden floor. "Take it slow and easy." His big, warm hand caught hold of hers. "Thirsty?"

"Yes." She almost nodded, but caught herself in time. Tucker let go, and a moment later she heard the soft chiming of water spilling into a metal cup. He put it in her hand and guided it to her lips. A soft moan escaped her at the blessed, sweet chill of the water filling her mouth. She hadn't realized how parched she was until a sensation nearly like ecstasy spilled through her.

Her grandmother's warnings filled her mind, so she sipped and swallowed slowly, letting the liquid soak into her mouth tissues, avoiding the jarring of sudden, cold wet in her stomach. All the time she sipped, until she emptied the cup, she felt Tucker's warm presence close by.

"Better?" He squeezed her hand before taking the cup. "Feel like eating?"

"How bad is it?" She envisioned horrible, deep cuts and gouges across her scalp and face, leaving scars like streaks of ice.

"Not as bad as we first thought. Scared Pucket of a year's growth, all that blood. And you being such a little thing."

"Not that little." If he said she was a "pretty little gal," she would... Ess wasn't sure what she would do. She had never felt so weak and helpless, not even when she was a baby. Not that she could remember that far back.

"No, you aren't." He sighed and caught hold of her hands again. "Mind telling me what your real name is?"

"You -- I'm --" She nearly asked why he hadn't looked through her journal, where she had put everything, including her name, her home, her family's names. "My name is Odessa Vivian Fremont. I'm nearly sixteen, and Sutter knows the truth about me."

"Uh huh. That explains some of the things he said when he assigned us to watch over you and Stockwell. Well, Odessa--"

"My friends call me Ess."

"Glad you still consider me a friend."

"Do you still consider me a friend?" Ess cringed at how weak, close to a sob, her voice sounded. She shook her head, and was surprised when the unwise motion didn't make her throb or feel sick again. "Where am I, and what happened last night? Is -- did they kill Mr. Stockwell? Please tell me he's all right?"

"I regret to inform you that Alexander Stockwell was killed in the wreck of his train two nights--"

"Two nights?" Ess shuddered, thinking of who had to tend her while she slept around the clock.

"And several members of the circus, who were trapped on board when it was stolen by a group of slavers trying to kidnap circus employees -- specifically young women." He pressed her hands together between his. "We're very good at lying, when it comes to protecting people we respect and admire. Starting with the colonel -- and don't even think of asking what his real name is. Dead men, and boys, as the case may be, aren't allowed to ask questions."

"So I'm dead, too?" Ess grinned when her question earned a snort from him.

~~~~~

The bandages were mostly to keep Ess's many shallow cuts covered, hold the healing ointment on them, the pressure to keep the flesh pressed together so it would heal without scarring. Doc Simpson only had to sew up four long, deep cuts. As he explained the day he unwrapped the bandages, scalp wounds bled horribly and closed up quickly. Pucket was wise to hurry her to medical help, so her many cuts were cleaned and salved, washing away the grit and dirty water that could have caused infections. If Ess had scars, they would be along her hairline, and would be easy enough to hide.

As far as anyone knew in the hundred or so miles surrounding the crash, Stockwell had died in the crash. Several members of the circus troupe who had tried to rescue him from the runaway train were either dead or had been badly injured enough to require being sent away by fast train to a hospital with the newest advances in medicine. Doc Simpson had insisted on going with the injured, and to escort his employer's body to burial.

Ess was impressed with how quickly Tucker and the other agents had taken over and how easily they fabricated a cover story that was totally believable. She tried not to resent the high-handed way in which she was swept along and moved around the country. For the first few days, she was content to stay in her bed in the hospital and sleep. It was enough for her to know Stockwell was safe, and Jasper -- who had decided to return to wearing skirts and be called Jasmine again. The great mistake she had made with Durgen had frightened her. Ess was only relieved to know that her friend and her grandfather would be safe. Sutter was coming from Washington and the four agents were charged with escorting the invalids to meet him.

From the hospital on the border of Florida and Georgia, the day after Doc Simpson left to return to the circus, the four agents spirited the three refugees west to Alabama. They stayed four days in a hospital run by a Dr.
~~~~~

Hytower, who had served in the war with Pucket and seemed to find great enjoyment in keeping secrets. Ess wasn't sure about him, but she trusted Pucket and Tucker. By the third day, she decided that despite all his winking and cryptic remarks, Dr. Hytower was a man of integrity and loyalty.

A messenger came by airship, summoning the traveling party of seven to Lexington. By this time, Ess was healed enough to be allowed to ride a horse. She could barely restrain herself from leaping up and hugging Tucker when he presented her with a set of riding clothes -- boy clothes. She wouldn't be confined in the wagon with Stockwell and Jasmine.

They made a merry party, taking their time going down back roads instead of main highways, riding from one medium-sized town to another instead of aiming for major cities. They stopped at small taverns instead of large, popular inns, and always traveled among crowds. Ess didn't understand that tactic at first. Didn't they want to avoid leaving many witnesses to their journey? She thought perhaps the numbers provided safety. Murderers might hesitate to attack when there were witnesses, and perhaps people willing to get involved and defend a fellow traveler.

"Hiding in plain sight," Tucker told her, when she asked her question, after a week of leisurely travel. "If you suspected the man you tried to kill had escaped with his life, wouldn't you expect him to be fleeing north out of your reach, as fast as he could?"

Leisurely, suspicion-killing travel included stopping to take shelter whenever the weather turned unfriendly. As they traveled north, rainy weather turned even more unfriendly, including snow and high winds. Their traveling party took advantage of enforced stops to go through shops and ask about tools and parts and tinkers and inventors, to attempt to repair Stockwell's leg. It was a work of art, a one-of-a-kind creation straight from Gus's incredible mind. The chances of repairing the leg without Gus's help were low, and Ess had been surprised when Pucket showed her the long wooden case that formerly held a small gattling gun, and opened it to reveal the dismantled clockwork leg. She even told him she didn't see how they could find anyone who could repair the leg. Then Pucket showed her the second case, holding all the spare parts -- springs and cogs and wires and winding keys and little boxes with incredible machines inside them, essentially self-winding clockworks to provide energy and motivation for the leg -- courtesy of Gus. Including multiple drawings of the leg, chronicling the prototype, and then all the changes and improvements and adaptations the inventor engineer had created through the years.

So in the evenings when they had some privacy, their party gathered around a long table, or simply spread a cloth on the ground, and they worked together to try to repair the leg. Sometimes they made progress, and sometimes they had to undo what they did the night before, and sometimes an experiment undid everything they had accomplished. Then there were the times when they would ignore the schematics Gus had given them, and create ridiculous machines that did nothing but roll around or take four steps and then bind up and explode cogs and springs. Those evenings were great fun for Ess. She hadn't realized how much she missed being able to laugh with people who knew her secrets.

~~~~~

Sutter reached Lexington before them. The Secret Service owned a farm so far from the city it could barely be considered part of it. Collins waited at a crossroads outside Lexington and escorted them around the city limits. He told them about the farm. The previous owner had retired from the Secret Service to marry and carry on his family's tradition of breeding fine horses. He had lost all four sons in the War Between the States. He ended up bequeathing the horse farm to his comrades in the Secret Service, as a place to rest and recuperate. Agents who had no homes to retire to could stay there, as long as they had a talent for horses. Collins seemed to find it amusing that eight of the most popular studs in the entire country belonged to the horse farm, and the purses won in racing took care of all the farm's expenses.

He stopped laughing after Tucker winked at Ess and rode up next to him and leaned across the gap between their horses to whisper to him. Ess stayed back with Pucket, who also grinned at her, while a fierce conversation went on between the two senior agents. Collins didn't say anything to Ess during the remainder of the ride, but he kept stealing glances at her over the next half hour or so. Gradually his disbelieving scowl relaxed into something sheepish, accompanied by a lot of head shaking. When they reached the gates of the farm, he made some comment to Tucker, dug his heels into his mount's side, and rode ahead. Ess then moved up next to Tucker.

"Well, I don't think you'll get asked to the spring dance, but he won't rip your head off, either," the agent commented, not looking at her.

"Wouldn't go anyway." She waited, watching him from the corner of her eye. When he finally gave in and looked at her, she fluttered her eyelashes at him. "No dress."

He laughed and snorted and nodded.
~~~~~

Chapter Twenty

Sutter was waiting when they came out from between two barns and approached the main house. The senior agent walked slowly up to the loading block where Stockwell brought the wagon to a stop. He snapped into a militarily precise salute, and held his parade posture until Stockwell dropped the reins, turned around in the driver's box and swung his legs over the side to slide down. He waved away the hand Sutter offered to balance him as he stepped down, so Sutter offered help to Jasmine. She still wasn't used to wearing full skirts -- granted, her newest dress was several inches too long and kept dragging and tripping her -- but she had recovered her spirits enough by this time to enjoy playing the part of "pretty but brainless chit." Ess had a hard time not laughing when Jasmine fluttered her eyelashes at Sutter and let out a trilling little giggle, and the man actually swallowed hard.

One of these days, Ess knew she would have to give up and wear skirts, at least during daylight hours. She would have to learn all the tricks that women had been using for centuries to befuddle men's minds, simply to keep them from noticing her other, less feminine activities. Common sense said to start practicing now, learning from Jasmine, who was certainly a good ten steps further down that road.

Finally it was Ess's turn to face Sutter and be greeted by him. There was something slightly satisfying about the way he searched her face when she dismounted and turned to face him. He had been concerned. She liked knowing there was someone in this world who worried about her.

Don't be a silly nit, she scolded herself a moment later. Despite his failings, Uly had to be thinking about her, feeling some guilt or worry. The same for their grandparents. They had the common sense not to be eaten up with guilt over whatever kept them from returning to her, but she knew they were worried.

Still, it was nice having that particular concerned person actually in front of her, looking at her, visibly relaxing to see her on her feet.

"I don't know if I should be relieved you're not a mass of scars, or worried," the agent said. That earned a squeak from Jasmine and a bark of laughter from Stockwell.

"You are not making that girl one of your couriers," the former circus owner said. Interestingly, most of his tone contained amusement, despite his attempt at a scowl and scolding. "Hasn't she earned a rest?"

"Courier?" Ess said, instantly interested. "What benefit would scars give me?"

"Helping in your disguise." Sutter waved away the questions ready to spill off her tongue. "Colonel, Miss Ambercromby," he winked at Jasmine when she let out another squeak. "Miss Fremont."

Ess guessed that Ambercromby was Jasmine and Stockwell's real name, since Sutter used her real name.

"Why don't we get all of you settled, and then have a war council over dinner?" He gestured at the main house, which looked big enough to house the entire population of the Academy, including the housekeeping staff and all the teachers.

Ess was delighted to discover that the main house had the latest conveniences -- including indoor plumbing. What a luxury, to fill a tub with steaming hot water pumped up to her room on the third floor by pipes, and know that no one had to haul the huge metal cans of water -- even if just from a dumbwaiter at the end of the hall. Even better, opening a stopper in the bottom of the tub would let that water pour down another pipe. No chance of spilling the dirty water on the floor, and no one assigned to the messy, unpleasant task. While she relaxed in a tub full of thick, lemon-scented bubbles, she decided part of the reasoning for such luxury was to provide the ultimate privacy. There was no excuse for anyone to come into a room on errands.

Sutter had announced that everything they would need had already been furnished in their rooms, so Ess hadn't bothered to explore her room before taking advantage of the bath. When she got out, dripping and glowing and feeling truly warm and clean for the first time in what felt like months, she wrapped an enormous bath towel around herself and left footprints from the bathing room -- each room had its own bathing room and toileting closet -- to explore the wardrobe. To her amusement and satisfaction, Sutter had provided her with several suits of clothes, both male and female. What sort of message was the agent sending her by giving her a choice? Perhaps she was to give him a message by her choices?

When she finished dressing, Ess found someone had slid a folded piece of paper under the door. She picked it up and opened it, read the two short lines. With the growing howl of an incoming storm, she had no way of knowing if anyone had knocked when they brought the note, or how long the sender had been waiting for her response.

She decided right then she would enjoy staying at the horse farm, for as long as it was necessary. The note asked her to come downstairs and help with final preparations for dinner. There were no hired servants, for security purposes, so everyone who stayed at the farm was expected to help with chores.

A strange pressure developed in her chest as she hurried to put on her boots and slide down the back stairs to the kitchen. Ess missed helping Hilda in the kitchen at home, teasing with Peggety. She had enjoyed running and fetching for her grandmother when Matilda took it into her head to experiment with the cuisine of other countries and cultures, and create a feast.

Jasmine had spent time helping in the cook tent at the circus, so she wasn't lost in the massive kitchen that was almost as large as the cooking tent. She had opted for trousers, just like Ess. Had Ashmore done the shopping for them? Ess found she missed the agents who had become her friends during that short adventure in Springfield.

"What you need is someone you belong to, who won't go away or who you don't have to leave," Jasmine remarked, when Ess confessed that thought to her, during a short time they were alone in the kitchen.

Collins had kitchen duty, and two agents who were assigned long-term to the horse farm, named Denton and Kitchell, along with their wives. As soon as Ess realized there were women on the farm, she revised her theory about who had provided their wardrobes. Mrs. Denton and Mrs. Kitchell were older ladies. She hadn't considered Secret Service agents being allowed to marry. Didn't they travel all over the country, constantly on the move, putting themselves in danger to protect the president and other government officials? How could they find women who would put up with constant absences?

Ess knew better than to ask such questions. At least, not until she had gotten to know the women better. She found them to be friendly, with good senses of humor. Maybe a woman married to a government agent had to have a sense of humor, or suffer from constant nerves. The seven of them served up an enormous meal in no time. Jasmine had been assigned to set the table, and Ess wondered what had taken her friend so long until they started ferrying the bowls and platters down the short hall to the dining room. Then she understood. The table was long enough to serve as a boarding school dinner table, with seating for at least twenty people. Jasmine was still pouring water into glasses when Ess came in, pulling a wheeled cart behind her.

Someone had set off a signal, because the rest of the inhabitants of the farm came into the dining room and helped unload the carts. Ess noted the somber expressions on Stockwell's and Sutter's faces and wondered what plans the men had been making. Sutter was likely in charge of Stockwell's and Jasmine's safety, perhaps creating new identities, finding them a new home and safe place to live. Would she have a new job waiting for her, as well?

Dinner conversation was pleasant enough, with the inhabitants giving the newcomers an idea of the surrounding area. Recommendations for a church to attend, amusements such as regular dancing parties, the largest lending library in the state, ladies social clubs, reading clubs and other activities. Ess and Jasmine traded glances, and she could tell her friend was thinking the same thing: Getting involved in the social life around Lexington, making themselves familiar, becoming known faces... was not safe.

Unless Sutter was planning on them settling there? It could be vital for their safety to become known and familiar, so they were part of the community and everyone would naturally look out for them.

Ess fought down the slowly growing sense of being trapped that tried to steal away her appetite. She could not, she would not, sit still in one place. She still hadn't found any clues to her brother's route when he had vanished from their home. As soon as the Pinkertons located Uly, even if it was just a cold, fading trail, she had to be ready to move, to chase him down. She needed her brother.

As the meal progressed, talk finally turned to plans for the future. Ess's theory was halfway correct. Stockwell and Jasmine would be staying at the horse farm, to run it and create a stronger sense of identity and continuity for the people living in the surrounding area. With the rebuilding of the nation, people were moving back into the area. Families were reclaiming ancestral farms. Fields that had lain fallow for years were being planted. With the advent of airships for travel and for civilian purposes rather than just military transport, aerial surveillance and security work, affluence was rising. People expected to see their neighbors more often than at social events, and they would notice if the faces at the horse farm changed too often.

As of that night's dinner, Stockwell was known as Colonel Bramwell and Jasmine was to be Jessica Bramwell. She was his great-niece, granddaughter of his brother, and their family had been wiped out in the influenza and cholera epidemics that had swept the country in the wake of the war. Stockwell would simply be known as the Colonel. He would be a Navy man who had lost his leg during an explosion of an ironclad in the early days of the war, soon after the South had fired on Fort Sumter.

"What about Ess?" Jasmine-Jessica asked, when her and her grandfather's new histories and identities had been thoroughly discussed and agreed upon. The Kitchells had made a quick trip into the kitchen for a lovely pudding made with dried fruit and mounds of sweetened whipping cream.

Several agents actually looked around the table, evidently not knowing either Ess's real name, or just the shortened version. The two girls traded grins.

"Odessa has earned some rest and recovery time, even though she is not officially a member of the Secret Service," Sutter said. "I would like to employ you as a courier, when you're ready to take to the road again. Totally your choice."

"What does a courier do?" Ess asked, trying not to fidget when it seemed like every pair of eyes at the table focused on her. "I know what the word means, but wouldn't airships or trains or even stagecoaches be faster, more secure?"

"That's why a courier, especially one no one would suspect, works better," Collins said. "There are some things we can't discuss by telegraph, and enemies of the country will be looking for official packets and agents who look and move like agents."

"They won't pay attention to a dirty boy who comes in the back door," Ess said, easily envisioning how she could get in and out of field offices.

"You'll do much of your traveling by horseback, or riding second or third class carriages," Sutter said. "Speed isn't worth anything if security is compromised. You'll be taking reports to consolidation offices, then taking reports and evidence, photos, anything else necessary from those consolidation offices to central offices. Whatever the agents you're reporting to need you to do. Sometimes they'll ask you to sneak around back alleys and hang outside windows -- you still remember how to do that?" A smile cracked his face for the first time. "The only reliable law of our kind of work is long hours of boredom broken by minutes of panic and life-threatening danger. You might spend an entire year simply carrying papers, and then one night uncover a Resurrectionist plot to blow up Congress." He folded his arms and sat back. "What do you think?"

"It sounds like the same old thing she's been doing," Jasmine-Jessica muttered, just loudly enough for everyone at the table to hear her.

"Sir, we all know what the child has accomplished," Mrs. Denton began.

"She may look like a child, especially with dirt on her face and ragged trousers, but Odessa is not a child. Our president greatly admires her, and wishes he had a dozen plucky young ladies just like her, to confound his enemies. Until the hide-bound traditionalists step down from power -- the ones who believe the world will implode in fire and flood when women are allowed to think for themselves -- we must proceed slowly. One talented young lady at a time. In disguise. At the fringes." Despite his smile, the amusement in his voice, Sutter struck Ess as being unutterably tired. She suspected he had seen far too much in his short time of service.

"I'm in," Ess said. "As long as you keep in mind that my first priority is, and always will be, finding my brother and our grandparents. My family comes first."

"As it should be," the newly renamed Colonel Bramwell said, nodding slowly.

~~~~~

Their traveling party had reached the horse farm in February. Ess stayed, watching her cuts and scars fade and helping the Bramwells set up their new lives, until the end of March. Then she set off on a sturdy two-year-old gelding to begin her courier duties. The latest report from the Pinkertons had yielded no progress on finding Uly. It was as if her brother had vanished into thin air. Sometimes she fancied an airship had hovered over their house the night after the big ruckus in town, and people had come down on ropes, straight into her brother's bedroom, tying him up and hauling him away. No footprints. No sounds of people going down the stairs. No wagon tracks in the dust. No witnesses on the roads leading away. For all she knew, Ulysses Fremont hadn't put his feet on solid ground since that day.

It was a ridiculous theory, but it was the best she could come up with. She supposed she was lucky that the Pinkertons had learned enough about Uly's disagreement with strangers in town, and the resulting ruckus, to prove
~~~~~

that he actually had existed at one time. Without that, they would have been justified in accusing her of sending them on a wild goose chase. Or perhaps more accurately a ghost hunt, chasing a figment of her imagination.

Ess's only argument with Sutter had been over the telegram she had sent to the Philadelphia Pinkerton office and Detective Horace Winslow, and then the packet of reports that came in the mail two weeks later. Ess didn't want anyone to know, and Sutter demanded that she share everything. She felt like a fool when she finally, grudgingly, showed him the report and admitted she had the Pinkertons working for her. Especially when Sutter apologized and seemed to be somewhat embarrassed. At least he hadn't been distrustful of her. He was concerned, rather than expecting her to get into trouble.

The head agent even went above and beyond, to make up to her for their argument, by requesting information from the U.S.'s ambassadors to South America. He requested their honest assessments of the situation, their estimate of when it would be safe for United States citizens to travel, and if they had heard anything about Americans being stranded or in trouble. He specifically searched for word of any unusual activities or sightings in the area around the last known archeological expedition camp led by Earnest and Matilda Fremont. The ambassadors and their assistants were very helpful. Unfortunately, much of the information they provided simply repeated everything Ess had learned already about the situation. South America might be an unstable region of the world for another decade, maybe two. Revolutionaries had developed cannons to shoot down airships, and had small fleets of their own, to guard their borders and assault other nations or revolutionaries who didn't agree with them. The borders of various countries could change from week to week, depending on who was in power and who was able to assassinate today's leaders by tomorrow morning.

Just before Ess headed out on her first courier assignment, gathering up reports from six field offices along the Ohio River and delivering them to a paddlewheeler traveling up and down the Mississippi, Sutter sent her one more, totally unexpected, present. He had asked the Secret Service office in Cleveland to be on the lookout for Hilda. The city was growing at an exponential rate and there were many places where a widow woman could find employment. There were any number of places where she could earn a living cooking or doing laundry or looking after children. Construction sites needed cooks. Shelters for orphans needed housemothers, cooks and laundresses. Charity shelters run by churches and mission organizations were still dealing gwith the emotional and mental debris resulting from the war. Plus, there was nothing about Hilda that would make her stand out in a crowd. There were literally thousands of squarely built, white-haired women with a slight European accent.

Ess knew very little about the arrangements that Hilda and Giles had made to keep in contact, and she knew even less about where she said she was going, who she was going to contact in Cleveland. Only that they were friends of her grandparents. The only clue she had to track down these "friends" was what she had seen and overheard of the people who came to claim Darius' body. It was pitiful little, and definitely not enough for Sutter or the Pinkertons to even begin an investigation.

Part of her wished Sutter hadn't tried, because it merely solidified what she had long suspected -- until she found her brother, or her grandparents emerged from the chaos in South America, Ess wouldn't find these alleged friends. Yet when her grandparents returned, she wouldn't need to find those friends. She needed to head west, visit the places that she had heard Uly talk about, the places he had dreamed of visiting. Somewhere along the road ahead of her, she would find someone who remembered her brother. Then she would have a starting point.

She sent a note back to Sutter, thanking him, and promised to send a telegram once she had made her first delivery. If all went well, every time she made a delivery, a new assignment would be waiting for her. She would keep moving, keep in contact with the Secret Service, slip under the very noses of those who plotted against the United States of America, and have the support of people who could pull her bacon out of the fire if she ran into trouble. Other than her brother's location, what more could she want in life?

Her third night out on the road, when she had to take shelter in the burned-out remnants of a barn on a farm that had been abandoned since the war, Ess had her answer. She had burrowed into a pile of moldy hay for warmth, feeling the spray from a fierce spring storm despite the body of her horse acting as a wall between her and the weather. Waking from a dream, for a few moments she had no idea where she was, what she was doing, and a whimper escaped her lips.

"Mama?" Ess caught her breath, startled at what she had said. Then as she oriented herself to the present instead of a child's sunny memories, she gave in and wept.

What she wanted most in life was her parents. What she wanted most was to go back to childhood, and the ability to convince her parents not to leave on that archeological expedition when she was seven. The expedition they had not returned from. If only it were possible to turn back the clock or the sundial, or whatever mechanism could control time. The ability to change time, walk her life path a second time, and retain enough memories to change what had happened nearly nine years ago -- what wouldn't she give in exchange for that power? Her life would be entirely different from what she had now.

As her tears dried, Ess knew such wishing was a waste of time and energy. Still, it was a pleasant enough diversion. Perhaps she would save the concept to discuss with her grandfather someday. What would Earnest say about the idea of a machine that could change history? Would he approve, or consider it yet another piece of evidence that all of humanity was becoming even more decadent, selfish, discontented, and lazy?

Earnest and Matilda Fremont, even to regain the lives of their only son and his wife, would never condone such a mechanism.

Oddly, Ess found great comfort in such certainty.

Ess enjoyed her nomadic life. On her sixteenth birthday, she wore a dress and borrowed braids, indulged in a room in a fancy hotel, and pretended to be offended and afraid when a man in fancy dress and a thick Creole accent tried to attach himself to her. First he approached her in the dining room, attempting to convince her that no, she most certainly did not want to dine alone. Then he insulted the waiter who came to her rescue, ordering the man to go away or he would "soundly thrash" him with his cane. Fortunately, Ess had already finished her meal -- though she did want to sample the desserts on the expansive menu -- so when the bounder would not go away after being asked four times, she was free to get up and leave the room. Fortunately, there were several men in the dining room who were true gentlemen, because they intervened to stop the determined rogue from following her. At the very least, they listened to the women with them, who insisted they intervene. Ess reached the first landing, heading for her room to hide and change into her boy clothes.

Then she overheard the man loudly proclaim that she was his wife and he had every right to follow her. When he demanded all three interfering men meet him for a duel at dawn, Ess ran back downstairs. She pulled her derringer from her pocketbook. Several women screamed when she stepped into the dining room, leading with the gun. The bounder went white and his eyes bulged. He stammered and shuddered, and couldn't come up with an answer when she challenged him to tell everyone her name. Surely he would know, if she was indeed his wife. Several people laughed, and the owner of the hotel came charging into the dining room with two uniformed hotel workers. He changed his story then, insisting that while the young lady wasn't his wife, a young woman alone was looking for trouble and had no right to say no to a man who wanted to have some fun. The hotel owner apologized to Ess, to the offended ladies, and had the bounder escorted across the street to the sheriff's office.

It was an interesting evening, and within a few weeks she was able to look back on the whole incident and laugh. However, that unpleasant encounter taught Ess that unless she had a drastic, desperate need to masquerade as a woman to save her life, she would avoid skirts until it was absolutely impossible to pass herself off as a boy. No matter how enlightened society had become, especially as more philosophers and scholars declared women had the intelligence and moral fortitude to participate in the process of government, a woman alone was still considered fair game for the predators of society.

Chapter Twenty-One

Every three months, Ess stopped somewhere long enough to contact the Pinkerton office in Philadelphia and have a report sent to her. There were a few possible sightings of her brother, but the young man who answered to the description didn't use the name Ulysses Fremont, and he was always gone from the place months before the investigator came with his or her questions.

That winter, she went to Lexington and spent the long, cold months from Thanksgiving until mid-February with the Bramwells. To her disappointment, her corset finally shredded. Ess had to concede that her maturing shape didn't fit into the shape-changing garment. She and Jessica had an interesting time trying to recreate the corset, and ended up devising something that was simpler to get into, but not nearly as comfortable or satisfying.

Whether the colonel reported on this problem to Sutter or something else was happening that Ess hadn't caught onto, Sutter didn't give her quite as heavy a load of courier work, when spring came. She found several days of leisure between each delivery, when she would go to a boarding house or even find a place to sleep in the building owned by the Secret Service, and wait until a new assignment came in. She wondered if Sutter would try to give her a sedentary job somewhere, or perhaps she should take pre-emptive action and hand in her unofficial resignation for her unofficial position with the Secret Service.

At the end of May, Sutter sent a message with the man who took delivery from her of a thick bag full of reports from ten field offices. A tricky operation involving tracking a gang of train robbers known as the Blue-Eyed Gang was taking up all his time. Offices in the surrounding states were involved. He wanted her to find a place to settle down, take some time off, and lay low. She was to contact him in one month, let him know where she was, and hopefully by then he would have an assignment for her. The message came with a wad of bills, a new costume, and a new identification pendant. Ess shivered when she saw it, because she could only think of one reason for changing the badge that identified her as a courier to the directors of the offices -- the enemy had infiltrated deeply enough to understand the code, and to even know of her existence.

Her new costume was a boy's set of much-mended but clean and neat clothes, rather than the Cavalry cast-offs that suited her lifestyle on horseback, and a carpetbag to carry her possessions. Since no one would believe a boy dressed in faded, mended clothes would be riding such a fine-blooded horse, Ess had to leave her mount with the office. Anyone seeing her riding that horse would immediately accuse her of stealing it. Again, Ess shuddered, wondering if Sutter was depriving her of the horse to make her harder to find. What if the agent was lying to her, and there was no gang of train robbers to chase, he was only doing this to protect her life? Even worse, the situation was so precarious, he couldn't even trust her to defend herself?

~~~~~

Ess sent for the next report from the Pinkertons before she moved on. A telegram came back within the hour. Detective Winslow was away on assignment and no progress had been made on her case. Did she want him to contact her when he returned, or wait until the next regularly scheduled check-in? Feeling disgusted with the world in general, Ess responded that she would contact them in three months. She left town two hours later, in her new disguise, riding in the baggage car of a train. Taking the risk of being caught, or getting hurt jumping onto the train at dusk suited her mood and the disguise. She would ride the baggage car until either she got caught and thrown off the train, or she ran out of the food. Then she would get off in the next town and find work. Boys with nothing to do somehow attracted much more attention than boys who were gainfully employed. She wanted to be invisible, as much as that was possible.

With three weeks until her seventeenth birthday, Ess got off the train in Watertown. She didn't like the looks of the people who lounged around the train station. Some of them had small wheeled carts, and she imagined they were gainfully employed -- or tried to at least appear that way -- hauling people's luggage to hotels or elsewhere. No one approached her, though a few of them eyed her and her thick, battered carpetbag. She knew better than to stare back or to hurry away. Sutter had taught her that those who were the least trustworthy always suspected everyone else of evil intentions. If she acted like she had nothing to fear, those who were looking for victims would assume that meant she was armed. Which she was, but only a fool would advertise the presence of the derringer. Still, there was nothing wrong with stacking the odds in her favor. When she saw a bulletin board loaded with posters advertising hotels and saloons and other entertainment and hospitality venues in Watertown, Ess picked the name of a hotel that struck her as respectable more than ostentatious. She walked up to the ticketing booth and asked for directions to the hotel, adding that her father was waiting for her there.

From the corner of her eye, she noticed two people look away, immediately losing interest in her. So, that was the size of things, was it? Should she keep moving, or find a place to settle in and make herself one of the locals and vanish that way? It would be nice to stay some place more than three nights in a row.

Life on the road wasn't everything she had imagined. What was wrong with her big brother that he still hadn't come home yet? Despite his wanderlust and eagerness for adventure, Ess couldn't imagine Uly enjoying
~~~~~

a rootless existence. Where was he and why wasn't he home yet? Had he found a place to put down roots, or was he wandering around, looking for her? She found some amusement, slightly tinged with bitterness, at the thought that she and Uly had been passing each other, roving up and down the countryside.

"That settles it," she mused aloud as she strolled down the sidewalk made of boards, raised a good six inches above the packed dirt street. "Time for one of us to sit still and hope the other passes by. Just for a little while."

She took it as a sign that no one chased her away the moment she stepped through the gates into the stable yard behind the hotel. Ess focused on a big, graying man sitting on the back porch, watching boys currying horses and shining carriages and a couple steam-powered carriages, and approached him to ask about a job in the stables. When he didn't chase her away immediately, but leaned back and looked her up and down a couple times, Ess took that as a sign that she had made the right decision.

By nightfall, she had a bed in the loft over the parking spot for long-term guests' carriages, breakfast and dinner, and steady work pumping water for the stable, kitchen, and the vast reservoirs of hot water to service the hotel guests. The well that had seemed to promise an unlimited supply of water when the hotel was built eight years ago had run out. Management didn't want the added expense of moving the great steam-powered pump to the new well that had been sunk a good fifty feet further back on the hotel property, just in case that well gave out as well. Ess joined a relay team of five boys -- she was the tallest -- who worked the treadmill that pumped water up out of the well to fill a hundred-gallon tank. When the water settled, the boys filled buckets from a spigot on one side, and hauled the buckets to the larger tank inside the hotel basement, where the central pump sent it to the water heater and throughout the newfangled sanitary sewage system. During her first afternoon of work, Ess thought of Gus and imagined four different ways the inventor engineer would have dreamed up a simple piping system to get the water from the well tank to the hotel's reservoir.

She knew better than to say anything to anyone about it. Why deprive herself and her new co-workers of necessary income?

The other five boys weren't talkative, but they seemed friendly enough. She speculated that they were glad to have a sixth member of the team, just to take the pressure off of them. Oswald, the man who hired her and was in charge of the stables and the maintenance team, informed her that the time of greatest pressure for water was first thing in the morning when the guests awoke and wanted hot water to start their day, then in early afternoon, when the hotel did the laundry, then late afternoon when guests were washing up for an evening out on the town, and indulged in hot baths.

During her first afternoon of work, Ess observed enough to understand the hierarchy among those who worked "below stairs," as Hilda would say; the maintenance and service people who never had actual contact with the hotel guests. She marked two young men who thought they were not only important, but going places. By the mutters among her fellows on the water relay team, the two, named Buckman and Scopes, had just recently graduated from their ranks and considered themselves authorities -- meaning they had the right and the duty to harass the younger boys whenever possible. Ess set herself to watch them.

Before she finished her duty shift and Oswald dismissed the team to get some dinner, Ess had seen a great deal. What amazed her was that no one else saw what she did. Either that, or no one cared that Buckman and Scopes had made a ladder out of the fancy façade of the hotel, where slabs of stone stuck out at irregular intervals -- and using that ladder, climbed up to the windows of rooms and let themselves in. Ess saw them quite clearly from her position on the treadmill. She watched them and timed them as they climbed to a room on the third floor, then visited a room on the fourth floor, spending at least fifteen, twenty minutes in each room.

With all the air traffic nowadays from airships and buildings climbing as high as fifteen stories in some cities, Ess expected more people to look up on a regular basis. Maybe no one behind the hotel thought it worthwhile to look upward? Then she considered the boys working with her, and how they looked away and hunched their shoulders or bowed their heads when the older boys came by. Were they afraid of Buckman and Scopes?

The two burglars -- what other reason would they have for climbing into guest rooms? -- reached the ground again just as Ess and the other boys were leaving the treadmill. She walked slowly, staying behind her coworkers, and watched the two as they huddled together in a shadowy corner off the back porch, showing each other what they had in their pockets. Definitely thievery.

If Agent Sutter were here, she would go to him and tell him what she saw, and he would do something. He wouldn't doubt her for a minute. Unfortunately, Sutter wasn't here, and he would be irritated if she wasted the cost of a telegram to send for him. He would tell her to go to the sheriff about the thieves. Ess knew, as a newcomer, the sheriff wasn't likely to believe her. The word of a newcomer against young men who were known? Hardly.

"There's no excuse for not helping when you have the means and the ability," Granny Matilda would have said right about then.

Then she would shake her head, roll up her sleeves, and stomp across the yard to confront the two thieves. An elderly woman in a righteous fury could accomplish miracles. However, Ess was just a young, seemingly homeless boy. No one would listen to her. While she knew some tricks of self-defense, it wasn't wise to deliberately put herself into situations where she needed to use those skills. What could she do to make sure those two thieves didn't get away with their loot?

"Take it back," her brother said in her mind, with a ghostly whisper of his laughter.

Why not? The Countess had taught her to be an admirable pickpocket.

Ess had the plan in her head, nebulous and half-formed, even as she went down on one knee and pretended to tie her boot laces -- right in the path of the two thieves, who were still examining their loot and not watching where they were going. One stepped on her foot while the other nearly gave her a black eye with his knee. They went down and she rolled, deliberately tangling her legs up with theirs. They cursed and thrashed and took swings at her. Ess added to the noise, wailing and flailing with her arms and pulling herself upright by hanging on their clothes. That just threw Buckman and Scopes off balance, so they never noticed her hands in their coat pockets. They cursed louder -- and louder still when Oswald's loud, rumbling laughter flowed across the open yard. Buckman, the bigger of the two, clenched his fist and swung down, aiming for Ess's face. She howled louder and threw herself away from him, turning a backwards somersault. Oswald grabbed Buckman's wrist. He added to the shouting with some curses of his own and twisted the captive completely off his feet. Scopes shut his mouth and ran. Oswald flung his partner after him. Ess stayed where she had fallen on the ground, cautiously tucking the items she had pilfered into her pockets. Her actions were hidden by her curled up body.

"You all right, lad?" Oswald said, bending down to grab hold of Ess by her shoulders and haul her to her feet with one swift tug upward.

"Fine." She wrinkled up her nose and tugged her clothes straight. "Bullies like them, all they care about is making someone yell, so I yelled like they broke me worse than a china teapot." She grinned cheekily, earning a bark of laughter and a gentle cuff against the back of her head from Oswald.

The big man warned her to stay away from those bullies, then strolled up onto the hotel porch and inside. Ess waited until she was alone in the yard, then she copied the thieves' route up the uneven slabs of stone decorating the hotel wall. When she reached the first room, she could see its single occupant was a man. She left a pipe, carved from what looked like ivory, and a gold pocket watch on the trunk at the foot of the bed. In minutes, she was in the room above the first. This was visibly occupied by a woman. The other items she had liberated from the two thieves were garnet earrings, a matching pendant, and a small hand-held mirror. Why the two bullies wanted the mirror, she couldn't guess. Unless one of them had a sweetheart he wanted to give it to. She left those items on the dressing table and got out of the hotel room as quickly as she could.

Her mistake was pausing in the hotel yard to look up at the rooms she had just visited and admire her handiwork.

"Ain't she something?" Oswald startled Ess, appearing seemingly out of nowhere as she stood in the yard, looking up at the hotel.

"Something, all right." She bit her tongue against the stupidity and arrogance of the architect and builders who gave thieves an easy stairway to help them break into rooms. Then again, there was something wrong with a hotel that didn't put locks on the windows.

"We're the tallest building in the town, but I don't doubt that won't last long. Eight stories. Had to go all the way to New York to find an elevator that'd go that high. Some folks were worried the engine to lift people so high would be noisy as all get out. Not at all. Other folks were afraid we'd scare customers away and give them nosebleeds from going up so high." He clapped her on the shoulder. "You did good work today, Josh-me-lad. Keep it up, you'll have a place here as long as you want."

"Thank you, sir."

"Ah, now, no 'sir,' here. I'm just Oswald. You better get on into the kitchen before the other boys eat up all the dinner." He gave her a friendly shove between her shoulder blades.

Ess hesitated, then caught movement from the corner of her eye and saw the two bullies stomping back down the long driveway from the side street entrance. They were glaring at each other in between studying the ground in front of them. Did those two buffoons honestly think they had dropped *all* their loot? She scurried to get up onto the porch before they saw her and remembered they had tripped over her. Just because they hadn't noticed her picking their pockets less than half an hour ago, that didn't mean they wouldn't remember now when they saw her again.

She heard a baritone chuckle from the guest side of the building as she went through the kitchen door. Then a shout of anger followed from the yard. Passing by the kitchen window, she saw Scopes take a punch at his partner. She grinned as the big, red-faced chief cook ordered her to wash up "right quick," and scampered over to the massive sink. The other boys were already sitting on the long benches on either side of the trestle table where the staff ate their meals.

Oswald and two older men took care of the stables and cleaned and made repairs to the various wagons and carriages and steam carriages of hotel guests. They were still talking about the fight "those two young idiots" had in the yard, when Ess and the boys came outside and went back to work to fill the tanks for that evening's bathing needs. Common sense said until the two bullies were fired for fighting, or they were caught thieving, they would keep robbing hotel guests. Ess set herself to stay vigilant. If she could frustrate their efforts, she would be making her grandparents proud, and keep sharp the skills the Countess had taught her. She might even have some interesting stories to tell Agent Sutter when next she saw him. At the very least, she might make him laugh.

Buckman and Scopes tried again the very next afternoon. The lull when guests were elsewhere in town or relaxing in the hotel parlor or music room, and weren't in need of transportation yet, was the best time to work relatively unseen in the yard. Hotel employees were for the most part busy with their various duties. Ess watched the two thieves climb up to rooms on the fourth and fifth floors this time. She stretched a thin cord between the decorative shrubs around the foundation of the hotel, and neatly tripped the two would-be thieves as they hurried to get away from the building. They were so flustered by the laughter of the other water boys, and then so angry, busy making threats, they didn't seem to notice when Ess slid up behind them from the shadows and neatly picked their pockets.

She considered them not only oblivious idiots, but dangerously stubborn -- dangerous for their own welfare, mostly -- when she found the same garnet jewelry and mirror in Scopes' pockets, and a sealed pack of playing cards, a silver cigar case, and a small bag of silver coins in Buckman's. This time the trip up the hotel wall was even faster, because she knew her way, and she didn't have to take clues from guests' belongings to know what stolen possessions belonged where.

Buckman and Scopes took a break from their thieving for two days. Ess knew better than to hope they had given up out of frustration. However, she did find some amusement in overhearing them arguing with each other over who had dropped their loot. She curled up in her cozy hole in the stable loft and listened to the thieves argue in the main aisle below her. Part of the argument was covered by the other water team boys whispering and laughing among themselves. After the second night of arguing, the two thieves inched toward accusing each other of cheating. They didn't say it outright, but they came close to "supposing," as her grandfather called it. How soon until some common sense blew in through the gaping holes in their brains and they decided someone else was to blame?

Maybe she needed to pick up and leave Watertown and find some other comfortable place to wait until Sutter gave her new work? Maybe she should just forget about her connections with the Secret Service and focus on finding her brother? Maybe she should take the chance the press had blown the turmoil in South America out of proportion, and hop the next steamship heading south?

By this time she knew better than to ignore the gut warnings, the certainty that trouble approached. Added to the nastiness of the arguing thieves, Ess had the growing sensation of being watched as she went about her duties. Maybe she should quit and go two towns further down the train line?

The next day, when she caught the two thieves climbing over the windowsill of a room on the second floor, she limited herself to running into them with two buckets of water, picking their pockets, and tossing the confiscated loot onto a luggage cart by the front desk. The fuss raised by the discovery of the stolen items was quite entertaining. Ess waited in shivering anticipation for the fight that would break out between the two partners after she and the water team had gone to their beds in the hayloft.

Nothing happened. The two older boys never came to their abandoned stall beds. She wondered if perhaps they had argued somewhere else, maybe even got into a fistfight and made such a ruckus they got caught. Maybe they even accused each other so much, the sheriff had enough evidence to arrest them?

The next day, however, Buckman and Scopes were back in their usual spots in the yard behind the hotel, sulkily running errands, spying on guests, and trying to avoid work, as usual. That evening, they returned to the stables, but they weren't arguing. Their chortles of glee as they made their plans chilled Ess. An elderly, wealthy woman had come into the hotel that afternoon, "dripping with jewels," in the words of Buckman. Ess could almost hear the drool spilling from his mouth in anticipation. The manager, Mr. Mortimer, danced attendance on her with twice the nervous obsequiousness he gave to other wealthy guests. Ess had noticed that, but she had also noticed the way the elderly lady smiled at him and patted his hand. She heard the manager slip up and call her "Auntie Gertrude," and saw how he blushed dark.

The two thieves plotting and whispering and snorting underneath her sleeping spot had also caught onto that relationship. It seemed to give them even more reason to plot the "heist of the century," in their own words, to rob the old woman. They despised Mr. Mortimer because he didn't put up with their protests that their assigned chores were either too hard or they were too old for such baby jobs. Ess agreed with Mr. Mortimer's response, when he asked them to make up their minds: was the job too hard, or was it for babies?

Ess kept watch on Buckman and Scopes all the next day, so much that Oswald scolded her twice for having her "head in the clouds." The two would-be thieves loitered too long and too often in the back yard of the hotel, and they studied the sixth floor room so steadily, Ess wondered that no one else got suspicious. Yet they never made a move. Had they grown some common sense, at long last? Maybe elderly Mrs. Sinclair's wealth intimidated them? Or had they simply learned some caution since their last failed attempt at theft? She almost didn't go to dinner, afraid the two older boys would make their move while her back was turned. However, when Ess came outside again, after a dinner of very good roast beef and noodles, they were still at their posts in the shadows of the stable, watching the side window of the suite that was their target.

Chapter Twenty-Two

She was halfway around the perimeter of the yard when Grimmly, the head porter, came down the alley to call for the carriage that had been prepared since before Ess and the boys went to dinner. Oswald stepped out of his office/living quarters at the far end of the stable and the two exchanged grins while the driver -- Rosco was on duty tonight -- scrambled to put on his long red livery coat and climb into the driver's seat.

"Mortimer's really intent on showing the old lady the town, ain't he?" Oswald said.

"When you've got an aunt rich enough to buy Watertown and half the county, and a dozen other cousins all trying to cozy up to her and get put higher in her will, you'd better believe it," Grimmly responded, and stepped up into the driver's seat next to Rosco.

Buckman and Scopes sauntered across the yard in the wake of the departing carriage. That, Ess realized, was the signal they had been waiting for. She had played with scenarios in her head all day, waiting for them to make their move, but for three seconds, she froze. What could she do to trip them up and distract them that she hadn't done before? Eventually, those two dunderheads would catch on that she was always in the vicinity every time they had an accident and then found their pockets empty.

Tyler called to her from the back porch as the other water team boys came streaming out after dinner. Ess turned and barely saw the ball streaking toward her in time to catch it. Oswald called out to them to be careful not to break any windows and stay out of traffic, then turned and went back into the stables.

No one noticed Buckman and Scopes climbing up, except Ess. She nearly got hit in the face three times, and her teammates jeered her twice when she didn't even try to go after the ball. When the two thieves climbed down again a good twenty minutes later, the game had devolved to the point it had no rules, except to steal the ball from whoever had it at that moment. That meant even less chance of anyone noticing the two on the wall. More than once, Ess had flung the ball to a boy who was on her team, only to have him turn and toss it to someone on the other team, and have the alliances rearranged in an instant. She laughed with the others and concentrated on keeping the roughhousing and running and yelling as close to the back wall of the hotel as possible. Eventually, someone had to look up and see the two thieves in action.

Of course, it looked like time was running out. She nearly got hit in the face with the ball when she paused too long to find the two thieves at the second floor window. She had to do something -- but what? Ess chased after the runaway ball, then darted out of the reach of two boys who tried to snatch it from her grasp. Her heart raced three times faster as she devised a hopefully simple plan.

Ess ran across the yard, keeping Buckman and Scopes in her sights as they reached the ground and paused a few seconds in the shadows of the ornamental bushes. Timing would be delicate, but just how delicate could she make it with three boys racing at her from three separate directions, intent on wrestling the ball from her in just a few seconds?

A shriek escaped her as two other boys, Sydney and Joe, stepped into the perfect position almost directly in front of the bushes and the thieves. Ess stretched her arm back as far as she could and flung the ball with all her might. It went over Sydney's head, into the bushes. He and Joe dove after the ball. The other boys let out cries of dismay, and it was all Ess could do to hold back a cheer as the ball hit Scopes square in the gut. He folded and the ball ricocheted. Buckman kicked at Joe as the boy tried to push past him. Sydney let out a shout and leaped at Buckman. The other boys roared, and in seconds they were all converging on the spot in the bushes. Ess stumbled for two steps before leaping into the tumult -- this wasn't what she had hoped for, exactly -- but it was exactly what she needed.

The shouting, punching, stumbling mass of arms and legs and furious boys finally getting some licks in against the bullies rolled out into the center of the yard. Oswald came running, and Jenkins the hostler. Two porters pulled dinner napkins out from their collars before leaping into the fray to pull the boys apart. Ess got pushed around and her clothes pulled on and punched in the gut and took a glancing blow on her cheek, but she emptied the two thieves' pockets as best she could. Breathless, she staggered into the shelter of the decorative bushes and went to her knees. She had lost her cap somewhere along the way. She certainly wasn't going back for it now.

Oswald herded the other boys into the stable, scolding them to wash up and threatening not to get Willy a piece of beefsteak for his black eye if he didn't settle down. Ess held her breath, waiting for him to notice she wasn't there and call out, or even come looking for her. She held as still as possible as the two thieves finally skulked down the alley right past her hiding place. They weren't chortling over their haul -- most likely because the two porters stayed on the back porch steps, calling out to them that they should know better than to pick on younger boys. Ess hoped they went far away before they dug into their pockets to look at their loot.

She grinned as she checked her pockets and inside her shirt, where she had tucked some of her takings for safekeeping. A pretty locket bordered with diamonds. A cameo of ivory on onyx. A pearl necklace. Nearly a dozen rings of gold and silver, some with precious stones. Ess was amused to realize she had also liberated a battered tobacco pouch and an equally battered coin purse, a dirty handkerchief and a tintype that she thought might be Scopes' sweetheart. She had heard him boasting that he had a sweetheart and a tintype picture of her, but hadn't seen it.

Leaving the two bullies' possessions on the ground under the bushes, Ess started up the precarious stairway to Mrs. Sinclair's sixth floor room. She silently vowed this would be the last time she risked her neck doing the right thing. The hotel designers and management should have had the common sense to put locks on the windows, or maybe even bars, so guests could get fresh air but no one could get in or out through them. At the back of her mind, she composed a scolding letter to leave with them -- or perhaps she should drop the letter at the newspaper office, instead? -- on her way out of town.

To her dismay, the decorative bricks didn't make quite as wonderful a stair, once she got to the fifth floor guest room windows. Ess panicked for several seconds when her questing fingers didn't find the bricks sticking out where she expected them. With the growing dusk, the alley was full of shadows and she couldn't see clearly. She gritted her teeth and stretched her arms as far as they would go, scraping her fingers on the bricks until they felt raw. Almost at the point when she thought she should give up, climb back down, and contrive to leave the jewelry at the front desk, she found the bricks sticking out. Ess muffled a sob of relief and stepped off the ledge of the fifth floor window.

As she headed up to the sixth floor window, it occurred to her to wonder if she would be able to get back down again, since it had been such a stretch to get out there.

"Go through the door, idiot," she muttered. Would it really matter if she was caught inside the hotel, inside the guest area? What was the worst that could happen? She would get fired -- and wasn't she planning on leaving town, anyway?

Ess had a moment of fright when she thought the shutters on the window of Mrs. Sinclair's room had stuck shut, but a shove hard enough to threaten her precarious perch on the ledge opened them. She settled down on the windowsill, legs hanging in the room, and caught her breath. Then she looked around the room and silently cursed Buckman and Scopes.

Unlike their previous thefts, they hadn't left the room looking untouched. Three drawers hung open, pillows lay on the floor in front of the settee, the vanity mirror lay backwards on its pivot, and if she wasn't mistaken, a fine layer of what was probably dusting powder lay over the contents of the vanity and the chair and the lovely Grecian key print of the rug. It was one thing to steal from people, but to make a mess and even break something belonging to their victims? That was extra cruel. These two deserved to be caught this time.

For about thirty seconds, Ess contemplated climbing down again and going to Mr. Mortimer's office to wait until he came back from driving his aunt around Watertown. She would have all the proof she needed in her pockets. If she didn't leave footprints in the room and didn't get powder on her boots, they couldn't put the blame for the robbery on her, could they? Too bad Buckman and Scopes hadn't left footprints.

No, she couldn't take the risk of not being believed. Better to put everything where it could be found and get out of here as soon as she could. What if she gave the jewelry to Mr. Mortimer and he called for the sheriff? Who would believe her when she asked them to contact Agent Sutter to testify on her behalf? If she was locked up, how long could she avoid someone realizing she was a girl? That was the ultimate question and the catastrophe she had to avoid at all costs.

"To work," she muttered, and slipped down off the windowsill. With the mess in the room, why try to put the lovely pieces back where they belonged? She should just lay them on the lovely silken quilt where they could be seen, and let Mrs. Sinclair and Mr. Mortimer wonder how they had gotten there. If she was lucky, they would blame it on thieves being caught in the act, fleeing and tossing aside their loot to avoid capture.

Thudding feet out in the hall made her pause. Ess swallowed hard and stepped across the room. Definitely, she wasn't stepping into that dusting powder and leaving footprints. Even worse than leaving footprints that were identifiably a boy's size, she might have powder on her shoes, and wouldn't that cause questions if she followed her plan and went down the stairs? She reached into her pocket for the first item and hissed as pinprickles of fire scored her fingertips. Ess pulled her hand out and stepped closer to the one lamp left burning on a round table in the center of the room. Her fingertips were bloody and raw where she had rubbed and scraped them on the bricks.

She reached into her pockets with both hands and emptied them out onto the bed. Ess wished she hadn't dropped the bullies' possessions outside. She would have loved to witness them stammering and swearing and sweating as they tried to explain how their tobacco pouch and tintype and other items ended up in Mrs. Sinclair's room, tangled with her jewelry.

The suite door banged open and boots clomped across the outer room.

"Hold it right there, lad," a man barked, as Ess turned around.

She had seen Sheriff Tucker several times, as he was a friend of Oswald. Even then, she would have known him by the shiny gold badge on his vest. Several men crowded into the doorway behind the sheriff, and at the back of the group stood Buckman and Scopes, one wide-eyed with surprise, the other scowling and looking like he would spit his fury.

~~~~~

Ess was the only occupant of the Watertown jail that night. She supposed she should be grateful for that, because a quick glance at the other three cells revealed only two had anything remotely resembling a mattress on the boards of what passed for a bed. She managed to reach into the next cell and snag the blanket from the unoccupied bed, so she was relatively comfortable. The blankets even proved to have been laundered within the last month or so, and didn't smell too bad.
~~~~~

Sheriff Tucker shooed away the onlookers who had come upstairs with him, and escorted Ess back to the jail in total silence. He didn't ask for an explanation and she didn't offer one. She could guess what had happened quite easily. Buckman and Scopes had stopped to check the loot in their pockets. Maybe they were paranoid after coming up empty the previous three times. When they realized their pockets were empty yet again, they probably raced back down the alley. Maybe they even saw her climbing the wall and realized what she was doing. Why they had gone for the sheriff instead of simply coming upstairs and confronting her, beating on her until she handed over the jewelry, Ess didn't know. Maybe they had tried coming into the hotel and someone had stopped them, and they had argued enough to draw suspicion. She couldn't imagine them being intelligent enough to actually turn the blame around.

Didn't anyone wonder how they knew exactly which room to come to, to catch the supposed thief in the act?

Ess planned what to say to the sheriff, lying there in the dark, chilly, utterly silent jail. If she could get Sheriff Tucker to listen to her, she could present enough facts, enough logical argument, to clear her name. What about the jewelry on the bed? What about the dusting powder, but no footprints that matched hers? Still, she admitted even she would find it hard to believe a water boy from the back yard of the hotel would go to so much trouble to put back jewelry stolen from a guest on the sixth floor. Trying to anticipate the sheriff's arguments and whatever lies the two bullies had told made her head ache. Despite all that, she actually got a few hours of sleep.

A man sat in a chair outside her cell, balanced on two legs and slowly rocking, when Ess woke up in the cold light of early dawn. The kerosene bite of smoke from an extinguished lamp hung strong in the air, meaning he had only recently turned down the flame. Ess lay still, waiting as the growing daylight moved across the back room of the jail and finally illuminated his face. She flinched a little, probably enough for him to see under the blankets, and knew it was useless to pretend to be asleep.

The last person in the world she expected to see: Horace Winslow, Pinkerton detective.

"Good morning, Mrs. Lewis." Horace settled forward, bringing the front two legs down to the floorboards with a bang. "Fancy seeing you here in Watertown." He raised one hand, and Ess was horrified to recognize her journal in his grip. It didn't take much thinking to realize the detective had found her sleeping spot in the stable loft and confiscated her few possessions.

"Did you enjoy what you read, Detective?" Ess sat up, pushed aside the blankets, and slowly swung her legs over the side of the bed. She felt as if she had slept in an ice house, after being pounded from head to toe with a rug beater. Odd, since Sheriff Tucker had been unusually gentle with her, considering she was a thief caught in the act. Maybe it was her restless night.

"Oh, indeed, very much." He tipped his head to one side, and a slow smile crept out from under his moustache. "How'd you like a hot breakfast, a hot bath, and a job?"

"Pardon me?" For two seconds, she wondered if she might be asleep.

"Young lady, I have been watching you make idiots out of those two would-be burglars. And as an added bonus, proving what I've been telling the owner of this hotel since I arrived last week. All that fancy decoration is just an invitation to trouble. It's been a rare treat all around. More fun than reading a penny dreadful with a good cigar and a bottle of smooth whiskey. Talent like yours shouldn't be wasted." He stood up and held out a hand to her through the bars. "What do you say, Miss Odessa Vivian Fremont? Care to come work for the Pinkertons?"

"Just like that?" Ess slowly stood and took two steps toward him, but she didn't hold out her hand to shake his just yet. She had already deduced that Horace Winslow was a man of his word, and a handshake was as binding for him as swearing on the Bible and signing a contract would be for other men.

"Hmm…" He winked. "Maybe not quite, but we can discuss the finer details once we get you out of here and clear your good name. Which one are you using right now?"

"Joshua." She laughed and gave her hand into his grasp.

~~~~~

Mr. Mortimer had been trying to tell the owners since before the hotel was built that the decorative facing was an invitation to thieves. He had even been scolded several times by the hotel owners for asking hotel guests to leave their valuables in the hotel safe and to keep their windows closed when they weren't in their rooms. Such caution, the owners felt, put the hotel into a bad light. He knew about Buckman and Scopes since the second robbery, when Horace told him what had happened. The stolen goods Ess left at the front desk after the third robbery had been all the proof he needed. Proof, however, was the sticking point. Mortimer had been willing, although nervous about the whole arrangement, to let the entire farce play out until he and Horace could weave together a solid trap for the two thieves.

Ess was only slightly amused to realize that she had been putting a crowbar into the mechanism of the trap, by returning the stolen items so thoroughly -- in essence, destroying the proof, other than the word of a senior Pinkerton agent. When Horace had caught up with Mr. Mortimer and his aunt only two blocks down the street and informed the hotel manager what window the thieves had gone into that night, the man had nearly gone into apoplexy. He had rushed out into the street, shouting for Sheriff Tucker, and the sheriff and two deputies had come running just in time for Buckman and Scopes to race into the hotel and hear what was going on.

The manager again had an attack of apoplexy, according to Horace, when confronted with the fact that the clever boy who had been single-handedly foiling the thieves was in fact a girl. When Ess came out of the bathing room in Horace's suite after the amazing experience of a hot shower,
~~~~~

dressed in a suit a young man of good family would wear on Sunday, she found Mr. Mortimer sitting with Horace at a breakfast table set for three. The hotel manager looked rather white around the mouth, and his eyes seemed somewhat larger than usual, and he had two spots of high color in his cheeks. His hand and voice were steady as he stood and held out a hand to shake Ess's, and thanked her for her efforts on behalf of the hotel and its guests, and especially his aunt. Ess obeyed Horace and related all the details of the four robberies and how she had managed to pick the pockets of the bumbling thieves and return the items each time. By the time she finished, Mr. Mortimer had regained his balance and proper color, and even managed to laugh.

"How did you learn such skills?" he asked, as he got up and went to the side table to retrieve the coffee pot to refill their cups.

Breakfast had been amazing, in Ess's estimation. She decided she had gone for too long on simple biscuits and lukewarm coffee or slightly cool milk, and maybe a bruised piece of fruit for her morning meal. Bacon and fried eggs and oatmeal, coffee heavy with cream, and out-of-season berries drizzled with honey made her feel as if she had stepped into a dream. If this was the kind of fare Pinkertons could depend on while on the job -- she assumed Horace was here in Watertown on some assignment, and not for a pleasure jaunt -- then she could very easily settle into such work.

"I traveled with a circus for several months, and learned sleight-of-hand from the magician," she said, nodding thanks, and offering the cream pitcher to him in return.

"Any other skills?" Horace asked around the cigar that seemed more important to him than the remains of the breakfast sitting on his plate.

"Trick riding." She shrugged. "Sharpshooting. Maintaining the steam engine and devising tricks with the engineer. Makeup and disguises."

No need to tell them she already knew how to shoot before joining the circus, and had learned quite a bit in the way of makeup and costume and changing how she moved and talked from Miss Talbot's acting troupe.

"What about those two bullies?" she asked, to ward off the in-depth questions she could see burning in Horace's eyes. "How are you going to finally lower the boom on them?"

"It should be lowering as we speak." Amusement glittered brighter in his eyes now.

"Aunt Gertrude thinks it's a grand lark to help trap them. She invited them to take breakfast with her, ostensibly to thank them for helping to capture the thief. The louts have no idea they incriminated themselves by pointing out what room had been broken into. How would they know unless they had done it?" He shook his head. "She put all sorts of costume jewelry out on display, along with a huge bag overflowing with fool's gold, sitting right out where anyone can see it." Mr. Mortimer actually chuckled now as he pulled out his pocket watch.

"Right this moment, my aunt is taking a morning constitutional walk through the center of town, her room unguarded, while Sheriff Tucker is waiting in the hall, one of his men waits in the wardrobe, and three others are hidden in the yard as witnesses to watch those two scoundrels climb up to the window." He nodded to Horace. "Detective Winslow kindly alerted us to the pattern of traffic through the back areas of the hotel, and the times when it is entirely empty with no one to witness nefarious activities. I was rather irritated with you, young man -- err, young lady." He winked at her.

"Yes, irritated that you didn't come to someone in authority, Oswald at the very least, with your discovery. Then it was pointed out to me that no one would believe you, the word of a newcomer over young men who had been serving here at the hotel since it opened."

"Common sense and flexibility." Horace stubbed out his cigar and reached to refill his coffee cup. "Work with what you've got, work around what you don't, and use the idiots' mistakes against them. All marks of a Pinkerton."

"Do tell," Ess murmured, and decided to indulge in the last two strips of bacon. Horace snorted into his cup, muffling laughter.

~~~~~

"It's not that easy, is it?" Ess said, after Mr. Mortimer had left in response to a summons, most likely the trap having been sprung.

"What is?" Horace settled back in his chair and patted his stomach. He had put away more than twice what she had eaten and didn't look at all as sleepy-replete as she felt.

"Becoming a Pinkerton."

"Somehow, I don't think you've quite made up your mind to accept the offer."

"I haven't. Need to know all the details. What sort of test do I need to pass? I assume I have to prove myself, to the upper brass, if not to you."

That earned a chuckle from him. He stretched his arms to the ceiling, then brought them down to clasp his hands behind his head, and leaned back to balance on the back two legs of his chair. Ess wondered if that was his preferred position no matter where he sat, and no matter with whom.

"Your test, as you so accurately put it, will be helping with what brought me to Watertown in the first place." A long sigh escaped him, when Ess thought he would launch into some explanation of the assignment. Horace narrowed his eyes at her. "Are your Secret Service friends going to throw up any kind of fuss if you join us?"
~~~~~

Chapter Twenty-Three

"I see I'm going to have to create a more complex code for my journal." She fought to keep her expression calm. Ess decided this was a lesson to her -- never record such delicate, dangerous personal information, even in code, if her journal could fall into the wrong hands. Maybe she should use one of the ancient Egyptian dialects her grandfather had delighted in teaching her before she realized she was actually learning something academic.

"Spent the war breaking codes used by the South and the British forces supporting them. Had an offer to join the Secret Service when everything calmed down, but all that bureaucracy didn't appeal to me. Allen Pinkerton was a friend from way back, so all the more reason to join up."

"I don't suppose you know any agents? Specifically, Agent Randolph Sutter?"

Horace's front chair legs hit the floor with a resounding thud. Ess laughed, and a moment later he joined in.

Horace was here to scout out the area and get a feeling for the people in Watertown, the loyalties, the histories, the relationships. Most important was finding a house to rent just outside of town, but close to the railroad tracks. A team of agents were due in Watertown that afternoon. According to the original plan, they weren't due to arrive for four more days. However, the gang of train robbers they were tracking had changed their pattern and routine. Those who had been spying on their activities and ordinary lives could only deduce that some sort of crisis had precipitated the change. Tensions were rising among the gang members. Allen Pinkerton himself had analyzed what five different agents had learned and made a calculated guess that the gang was either about to splinter into smaller groups, or retire from the business. Part of that was the result of the Secret Service bearing down and making it harder than ever for the Blue-Eyed Gang, as the robbers were called, to operate.

The two cousins who headed the gang were the type who would want to go out in a blaze of glory. While the Secret Service was focusing on another part of the state as the possible location for the Blue-Eyed Gang to go out in a blaze of glory, Allen Pinkerton believed the monthly payroll shipment that came through Watertown was their target. To throw the gang off balance and force them to act quickly, he had convinced the owners of the railroad to ship the payroll early. It was now or never to catch these men, before they faded back into their ordinary lives, with no solid evidence to use against them.

Ess would be part of the trap for the gang. However, while Horace thought she could handle the job before she was officially a Pinkerton, she had to prove herself to the other agents involved. Horace sent Ess in her fancy new boy suit to wait at the train station when the other agents came in. He had described them to her, but had no pictures to help her identify the men. They would come in on the same train, but not together. Her assignment was to watch the passengers disembark, identify the Pinkertons, and pick their pockets before they reached the hotel. Horace would not be waiting in the lobby for them as arranged, but at a rented house. When Ess picked their pockets, she would slip a note into the pocket of each man, with the address of the house. In the hotel lobby, she was to leave their possessions for the front desk clerk to return to them, prompting them to search their pockets and find the notes.

"What if they don't think it's funny?" she asked, after thinking about her instructions for some time in quiet. Meanwhile, Horace finished another cigar and wrote up a report on the entire wall-climbing thieves incident.

They had waited until Buckman and Scopes were hauled off to the jail, protesting loudly that the trap was unfair, then vacated the hotel suite to go to the rental house.

"Why would I want them to think that?" Horace snorted and stubbed out his cigar in the garish bowl that tried to imitate a seashell. Why someone would want a bowl that looked like a polished seashell big enough for a cup of coffee, Ess had no idea.

"If I'm going to be working with them, I don't want them angry with me. I've seen what happens when new girls at school irritate their classmates."

"Hmm, hadn't thought of it that way." He examined the smoking stub, lips pursed, while the seconds ticked by. "So if they laugh, you think they won't be sore with you?" Smile lines crinkled around his eyes, for a few moments reminding her so much of her grandfather that it hurt and stole her breath. "Know what an elephant is?"

"I rode one at the exhibition in London, when I was six."

"Do tell?" He nodded, eyes twinkling. "Pinkertons need skins thicker than an elephant's hide. Need a wicked sense of humor." A snort. "Need to know how to play poker to pass the time when you're stuck on a long, dead-boring watch duty. My associates coming into town today are the sort who'll be downright tickled that you got the better of them, and then flabbergasted when they realize you're just a slip of a girl."

"I'll be seventeen in two weeks."

"Then it's high time we got you into a different line of work. Not sure how much longer the disguise of ragged, footloose boy will work for you. Better learn more disguises. I'm thinking we'll put you on the train with the payroll shipment, looking like a fluttery, fussy little bird, cinched up so tight you can't breathe, without a thought in your pretty little head. The gang is evenly divided between the ones who'll be staring and tripping over their tongues, and the ones who will dismiss you as not worth their bother or notice."

"Until they trip over me?"

Horace chuckled and saluted her with his coffee cup.

At four that afternoon, nineteen people got off the train. Ess identified the five Pinkerton agents by the simple expedient of noting who avoided looking at each other. Three of them almost slipped past her, because they cleverly attached themselves to other passengers: an elderly lady needing assistance with her baggage and stepping down from the car, and two women with children.

She had spent the time waiting for the train to arrive making a nuisance of herself, rolling a hoop up and down the length of the platform, regularly rapping the hip-high metal ring with the guiding stick hard enough to make it ring. Just as regularly, she tripped over her own feet and lost control of the hoop. The porter on the platform just laughed and encouraged her to keep trying, and kindly warned her to step out of the way of the passengers when the train arrived. Ess heard him sigh loudly when she aimed the hoop at the first identified Pinkerton agent, and to her delight, the porter laughed when it rolled straight into the man.

"Sorry, mister," she said, breathless, and squinted at him through the thick, scratched lenses of the spectacles she had retrieved from the bins behind the hotel four days ago. The Countess had taught her to always look for "props" to help with disguises in the future, and Ess thought it amazing luck to find the spectacles. Then she had second thoughts, when she put on the glasses and realized that they hadn't been ground in any way to help the wearer's vision -- the lenses were plain glass. Someone else, most likely, had been using them for a disguise until they were too scratched to be useful.

To complete her disguise, Ess had inserted pads of cottonwool into her new suit of clothes, to make her look plump. A sweaty, fat boy with thick spectacles was the epitome of harmlessness and easily ignored.

"Careful there, lad," the Pinkerton said, and kindly bent down to retrieve the hoop for her.

Ess swallowed her frustration at having the chance for physical contact removed, and tripped over her feet. She fell into the man and dropped the rod between his feet. Another of the suspected Pinkertons actually broke his pretense of not knowing him, and took two steps toward them. Ess's target -- if she was right, his name was Butler -- shook his head slightly and bent down to pull her back up onto her feet.

By this time, she had already slipped a thin flask from his outer coat pocket and replaced it with the first of Horace's notes. She stumbled away, apologizing profusely, darted back to retrieve her hoop and rod, and ran the other direction. This took her straight into the second Pinkerton -- the long scar bisecting his copper-colored beard marked him as Henshaw. She yelped and hit him square in the chest, and clutched at his coat long enough to slip his pocketwatch free of the inner pocket of his vest. The note almost didn't go down into the little pocket and Ess stumbled away, nearly stammering for real as she envisioned the note falling to the platform. She refused to fail so early by getting caught.

She darted down the steps from the platform and found the third man, still disentangling himself from the woman with three children. The youngest had wrapped her arms around his lower left leg and sat on his foot. He was turning an interesting shade of red and brushing off the young mother's almost tearful, embarrassed apologies. Remembering Horace's comment about Pinkertons needing a hide like an elephant made Ess want to laugh. She decided he was anchored there at the station for a while, so she could take the risk of making the switch on the other two. Yates was the tall, pale-haired man with a strong resemblance to President Lincoln, and he had remained with the elderly lady he championed, escorting her to a pony cart waiting out front of the station. Ess sent her hoop rolling in his direction. He didn't jump when the hoop banged into the cart's side while he and the driver, a young man who addressed the lady as Granny, got her settled. Feeling a little trepidation at this evidence of the agent's alertness, Ess toned down her stumbling, stammering act, and darted in to retrieve the hoop.

A long-fingered hand caught hold of her wrist with an iron grip. She swallowed down a yelp and let Yates pull her up to her feet. Sweat dripped into her eyes and her cap sat askew, low on her forehead.

"Sorry, mister," she mumbled.

"Be careful, lad. You don't want to hurt someone."

"Timothy O'Leery, is that you?" the elderly lady said, chuckling.

"No, ma'am. Sorry. I'm new to town. Just moved here with my uncle Jasper." Ess hooked her thumb over her shoulder in the opposite direction of the rental house. Yates finally let go of her wrist and she rubbed at it. A flicker of something softened his stern expression for a moment. Ess took it for regret and decided she might like him after all. She hoped he was one of those who would laugh loud and long when he realized the trick played on him, as Horace had promised.

"Move along, lad," Yates said, and caught hold of her shoulder to turn her around.

Ess had managed to snag his handkerchief -- fortunately, still clean and unused -- from his outer pocket. The note had seemed to crinkle extra loud, as if in defiance, when she slipped it into place. She felt a little wobbly as she clutched hoop and rod in one hand and darted away. Now where was the fifth man, Miller?

She found him shaking hands with a man who had to be the husband of the woman Miller had escorted -- he was holding the little girl perched in the crook of his arm and laughing at whatever the Pinkerton had just said. Ess was tired of rolling her hoop into people. After all, how many times could she get away with it before someone got suspicious? Then the little girl dropped her doll when Ess was only a few steps away. In a split second, she saw the sweet porcelain face and knew from bad experience the sound it would make when it hit the brick pavement in front of the train station.

Dropping her hoop and rod, Ess dove, stretching out her hands for the doll that fell head-first. Her ribs hit first, knocking the breath out of her despite the cottonwool padding. She could have sworn that three bricks in a row stood a good four inches higher than all the others, hitting just right. Gray haze surrounded her vision as she felt the doll land safely in her fingers, at the same moment the little girl let out her first shriek of dismay.

Big hands caught hold of her by her collar and the back of her belt and hauled her upright. Ess couldn't seem to breathe or even get her arms and legs to move. Her glasses fell off and hit with a solid crack on the bricks. She felt the doll slipping from her hands and clutched it tight, then a moment later realized the little girl was trying to take it back.

"Oh, thank you!" the mother cried, while her husband bent to pick up Ess's glasses and Miller gripped her shoulders, keeping her upright when her knees tried to fold. "Her grandmother just gave her that doll. She would be heartbroken to lose it so soon."

Ess managed to wheeze a response. Suddenly her lungs figured out how to work again and she gladly leaned into Miller's support while she caught her breath. He was so kind, she felt guilty relieving him of his coin purse. Then she panicked when he remarked that it wasn't right that she sacrificed her glasses for the sake of a doll and his hand started to go toward his coat pocket.

"Don't worry about it, mister," she blurted. "I can see fine, but my Granny thinks my eyes are weak from the fever last winter. I'd just as soon they were broke, if you know what I mean."

"Aye, lad." Miller winked. "I do indeed. Not much fun when they treat you like a baby on leading string, is it?" He patted her shoulder and walked away, leaving her at the mercy of the grateful family.

The little girl clutched her doll close and hid her face against her father's shoulder, taking brief, scowling glances at Ess while the parents thanked her again. Maybe she thought Ess would try to take the doll back? Ess was more than relieved when they said their farewells and she was free to return to her fifth and final target.

Who, of course, wasn't where she left him. Ess stumbled, the racing of her heart coming from panic, rather than her too-warm disguise. Why did it mean so much to her to pass Horace's test to perfection?

One thing she knew -- remaining any longer at the train station would attract attention. She didn't need to attract the attention of men trained to pay attention to their surroundings. She headed away from the train station, toward the hotel, and willed the last man, Cooper, to appear before her. Putting her hoop down, she rolled it along the edges of the brick-paved main street, paying more attention to the people ahead of her than the hoop. For some reason, the stubborn toy cooperated, letting out an almost melodious chiming sound when she tapped it with the rod to make it keep moving.

A knot of people parted around her, and she glanced down to guide the hoop in a detour, looking up just in time to realize Cooper had stopped to talk with someone standing on the wooden sidewalk a good eight inches higher than him. Ess let out a yelp and skidded to a stop. She nearly caught hold of the hoop to stop it from running into him before she remembered that was what she wanted.

Cooper laughed and snatched up the hoop while it was still wobbling crazily, unwinding itself like a top, before it lay flat on the brick pavement. With his back turned to her, the pipe in his pocket stuck up through the side flap of his coat. Ess snatched it.

"Hey -- thief!" the man on the sidewalk cried. He dove at Ess, at the same moment Cooper turned to hand her the hoop. Man and hoop collided and the hoop went tumbling. Ess still clutched the last note in her other hand. Unthinking, she handed it to Cooper. He took it. She turned tail and ran.

A giggle rose up in her throat, threatening to choke her. Nine out of the ten steps without getting caught wasn't bad, was it? She stretched out her legs as far as she could and gasped for breath. If she could have paused to shed the cottonwool padding to make it easier to move and breathe, she would have. If she could get to the lobby of the hotel and duck out of sight before Cooper or the other Pinkertons arrived, she would consider the test passed with flying colors. Maybe Mr. Mortimer was on duty and would hide her?

To her delight, the manager was just coming out of his office as she fled across the blessedly unoccupied lobby. He spotted her and paused, his mouth dropping open. Ess grinned cheekily and flew past him, straight into his office. She skidded to a stop in front of his big, paper-strewn desk. Gasping for breath, she snatched at the visitor's chair sitting there when her legs suddenly went as wobbly as German egg noodles. Then she nearly choked on laughter at the look on Mr. Mortimer's face, slowly changing from shock to a grin as he stepped back into the office and closed the door. She held out the pipe to him, but it took a few more seconds before she could get her breath enough to explain.

"Any second now -- a gentleman in a brown waistcoat, with silver spectacles and a curled moustache, will get here, looking for the boy who stole his pipe. Could you give it to him?"

"Why did you steal his pipe?" Mr. Mortimer took it from her, looking only curious, not confused.

"Detective Winslow told me to." She swallowed and wiped her sweaty face. "Well, he didn't specifically say to take his pipe, but I had to pick his pocket and leave a note. Five gentlemen, altogether, and they should all be arriving soon. I imagine things could get interesting out there any minute now." She divested herself of the other items she had taken, dropping them onto his desk.

Mr. Mortimer narrowed his eyes in thought, crossed his arms and cupped his chin, then tipped his head back and laughed. He pointed at the door on the other side of his office, told her it would take her to the back hallway leading to the kitchens, and then opened the front door and stepped out into the lobby. Ess took the time to shed the cottonwool padding before exiting the hotel. She felt only slightly disappointed that she didn't see Oswald or any of her friends from the water crew.

She reached the rental house and reported everything to Horace scant seconds before several pairs of booted feet clumped on the front porch of the house and someone banged on the front door. Horace made no move to get up from his spot at the long kitchen table. Ess had a fearful moment when she actually thought he would make her answer the door. Then the front door creaked open. She half-rose from her chair, and nearly knocked over the wooden mug of water Horace had pumped for her.

"Stay put." Horace tipped onto the back two legs of the chair. He caught one booted foot around the leg of the kitchen table, balancing himself perfectly.

Henshaw led the way, all five Pinkertons arriving together. He stopped three steps into the kitchen, after giving Ess only a passing glance. His glare unloaded its full force on Horace, who just nodded to him as he pulled out his cigar case and penknife and prepared another cigar for smoking. The other four detectives stepped into the kitchen, shaking their heads, lips pressed flat in various degrees of disgust.

"Pay up," Yates said. Butler handed him several coins and stepped over to the pump to fill a mug of water for himself.

"Who bet against me?" Horace asked, tossing the end of the cigar toward the dry sink.

"We all did," Henshaw growled. He yanked out a chair, dropped heavily into it, and turned to Ess, looking her up and down three times. Then abruptly, his face dissolved into laugh lines and he slouched in the chair. "You're good, boy. Very good. I'm guessing Horace is recruiting you?"

"Allen'd have my head if I let talent like hers slide out of my grasp."

"Hers?" Butler yelped, choking on his water.

The others all laughed, and Horace gave her an "I told you so" grin as he sat forward and slammed the front legs of his chair down to the floor.

~~~~~

Horace hadn't been joking or exaggerating when he described the costume that Ess found herself in the next day. She entertained herself on the three-hour train ride back to Watertown speculating how many sets of lace window curtains had been sacrificed to make her ridiculous, fluttery, wasteful costume. What sort of fool would wear yards and yards of white lace on a train in the heat and dust of summer? The only positive point she could see in her draping costume was that the sleeves were wide and hung down nearly to her fingertips, all the better to conceal the small pistols strapped to both forearms. All the pouf and airiness of her ridiculous dress actually allowed for air circulation, so she didn't swelter nearly half as much
~~~~~

as the women around her, all of them dressed in sensible linsey woolsy and homespun, in dark colors that didn't show the cinders and dust and coal smoke coming through the open windows. Along with the pistols, her arsenal included a gold, white, and sky blue Chinese fan, the panels of which separated to become throwing knives. The overflowing skirts hid a pistol tucked into a specially made holster just above her left knee. On her right leg, she had a pouch of bullets. Ess tried not to speculate on just what kind of situation this whole operation would turn into, that she would have both the need and the opportunity to reload her three guns. The detectives all agreed she was there as a backup precaution only, in case things "turned southerly" as Yates put it, when they closed in to confront and capture the Blue-Eyed Gang.

On a more positive note, Butler actually apologized when he handed her the rest of her props, to fill in the character she pretended to be. First, an utterly useless, tiny reticule, barely large enough to carry a paper packet of sweets, a bottle of smelling salts, and two handkerchiefs. What was she supposed to do with them? Turn the handkerchiefs into a slingshot and try to mimic David, using the sweets in place of the five smooth stones? Which one of the gang would stand in for Goliath? Next was a carpetbag packed with several ladies' journals, offering advice on fashion per the standards on the other side of the Atlantic. Or essays on the rising quality of public education and the benefits of trusting her health to the slowly growing numbers of female physicians being graduated on the East Coast. Or advice columns dealing with courtship, the perfect wedding festivities, and raising children who would be ready to face the glorious new world. Or preparing children to face the hazards of the grim future, depending on the viewpoint of the authors.

What Ess found only slightly amusing was that both authors blamed all this on the increase of technology that offered wonders such as labor-saving devices and swifter transportation, thanks to steam and airships. One author warned that disease would spread around the globe and devastate the populations of nearly every country, thanks to the ease of importing foreign foods and fresh foodstuffs straight from the orchards and fields and forests.

If she had anticipated the shallow mindset and simplistic writing, Ess would have asked for something more meaty to read. Even a volume of history she had read before would have been more enjoyable. Although she supposed if she had managed to get hold of something on Ancient Egypt -- what were the chances of that, this far from a major city with a worthwhile museum of antiquities? -- that would have clashed in horrible discord with the fluttery, spun-sugar image the Pinkertons wanted her to project.

Chapter Twenty-Four

She had to go into the bushes to change into her costume, two miles away from the station where she was to board the train. Miller laughed at her when she emerged in all her fluttery white glory. Ess hoped he was cramped and stifling in the massive trunk that her persona, Miss Amelia Forsythe, had loaded onto the train when she boarded -- and the porters handling it had dropped it three times when they loaded it. She hoped the lock didn't open immediately from the inside as Henshaw had promised it would. Not that she wanted Miller stuck inside there. He needed to be out and positioned in hiding for the moment the Blue-Eyed Gang members threw open the doors of the baggage car, looking for the payroll safe. She simply wanted him to be inconvenienced, a little panicky, and as uncomfortable as she felt right now.

"Well, don't you look good enough to eat?" a low voice drawled, while a shadow passed over her and a cloud of some heavily spiced cologne threatened to choke her.

Ess looked up, fluttering her fan at twice the speed. Her gaze met the deepest blue eyes she had ever seen, surrounded by long, thick, almost obscenely curled lashes. Why did men have such gorgeous eyelashes, while women in their family line had short, stubby things?

That's one. Ess almost laughed when she recognized one of the gang. She hadn't quite believed the description of the eye color they all shared, until now.

"I assure you, sir, better men than you have tried. My daddy and my brothers have sent them all packing." She fluttered her fan faster and turned sideways just enough on the seat that a man of higher society would have recognized the social "cut," and repented of his vulgar words.

"Sugarplum, I don't see your daddy or your brothers," he said with a chuckle, and slid into the seat next to her. He didn't even bother removing the journals filling the seat, but settled on top of them. "Now ain't that sweet? Been a long time since I seen a lady blushing." He leaned closer, gusting breath filled with a mixture of rum and peppermint into her face.

Ess bit back the retort burning on her tongue, that she doubted he had ever seen a real lady in his life. The idiot couldn't tell the difference between a blush and a red wave of fury -- granted, her heart was racing with some tense excitement. The Secret Service had been wrong, the Pinkertons were right, and the trap would indeed close on the gang today. Not that it mattered one whit to her that she wouldn't have to suffer through another trip in this horrific dress. She fluttered her fan higher, concentrating on being a witless, high society, spun sugar confection no one would take seriously until she shoved her pistols up their unfairly patrician noses.

"Just how far down does that pretty pink wave go, anyway?" he added, and waggled his eyebrows at her.

Did this fool think he was being charming? Unfortunately, she knew of a dozen girls right off the top of her head who would swoon at such crude flirtation.

Ess raised the fan higher so only her eyes could be seen over the lacy edge. She turned, catching movement over her uninvited seatmate's head. Another young man, with the same chiseled cheekbones and deep blue eyes, stepped up next to their seat and slapped the first man's shoulder.

"None of that, Beau," the second man said. He nodded to Ess and touched the brim of his Stetson. "Sorry about the imposition, ma'am."

She nodded to him and lowered the fan enough for him to see her simper -- at least, she hoped it was a sticky sweet simper -- and fluttered her eyelashes at him. Whatever expression she managed to paste on her face, it irritated her erstwhile suitor and made his brother or cousin flush a little. The first man got up and stomped away without a backward glance, while the one who retrieved him nodded again to Ess. He looked back once, meeting her gaze, before the two opened the door and stepped out to cross the connector to the next car.

"Ain't he a handsome one?" a girl whispered a seat or two back behind Ess.

"Which one?" another girl responded, her voice slightly louder. They both giggled.

Ess contemplated the unfairness of physical form not matching the spirit and soul within the body. If the changes in a man's morals, the choices he made in life, could be reflected in his face and form, that would solve a great many of society's ills. People would be warned with one glance what type of person they dealt with, and a great many quacks and patent medicine salesmen and other such deceivers would be deprived of their prey.

A steam whistle's scream, almost simultaneous with a jolt and the shriek of brakes, interrupted her thoughts. Her face warmed, as she realized she had let herself get distracted. Shouldn't the appearance of two of the six robbers have warned her to be doubly alert? What kind of a Pinkerton was she going to be? Granted, Horace told her to stick to her role of a useless ninny, and even feel free to shriek or faint or have a cataleptic fit, if the situation so demanded, but that was no excuse.

The one-third occupied car around her erupted with cries and chatter as the train screamed to a halt. One glance out the window told Ess the train was still three miles outside of Watertown. That fit in with Horace's belief that the Blue-Eyed Gang made their home in the surrounding area, and they used their familiarity with the hills and ravines and forests to assist in their getaway. Right now, the rest of the gang approached the train.

Gunshots outside answered that thought. Ess tugged her wide-brimmed hat down further on her head to shield her face as she peered out the window. Maybe Horace hadn't been playing games with her when he saddled such an enormous, wasteful piece of headgear on her. Between all the lace and bows and the ridiculous curls of the strawberry blonde wig she wore, her face was in shadows. No one would know where she was looking -- and hopefully couldn't see her expression, if it gave away what she was thinking and planning.

The train was only six cars long, besides the engine, coal car, and caboose. There was one passenger car ahead of Ess's, then two baggage cars, and two holding horses, supposedly going to the Army garrison fifteen miles on the other side of Watertown. The sound of a baggage car door sliding open came clear through the dying squeal of brakes and wheels slowing and the hiss of steam escaping the engine.

"Everybody out!" a cheerful baritone voice called, and Ess's unwanted suitor strolled back through the car, revolvers in both hands, gesturing like the conductor of some barbaric orchestra.

The other passengers cowered back in their seats, shrieking, but obeyed quickly enough when he gestured with the guns. Ess debated pretending to faint, then his gaze met hers and something in his deep blue eyes told her not to give him any excuse to touch her. She got to her feet, clutching her fan and abandoning everything else. All the traffic to exit the car went past her seat, and she was blocked in for a crucial few seconds.

"No you don't, sugarplum," he drawled, reaching across two seats to catch hold of her sleeve when she was about to step into the aisle. "Pretty lady like you deserves special treatment. You're my special guest for the most important party of my whole life." He twisted her arm behind her back, making it painfully easy to guide her down the aisle, through the door at the back of the car, and down the steps.

Two steps from the bottom, Ess deliberately missed the step and fell. Her scream was utterly genuine when her escort didn't let go of her arm. Granted, he did loosen his grip so her shoulder wasn't dislocated by the fall, but she promised herself she was going to kick him where Uly told her it would leave a lasting impression. She stayed on her knees in the cinders beside the track as the robber stepped down behind her. All the other passengers clustered together, their eyes big, frightened into silence by her scream.

"What'd you go and do that for? Mess up that pretty dress." He bent down and looped his arm through hers to yank her back up to her feet.

At the next car, two men on horseback climbed from their saddles through the open sliding door. Two more men on horseback came from the front of the train. Ess guessed that they had been sitting on the tracks, to force the engineer to stop the train. The sixth man of the gang came down the steps from the car ahead of the one in which Ess had been riding. All six members of the Blue-Eyed Gang were present and accounted for. Movement in the corner of her eye brought a glad leap to Ess's pulse. It took all her self-control not to look to the top of the train where, per the plan, Horace and Henshaw now ran from where they had climbed up, between the baggage cars. The sliding door of the horse car banged open as Butler and Yates leaped out on horseback. Gunshots blazed from the baggage car, and Ess prayed Miller and Cooper were the ones who had shot first.

Butler and Yates raced past her, as her captor loosened his grip in shock. The two men on horseback swore and turned as one to flee. Ess cringed at the deafening gunfire.

"Hold it right there, McGuire!" Horace barked, coming to a stop and pointing his gun at the man standing behind Ess and her captor.

"Which one?" the man holding Ess sneered. He yanked harder on her arm, twisting it again. "Got me a pretty--"

Snarling fury, Ess twisted around, dropping her fan and snatching at his belt with her free hand. Using that as her pivot point, she flung her legs up in the air, as she had learned to mount a horse trotting around the circus ring. He *oophed* most satisfactorily as the force of both legs slammed into the side of his head. Down he went, with Ess on top of him. Gunfire exploded around her and she spotted a man dropping down from the top of the train. She hoped that was Henshaw. Most of the women shrieked, but Ess distinctly heard several of the men laugh and whoop. She bounced on the downed man's chest and managed a blow to his face with each fist before rolling off him.

Her foot landed on her dropped fan, making it crunch and crack, and she stumbled, going to one knee. A sense of movement from behind her had her dodging, tumbling forward, hampered by her skirts. She snatched at the pieces of her fan as she twisted and went sideways, rolling down the incline from the tracks. The world tumbled around her for a few seconds, and as she struggled to her knees and then to her feet, she looked up, straight into the eyes of her unwanted suitor. He snarled, his handsome face twisting so it did indeed, just for a heartbeat, reflect his soul. He brought up his revolver.

"Down, girl!" Horace shouted.

Later, Ess didn't know why or even how she managed it. She flung the pieces of the fan straight into the man's face, aiming for those ugly, blazing blue eyes. Simultaneously, a roar deafened her and an incredible force slammed into her hip, twisting her around and slamming her into the ground. Her hat flew off, despite the pins holding it to her wig and despite the pins and clips holding the wig to her hair. Her head slammed into the ground and she saw stars.

Fire flashed through her body, radiating from her hip, before she could get her breath back. Ess struggled upright -- difficult when her hip ached so fiercely and she lay on an incline with her feet higher than her head. Men were shouting and cursing around her and more guns fired. She scrambled to get her revolver from the holster around her knee, blinking tears from her eyes while the stars slowly faded. Her hands shook in time with the throbbing in her hip as she looked for someone, anyone, to shoot.

She nearly shot at Yates before she recognized him. The concern wrinkling his face turned to alarm, which made her feel distinctly queasy. Ess knew better than to look at the source of the throbbing fire. She held up her revolver with one hand while she tried to brace herself with the other and get turned around so she could stand. What was the idiot man doing, just staring at her? Didn't he know there were six armed train robbers that needed capturing?

"Stay down," Yates said, reaching for her with both hands, as if he would hold her down. He spilled a string of curses, so fast she almost couldn't tell words apart.

Slowly, it dawned on Ess that the gunfire had stopped. That had to be a good sign. Yates' curses stopped when Horace stepped into her field of vision. Slowly shaking his head, he went down on one knee next to her.

"You want to tell me where you learned to move like that, girl?" He didn't wait for her to respond, but nodded to Yates. The two of them put an arm around her back, and the other arm under her knees, and lifted her.

"Oh, didn't I mention?" Ess gasped, feeling as if her head wanted to separate from her shoulders as they started up the incline to the train. "I learned trick riding--" Several quick, deep breaths fought the queasies that knotted her stomach. "Riding at the circus."

"How about knife throwing?" Yates growled.

"Not -- not so good."

"Not so good, she says," Horace muttered. "Heaven help us when she does get good."

Later, Butler gave her a sketch he had done of the aftermath of the short, bloody fight. One of the knives from her Chinese fan had gone into Beau's left eye. Another had caught in the fleshy part of his throat, just before the hinge of his jaw, and a third stuck in the soft indentation above the dip of his collar bone. Massive splotches of black ink filled in for the puddles of blood that erupted from the man's slit throat.

Henshaw had some surgery experience gained during the war, when it had been vital to remove bullets on the battlefield, rather than waiting to get a wounded man to a surgeon. All the passengers were crowded into the first passenger car while the Pinkertons sequestered their bound and gagged prisoners in the baggage car. Horace stood over Ess, making her down one shot glass after another of bourbon until her extremities went numb and her eyes went hazy and all the sounds around her reached her ears through cottonwool a foot thick. He held her down and badgered her to sing filthy saloon songs with him while Henshaw dug the bullet out of her hip. Then he held her hand until she passed out at last, while the other Pinkerton did a crude sewing job with a curved needle and quilting thread borrowed from a passenger's abandoned belongings.

When Ess woke up, Horace was still holding her hand, though she assumed he had to let go at some time. It would have been awkward getting her off the train in Watertown, then carrying her to the doctor's office, then getting her out of her bloody dress, redressing her wound, and putting her into a nightshirt. He offered her a foul-tasting, gritty tonic when the first attempt at moving her head sent a seasick throbbing down her throat to her stomach and then out through the rest of her body. Ess didn't know if it cured her hangover by simply making her sick in a new way, or it did sweep the residue of the alcohol from her blood. She was most grateful that she kept it in her rebelling stomach, positive that hurling it back up again would be even worse than getting it down.

Horace proved just how insightful he was, when he didn't ask her any questions, didn't make inane comments promising she would feel better soon. He brought her a bottle of chilled sarsaparilla to sip, which washed the foul taste from her mouth and helped settle her stomach more. Then he proceeded to tell her all the important details of the gunfight and capture. Essentially, the Blue-Eyed Gang had been captured. Only one had surrendered without needing to be shot or punched into submission. Two of the cousins were dead. One, from Ess's fan-knives, and the other from his horse rearing up and falling backwards on him, cracking his skull and several ribs. Doctor Sullivan hadn't determined yet if it was the blow to his skull that killed him or broken bones had pierced vital organs and he bled to death. All they were sure of was that he had lost consciousness on the short ride to Watertown and died while waiting for Dr. Sullivan to finish tending to Ess.

"Hope you don't mind," Horace said, after they had sat in quiet for several minutes, while Ess digested the outcome of the amazingly quick skirmish.

"Mind what?" She smiled at the cracked, wheezing sound of her voice. A mouthful of sarsaparilla remained in the bottle and she saluted him with it before drinking it to moisten her throat.

"Well, it's hard to keep events like last night out of the newspapers. Confounded telegraph was bad enough, but now newspapers have ponied up big money to keep reporters traveling all over the country with photography equipment or artists who can draw good and fast, and they use airships to get stories everywhere in one tenth the usual time. I can remember when we thought the Pony Express was too fast." He shook his head, then slapped his knee for punctuation. "We can't keep it out of the news that a woman was involved in the capture of the Blue-Eyed Gang. Not with all the witnesses."

"What did you tell them?" Ess took a few deep breaths, fighting a new surge of nausea that had nothing to do with her hangover and the background throbbing of her hip. She blinked hard, surprised by the tears that came at the thought of her grandparents' reactions -- or worse, Uly's -- if they read her name and a description of her actions in a newspaper account.

"Basically... I lied." Horace winked and squeezed her hand. "I told them

Mrs. Flora Lewis, a Pinkerton agent for the last three years, participated in the operation. I told them you were twenty-six, widow of a Secret Service agent who died on a raid on a Resurrectionist hideout in Oklahoma territory. Too bad your wig came off in the tussle, otherwise we could hide what you look like."

Ess laughed. Not for long, but it felt good to laugh -- at least, until the throbbing resumed in the base of her skull.

The sound of her laughter brought the rest of the team from the outer room of the doctor's offices. The other Pinkertons were in their shirtsleeves, hair mussed, food stains on a few shirts. Their voices were subdued, but their faces brightened as they pulled up chairs or found places to perch, and Ess found herself suddenly close to tears with the realization that they were worried about her. Cooper reported that the US Marshall had sent a team of men to take the remaining four members of the Blue-Eyed Gang into custody. Several telegrams had come from the Pinkerton central office, commending the team for their success, authorizing a transfer of funds to pay for their expenses, and telling Horace he was "spot on."

Ess felt a tightening in the atmosphere at that pronouncement, and found everyone looked back and forth several times between her and Horace. She held her breath, sensing something momentous had happened.

"Didn't doubt it for a minute," Horace said, his somber expression slitting into a grin. He held out his hand for hers, and pumped her hand three times. "You made it, Odessa. You're officially a Pinkerton."

As the others grinned and laughed and shook her hand and congratulated her, Ess realized that no one had asked if she really wanted to be a Pinkerton. It was just assumed. Some of the tightness in her gut fled when she realized that was more than just fine with her. She couldn't think of anything better she wanted to do with her life. That is, until the situation settled down in South America.

"We've got men on the lookout for your brother and listening for news on your grandparents, don't you worry," Horace said, as if he had heard her thoughts. "You're one of us, and we take care of our own."

"Pardon me for pointing out the obvious," Yates said, drawing out his words, "but just how do we take care of Odessa when we don't know what in tarnation you're talking about?"

"I can make a pretty good guess, filling in the holes where I don't know the facts. Want me to tell them, or do you want to do the honors?"

"You tell them, and I'll fill in the holes as you go along," Ess said.

Horace started with the day she came into the Philadelphia office in disguise. He sighed loudly and muttered about having a bad day, that he couldn't see the fourteen-year-old girl underneath the widow's garments and makeup. The others made comments, teasing, and Ess had to fill in and explain the help she had with costume and makeup. That led to backtracking to detail her time at Miss Van Hastings' Academy, and then telling how she had discovered the Resurrectionist headquarters underneath the school. Horace described what little he had been able to learn about Uly and the paucity of information he had been able to obtain about the elder Fremonts' activities in South America. Ess then had to explain her grandparents' archeological work and the books they had written.

By lunchtime -- broth and custard for her, until they could be sure her stomach would behave -- Horace had described the entertainment Ess had provided, foiling the burglary attempts at the hotel. Then she had to backtrack and explain her time at the circus, the skills she had learned in sleight of hand, trick riding, trick shooting, and assisting with the steam engines and other mechanisms that provided the illusions and tricks for circus performances.

She actually earned several whistles and a few soft-voiced curses, all entirely respectful, when she had to explain her association with Agent Randolph Sutter, recognizing Resurrectionists who were about to make an attempt on President Lincoln's life.

"How old are you again, Odessa?" Cooper said, after they had laughed together over the test Horace had given her, and how she had managed to irritate them all and pick their pockets just two days before.

"My friends call me Ess," she said, "and I'll be seventeen in two weeks."

"Girl..." He shook his head. "You've crammed a lifetime into the last two years. Why aren't you looking for some peace and quiet for a change?"

"Doing what?" She braced herself for suggestions of going back to school, taking a tour of Europe and attending a finishing school, or even finding a husband and settling down to raise a house full of children.

"Boys, you don't put a fine race horse to pulling a dairy wagon, and to a man, all of you would cuss out anyone who suggested you do anything other than what you are now." Horace nodded to Ess. "The girl is where she belongs, doing what the good Lord made her to do. Am I right?" He winked at her as the other five agents agreed nearly in unison.

The End

About the Author

On the road to publication, Michelle fell into fandom in college and has 40+ stories in various SF and fantasy universes. She has a bunch of useless degrees in theater, English, film/communication, and writing. Even worse, she has over 100 books and novellas with multiple small presses, in science fiction and fantasy, YA, suspense, women's fiction, and sub-genres of romance.

Her official launch into publishing came with winning first place in the Writers of the Future contest in 1990. She was a finalist in the EPIC Awards competition multiple times, winning with *Lorien* in 2006 and *The Meruk Episodes, I-V*, in 2010, and was a finalist in the Realm Awards competition, in conjunction with the Realm Makers convention.

Her training includes the Institute for Children's Literature; proofreading at an advertising agency; and working at a community newspaper. She is a tea snob and freelance edits for a living (MichelleLevigne@gmail.com for info/rates), but only enough to give her time to write. Her newest crime against the literary world is to be co-managing editor at Mt. Zion Ridge Press and launching the publishing co-op, Ye Olde Dragon Books. Be afraid … be very afraid.

And please check out her newest venture: Ye Olde Dragon's Library, the storytelling podcast. Each week, listeners are invited to join Michelle on her blog to ask questions and give feedback and suggestions. Interspersed between the chapters will be interviews with authors of fantastical fiction. Listen to the podcast on your favorite podcast app or listen on the website: www.YeOldeDragonBooks.com, and click on the Ye Olde Dragon's Library link. Then go to her blog to interact: www.MichelleLevigne.blogspot.com

www.Mlevigne.com
www.MichelleLevigne.blogspot.com
www.YeOldeDragonBooks.com

<u>www.MtZionRidgePress.com</u>

Look for Michelle's Goodreads groups:
Guardians of Neighborlee
Voyages of the AFV Defender

NEWSLETTER:
Want to learn about upcoming books, book launch parties, inside information, and cover reveals?
Go to Michelle's <u>website</u> or <u>blog</u> to sign up.

Thanks for reading!
If you enjoyed this book, would you help Michelle by posting a review on Goodreads?

Are you a member of Book Bub? If so, please follow Michelle on Book Bub, and you'll get alerts when new books are coming out.

As a way of saying thanks, Michelle invites you to the Goodies page on her website. It will change regularly, offering you a free short story, a sample audiobook chapter, sneak peeks at new cover art, inside information on discounts and new release dates, etc.

Please go to: Mlevigne.com/good-stuff.html

Also by Michelle L. Levigne

Guardians of the Time Stream: 4-book Steampunk series
The Match Girls: Humorous inspirational romance series starting with **A Match (Not) Made in Heaven**
Sarai's Journey: A 2-book biblical fiction series
Tabor Heights: 18-book inspirational small town romance series.
Quarry Hall: 11-book women's fiction/suspense series
For Sale: Wedding Dress. Never Used: inspirational romance
Crooked Creek: Fun Fables About Critters and Kids: Children's short stories.

Do Yourself a Favor: Tips and Quips on the Writing Life. A book of writing advice.

To Eternity (and beyond): *Writing Spec Fic Good for Your Soul.* A book defending speculative fiction.

Killing His Alter-Ego: contemporary romance/suspense, taking place in fandom.

The Commonwealth Universe: SF series, 25 books and growing

The Hunt: 5-book YA fantasy series

Faxinor: Fantasy series, 4 books and growing

Wildvine: Fantasy series, 14 books when all released

Neighborlee: Humorous fantasy series

Zygradon: 5-book Arthurian fantasy series

AFV Defender: SF adventure series

Young Defenders: Middle Grade SF series, spin-off of *AFV Defender*

Magic to Spare: Fantasy series

Book & Mug Mysteries: cozy mystery series

Quest for the Crescent Moon: fantasy series starting in 2023

Steward's World: fantasy series reboot and expansion

The Enchanted Castle Archives: fantasy series, Liars' Quest, 1st book in the Ye Olde Dragon's Library podcast